RENNY'S DAUGHTER

By Mazo de la Roche

★

Chronicles of the Whiteoak Family

THE BUILDING OF JALNA
MORNING AT JALNA
MARY WAKEFIELD
YOUNG RENNY
WHITEOAK HERITAGE
THE WHITEOAK BROTHERS
JALNA
WHITEOAKS
FINCH'S FORTUNE
THE MASTER OF JALNA
WHITEOAK HARVEST
WAKEFIELD'S COURSE
RETURN TO JALNA
RENNY'S DAUGHTER
VARIABLE WINDS AT JALNA
CENTENARY AT JALNA

RENNY'S DAUGHTER

MAZO DE LA ROCHE

MACMILLAN

SBN 333 08561 2

First Edition 1951
Reprinted 1953, 1955, 1960, 1963, 1967, 1970, 1972

Published by
MACMILLAN LONDON LIMITED
London and Basingstoke
Associated companies in New York, Toronto,
Dublin, Melbourne, Johannesburg and Madras

Printed in Great Britain by
LOWE AND BRYDONE (PRINTERS) LTD., THETFORD

CONTENTS

THE WHITEOAK FAMILY

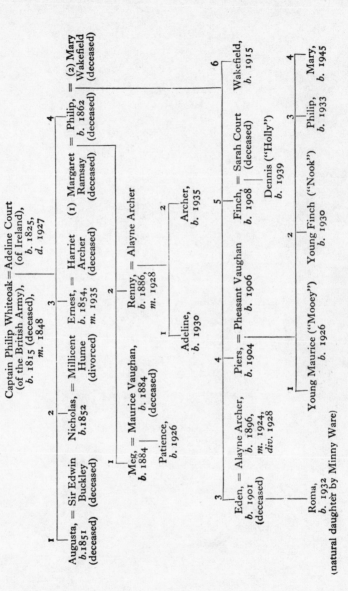

Captain Philip Whiteoak=Adeline Court
(of the British Army),   (of Ireland),
b. 1815 (deceased),   b. 1825,
m. 1848   d. 1927

1
Augusta, = Sir Edwin
b.1851   Buckley
(deceased) (deceased)

2
Nicholas, = Millicent
b.1852   Hume
            (divorced)

3
Ernest, = Harriet
b. 1854,   Archer
m. 1935   (deceased)

4
(1) Margaret = Philip, = (2) Mary
Ramsay   b. 1862   Wakefield
(deceased)   (deceased) (deceased)

1
Meg, = Maurice Vaughan,
b. 1884   b. 1884
          (deceased)

Patience,
b. 1926

2
Renny, = Alayne Archer
b. 1886,
m. 1928

1
Adeline,
b. 1930

2
Archer,
b. 1935

3
Eden, = Alayne Archer,
b. 1901   b. 1896,
(deceased) m. 1924,
          div. 1928

Roma,
b. 1932
(natural daughter by Minny Ware)

4
Piers, = Pheasant Vaughan
b. 1904   b. 1906

1
Young Maurice ("Mooey"),
b. 1926

2
Young Finch ("Nook"),
b. 1930

5
Finch, = Sarah Court
b. 1908   (deceased)

Dennis ("Holly"),
b. 1939

6
Wakefield,
b. 1915

3
Philip,
b. 1933

4
Mary,
b. 1945

RENNY'S DAUGHTER

I

STIRRINGS OF SPRING

THE ROOM could scarcely have been more snug for two very old men. The birch logs in the fireplace had blazed brightly and now had been resolved into glowing red shapes that looked solid but were near the point of crumbling. Soon a fresh log would be needed. There were plenty of them in the battered basket by the hearth. The February sunshine glittered on long icicles outside the window and the steady dripping from them played a pleasant tune on the sill. It was almost time for tea.

The two old brothers, Nicholas and Ernest Whiteoak, were quite ready for it. They ate lightly but liked their food often. Tea was their favourite meal. Nicholas looked impatiently at the ormolu clock on the mantelshelf.

"What time is it?" he asked.

"A quarter past four."

"What?"

"A quarter past four."

"Hm. I wonder where everyone is."

"I wonder."

"Winter's getting on."

"Yes. It's St. Valentine's Day."

"I have a valentine." The clear pipe came from the hearthrug where their great-nephew Dennis was lying with a book in front of him.

"You have a valentine, eh?" exclaimed Ernest. " And do you know who sent it you? "

"No. That's a secret. But I guess it was Adeline." He rose and stood between the two old men like a slender shoot growing between two ancient oaks. He wore a green pullover which accentuated his clear pallor, the blondness

I

of his straight hair and the greenness of his long narrow eyes.

Ernest said, in rather halting French,—"I have always considered those eyes of his rather a disfigurement. They're altogether too green. Certainly his mother's eyes were greenish but not like this."

Dennis said, in English,—"I understood every word you said."

"What did I say then?" demanded Ernest.

"You said my eyes were too green. Greener than my mother's."

"I'm very sorry," said Ernest. "I apologize. I forget that you're not just a very small boy."

"I was nine at Christmas."

"Eight. I well remember when I was eight. I had a beautiful birthday party, in this very house."

"How old are you now, Uncle Ernest?"

"I am ninety-four. That seems quite old to you, I daresay."

"Yes. Pretty old."

"Yet I remember my eighth birthday as though it were just a month ago. It was a lovely spring day and I had a new suit for the occasion. There had been a heavy rain the night before and, as I ran out to welcome the first guest, I tripped and fell into a puddle on the drive. The front of the jacket was all wet with muddy water! Even my lace collar was wet."

"Lace collar!"

"Yes. Boys dressed differently in those days."

Ernest would have liked to go on talking about the past but the door opened and a young girl came in. She was the daughter of the old man's eldest nephew, Renny Whiteoak. She went to the brothers and kissed them in turn.

"Hullo, Uncles," she exclaimed. "You look beautiful, bless your hearts."

"All spruced up for tea," rumbled Nicholas. "And tired of waiting for it."

Adeline stroked his upstanding grey hair which the onslaught of the years had failed perceptibly to thin. "I love your hair, Uncle Nick," she said. "It looks so massive."

At once Ernest felt a twinge of jealousy. He passed a hand over his thin white hair and said disparagingly:

"I don't know why it is but your Uncle Nicholas' hair never looks as though he ran a brush over it."

"That's the trouble," said Adeline. "He runs the brush over it, not through it. I'll have a go at it one of these days and show you how handsome he can look."

Nicholas looked up at her adoringly. He took one of her slim, strong hands in his and held it to his cheek.

"You've been outdoors," he said. "I smell the frosty air on your hand."

"Yes. I've just had the dogs for a walk. I'm starving."

"Here comes the tea!" cried Dennis.

Through the door which Adeline had left open behind her, a small thin man, with close-cropped grey hair and an expression of mingled resignation and aggressiveness on his sallow face, came in, carrying a tray. Adeline sprang to his assistance and drew the tea-table between the two old men.

"Good," she exclaimed. "Plenty of bread and butter and blackberry jam. I believe I like bread and butter better than any other food." She took a piece from the plate and began to eat it. Dennis at once stretched out his hand to do the same.

"Don't do that, young man," said Adeline, her mouth full. "It's one thing for me to have bad manners. Quite another for you."

Adeline's mother now entered. She was in her early fifties, her look of calmness and self-possession the achievement of many years of struggle. The smile on her lips was not reflected in the clear blue depths of her eyes. She seated herself behind the tea-table, her hands moved among the cups and saucers. Dennis came and stood by the tray.

"May I pass things?" he asked.

"If you're very careful." She began to fill the cups.

"Where is Renny?" asked Ernest.

The man, Wragge, spoke up. "'E's in 'is office, sir, going over accounts, but 'e said to tell you he'd be in directly."

"Thank you," said Alayne Whiteoak, with an air of dismissal.

He did not go at once, however, but lingered to set a chair in place, to adjust a curtain, to empty an ashtray into the fireplace. It was as though he remained to irritate her. When, at last, he had gone she said:

"I wish Renny would ever be on time."

"He has the accounts to do," Adeline said, defensively. "He can't very well leave in the middle of doing them."

Ernest remarked, to bridge the moment's tenseness between mother and daughter:

"The fire needs fresh logs."

"I'll put one on," cried Dennis. He heaved the largest log on to the fire which sent up a cloud of sparks. Small eager flames beset the log as it settled on to the glowing foundation.

"Good boy," said Nicholas. He stretched out his hand to raise the teacup to his lips but miscalculated the distance and overturned the scalding tea on to the rug. "Well, well!" he exclaimed ruefully. "That was stupid of me." He took out his handkerchief and began to mop up the tea.

"If you would only keep your mind on your movements the way I do," said Ernest, "you would never upset things."

Nicholas blew out his cheeks. "Can't keep my mind on anything," he rumbled. "Got very little mind left."

"Uncle Nick," cried Adeline, "you have a wonderful mind! Don't worry about the rug. I'll fetch a towel from the dogs' room."

Alayne said,—"I'll pour you a fresh cup of tea, Uncle Nicholas." But her hands trembled with irritation as she poured. She kept saying to herself,—"We shall not have him with us much longer. Be patient."

Adeline brought a towel and a basin of water, Nicholas and Dennis watching her with concentrated interest as she mopped up the wet spot. Things were barely in order again when Renny Whiteoak entered, bringing with him a gust of cold air.

"I thought you'd like a little fresh air," he said. "It's terribly hot in here."

"Please don't leave that door open," exclaimed his wife.
"We shall freeze."

"I should certainly be forced to go to my room," said
Ernest.

Nicholas was silent, brooding on the spilt tea, though he
had a freshly-filled cup in front of him.

"It's like spring outdoors," said Renny. "The birds
are chirping. It would do you good to get the air." He
stood beside the tea-table smiling down at them, tall, wiry,
his dark red hair lightly touched with grey at the temples,
his high-coloured face animated by a teasing smile.

Alayne thought,—"How can he look younger than I,
when he is much older! It isn't fair. And yet it is fair
because he has the power to do what I have not the power
to do—draw happiness out of some deep well within himself—out of some pagan link with the primeval." She rose
and, with her graceful walk, went to the outer door and
firmly closed it. When she returned to her place Renny
sat down and took Dennis on his knee. "How often,"
thought Alayne, "I have seen him with a child on his
knee! A child on his knee or sitting astride a horse—those
are the two ways I picture him most easily. I'm not particularly fond of children. I don't very much like horses,
but Renny still fascinates me." She poured a cup of tea
for him and handed it to him with a smile.

Nicholas had regained his spirits. There was a deliciously
soft fresh cake and he was eating it with relish. His few
remaining teeth, which were mercifully hidden behind his
drooping grey moustache, were capable only of masti-
cating soft food. He said:

"It's high time this young lady of ours saw something
of the world. I was saying to Ernest less than an hour ago
that it's high time she saw something of the world."

"I couldn't agree with you more, Uncle Nick," said
Adeline.

"What Adeline should have been doing in these past
months," said Alayne, "is to have gone to a university. I
very much wanted to enter her at Smith, as you know."

"Never heard of it," declared Nicholas. "Where is
it?"

Nicholas had, since the war, become tremendously anti-American. No one quite knew why. He took no trouble to conceal this feeling, for he could not remember, no matter how often he was reminded, that Alayne was an American. Though she had spent almost half her life in a British country she still was very conscious of her American roots. She subscribed to the more intellectual of American periodicals. She kept in touch with what was going on in the political scene. It was seldom she allowed herself to be stung by any of the old man's remarks but, for some reason, this last remark of his did annoy her.

"It is the most notable women's college on the continent," she returned.

"Never heard of it," he persisted, and emptied his teacup with audible gusto.

Ernest's loved wife had been an American and he now said,—"How well I remember my dear Harriet's descriptions of her life there. They were both enlightening and entertaining."

Nicholas heaved himself about in his chair to look sceptically at his brother. "Never heard Harriet speak of it," he said.

"I myself am a graduate of Smith College." Alayne spoke with a little asperity.

"Ha," returned the old man. "That accounts for the only fault you have."

Alayne looked enquiringly at him.

"An air of superiority, my dear."

Alayne flushed a little. "It is remarkable," she said, "that I should still retain that, after more than twenty years at Jalna."

Renny laughed. "But you do," he declared. "You do."

"Adeline," put in Ernest, "matriculated with honours. It is a great pity that she has not gone on with her education in a university."

"I didn't want to," said Adeline. "I mean I'm not that sort of girl."

"But you are," insisted her great-uncle. "Otherwise you would not have done so well in your exams."

"I know enough now," returned Adeline laconically.

"There you show your ignorance," said Alayne. "If you want any sort of career—but"—she gave a little shrug—"we've been through all this before. I know you think life at Jalna is career enough for you. I only hope you won't regret it."

"Never fear," put in Renny. "She won't regret it. She's her father's daughter. Not one of the boys has been as keen about horses as she."

He often spoke of his brothers as though they were his sons, of which he had only one, a boy of almost fourteen, at a preparatory school.

"The point is," said Adeline, "that I am dying to go to Ireland with Maurice."

Nicholas had finished his tea and his chin had sunk to his breast. He was indulging in a short nap. Now he brought himself up with a snort, subconsciously aware that something of real interest had been said.

"What is that?" he demanded. "Ireland? Who's going to Ireland?" The very name of Ireland uttered was enough to rouse him from sleep, for from there had come his strong-willed mother as a young woman, to there she often had returned to visit; Ireland she had constantly elevated as the greatest of countries, its speech had coloured her own, and though she never had been able to get on with her relations there, she had boasted of them as superior in wit and breeding to the Whiteoaks.

"Ireland," Nicholas repeated. "We haven't a living relation there now—except old Dermot Court."

"He died years ago, Uncle Nick, and left his property to young Maurice. Don't you remember?" Renny looked anxiously into the old man's face. "Maurice goes over this spring to claim it."

Nicholas' brow cleared. "Ah, yes. I remember now. And a very nice property it is. I saw a good deal of Dermot at one time. Best manners of any man I ever knew. Who's going to Ireland, did you say?"

"Me!" Adeline gave a daring look at her father.

"I wish you would try not to be aggressive," said Alayne.

"I do try. But you've no idea how hard it is."

She now threw a coaxing look about the circle of grown-ups. "It will be such a wonderful opportunity for me to see something of the world. You know the war kept me from ever being taken anywhere. I actually don't know anything of life outside Jalna, do I?"

"The thing for you to do," said Ernest, with a sly smile, "is to marry Maurice and go to Ireland on your honeymoon."

The suggestion of marriage for Adeline was distasteful to Renny. He expected that, in due course, she would marry but he looked on that time as years distant. He regarded Adeline as a child. He did not want Adeline to marry till the perfect mate for her appeared—if such a one existed. He did not think Maurice and she were suited to each other. He was not even sure that Maurice cared for Adeline except as a cousin. Alayne, on the other hand, would have liked to see her daughter's future secure. She was convinced that Maurice was attracted to Adeline, and, in truth, felt that, if there would be any unsuitability in the match, it would be because he was finer fibred and more sensitive than Adeline. The young girl, with her passionate love of country life, of horses and dogs, her tardy approach to things intellectual, was not and never had been a congenial companion to Alayne. She had been surprised and pleased by her excellent standing in her studies but it had been disappointing to find that Adeline's attitude towards scholastic achievement seemed to be that she could do well anything she chose but that, once she had mastered what was in the books, she had little further interest in them. Alayne's hopes for intellectual companionship lay in her son, whose school reports showed that he was already impressing his teachers with his ability. Archer was an omnivorous reader. Adeline liked the old romantic novels she found on the bookshelves in the library. Many of these had belonged to her great-grandmother for whom she was named, and Alayne sometimes suspected that part of the child's interest in them was because they had been handled and read by the woman whose portrait she so much resembled. She had devoured the old copies of the *Boys' Own* and the books of Talbot

Baines Reed that were heaped in a corner of the attic. Not long ago Alayne had discovered her reading *Tom Jones*. "Do you like it?" Alayne had asked, herself hating the book excepting in an academic fashion. "Oh, yes," Adeline had answered. "Those were the days! I wish I'd lived then." "Well, don't give it to Archer," Alayne had said. "Of course not," Adeline had agreed promptly. "But he probably knows more than you think."

"Yes," Ernest now repeated. "Marry your cousin and go to Ireland on your honeymoon."

"She'd better not suggest such a thing to me," said Renny.

"I can't very well till Maurice suggests it to me," laughed Adeline.

"Come now, come now——" Ernest shook his head teasingly at her.

She flushed. "I want to go to Ireland for fun," she said. "Not on a honeymoon."

"No better fun," rumbled Nicholas, but stopped himself at a look from Alayne.

"I want to go to Ireland," Dennis said in his high clear voice. "My mother came from Ireland."

"Did she!" Adeline exclaimed. "I always thought she was an American like my mother."

Nicholas gave a thump on the arm of his chair. "The ignorance of these children is unbelievable," he declared. "Dennis's mother was a Court. She was of a good old Irish family. Nothing American about her."

"I wasn't ignorant," said Dennis. "I knew she was Irish."

"But she died in the States, didn't she?" Adeline asked.

"Yes," Renny answered curtly. Then demanded,— "What has put the idea of going to Ireland into your head?"

"Well, I went there once with you," she said, "and it was the best time I've ever had in my life."

"You said," put in Dennis, severely, "you'd never been anywhere."

"Don't be cheeky," ordered Nicholas, and put a piece of cake into Dennis's hand.

"What I meant," said Adeline, "was that the war had stopped me going back to Ireland. Oh, I do so want to go when Maurice goes and I don't see what's to prevent me."

"If Maurice's mother were going as she planned to do, it might be possible for you to go too," said Alayne, "but she can't get away, any more than I can."

"I don't see why it wouldn't be proper for two young cousins to go on a voyage together."

"It would be highly improper," said Ernest, "un-less——" He could not keep his mind off the thought of the marriage.

"We are always talking about going to Ireland," Adeline muttered, "yet nobody goes."

Ernest patted her knee. "Maurice is now his own master. We shall see what happens. You may be able to go with him in a relationship that will please everyone."

"Did I hear my name?" asked a voice from the doorway. All turned to look at Maurice Whiteoak.

II

THE COUSINS

HE WAS a slender, graceful young fellow, with a sensitive face, a contrast to his father, Piers Whiteoak, who in middle age had grown thickset and who looked on the world with a challenge. When no more than a child Maurice had been sent to Ireland to live, at the invitation of a childless relative, Dermot Court, in the acknowledged hope that he would be made the old man's heir. What might have been a boring experiment for the man and a tragic experience for the boy had turned out well. Each had been happy in the other's company. A deep love and understanding had grown up between them, and when, five years later, Dermot Court had died, Maurice had inherited from him his large house which was in fair repair, and an income sufficient for its maintenance. He had returned to his parents' house, a stranger, a shy, proud stripling of seventeen, financially independent of them, but vulnerable as ever to his father's sarcasms.

Now Nicholas said to him,—"We're wishing we might go to Ireland with you, Mooey."

"Especially your cousin Adeline wishes it," Ernest added.

"I should be glad to entertain all of you," said Maurice. "You'd be welcome at Glengorman."

Dennis carried the plate of cakes to him. "Have one," he said, ingratiatingly.

"Bread and butter first, thank you." Maurice helped himself to a piece, then sat down beside Adeline.

Nicholas said,—"Your Uncle Ernest and I will never see Ireland again. Nor England."

"Alas, no." Ernest drew a deep sigh.

"Nonsense," exclaimed Renny. "You may at any time now. The change would do you good."

"I hear," Ernest said, "that travelling is most uncomfortable. I even hear the word austerity used in connection with it—a word I have always disliked."

"I wasn't aware you knew the meaning of it," said Nicholas.

"It is extraordinary," Ernest spoke with severity, "that you should choose to belittle what I endured during the war. I did without many comforts to which I was accustomed, didn't I, Alayne?"

"You did indeed, Uncle Ernest."

"Once you arrive in Ireland," said Maurice, "you shall have everything you want."

"That is very kind of you." Ernest leant forward to pat his great-nephew's knee. "Very kind indeed. Well . . . I'll consider it. But, you know, I shall be ninety-five in the spring. It's pretty old for travel. Still—if you'd like to have me, Mooey."

"I should indeed," said Maurice. He was particularly fond of this old uncle who always had shown kindness to him and understanding of the traits in him which were irritating to Maurice's father, had sympathized with his preference for books above horses, had encouraged his attachment to Adeline.

"Go ahead, Ernie, and have your last fling!" Nicholas' voice, singularly robust for his age, boomed into a laugh. "Go ahead, and take my love to the gals we used to know there—if any of 'em are above ground."

Adeline laughed across the chasm of years that separated her from Nicholas.

"I'll bet they are, Uncle Nick," she said. "I'll bet there's many a lonely old lady in Ireland who would like to get a nice message from you."

"Well, well," he said, "I'll never see 'em again."

"We gave a pretty good coming-of-age party for you," Ernest remarked to his great-nephew. After a pause, he added,—"The last Whiteoak to inherit a fortune on his twenty-first birthday was Finch. How well I remember the party we gave for him! We had a dinner party and a dance.

Finch made a speech. He was very nervous. After all the guests were gone he and Piers, you and I, Nicholas, sat up for a long while talking and drinking. It was then that Finch suggested that Nick and I should go to England for a visit at his expense. And now here is this dear boy, Mooey, offering to take us to Ireland."

"You four got pretty tight that night," said Renny. "Do you remember? I was waked by your singing and I came downstairs and took you off to bed."

The two old brothers laughed, as at the recollection of a good joke. Young Maurice regarded them anxiously. The thought of paying their travelling expenses to Ireland had not occurred to him. Adeline, seeing his discomfiture, gave him a teasing smile. He ignored it and said to her:

"I have some rather good new records. Like to come over to our place and hear them?"

"I'd love to." She got up, gave herself a small stretch and asked,—"Does anybody want me for anything?"

Nobody did and she and Maurice went into the hall.

"Did you come in a car?" asked Adeline.

"Yes."

"I thought you would. Lazy dog."

"Surely you wouldn't expect a fellow to walk through slush to his ankles!"

"You could wear rubber boots."

"Don't you like a car?"

"Certainly I like a car. But I think a walk would do you good. You're soft."

"You're always criticizing me," he said, resentfully.

Adeline laughed. They jostled each other as they passed through the door into the porch. Antagonism and attraction struggled between them. "If only she were different," he thought, "I could love her with all my heart." "If only he were different," she thought, but she did not think of love. He wanted her to be like the girls over whom he brooded in his solitude. Physically she was perfect to him. Her smile enchanted him. Why should she be so careless of those charms, bestowing her smile where it was not appreciated, for Maurice felt that no one but himself appreciated her! Yet on him she looked critically. She wished, he was sure, that he were more like her father. Once he had told her so.

"Goodness, no," she had said. "One of him is all I can cope with."

"Still you'd like me better if I were," he had insisted.

"One of him is all I want," she had repeated.

Now he said,—"Aren't you going to put on a jacket or something? You'll freeze."

"I suppose I'd better." She darted back into the house and returned with a jacket.

A flock of pigeons flew from the roof towards her. They sought to alight on her head and shoulders. Holding up her arms to protect herself from this demonstration of their affection she ran to the car and scrambled in. Maurice sprang in after her and slammed the door. The pigeons circled above the moving car, then were about to return to the roof when a long glittering icicle fell from the eave to the steps, with a sound as of splintering glass. The pigeons swept away in the direction of the stables, their plumage shining in the sunlight.

Maurice was happy to have her in the car with him. In its isolation he had a feeling of possessiveness over her. She sat acquiescent in the seat beside him, her burnished chestnut hair waving close about her head; the formation of her nose and chin which, in middle age, would show the strength of her great-grandmother's profile, was now softened by youthful curves. Her lips, Maurice thought, looked unusually sweet-tempered. Conscious of his scrutiny she turned to him and smiled.

The car bumped over a rut in the snow-drifted road. The two were bounced on the seat.

"I hate the winter," he exclaimed.

"I thought you liked ski-ing."

"I do. It alleviates the monotony of cold and snow outdoors and dry heat indoors. I was made for a temperate climate, moist and gentle and green. I like tranquil people."

"People like me?"

"I don't *like* you, Adeline."

"What do you think of my going to Ireland?" she asked hurriedly.

"I've always intended you should come."

She gave a little grunt of surprise and exasperation.

"You are the most supercilious person I know," she exclaimed. "You look so gentle and you speak so gently, yet you're terribly superior inside. I guess it was your life in Ireland with that old Cousin Dermot. He spoilt you terribly. Everybody says so."

"What about you? You're a spoilt child."

"Me? I've been very strictly brought up."

Maurice turned the car into the driveway of the grey stucco house.

"Mother and Dad are out," he said.

He glanced sideways at Adeline to discover whether she were pleased or disappointed that she was to be alone with him. She showed neither feeling. Simply she wore an expression of pleasurable anticipation at the prospect of hearing a new record. They went into the comfortable living-room which clearly showed one woman's struggle against four males to preserve the freshness of its chintz, the plumpness of its cushions, the firmness of its upholstery. She had not quite succeeded or quite failed. It was a long narrow room, and in one corner stood the radio-gramophone and record cabinet.

Adeline whistled. "Goodness, you have a lot of records! They must have cost a pretty penny."

"I've made rather a hobby of collecting them," he said. "It's something to do."

"I should think you'd have plenty to do with your university work."

Maurice gave a faint shrug. "Oh, I don't work very hard. And you must remember I'm just getting over a bad attack of 'flu."

"You do catch things, don't you?" she said.

Maurice thought there was a little disparagement in her voice. He answered quickly:

"No more than most people. You're almost too healthy."

Adeline laughed. "One of us has got to be strong," she said.

"Just what do you mean by that?" he asked eagerly.

"Nothing—excepting that the new generation can't afford to be delicate and elegant."

"I'm not delicate," he returned hotly. "But just because I've never been keen about horses and sports, you think I am."

"You get annoyed," she said, "if I suggest that you're delicate. Yet you said, a moment ago, that I'm too healthy."

"Forgive me, Adeline." He put his arm about her. "I wouldn't for worlds have you different."

Something in his voice made her feel their isolation in the house. Detaching herself she turned on the radio. The voice of a male crooner came out, whiningly, urging his loved one to surrender.

The two young people, with expressionless faces, stared at the radio.

When the song was finished Adeline said,—"Imagine surrendering to *that*!"

"I don't believe you will ever know what surrender means."

"I don't think I shall," she returned serenely.

Maurice turned off the radio and adjusted the machine for records. He put on the waltz from Tchaikowsky's Serenade for Strings. Adeline felt that here was music she could understand, very different from the lifeless sounds that had just come over the radio. She pictured Finch bending above the keyboard of the piano at Jalna. She stood by the window looking out at the snowy scene, the bare black limbs of the trees, each limb topped by a sharply defined rim of snow, the sky red in the burnished sunset.

"That music makes me happy," she said, at the end. "I could fly—I could dance like an angel to it."

"You do dance like one."

"Thanks."

"Would you like to dance now?"

"I thought I came here to listen to records."

"We can do both."

"Let's have the records first."

Maurice put on several classical records. She gave her judicial attention to each. She said:

"I like the Tchaikowsky one best."

"I knew you would. You see, I can guess your taste."

"We don't go in for records."

"Adeline, will you dance?"

"No. I'm not in the mood," she answered tersely.

He offered her a cigarette and they sat down side by side on the sofa.

"I can't tell you," he said, "how excited I am at the thought of going back to Ireland. You know I should have gone when I came of age but my mother was ill. Wouldn't you like to visit me in my own house, Adeline?"

"Of course I should! We've always planned it. I'll persuade Daddy to come too. See if I don't."

Maurice said dreamily—"Everything is going to be different from now on. I shall be my own master. So long as I am under this roof I'm conscious of my father's authority."

Adeline gave a little sympathetic grunt. Then she said,— "Mooey, you haven't changed a bit since you came home. Excepting, of course, to grow up."

"The years I spent in Ireland were the happiest of my life," he said, in the reminiscent tone of an elderly man.

"I think it was a very queer thing," declared Adeline, "for your parents to do. I mean to let you go all that distance to live with an old forty-second cousin. Why, you might have died of homesickness. I'm sure I should have."

"It was pretty bad at first."

"Still, it turned out well, as he left you all his money."

"Adeline, you are a materialistic little beast."

"No, I'm not. I just look facts in the face. You live in a kind of dream. You like to pretend that you don't care about money but you like it just as well as anybody."

A motor car turned into the drive. In a moment the front door of the house was thrown open. Piers Whiteoak, his wife, and his youngest child, entered the hall, with a stamping of snowy feet, and the barking of a small dog. Child and dog ran into the room.

This baby girl was Adeline's favourite and pet. She snatched her up and kissed her.

"Do you remember," she asked Maurice, "how, when Baby was born, you and I agreed never to marry but always to be friends and have her for our child?"

"I never agreed to any such thing. It's an idiotic idea."

"It would save a lot of trouble."

"Don't be silly."

Adeline opened her eyes wide. "Why, Mooey, I thought it was all arranged."

Piers and Pheasant came into the room. Piers, at forty-four, still retained his fresh-coloured complexion, the brightness of his blue eyes. Pheasant, two years younger, had the figure of a slim girl, an eager questioning look in her eyes. What that question was she did not herself know. Even the devoted love she gave Piers did not answer it, nor even his loyal love for her.

Piers said to his son,—"That car of yours was left directly in my way. The result was that your mother had to wade through deep snow to get round it."

"Oh, I'm sorry," exclaimed Maurice contritely but with a tremor of anger in his voice at the anger in Piers'.

The little girl said proudly,—"Daddy carried Baby in. Baby didn't walk in the snow."

Pheasant sat down facing Maurice and Adeline. "Where do you suppose we were?" she asked. "We were at the Clappertons'! Really it is the strangest household! I almost feel sorry for the old fellow. I don't think he realized, when he married that odd girl and took her odd sisters into the house, what he was letting himself in for. The house is like a menagerie. Pets of all sorts—all over the place. And it's so untidy! And poor Mr. Clapperton has a cowed look."

"He looked bad-tempered to me," said Piers.

"I wish I might be hidden there," she continued, "and hear what goes on."

"For one thing," said Adeline, "they can't get any proper help. Maids won't stay there. It was the youngest sister who did most of the work and since she's married Mr. Clapperton's nephew and gone to the States, things get worse and worse. Neither Mrs. Clapperton nor Althea is able to do much."

"They have a D.P. now," said Pheasant, "who can speak only a dozen words of English. You'll never guess what Mr. Clapperton whispered to me, Piers."

"What? I saw a good deal of whispering between you."

"He told me he's planning to get on with his model village in the spring!"

"Why—he promised to give up the idea of that, to please his wife!"

"I guess he's tired of trying to please her. Anyhow that's what he said."

"Renny'll never allow it."

"I hope he can stop it but, for my part, I don't see much harm in a pretty little model village."

Piers gave her a look of disgust. "A pretty little model village—right on our doorstep! Teeming with undesirable people—screaming children all over the place—I can tell you it would lower the value of our property in no time."

"There is a terrible need for houses." Maurice thoroughly disliked the thought of the village but some antagonism he could not resist impelled him to be in opposition to Piers.

"Let them build somewhere else," Piers said hotly. "There's plenty of room."

"If Mr. Clapperton builds a lot of houses next door to us," said Adeline, "Daddy will pull them down with his own hands. And I'll help him."

"Mrs. Clapperton will never let him do it," declared Pheasant. "She has the upper hand, it's easy to see."

Adeline stood up very straight. "I'm going home," she said, "to tell Daddy and the uncles."

The baby girl clung to her. "No, no, Adeline stay with Mary!"

"I'll come back tomorrow."

"Stay to supper," urged Piers.

"I'll stay tomorrow, if I may."

Driving to Jalna Maurice said petulantly,—"Why did they have to come home, just when we were enjoying ourselves alone!" He had a feeling that if he had been left alone with Adeline the barrier that separated them might have disappeared. He had many opportunities of being alone with her yet always experienced the same feeling of frustration, of inability to draw spiritually close to her. Sometimes he told himself that this would be for ever impossible, that they never could be more to each other than they now were—cousins—friends—but lovers, never. Sometimes he told himself that the trouble lay in her youth. She was, in many ways, young for her years, while he felt himself more mature than his parents. Yet he knew that in their eyes he had not touched even the fringe of experience. He knew that to Piers he was no more than a callow, rather irritating youth, to Pheasant her little son, growing up, of course, but still her little son. One thing Maurice was sure of—Adeline would never grow up in the way he wanted her to, while she lived at Jalna. He was the outsider and he wanted to draw her outside with him. If he could take her to Ireland with him everything would be different. She wanted, with all her might, to go to Ireland —but not for the sake of making anything different.

In the drawing-room, with the curtains drawn against the evening, Renny and the two old uncles sat close together in front of the fire whose light made a fragile cameo of Ernest's face, mysterious caverns of Nicholas' eyes, glinted on his massive seal ring and intensified the high-coloured hardiness of Renny's face, Adeline stood regarding the three with the sombre look of one who bore tidings which would take the smiles from their faces.

"Mr. Clapperton," she said, "is at it again."

"At what?" demanded all three.

"His village. Uncle Piers and Auntie Pheasant just came from his house and he told her he's getting on with it in the spring."

Ernest struck the arm of his chair with a slender clenched fist.

"He can't do it," he said, his voice breaking with anger. "I will not allow it!"

Nicholas cupped an ear with his hand. "What's this?" he demanded. "What's that horrid old fellow up to? Ill-treating his poor young wife, I'll be bound."

Adeline came and perched on the arm of his chair. "No, Uncle Nick—something far worse. He's talking of building more bungalows. His model village, you know."

"But we stopped that years ago."

Renny gave a short laugh. "He perennially brings up

the subject, but his wife will never let him go on with it. He's completely under her thumb."

"And the right place for him too," said Nicholas.

"I shouldn't be too sure of that," Ernest said judicially. "I should look into the matter. Tell him I will not allow it."

"A lot he cares for you," chuckled his brother.

"He has the greatest respect for my opinion, as he has told me on more than one occasion."

"It was a bad day for everyone when he came into the neighbourhood," said Renny. "I hate the sight of him. I think I'll go straight over and see him."

III

A TRIO AT HOME

AFTER Piers and his wife had left Vaughanlands the three people who made up the family sat silent for a short while, each occupied with thoughts which their calm exteriors belied. Eugene Clapperton, grey-haired, rigid, thought— "Why did I tell Mrs. Whiteoak I was going to start building again? Gem would never agree to it. But I had to tell her. It made me feel better. It made me feel my own master again. And certainly if I want to realize my life's dream I'll not let her prevent it. God, when I think what I've done for her—and her ingratitude! It makes me sick. To think she wouldn't have been able to take a step today, if it hadn't been for me! Look at the luxury I keep her in, and she was poor as a church mouse. If only I knew what is in that head of hers! Ingratitude and conceit. You'd think she owned the house. She likes to put me in the wrong—make me look small. . . . If only I didn't love her it wouldn't be so bad! But she'll try me too far. . . . There's a limit even to my endurance." He sat smiling a little, his eyes blank, his thin ankles interlocked against the front of his chair.

His wife thought,—"What was he whispering to Pheasant? Some foolish boasting I'm very sure. But she seemed worried by it. What could it have been that would make her look anxious? I wish he would go and leave the fire to Althea and me. His presence in the room irritates me. The way he holds his legs. The way he keeps rubbing the back of one hand with the dry palm of the other. . . . Yet, if his hands were moist—how horrible! I dislike Eugene's hands. The fingers are too short for his height. The thumb is coarse. . . . When I have him alone I

22

will worm out of him what he was saying to Pheasant Whiteoak."

Althea, fair and ethereally slender, sat watching a dark corner of the room. She was thinking,—"I believe I heard the tortoise move. How thrilling if he's awake! I'm glad I brought him into this warm room. He has slept long enough. This is just the place for him. As far as I'm concerned it's my favourite room in the house and I could make it beautiful, if I could get rid of those hideous pictures of Eugene's and put up some good ones. That fat woman knitting. That shipwreck off an incredible coast. Those cows in that repulsive meadow. I should burn them all! And Eugene with them!" She gave a little laugh.

"And what do you find amusing, may I enquire?" asked her brother-in-law.

"The tortoise. He's waking. Don't you hear him?"

A steady thumping and bumping came from a small wooden box at the end of the room.

"You have brought that creature into the best room!" Eugene Clapperton exclaimed angrily.

"It's the best room for him. It faces south. It's always warm. He's been cold long enough."

"I don't like it at all."

Althea turned to her sister. "The tortoise does no harm, does he?"

"Not a bit of harm. I adore him."

The two young women sprang up and hurried to the box where the bumping continued, Althea with long, silent steps, Gemmel making sharp sounds with her high heels. They bent over the box where convulsive movements were taking place inside a piece of flannel. Althea tenderly unwrapped the creature. From between his shells his greenish legs stretched forth, feeling for security. His little snakelike head protruded, his mouth stretched in a pink yawn. He was the size of a tea plate.

"Oh, the darling!" cried Gemmel.

Althea held him rapturously in her long white hands.

"You have slept so long," she whispered to him, "and now you are hungry. You shall have a dandelion. I have them growing in a box upstairs. Watch him, Gem, while I fly up and get him one."

Noiselessly she left the room and they did not hear her run up the stairs. She had set the tortoise on the floor and now he began, with prehistoric deliberation, to cross the room.

"I don't like animals crawling over my rugs," said Mr. Clapperton.

"Oh, Eugene, I think he's sweet."

"He's disgusting to me. All those animals your sister and you bring into the house are nasty. There was that enormous worm that wove its cocoon in a window curtain and in the spring a moth came out and laid eggs and the eggs turned into grubs. There was the nest of young skunks! There are the dancing mice and the toad!"

"No one," declared Gemmel hotly, "could reasonably complain of any of those excepting the skunks and we got rid of them."

"But not of their odour." With disgust he watched the tortoise creeping towards him. He drew up his feet. "Take it away," he ordered.

"Oh, how funny," she laughed. "What a picture!"

He kicked at the tortoise, rolling it over on its back. Althea came into the room carrying a dandelion in her fingers. She gave a cry of dismay and dropped to her knees beside the tortoise whose legs weakly sought a foothold in the air.

"Poor darling!" she cried and righted it. "Oh, Eugene, how could you be so cruel?" She stared with hate at her brother-in-law who returned the look with no lessening of that quality.

"I didn't hurt it."

"You did! He's lame."

"Nonsense."

Althea offered the dandelion and the tortoise, ending his long fast, opened his mouth wide and, with a hissing sound, drew in the blossom. The three watched him, fascinated. Then, quite uninjured by the kick, he resumed his purposeful walk.

"I want you," said Eugene Clapperton steadily, "to take

him upstairs and keep him there. I want you to keep all your pets in your own room."

She answered, in a shaking voice, "I will. And myself too." She snatched the tortoise, his flannel wrapping, his box, and fled.

There was a silence after she left, embarrassed and angry on the husband's part, amused and angry on the wife's. After a little he said:

"That girl irritates me so I say more than I should. She's enough to drive a man crazy."

"You knew what she was when I married you."

He returned bitterly,—"It's no fun marrying your wife's relations. In your case, two queer sisters."

"One of them is gone. Some day Althea will marry."

He gave a derisive laugh. "I'd like to know who would marry her."

"Oh, she's had her chances! She's not like me—jumping at her first offer."

He answered angrily,—"I have been indulgence itself to you, haven't I?"

She looked at him in cold silence.

"Haven't I?" he repeated. "I did a lot for you before we were married and I've done a good deal since. I gave up building my dream village for you and I've regretted it."

"Is that what you were muttering about to Mrs. Piers?"

"Muttering, eh? *Muttering!*"

"Well, you weren't talking in an ordinary tone."

"I daren't choose my way of talking," he said harshly, "in my own house!"

"I'm sorry, Eugene," she returned coaxingly. "I should have said you spoke in a low tone. I caught a few words that made me guess you'd brought up the question of the village again."

"I was only telling Mrs. Piers how I regret the project. You should not have made me give it up."

"But, my dear, you asked me what I should most like for a wedding present and I said at once I'd like to know that never, never would any more small houses disfigure the property. That's true, isn't it?"

B

"Yes."

"And you gave me your word to stop building, didn't you?"

"I was a fool, if ever there was one. That village had been my dream. Besides there was money in it. A good deal of money. It would have been a benefit to the community."

She laughed derisively. "A benefit! All the neighbourhood would hate you for it."

"The neighbours don't care much for me, as it is. I've never fitted in. Nowadays I don't fit into my own house. That tortoise is more at home here than I am. That great brute of a dog growls at me every time he sees me. Why Althea should want to keep a Great Dane I can't imagine."

"She has always liked animals better than people."

"She certainly likes him better than she likes me."

His wife came and sat on the arm of his chair. She stroked the back of his neck. "Poor old Tiddledy-winks," she said, using her ridiculous pet name for him.

His hand was against the fulness of her breast, her heartbeats thudded in his ear, beating coherence out of his thought, filling his mind with sensual longings. "Oh, Gem," he breathed, "I wish you'd have a baby. Things would be different somehow, if you had a baby."

"You're baby enough for me." She held his head closer. He was soothed and mollified.

They sat quietly for some time.

Upstairs the dog began to bark. Eugene Clapperton said peevishly:

"I've never before had a dog in the house. I've never liked them. Every time I meet Renny Whiteoak I'm annoyed by the dogs that surround him."

"Yes," said Gem, "a bulldog, a bob-tailed sheep dog and a Cairn terrier. They're sweet."

"Not to me. They're a nuisance from the day they're born till they die. Why is that brute upstairs making so much noise?"

"Althea is getting ready to take him for a walk. He's excited."

"He has a brutally coarse bark, that's all I can say."

The barking grew louder and louder as the two descended the stairs. It was deafening as they passed through the hall. Althea looked shyly in at the Clappertons and said something but it could not be heard. Now the barking was outdoors. Now there was silence.

"This is how we should be all the time," said Eugene Clapperton. "Alone together."

She got up and moved restlessly about the room.

"I was a very foolish man," he could not help saying, "to make you such a promise."

"Well, it's made and must be kept." Now she had put on what he called her "sulky face", but whatever expression she wore it was fascinating to him.

"I might remark," he said, "that you promised to obey me when we were married. Have you kept your promise?"

"Oh, that!" she exclaimed contemptuously.

One of their long, wrangling discussions began. An unseen listener might have thought they did it to pass the time, so persistent, so purposeless, was the pattern their argument took. Althea and her dog returned from their walk and went quietly upstairs. Then the winter twilight fell and Gem turned on the lights. There was a special light under the painting of the shipwreck. The lurid sky, the white-crested waves now dominated the room. Eugene Clapperton absorbed the scene with satisfaction. It gave him who had spent all his working life in offices, a sense of peace and manly power. Nothing would induce him to part with the painting. The artist, a Victorian painter whose name did not live after him, meant little to Eugene Clapperton. It was the picture that mattered. He had bought it in an auction sale of household furnishings and, from the moment of its purchase, it had become an important thing in his life.

The lights had been on only a short while when a ring at the doorbell brought the Polish displaced person who acted as maid hurrying from the kitchen. In a moment she announced Renny Whiteoak. Eugene Clapperton, pleased by this interruption to a tiresome talk, yet a little suspicious of the reasons for such a visit, rose stiffly from his chair.

He watched his wife as she gave her hand to the Master of Jalna, jealous that she should so casually touch the flesh of another man.

They talked of the weather and of how spring would soon be coming to relieve the harshness of winter. It was then that Renny remarked,

"There's going to be a lot of building this year and certainly it's needed. People—lots of them—can't find a roof to cover their heads."

"True, true," said Eugene Clapperton, sententiously. "I think that the way people are crowded together is very bad indeed. Bad for health. Bad for morals."

"Let's hope these development schemes will keep away from here." There was something almost threatening in Renny's tone. Clapperton replied:

"I quite agree that building in our neighbourhood might be a misfortune."

"*Might be!*" Renny repeated vehemently. "God knows it has been and is. Much of what was lovely country is ruined—what with putting up and cutting down. Do you remember the magnificent oaks and pines that were butchered—just to give some contractor a job to widen the road? But no, that was before you came here."

"*Sad*, very sad," said Eugene Clapperton sympathetically. "I've always liked a nice tree."

His wife sat in silence, staring at him.

He went on,—"The model village I had in mind was a village of trees and flowers. Nice little houses, with nice people in them."

"You built three little houses and you haven't had particularly good luck with your tenants."

"They pay their rent."

"Yes. But one of them drinks and makes himself a nuisance. One has screaming children and a slovenly wife. One keeps his radio running all day and a part of the night."

"You seem to know a great deal about my tenants." Eugene Clapperton's voice had a jealous note in it.

"I do. They're within a stone's throw of my stables. In fact, I've become very friendly with them. But there must not be any more. You agreed to that."

A smile crept over Eugene Clapperton's face. He clasped
one bony knee in his hands, which were rather surprisingly
coarse and strong. "Every man," he said, "sets himself
some sort of ideal and clings to it, more or less, through
his life. My ideal was to be a benefactor, if you know what
I mean. I wanted to make lots of money and I wanted to
help others with my money. I've tried to live up to that,
Colonel Whiteoak."

"You old humbug," Renny thought. But he grinned
with apparent geniality at Clapperton who went on to say:

"I'm not going to relate the benefits I've conferred on
others. One of them you know of," and he smiled with
tenderness at his young wife.

She entered the conversation for the first time.

"No one is likely to forget," she said, her voice coming
gaspingly, as though she had been running, "how it was
through you I had the operation on my spine and so was
able to walk. You paid for everything, didn't you?"

"Please don't mention expense in connection with that,
Gemmel," returned her husband hastily. "You have
repaid me a thousand times in becoming my wife."

"But money did enter into it," she protested.

"It enters into all good works."

Renny regarded them with a good deal of curiosity.
How, he wondered, could the girl endure him.

Eugene Clapperton continued,—"I have my ideal and
you have yours. Mine is to help others. Yours is——" he
hesitated, running his hand over his smooth grey head.

"To look out for myself," finished Renny.

"Well, if you like to put it that way. What I was going
to say is that your ideal is to keep Jalna the same as it was
when your grandfather built it a hundred years ago."

"You're right."

"A hundred years is a long time. You've got to take
account of the changes that take place in our civilization,"
and Eugene Clapperton beat with the soles of his shoes on
the carpet, as though he were a leader in the march of
civilization.

The Master of Jalna tied a knot in his weatherbitten
forehead. "I don't think much of civilization," he said.

"We go away to the wars to fight for it and, when we
come home, do we find things any better? No. There are
shoddier and shoddier houses being built. Shoddier goods
are being made, with more and more high-falutin' names
given them. You can't ride on the roads with comfort
because of trucks and motor cars. Thank God, I have
enough paths on my own estate to give me a gallop when
I want it. Inside my own gates I keep things as they
were."

Eugene Clapperton stopped tapping his soles on the
floor, as though at the mention of Jalna the march of
progress had ceased, but he said:

"And I admire you for it. But—my property is my
own affair. It is my own business, Colonel Whiteoak, what
I put on it. I wouldn't allow even my dear wife to interfere
with that." His eyes rested commandingly on his wife.
He felt a new power welling up within him.

"But, Eugene," she broke out, "you promised—you
promised!"

"What did I say, Gem? I promised that it would be a
long time before I'd ever turn my thoughts to building again.
And it has been. Quite a long while."

"Not four years."

"Ah, but four years can seem a long while, girlie.
You'll be proud and pleased to see my building project in
operation."

Renny Whiteoak did not know how to talk to this man in
his present mood. He had but one wish and that was to
insult him. He restrained his rising temper and said,—
"Well, if Mrs. Clapperton is not able to influence you, I
cannot expect to."

"No one can influence me. My mind is made up."
With a tremor of excitement Eugene Clapperton realized
that his mind had been made up only since Renny had
entered the room. Here was a man, he thought, who
brought out the fighting qualities in him. Here was an
opponent worthy of defeat.

"The house you live in," said Renny, "was built before
Jalna. Mr. Vaughan, who built it, would turn over in his
grave if he knew that you were planning to build streets of

ugly little houses on Vaughanlands. There are already far too many ugly little houses and ugly big factories about. Once it was one of the loveliest parts of the Province."

"I've heard all that before," returned Eugene Clapperton.

"The truth about you is," said Renny, "that all this talk of ideals and dreams is bosh. It's plain greed that moves you. You know there's lots of money in these jerry-built bungalows and you want it."

Mr. Clapperton began to tremble all over. His knees could be seen shaking inside his pin-striped trousers.

Renny looked apologetically at Gemmel Clapperton whose crooked smile was an odd mixture of forgiveness and applause. The door from the hall was thrown open by the Great Dane who pressed his shoulder against it as a man might and stalked to where Renny sat. Eugene Clapperton hoped he would spring on Renny, give him a fright or, at any rate, utter one of his blood-freezing growls. The Great Dane rose, placed a paw on either of Renny's shoulders and looked into his face.

"It's all right," said Gemmel, and sprang up to grasp the dog's collar. He growled.

"Let him be." Renny gently pushed away her hand. He raised his hard aquiline profile to the Great Dane's muzzle and it bent and drew its warm wet tongue across his forehead.

"I've never known him make friends before," she exclaimed.

Her husband gave her an angry look. He said——

"Please leave the room. I have something to say to Colonel Whiteoak that can't be said in front of a lady."

Renny rose, and the dog dropped his forefeet to the floor with a soft thud. "There is no answer," he said, "to anything I've accused you of. You know it's true."

Eugene Clapperton's voice came with a choking sound. Temper was upsetting to him and he did his best to keep cool. "There's not a word of truth in what you say. Money doesn't matter to me. I've all I want. I'm not like you, Colonel Whiteoak—always pressed for money. From what I've heard there's little you wouldn't do to get hold of a few extra dollars."

His wife now hurried from the room.

The men stood facing each other. Renny said,—"You're right. And at this moment I'd shake the weasand out of you for next to nothing."

He grinned into Eugene Clapperton's grey face and strode out of the house.

IV

HUMPHREY BELL

THE NEW moon that looked bright and cold as ice, seemed perched on the bare branch of the oak. Actually perched on the branch was a small owl, staring out of golden eyes at Renny Whiteoak as he appeared on the snowy path. The air had turned colder, and the snow that had been melting was now a hard crust crunching beneath his heavy boots. Leaving Eugene Clapperton he had turned his angry steps across a field and into this little bare wood where was a small house named the Fox Farm, because people who bred foxes once had lived there. Later it had been occupied by Gemmel and her sisters. It was here that Eugene Clapperton had met her and from here she had been married. After that the house had stood lifeless and empty for a time. It belonged to Renny and he regarded it as not at all like the bungalows Eugene Clapperton was building but as a pleasant little house, isolated in a bit of woodland, of which the tenants must be congenial, it mattering little what rent they paid. In truth, he preferred that they should pay a low rent because, in some mysterious way, the less they paid, the closer the small house was drawn into Jalna.

For the past six months the Fox Farm had been let to a veteran of the war, Humphrey Bell. He lived there but had made no appreciable impression on the place. His soft voice, his insignificant personality, were powerless to overcome the imprint the former tenants had left upon the house. Three sisters had preceded him. Uncle Ernest and his wife, during the short term of their elderly married life, had occupied it; and, before them, a mother and daughter, Renny having loved the mother and the daughter having loved

33

Renny. The faces of these past tenants seemed always to
be peering from the windows, the skirts of the women
fluttering as they moved in and out of the doors, their
voices still echoed in Renny's ears when he entered the
house, the voices of the three Welsh sisters that were sweet
as music, the precise New England voice of Uncle Ernest's
wife—how dear that little old woman had been to Renny—
the voices of Clara Lebraux and her young daughter,
Pauline! The voices of the six women came to Renny's
ears like the sound of distant bells as he drew near the
house.

Evidently there had been no stirrings outside the house
during the day, for the glistening crust of the snow was
unbroken by any footprints except on the window-sill of
the front room, where the snow was marked by tiny prints
made by the claws of small birds, as they ate the crumbs
scattered for them. The sill was made visible by the ruddy
yellow light that streamed across it from the room within.
The house, set down like a box, with two pointed gables
added, in the seclusion of snow and snow-decked trees,
had an air of repelling any intrusion on its fastness.

Yet, the next moment after Renny had knocked, the
door was thrown open and Humphrey Bell welcomed him
with obvious pleasure. Over-heated air poured out from
the room, yet Bell himself seemed not too warm in a heavy
grey sweater. He was a small slight young man, so admirably proportioned that he might have been almost impressive had his hair and face been less colourless. Indeed, at
first glance, he might have been taken for an albino, till
it was seen that his eyes were a clear flower-like blue and
well able to bear the light.

"So it's you, Colonel Whiteoak," he exclaimed. "Just
the man I'd like to see."

"Don't 'Colonel' me," Renny said. "War's over."

"I'm glad you feel like that. I hate everything military."

Renny came in and Bell slammed the door against the
winter night.

"Yet," said Renny, "you stood up to it pretty well.
You'd a long time in a German prison camp too."

Bell drew up a chair for him beside his own, so that the

two faced out of the window where the moon, in its first
power of shadow-casting, threw the blue silhouette of a
young pine on the snow. Behind them was the small,
cheaply furnished room, to which Bell somehow managed
to give an air of cosiness. Perhaps it was because he was
obviously so happy to live there. The war had turned him
into a different path from the one on which his feet had
first been set. He was the son of a doctor in a New
Brunswick town, the only son in a family of four daughters,
all considerably older than he. A late arrival and the darling
of his father's heart, he was destined for the study of medicine. He had had no inclination towards that profession
but had accepted it because six natures, all more dominating
than his own, had urged him to it. When the war came
he was in his first year in a medical college. In spite of all
his family could do to dissuade him he took a course in
flying at a time when the life of the average flyer was very
short. It was his duty to join a medical unit, his sisters
thought, anything on land or sea would have been better
than aviation. He had survived his first months of flying to
be shot down in Germany and to be a prisoner till the end
of the war. In the cloistered life of the camp, surrounded
by men, some of whom would have been obnoxious to
his family, he discovered himself. After the war he wanted
to live as far as possible from that family. He discovered
that, though he loved his parents, the atmosphere of the
town where he was expected to settle down and become
a partner in his father's practice was suffocating to him.
The thought of devoting his life to treating the ailments
of the sick repelled him. He found in himself no dedication
to that service. When he returned home the glad anticipation of the reunion became a bewildered disappointment
to the family. Even the three brothers-in-law he had
acquired during his absence were disappointed in him,
though they had never before met him. There was disappointment all about him, mounting higher every week,
like a quick-growing hedge, closing him in. He did not
know how to escape, yet escape he must. He was constantly
aware that the eyes of nine disappointed people were on
him, wondering what he would do. Do I look like a doctor?

he would ask himself. Would any patient have confidence in me? Miserably he compared his own qualities with the staunch qualities of his father.

Suddenly and from an unexpected quarter the way was opened to him. An old friend of the family, a bachelor, died, leaving him a legacy sufficient to support him for several years, if he were careful. He made up his mind to go to some distant place, perhaps the West Indies or Mexico, and try to write. He would write something that would make his family realize that he had done well to give up the study of medicine. If he never was able to write anything worth printing, still he had done well to give up medicine. He had gone down to Boston and there he had heard Finch Whiteoak play the piano, in one of a series of concerts. After the concert he had met the pianist in the house of a New Brunswicker living in Boston. Bell was so moved by Finch's playing that he feared to meet him, lest disappointment should follow. He shrank from small disappointments for himself even more than he shrank from inflicting large disappointments on others. But Finch Whiteoak was fascinating to Bell. He could not keep his eyes from Finch's hands. There was an inspired look in Finch's long, grey-blue eyes, Bell thought. He found himself talking freely, gladly of the formless, pent-up thoughts within him. After the years in school, after the years in the army, the prison camp, and after that, his family's plans for him rising like a barbed-wire fence round him, their disappointment like a dark deep ditch— now his freedom lay in his hands and he did not know where to place it. He was like a man carrying a sapling in his arms over a piece of bare land, trying to choose a place to plant it. From the sheltered corner of the room Bell had looked out defensively at the other guests, willing them to keep away.

"I thought of going to the West Indies or Mexico or even to some island in the Pacific," he said, feeling the weight of his plans in his chest. "I thought my money would last longer there and I could write—try to find out what I'm good for."

"You'd not be good for anything very long—on an

island in the Pacific. You'd marry a native and have a lot of funny-looking kids and get lazier all the time. You're a Northern type. You need sharp winds and frosty air."

"Perhaps you're right," muttered Bell. "But it must be somewhere that doesn't cost too much."

Finch ran his hand over his forelock, pushing it back. "Look here," he exclaimed, "I have an idea. My oldest brother owns quite a big place in Ontario. Certainly it's not as secluded as a South Sea island but he has five hundred acres and quite a lot of it is in woodland. Fine trees there. Do you like trees?"

Bell nodded. "I think I do."

"Well, there's a small house on the place, completely hidden among oaks and pines, which my brother is willing to let for a low rent to the right tenant. No one would trouble you there, unless you wanted."

Bell was excited. "It's the sort of thing I'd like, though it's a long way from the South Seas."

"You might try it," said Finch. "Perhaps it wouldn't suit you at all." He was easily rebuffed. "Better not risk it." He glanced at his wrist-watch. He was tired and there were other people here who wanted to talk to him, an aspiring young girl pianist who was panting to pour out her soul.

"But I want to try it!" Bell said eagerly. "I'm not at all set on going to an island."

"There's nothing picturesque about the place I'm telling you of," said Finch. He was already standing up. "It's just that it is a place you might like to write in. You'd find something just as quiet anywhere in the country."

Bell could not say that he wanted to be where he might see Finch sometimes but he asked:

"You spend a part of your year at home?"

"Oh, yes." Finch's thoughts already seemed removed far from this room. Young Bell felt like saying,—"I'd like to be somewhere near you," but he could not. Instead he asked,—"What sort of man is your brother?"

Finch was suddenly very much in the room. He gave a little laugh, as though at some heart-warming remembrance, and said:

"He's past sixty but he's the best horseman I know. He's got red hair and not a single white one in it—that I've ever seen. You might not like him. Some people don't."

"But you do!" exclaimed Bell warmly. "I can see that."

A smile lit Finch Whiteoak's face. "He's been a father to me," he said.

And now here was Bell opening the door of the Fox Farm, like a host, padding into the living-room in old grey felt slippers and placing a chair for Renny Whiteoak to face the intricate fragility of the snow-decked boughs of the evergreens, the twigs of the oaks, against the burnished afterglow in the West. He had lived at the Fox Farm for only six months. He would have told you this was the happiest time of his life, looking back no further than the beginning of the war that had made his boyhood seem another life scarcely remembered. This was his first winter, a mild one, and he had been very snug, delighting in his aloneness in the little house in the woods, in being cut off from his family, in making new friends, of whom he never saw any more than he wished to. In those months he had written three short stories, all of which lay in a drawer of his writing-table, each twice rejected. He had not yet made up his mind to send them out again. He was in no hurry, indeed he had not much faith in his powers. Or perhaps it was that he so enjoyed his present way of living that he shrank from disturbance of it.

When Renny Whiteoak came to see him it was his habit to place the two shabby, comfortable old chairs with their backs to the room and facing the woods, he himself taking the one with the sagging springs. He would then produce two glasses of whiskey and water and the two would settle down for an hour's talk. This happened twice a week, and once a month Bell took dinner at Jalna.

"Well," said Renny, genially, "how goes the writing?"

He was the only person to whom Bell had spoken of his hopes and that under a promise of secrecy. Renny was flattered by Bell's confidence. He looked gravely judicial when Bell would read one of his stories aloud to him. Though they weren't the sort of stories he himself liked, being concerned with odd and even macabre experiences of the mind, he thought they were good. Secretly he hoped Bell would outgrow the desire to write such peculiar stuff and turn to something showing more of the virtues of a man.

"How goes the work?" he asked, when they were settled.

"If you can call it work," said Bell, his small face set in a comic sneer.

"Damned hard work, I should say," persisted Renny. "I'd hate to tackle it."

Bell sprang up and went to the mantelshelf. "This is all I've done today," he said. He put into Renny's hand a peculiarly-shaped knot of wood from a branch of cedar that he had carved into the likeness of a chipmunk, so alert in its posture, so bold and yet timorous, that Renny laughed and curved his hand about it in pleasure.

"It's good," he said. "It's capital. Now there *is* talent!"

Bell made a little grimace at the unintentional implication. "I like my menagerie," he said. On the mantelshelf there were a dozen carvings of other small animals, contrived from oddly shaped pieces of wood.

"Why don't you try your hand at a human head?" Renny asked.

"I'd like to do yours—if I were able." He gave an admiring glance at the hard-looking head set with such spirit on the lean shoulders.

"What about old Clapperton!" laughed Renny. "I wish you'd find a particularly ugly knob of wood and make a suitably sinister head of him. God, how I dislike that old fellow!"

"What is his latest?"

"Oh, he's begun whining again about his ideals and his dreams. Asinine old crooner!"

"And what do his dreams portend?"

"Another go at his model village. I've told you how his wife persuaded him to give up the idea. Now he is playing with it again and in deadly earnest, I'm afraid."

"Have you been to his house?"

"I just came from there."

"I have the impression that his wife and her sister keep him very much in his place."

"They do. But he's getting tired of it. He had his own way for too many years. He's becoming restive."

"When I meet him," said Bell slowly, "I feel like running the other way. He strikes a false note here. He doesn't belong." A mischievous smile hovered across Bell's face. "Let's get rid of him."

"I wish we could," Renny returned sombrely.

"He never meets me," Bell stroked his tow head, "without rubbing me the wrong way," and he stroked more firmly, as though to rub himself the right way. "He advised me, the other day, to see a psychiatrist. I'm in a despondent state, he says, brought on by the war. I almost told him that I'm despondent only when I'm with him."

"I'll get him out of here yet," said Renny, but his words brought no conviction to himself or to Bell. Eugene Clapperton was too firmly entrenched.

Through the window they now saw Adeline coming towards the house. She wore a white pullover and a pale grey skirt. Large flakes of snow were falling and some had come to rest on her head forming, as it were, a wreath of white flowers. It was as though one of the young silver birches had refused longer to be earth-bound and, its roots being released, was moving lightly through the snowy wood. They saw her in the pale twilight place her feet in her father's footprints, in an almost symbolic following of him.

"She's been following me," Renny said, with a pleased paternal look.

Bell jumped up. He said,—"I must open the door."

"Let her wait. She won't mind." They could see her, leaning against an oak, her arms folded, prepared to wait.

Bell moved nervously about the room. "It's so untidy," he muttered. He had always hoped she would come, and now that she was here he felt unprepared. Renny settled it for him. He leant forward and tapped on the window. Adeline looked over her shoulder smiling, then, with a swift gesture, she touched first her breast and then the trunk of the tree, to indicate that she was satisfied to wait where she was. But Renny rapped on the pane again and beckoned. He strode into the little hall to open the door.

Bell looked wildly about the room, wishing that he might transform it into something that would surprise and delight her. But the room remained shabby and small. "Like me," he thought.

Father and daughter entered together, the resemblance between them so strong that an observer would not have pictured any other man who could have begot her, yet she was delicate of flesh and appealing of outline, where he was weather-beaten and sculptured with a fierce flourish.

Bell had turned on the unshaded electric light. Beneath it his head gleamed silvery, even his eyelashes, but his eyes were blue and inviting.

"Come in, come in," he said, and tried to sound as though he weren't afraid of her coming.

They shook hands, then Adeline's eye was caught by the carved chipmunk still cradled in Renny's hand. If Bell wished to delight her he had done it.

"Oh," she exclaimed and, when Renny had put it into her hands, she held it at a distance to drink in its charm, then, holding it close, she bent her head to kiss it. "I've never seen anything so sweet," she murmured.

"Look," said Renny, "he has made others." He indicated the collection of small beasts and birds on the mantelshelf.

"Darlings!" cried Adeline, to first one and then another. "But I like the chipmunk best."

"Better than the squirrel?" asked Bell.

"Much better. Squirrels have hard cold faces, cold greedy eyes, but the little chipmunk has eyes like a fawn."

"Keep it, if you like it," said Bell.

"Really?"

She was genuinely delighted and lingered behind Renny a moment in the room to thank him again. Bell watched them disappear into the wood that was now almost dark. He went back to the living-room and rested his forehead against the mantelshelf. . . . "You fool," he said to himself—"you blasted thundering fool."

He went to where a small looking-glass hung and stared at his reflection. "I won't let her do this to me," he said, scowling at the young man's face that stared back at him.

"I won't give in. It's not as though I had anything to offer her. Good God! A carved *chipmunk*! And she cares more for it than she does for me. . . . She doesn't even know she is doing anything to me." He pressed his hand to his forehead, as though to press back the confusion of his thoughts. He went to the window and saw that all through the wood there was a new consciousness of the moon. Now the smallest twigs showed themselves conscious of her presence, casting their minute shadows on the crusty surface of the snow. His own cat came out of the wood and looked up at the window, the moonlight shining greenly in her eyes. She mewed silently, her tail limp from cold.

Bell went to the door and let her in. He thought,—"This is what I'm headed for . . . an old bachelor, living alone with his cat! Probably Adeline thinks of me as just that. . . . A white-haired old fellow living alone with his cat. . . . Doing a little carving—trying to write. God, I hope her father hasn't told her I'm trying to write. . . . I needn't worry. They'll never talk of me. . . ." He picked up the cat and held her against his breast. She smelt of frosty fur. "Poor pussy—poor pussy!" Her whole sinuous frame shook with the energy of her thankful purring.

"I'll warm your milk tonight," he assured her, and smiled at the picture of himself warming milk for his cat, in a little saucepan, in his little kitchen.

But, lying on the sofa, with the cat purring on his chest, he felt a great unharnessed power within himself. It surged up to write a poem to Adeline, to write a play about her or sculpture in marble her lovely head. Or was the power nothing but a wild desire to have her alone with him in this small house—to offer his love to her as the dark wood offered itself to the moon?

V

THE EVENING

THE TWO figures crossed the ravine, the man and the young girl, breaking the crust of the snow, sinking to their calves in the soft snow beneath. They went through the ravine, stopping on the bridge that spanned only snow, the stream's way traced by bending bushes and the dry stalks of cat-tails. Renny said:

"I remember when I first carried you down here as a baby and you were so excited to see the running water that you almost jumped out of my arms."

"What fun! I wish I could remember it. Isn't it strange how this little stream and the bridge across it are so much a part of our lives?"

"I'm glad you feel that way about it."

"Oh, yes. I can't imagine the time when you and I will not stand on this bridge together."

"Yet some day that time will come." He gave a little laugh, at the same time holding her hand tightly in his, as though to deny the possibility of such a parting.

"Never!" she said emphatically. "I'll not let it."

She raised her face to his, the flesh both rosy and cold. He smiled down at her. "You have great faith in yourself."

"Daddy, don't you believe that, if you wish things strongly enough, you can make them happen?"

"We'll try it," he said. "We'll make a pact. We'll wish that spring will come and stream will run again and that Mr. Clapperton will fall in it with all his winter clothes on."

"I was being serious," she said.

"So am I."

"All right then. Let's hope he drowns."

They laughed together at the thought of Eugene Clapperton floundering in the stream which, at its highest, was never more than two feet deep. They saw coming towards them through the ravine the figure of a man, tall, a little bent, with a gentle, hang-dog expression and an ingratiating smile.

"Who is the fellow?" asked Renny.

"He's Mr. Clapperton's new man—Tom Raikes. He's a nice man."

He came closer now and they saw that he carried a gun. He carried it with an air that seemed to say nothing on earth would induce him to fire it.

Renny said,—"You know I don't allow any shooting about here."

Raikes answered, in a soft Irish voice,—"I do know that, sir. I was only after rabbits on Mr. Clapperton's place. I had no luck at all."

"What are you doing here?" Renny asked abruptly.

"Just taking a stroll. I hope you don't mind." He looked at Adeline and smiled shyly. "Miss Whiteoak and I had a little talk one day, and she kindly gave me some advice about pigs."

"Pigs!" Renny stared in astonishment.

"I know quite a lot about them," said Adeline stoutly.

"Yes, indeed," continued Raikes. "Mr. Clapperton, he thought that perhaps I didn't understand rearing the young ones in this country, but surely it would be the same here as in Ireland."

"How long have you been out?"

"Six years."

"Farming?"

"Well, no, sir. Not till I came to Mr. Clapperton's. I've worked at a good many jobs. But I farmed for years in Ireland."

"What's the matter with the pigs?"

"It's the young ones, sir. They all died."

Renny clicked his tongue. "Too bad. Perhaps you'll have better luck next time. And, if you want advice, go to my brother. He's lucky with pigs." He was turning away when the man spoke again.

"Mr. Clapperton," he said, "has bought the land on the other side of Jalna."

Renny wheeled. "The Blacks' little farm?"

"That's it. About sixteen acres. He's going to build something there. I don't know what."

"I hope it is not going to be more bungalows," said Adeline.

"I think not, miss. I think it's just as a speculation."

Renny's brows drew together in a frown. He was silent a moment, then he asked,—"Where do you live?"

"In Mr. Clapperton's house, sir. I'm unmarried. Good evening." With a bow he moved away through the ravine, the gun drooping in his hand.

"Isn't he polite! And they say he's a good worker," Adeline exclaimed as they mounted the steep path towards the house.

"Yes. I wish I might have got hold of him first. Good men are scarce."

"Perhaps he'll get tired working for Mr. Clapperton. I can't imagine any man wanting to stay with him. Their D.P. cook is going to leave because she found a white mouse in her bedroom. Althea simply can't keep her pets under control, and Mrs. Clapperton is always on her side."

In the house Renny found Alayne in her bedroom. She was sitting by her dressing-table tidying the contents of a small drawer. The light from under a pale green lampshade fell over her, the cool profile, the silvery hair. She had the beauty of a cameo, he thought. She was past fifty but he could not get used to that silver head. He wanted it still to be gold. She turned and smiled at him, yet asked a little anxiously:

"How did the interview go? I hope you were able to keep your temper."

He grinned. "No. I just told him that, for very little, I'd shake him by the weasand."

"Renny!" she cried aghast. "How could you use such language to him! Why, you've probably made an enemy of him for life and everything has been comparatively peaceful between you since his marriage."

Renny smiled tranquilly. "He doesn't know where his weasand is, I'm sure of that."

"Nevertheless," Alayne spoke with what Renny called her schoolmistress air, "he will not relish the thought of being taken by it."

"His latest is the purchase of the Blacks' place."

"Oh, well . . . that can't interfere with us—no matter if he does build bungalows on it. There are the fields and woods between."

"Everything matters that spoils the surrounding country. It's the same everywhere. Corporations and speculators hate beauty. What they really enjoy is to cut down magnificent old trees to widen roads so that there can be more motor traffic—I'd blast every car from the face of the earth if I had my way."

She was astonished. "Yet you are very pleased with your new car."

"I know. But, if they were all blasted off the earth, I'd not need one."

She laid down the bright-coloured scarf that she was folding. It was always a pleasure, he thought, to watch Alayne handle things—surely few women had such pretty wrists.

"I dropped in at Bell's on the way home," he said, "and Adeline followed me there. Bell admires her greatly, you can see that. Poor devil—I believe he's in love with her."

Alayne said coolly,—"He's a very foolish man if he imagines that Adeline is interested in him. She's not interested in any man but you."

Renny tried not to look too pleased. "Do you think so? Well, she is fond of me. She's a good child. You must acknowledge, Alayne, that she gives no trouble at all, considering that she's the very spit of Gran. Why, when Gran was her age she had half a dozen fellows after her. Her mother was almost distraught. Gran told me so."

"Your grandmother did not adore her father, as Adeline does you. I have a feeling that, when she does fall in love, it won't be an adolescent affair. I only hope it won't be the wrong sort of man." She had finished tidying the drawer and now decisively shut it while adding,—"But I expect he will."

Renny laughed. "You are pessimistic, aren't you?"

"Well, things usually turn out that way with girls."

"You mean they turned out that way with you?"

A small secret smile was her only response.

He said,—"I'll wager your parents would have looked on me as the wrong sort of man."

"Auntie didn't."

"No—bless her heart!" Tender recollection softened his features, but they hardened as he added,—"In spite of all she'd heard against me."

How could he refer to that terrible time when she had left him, as she thought, for ever, to live with that elderly aunt in her house outside New York? She turned to face him, her eyes bright with anger.

"Renny, how can you?"

"Well, it's all in the past."

"Then don't let us have painful resurrections."

"What I said was that your aunt liked me, in spite of all she'd heard against me."

Alayne gave an ironic smile. "All you had to do was to expend a little of your fatal charm on her."

"Charm is the last quality I thought I had."

"Oh, you've masses of it where women are concerned." She paced up and down the room trying to calm herself.

"There's one thing certain. Since that time you have nothing to accuse me of."

"Do you expect me to compliment you on not having affairs with women?"

"Good Lord!" he exclaimed, irascibly. "How did we get to this point?"

"We got to it through no will of mine."

He took her hand. "Alayne," he said, trying to make her look at him, but she drew sharply away.

"You're determined to be angry," he accused her.

"Please leave me for a while."

"Very well." He spoke with baffled resignation. "Though I don't know what this is about." He went to the door and stood there with his hand on the knob, hesitating, thinking that, if he left her now, their next meeting would be embarrassing. She pretended that his physical presence was no longer in the room. She took the pins from her hair and let its silken silver mass fall about her shoulders.

"Do you still want me to go?" he asked.

"Yes." She began to unbutton her blouse to get herself ready for the evening meal.

He left, closing the door quietly behind him, and crossed the passage into his own room now palely lit by moonlight. He stood by the window looking out at the shapes, so familiar to him, even in the mysterious distortion of this light. "Fifteen years ago," he thought, "and still she can get so upset over it." He began to whistle,—"A hundred pipers and a'." He had left the door of his room open behind him and the clear clean insistence of his whistling came to Alayne's ears. This tune was singularly irritating to her. It seemed to meet itself at the finish and begin all over again, in endless possibilities of repetition. Subconsciously it was comforting to him. He drew a good breath and the whistle came more loudly. It was as though the hundred pipers, with swinging kilts, advanced through the ravine.

Rags, now sixty-five, and more bent than any man has a right to be at that age, began a muffled beating on the gong in the hall below. Renny went into the bathroom to wash his hands. He heard Ernest coming very slowly up the stairs. With hands half dried he went to meet him, putting an arm about his waist and almost carrying him.

"Thank you, dear boy," said Ernest panting. "I find the stairs trying."

"Tell you what, Uncle Ernest, I'm going to have a lavatory put in downstairs, next spring, for you and Uncle Nick."

"Ah, that will be nice! I cannot think of anything I should like better."

At the top Renny said,—"I shall wait here and take you down again."

"Thank you, dear boy."

They were about to descend when Alayne appeared

from her room. Ernest made her a little admiring bow.
"How nice you look, Alayne!"

She smiled at him, avoiding Renny's eyes that were
bent on her. She went down the stairs ahead of them,
hearing their slow progress behind. Ever since she had
come to this house, she thought, she had seen very old
people moving through that hall. First Renny's grandmother who had lived to be a hundred, and now her two
sons who seemed likely to achieve an equal age. And
always there had been Renny at their side, accommodating
his vigorous step to the creeping step of extreme old age,
behaving as though all this burden were a pleasure to
him; and yet how little it took to chafe him in other ways.
His attitude towards all these ancients was admirable, she
granted that, but for herself she sometimes felt suffocated.
Even more of a strain, she thought, were those who were
too young—Adeline, Dennis, and, when they were home
from school, Roma and Archer. Piers' little girl came
every second day and was a spoilt child. Too many of those
at Jalna, Alayne thought, were either too old or too young.
She herself would not see her fiftieth birthday again—
almost half her life had been spent at Jalna. For an instant
the two moving slowly behind her faded from her consciousness and, in their place, she saw herself as she had
first come under this roof—dead Eden's bride—they two
running lightly down the stairs together, hand in hand.
For an instant she saw the light gleaming on Eden's hair,
heard his voice so clearly she wondered Renny did not
raise his head to listen. But looking up from below, she
saw his head bent as he guided his uncle's steps. "Steady,
now—steady," he was saying. How happy she had been
in those far-off days, and of how short duration had been
that happiness. How far too soon her passion for Renny
had, like a brilliant-hued, formidable plant, thrust aside
the fragile flower of her love for Eden! And how still he
was the lodestar and centre of her thoughts! How still
the sight of his sculptured head, the line of his neck and
shoulders as he descended the stair, moved her! He was
saying,—"I weigh within five pounds of what I weighed
the day I was married"—and Uncle Ernest was replying,—

c*

"Ah, you and I are not the sort to lose our figures. Now I weigh . . ."

Uncle Nicholas was heaving himself out of his chair with creakings and gruntings. She could not bring herself to go to his help. But he arrived safely at the door of the drawing-room without aid and gave her his warm, masculine smile. "He must have been a charmer when he was in his prime," she thought, and went to him and linked her arm in his, but not with ostentatious helpfulness. He took hers, almost with the air of assisting her, and managed to straighten his back. "Been sitting too long," he grunted.

Renny met them. "I was just coming to give you an arm, Uncle Nick," he said, and his eyes moved warily to Alayne's face. It was set forward, ignoring him.

"We don't need your help, do we, Alayne?" said Nicholas. He sniffed the appetizing smell in the dining-room. "My, how nice!" he exclaimed. He moved zestfully towards his chair.

Adeline had placed the chipmunk carved by Bell in the centre of the table beside the silver dish of apples and grapes. The little creature, poised in an attitude between fright and daring, seemed about to drop the acorn he held to his breast and dart across the table.

"Very pretty, very pretty indeed," said Ernest, leaning forward to look and dribbling riced potato from his trembling fork.

"A clever fellow, that young Bell," agreed Nicholas.

Renny said,—"Bell likes Clapperton just about as well as we do. He's a shy fellow, you know, and whenever Clapperton meets him on the road he stops him and pours out a lot of unwanted advice. Some day Bell will be roused to the point of telling him to mind his own business. I wish I might be there."

The small chapped hand of Dennis was creeping across the tablecloth towards the chipmunk.

"Clapperton," declared Nicholas sententiously, "is a horrid old humbug. He fancies himself as a lover of the countryside and doesn't know one sort of tree from another."

"He fancies himself as a lover of art," sneered Ernest, "and you should see his pictures."

"He's gone into breeding pigs," said Adeline, "and an entire litter has died. Raikes told me so. Raikes says he's always interfering with the feeding."

Alayne said,—"Mrs. Clapperton tells me that this new man is the best they've ever had. He has given them a feeling of security. I'm so glad, for they've had very bad luck."

"Their D.P. is quite good," put in Adeline, "though she hasn't half a dozen words of English. She says 'please' and 'can't do', and 'want to go home'."

"Poor thing," said Alayne.

The small hand reached the chipmunk. Dennis drew it to him in an ecstasy of pleasure and snuggled it beneath his chin.

"Now, sir," said Ernest, with his clear blue eyes fixed on Dennis.

Dennis wriggled in the joy of possessing the chipmunk. He defied Adeline, clutching it tightly.

"Drop it," she said, and uncurled his fingers. She set the chipmunk back in its place.

"Very annoying habit children have," observed Nicholas, picking up the little animal, "of always wanting to handle things."

"They should be taught better when they're very small," said Ernest.

"I have never known a child," Alayne spoke in a detached tone, "so given to handling as Dennis."

The little boy bent his head, turning his gaze inward, considering himself.

"I had a letter today," said Renny, "from Finch."

Dennis was alert to the name of his father.

"He'll be coming home soon. Says he needs a rest. I expect that concert work takes a lot out of him. But then he's the sort of chap that any sort of work takes a lot out of. He is not like the rest of us."

"Favours his poor mother," said Nicholas, mumbling on a bit of gristle.

"Do I favour my poor mother?" asked Dennis.

"You do and you don't," answered Ernest.

"If I gave you that answer would you call it straightforward?" asked Dennis.

Renny chuckled. "He's got you cornered, Uncle Ernest."

Unperturbed Ernest replied,—"The obligation to be straightforward ends at seventy, Dennis."

"It will be nice to see Finch," said Alayne.

"Why do people always come home when they're tired?" asked Dennis.

Ernest eyed him repressively. "You finish your pudding, my boy, and stop asking questions."

"How can I learn if I don't ask questions?"

The eyes of the two great-uncles were on him. He subsided but his hand stole towards the chipmunk.

"It's a curious thing," said Renny, "how all my younger brothers but Piers had a bent for the artistic. There was Eden—a poet."

"Poor dear boy." Ernest drew a sigh remembering Eden.

Dennis asked,—"Was he poor because he was a poet or a poet because he was poor?"

Both great-uncles stared at him.

To make things better he asked,—"Was he a poor poet?"

"Certainly not," answered Nicholas. "He wrote very fine poetry. If he'd lived he'd have made a great name for himself."

Alayne sat silent, turning her wedding-ring on her finger.

"Then there's Finch," Renny went on, "a musician. Has never cared much for anything but music."

Ernest nodded assent. "If Finch were separated from his music I do not think he could live."

"He was separated from his wife," said Dennis, "and he lived."

Nicholas gave one of his subterranean laughs. "Marriage is the least of the arts," he said.

"But if they hadn't married," reflected Dennis, "I'd be nowhere."

"And a very good thing." Nicholas looked at him with severity.

Renny continued,—"Then there's Wakefield—an actor."

Dennis put in,—"Rags says that Uncle Wake was a bad actor when he was a little boy."

"Dennis," said Alayne, "you have finished your pudding. You may go to your room and get ready for bed."

"May I take the chipmunk with me for a treat, Adeline?" he asked.

"Oh, bother! Can't I have anything in peace?" she exclaimed. "Very well. Take it."

Holding the chipmunk close he ran up the two flights of stairs to his room. It was dark and cold but he was not afraid. He drew back the window-curtains and let in the moonlight. He sat down in its light on the side of the bed. He held the little animal to his mouth. "Oh, you dear little sweet thing," he murmured. It was warmed by his hands. It seemed almost alive. He liked it better than if it were alive, for he could do what he wished with it.

Downstairs, the two old brothers, having enjoyed their food, felt better than they had all the day. They walked strongly back to the drawing-room where a bright fire was blazing. Adeline went into the library and turned on the radio. For a wonder there was music not objectionable to Alayne. In the dim hall she looked up into Renny's face. His face was softened into gentleness as he looked at her, into remorse for ever having hurt her, yet there was chagrin that she should be so easily hurt—so often hurt by him. He bent and kissed her forehead and then her lips. "Smile at me," he said, and she brought herself to smile.

VI

"SOBER AND INDUSTRIOUS"

RAIKES moved quietly through the ravine, the gun drooping in his hand. At the far end he went to the clump of bushes where he had hidden the cock pheasant. He took it by the feet and drew it out. Its plumage glistened in the moonlight, its proud crested head, its proud neck, with the clearly marked collar of dark blue and dazzling white, hung limp. The feathers of its tail floated gently as he carried it.

He went to the farthest of Mr. Clapperton's bungalows and tapped at the back door. It was opened by a stout woman and behind her stood a stout crimson-faced man in his shirt sleeves.

"Oh, good evening, Mr. Raikes," she said. "Come right in. And what have you there, I'd like to know? A pheasant! Well, I declare!"

"It's for you, Mrs. Barker," Raikes said, in his soft Southern-Ireland voice, and he put the pheasant into her hand. Her fingers closed gladly about the claws.

"Goodness, isn't he pretty!"

"Indeed and he is." Raikes gently stroked the bird's bright plumage. "I'd roast him if I was you."

"I'll stuff him and roast him and have cranberry sauce with him. Look, Jack."

"Fine," said her husband, in a drink-wheezy voice. "Just fine."

"Come in, won't you, Mr. Raikes?" she urged.

"Thank you, I will for a bit. It's cold for you with the door open." He entered, with his air of grave politeness, taking off his battered hat and showing his thick black hair.

The two men stood close together looking at each other. Barker's lips formed the words—"Have a drink?" His wife's back was turned but she knew.

"No drinking here," she said loudly, while she well knew that her bullying tone would have no effect whatever. She went about the work of plucking the pheasant, grumbling all the while about the drink.

Barker went to a cupboard and took out a bottle half full of rye whiskey. He sang softly in a husky voice,— "Have a wee drop and Dorcas, afore ye gang awa'."

"That's wrong," said his wife.

"What's wrong?" he asked belligerently.

"The words. They don't make sense the way you've got them."

"The words don't matter. It's the tune that counts *and* the sentiment. I've got the sentiment all right, haven't I, Tom?"

"You have the sentiment fine," answered Raikes, "but Mrs. Barker is right about the words." He gave her a little smile as he took the glass of whiskey and water from Barker. He asked:

"Wouldn't you like me to pluck that bird for you, Mrs. Barker? Sure you'll spoil your hands."

"Oh, no, thanks. I'll manage fine." But she threw him a grateful, an almost tender look, as she sat down with the pheasant between her thighs and began to tear the bright plumage from his breast.

The two men sat on either side of the table covered by a red cloth on which was a pack of soiled playing cards and, in the centre, a pink vase holding a pink artificial rose. Barker smacked his lips loudly at each mouthful, as though to affirm his enjoyment and defiance, but Raikes gazed pensively into the liquor remaining in the bottle and sipped without sound.

"My, it's a nice fat bird," exclaimed Mrs. Barker. "Where did you say you shot it?"

"I didn't say," replied Raikes, "and I wouldn't say, and, if I was you, I wouldn't ask. There are some that are very fussy about their pheasants."

"Colonel Whiteoak," said Barker, "did a funny thing last fall when the open season for pheasants began. He sprinkled corn over the floor of his barn and left the doors wide open. The pheasants smelled it out and they went for it—about sixty of them—and he locked the doors and kept them shut up there till the three days was over."

"I guess he wanted them all for himself," said Mrs. Barker. She began pulling out the pheasant's tail feathers. "Look, ain't they pretty? I'm going to have them in a hat." She held them against the side of her head and smiled coquettishly at Raikes.

"Women never learn," said Barker, pouring himself another glass, "when they're too old for dolling up."

"Mrs. Barker certainly isn't too old," said Raikes gallantly. Her eyes were on him and, when Barker offered him another drink, he refused. "I have to go into the house and see the boss. I mustn't be smelling of liquor."

"I'll give you a pinch of coffee to chew," said Barker. "That deadens the smell."

His wife burst into derisive laughter. "I can smell a whiskey breath a mile away—coffee or no coffee."

"You know it all, don't you?" said Barker sulkily, then asked,—"How's the old codger, Tom?"

"Just the same. Ah, he might be worse. I'm quite content with my job. The young ladies are very kind."

"That Althea is a bit touched here." Mrs. Barker put her fingers to her forehead. "I saw her sitting in front of a tree the other day, painting as if it was summer."

"I know," laughed Raikes. "She'll come in after a walk, tired out, and her skirts clogged with snow. But she don't mind about anything, so long as her pets are warm and fed. She's an odd one all right."

"Tom," asked Barker in an undertone, "will you be able to get the car tonight?"

"Sure. I'll be here for you about nine."

"I do wish you two would stay at home!" Mrs. Barker glared at them, down from under the pheasant's feathers clinging to her hair and even on one eyebrow. "You think of nothing but getting out with the car and drinking and gambling. One of these times Mr. Clapperton will find out and then where'll you be?"

"Just where I am, mark my words," laughed Raikes. "Come now, Mrs. Barker, don't you be cross and will you give me that pinch of coffee you recommended?" He gave her his gentle rather sad smile. She could not resist his nice ways, so in contrast, she thought, to her husband's gruffness.

"You get it for him, Jack, I'm stuck all over with feathers." She began to gather the glistening metallic plumage into a newspaper. She picked up the naked bird by his legs and viewed him at arm's length. "We'll have him roasted tomorrow night," she said, "and you must come and help eat him."

"Thank you kindly. I hope he's tender."

"Sure he is. I can tell by the feel of his breast-bone. We'll have him for supper and, mind you, there's to be no running away afterwards."

"Don't you worry, Mrs. Barker," said Raikes, munching coffee. "We won't run away."

He went off through the snow, carrying his gun. He crossed the narrow road lined with maple saplings, threw his leg over a low fence and was in one of Eugene Clapperton's fields. A path made by himself led to the barn. It was a large barn built a hundred years before, but so far the present owner had gone but cautiously into farming. Raikes entered the barn, took a lantern from a hook and lighted it. He climbed the ladder into the hayloft. A great mound of hay confronted him like a dry sweet-smelling mountain. He skirted its base and behind it cast the light of the lantern on a small pen in which nine piglets slept curled close together for warmth. Disturbed by the light they moved and snuffled, twitching their plump pink legs. A grin, half-tender, half-mischievous, lighted Raikes' face.

"Are ye warm enough, ye rascals?" he whispered. "Well, here's some nice fresh straw." He fetched an armful of straw and strewed it about the little pigs. He bent over them and patted a plump side. "Well," he said, "I must soon be getting you out of here—you're too noisy. Now mind what I say and be good and quiet." They snuggled closer together with comfortable grunts and he descended the ladder and went to see that all was well in the stable.

The Polish woman was in the kitchen as he passed through. She was doing her last job of the evening, leaving things ready for breakfast. She gave him a look askance to see if he had brought in snow on his boots. He smiled ingratiatingly at her. He said:

"Divil a bit of snow have I on me. I'm a good boy, isn't that so?"

She gave him her puzzled, yet aggressive look. "Please," she said. "I can't do."

"Nobody asked you to, old dear. All you have to do is to mind your own business and lave me to mind mine." He went along a narrow passage and into his own little room, his haven. It had nice clean curtains, a yellow pine chest of drawers with a small looking-glass, a patchwork quilt on the bed and under the bed his tin trunk, on which he still preserved the torn steamship label, for it seemed a kind of link with the old land—not that he ever wanted to go back there.

He bent to look in the mirror, took a comb from his pocket and combed his black gypsy locks. From a hook on the door he took a decent black overcoat and Homburg hat. With them on his arm he returned to the kitchen. The woman was gone to her own room. At the sink he washed his hands in the running water and even splashed it once across his mouth and chin. He dried himself on the roller towel that hung on the door. Then putting on his overcoat and carrying his hat in his hand, he tiptoed along the passage to the hall and tapped on the door of the living-room.

Eugene Clapperton's voice, reading aloud, ceased and he called out,—"Come in."

Raikes opened the door just wide enough to enter and stepped inside. In appearance he was transformed into a man making an evening call but his manner was deferential. He said:

"Excuse me, sir, but would you be wanting me to go to the vet's at Stead for the medicine?"

"How is the cow?" Eugene Clapperton asked irritably. "Animals seem to always be getting something wrong with them. First it was the young pigs dying and now this cow sick. I wish I hadn't a cold. I'd like to go out and see her."

"The stable would be a bad place for you, sir. The cow is no better. The creatures are like us. They have their ills. But the medicine I was telling you of will fix her up. I think it would be well for her to have it tonight. Had I better be taking the car to Stead, sir?"

"Yes, certainly. And let me know in the morning how she is."

"I will indeed, sir." As he stood smiling a gentle comforting smile at Mr. Clapperton, Gemmel, playing a game of Patience beside a rose-shaded floor lamp, contrasted the two men, to the cruel disadvantage of her husband. His grizzled head that she always thought of as a mean shape, his dry skin, his bluish lips and dark teeth, she contrasted with Raikes' black locks, his skin tinted warmly by the good blood beneath, the rim of his gleaming white teeth, just visible. Eugene was too consciously straight like someone who was determined never to die. Raikes drooped a little glancing sideways. A man, she thought, who would go anywhere over the world and not consider either life or death.

When he had gone Eugene said,—"In the time we have lived here I have had four men. Yes, this is the fourth. It's a terrible reflection on conditions today, that it's next to impossible to hire a decent respectable man. This man gives me a sense of security I haven't had since I came here. Not till now. You will remember that I advertised for a man that was *sober and industrious*. Those were my words." He savoured the words as though he had invented them. "Yes, *sober and industrious*. And when this man appeared and I talked to him I realized that here at last was a man I could trust. He gives you that feeling too, doesn't he, girlie?"

"Oh, yes," she answered vaguely, then she added, —"That reminds me I must ask him to get some cough mixture for Tania. Her cold gets no better."

"The druggist won't be open at this hour."

"Perhaps not but I'll ask Tom to try."

"Tom?"

"Yes. Tom Raikes."

"Let him get her a dose at the vet's. That'll do her. Just the thing for her."

Gem went through to the kitchen. Raikes was standing with his hand on the doorknob ready to turn it. He had his hat on, the brim casting a dark shadow over his eyes, but he took it off, with a polite little inclination of the head, as she entered.

"Oh, Tom," she said.

"Yes, Mrs. Clapperton?"

"Could you get some cough mixture for Tania?"

"I'm afraid the drug-store won't be open. But Tania wouldn't take it anyway. I offered her a dose of mine and she wouldn't have it. She's like that."

"Then we can't do anything about it."

"I'm afraid not. She's a quare woman." He smiled good-humouredly.

She noticed the length of his eyelashes and how they cast a shadow on his cheek. Yet strangely they did not take from his look of careless masculinity. He stood with his hand on the doorknob waiting to go, waiting politely for her permission to go.

"Well," she said and hesitated.

He raised his black brows enquiringly.

For a moment she could think of nothing to say, then, —"My husband was just remarking how pleasant it is for us to have a man we can trust about the place. I hope you're quite satisfied, Tom."

His face lighted happily. "I'm well satisfied, ma'am. I hope to work for you and Mr. Clapperton many years."

"I'm glad of that. Good night, Tom."

"Good night, ma'am, and thank you."

A rush of icy air entered the kitchen, then the door closed behind him. She heard his feet crunch in the snow, then the opening of the garage door and the engine of the car throbbing . . . Since early childhood she had been a cripple, unable to walk because of a fall, until she met Eugene Clapperton, and his generosity had made possible the operation on her spine. He had made it possible for her to walk strongly and quickly, to be like other girls. He had made her his wife. No matter how long he lived she never could do enough to repay him. She went back into the living-room and saw him sitting there. He looked up at her with his amorous smile.

"Come, girlie," he said, patting his thigh, "come and sit on my knee."

Behind her clenched teeth, under her breath, she told herself,—"Like hell, I will! I've done too much for you already." But she said, in her sweet Welsh voice that honeyed all her words,—"Oh, you silly Tiddledy-winks, you're always wanting attention." And she went and sat on his knee.

It was after midnight when Raikes and Barker returned over the snowy ruts in the road towards Vaughanlands. They talked loudly, sometimes in argument, sometimes in boasting of the clever things they had said and done in the bar-room of the club they belonged to. They had made themselves rather a nuisance there that night and their argument was about whether or not they should have heeded the bar-tender's urging of them to depart. Up and down over the snowy ruts of the road they bounced, recking nothing of the springs of the car. Sometimes Raikes waved one hand in the air to emphasize his boasting. Sometimes he waved both hands. And still the faithful car rocked on. It seemed a miracle that they reached the garage in safety, where it stood secluded, its roof grotesquely deep in snow. It seemed a miracle that Raikes was able to guide the car through the doorway, but he did.

Suddenly he became very polite to Barker and assisted him to alight. Solicitously he guided him in the direction of his home and bade him a loving good night. He locked the garage and went rather unsteadily into the house. Still wearing his coat and hat he lighted the stove and put on the kettle to make himself a pot of tea. While the kettle was boiling he went softly through the pantry into the dining-room. He stood listening. There was a muffled middle-of-the-night stillness in the house. Upstairs in the big mahogany bed the Clappertons slept. On the top floor Althea and the Great Dane, and near her in a little room with a sloping roof, Tania.

Raikes opened the sideboard and took out a bottle of brandy. Eugene Clapperton disapproved of alcohol but he kept one bottle of brandy in the house for emergency. Now Raikes filled a flask he carried in his pocket from the bottle and ,returned to the kitchen. He made the tea, fetched milk from the pantry, and poured himself a cup. Half-sitting, half-leaning against the sink, he drank two cupfuls. He had pushed his hat to the back of his head and the unshaded light fell on his long face which wore an expression of gentle melancholy. Above his head the kitchen clock, with roses on its massive face, ticked loudly. Its hands pointed to two o'clock.

He took the teapot into the dining-room and replenished the brandy bottle with tea. His hands shook and he winced as some of the hot liquid was spilled over his thumb. Now the sideboard was closed, and he gave the room an admiring glance before he left. He wished he owned a grand house like this, with furniture as fine. He felt sorry for himself— a lonely man, with no one to love him—a lonely Irishman, in a strange land. He thought of Mrs. Clapperton and the odd way she had looked at him that night, and not only on that night. Well—in him she could see a real man, not a pimp like old Clapperton.

VII

THE CONCERT PIANIST

THERE was no greater pleasure than walking, Finch Whiteoak thought. At this moment it was a more profound
pleasure than playing the piano. Seated before the instru-
ment, even at his best, there was the mind alert, ready to
pounce on the fingers if they faltered, ever so slightly.
There was the mind, conscious of his audience, quivering
with anger if everything was not right in the concert hall.
Even when he played in solitude, there was the mind,
exalted, fiery, casting its shadows on the keyboard. But—
in walking through these wintry woods—the mind was
gone. It was scarcely there to direct the legs. There was the
blood coursing hotly through the body, the eyeballs cool and
relaxed, the nostrils widening to draw in the icy air. He
had tramped for five miles along the country road. Now
returning through the woods of Jalna, the pines, the oaks,
the slim naked birches, stood waiting for him as friends.
Willingly would he spend the rest of his life among them.
He had had enough of people. Their inquisitive eyes, their
mouths saying the same things over and over.

Scarcely aware of what direction he took he passed the
house, turned down into the ravine and up the opposite
steep, a little breathless, for here it was heavy going,
towards the Fox Farm. In the still of the sunless day, with
the sky drooping heavy with more snow, snow that would
bring deeper, thicker silence to the wood, the house looked
like one in a German fairy tale. The door might have opened
and a strange dwarf looked out, or a little old woman with
a shawl over her head. Surely the smoke that rose from the
chimney was remarkable. It rose slowly, downy and white,
and spread itself like a toadstool above the house. This was

the first time Finch had been home since the coming of young Bell. It seemed strange to find him here. Yet quite ordinary everyday occurrences often seemed strange to Finch. The power, or weakness, of wonder had been given him at birth. How strange, he was for ever thinking to himself. Some combination of sounds on the piano which he had heard a thousand times would suddenly strike him, as though it were the first, and he would pause, in that delicious wonder. Now this smoke that curled so closely at the chimney's mouth, then spread itself like a greyish-white toadstool, held him. His face wore what Renny called his idiotic expression.

Watching him through the window was Humphrey Bell. He kept himself concealed and watched. He felt a quickening of the pulse at the sight of that long sensitive face which had been imprinted on his memory since their meeting. Often he had wondered if the face were as interesting as he had thought and now he said to himself almost joyfully—it is!

Finch moved slowly towards the door and by the time he had reached it Bell stood there to welcome him. They exchanged greetings and Finch stared about the room with an air of approval.

"So," he said, "you've dug yourself in, and mighty snug you are."

The stove was glowing almost red hot.

Bell said,—"I'm sorry if it's too warm but the truth is I was so long nearly frozen in prison camps that it seems as though I can't be too warm now. Won't you take off your windbreaker?"

Finch took it off and Bell placed two chairs side by side facing the window.

"Do you mind?" he asked shyly. "I always set the chairs this way when your brother comes."

"That is fine," said Finch. "Which brother?"

"Renny. The other one has never been."

"Piers is wrapped up in his work and his family. How do you like Renny?"

"He's just like you said. To see him cantering on horseback—well, it's just poetry."

"And you like living here?"

"You couldn't have done a better thing for me than to send me here. I've dug myself in as completely as a rabbit in his burrow."

The simile was almost too good. Finch chuckled. Then he said,—"The family tell me you have dinner with them occasionally. I'm glad of that."

"They've been mighty kind to me. Not only Colonel Whiteoak—but Mrs. Whiteoak and the two old uncles. I'd rather go there than to any other house I've ever been."

"What about Adeline?"

Finch had seated himself but Bell stood leaning against the window-frame, his hands in his pockets, his eyes on the pallid scene outside. "Oh, she," he answered. "She's so serene and untouched by life that I daren't think of her."

"She's really just a big child. She'll be an interesting woman some day."

"She has the most lovely bones," said Bell dreamily. "Her good looks aren't just pretty flesh and fine eyes and chestnut hair."

"She's like my grandmother. I can tell you, Bell, she had an arresting face when she was a hundred. Age could not change her bones. Lord, I remember her old hands and how wrinkled and yet how shapely they were! She wore a lot of rings."

"I wish I'd seen her. I have seen her portrait."

"I only knew her when she was very old." After a moment he added impulsively,—"She left me all her money."

"You were her favourite?"

"Gosh, no. I never quite knew why she did it. I wished she hadn't." He sat, lost in thought for a little, his long grey-blue eyes darkened by some painful memory. Then he asked abruptly,—"What do you do to pass the time?"

"Oh, I write some rather feeble short stories. They must be feeble, I suppose, or they'd get accepted. I don't write the bitter disillusioned stuff that most literary guys who've been to the war can turn out in words of one syllable and no punctuation. I like long words and I like the niceties of punctuation, and I like to embroider and elaborate. Neither can I write about sex. I'm too restrained and vague."

"Give yourself time," said Finch. "You've only been at it six months."

"The thing for me to do," said Bell, "is to stick to carving silly things like those," and his eyes moved from the scene outdoors to the small carvings on the mantelshelf.

"I don't believe you're happy here—in spite of what you said about being as snug as a rabbit in its burrow."

"Oh, yes, I am," Bell protested quickly. "I've never been so almost completely happy." He began to laugh silently, rumpling his silvery tow hair till it made a halo round his head. "But—I have one headache and it's an aggravating one, I can tell you."

"What?"

"Mr. Clapperton."

"Oh, him! You and my Uncle Nicholas should get together."

"We have. Your uncle invariably says Clapperton is a horrid old fellow."

"What has he done to annoy you?"

"Now, listen. He never meets me on the road or in the village but he stops me and begins to pour out his obnoxious advice." Bell spoke in a high afflicted tone. "He says I'm mentally ill. That it's proved by the way I shut myself up alone here. By the way I look and talk. He says that I must see a psychiatrist. He says that fifty per cent of the people one meets are mentally ill. He says that one out of every ten should be in a mental home. By God, I'll be in gaol for doing him an injury, if he doesn't let me alone!"

"Why don't you avoid him?"

"I can't. He smells me out. He's everywhere—with his know-it-all smirk and his cheap philosophizing."

"Have you met his wife and her sister?"

"Once he dragged me almost by force to his house to see his pictures. I suppose no worse collection of pictures exists anywhere. Yet they inspire him to live a finer life, he says. I don't know how the two women endure him. They're quite nice, though a little odd."

Bell really was worked up, but in Finch's presence he calmed himself, brought whiskey and sat down facing the window.

It was March and should have been spring but there was no sign of it in these woods. The snow was deeper than it had been all through the winter, the air thicker in portent of more snow. There was a deeper silence. No small animal ventured from its burrow to leave a footprint on the snow. Of the migratory birds crows had thrown their challenge across the sky and one morning a robin had been seen. "The first robin!" Adeline had cried. "Now I must wish on him." And she had, combining superstition and religion, murmured,—"Please, may I go to Ireland, oh God!"

Finch said,—"Young Adeline is dying to go to Ireland."

Bell looked surprised. "I thought she was perfectly happy here. Why should she want to go to Ireland—of all places?"

"She was there once, with her father, and she wants to go again. My nephew Maurice is going this spring. He owns a place there. If she goes someone must go with them from here. Perhaps Renny. Perhaps me."

As he spoke Finch was looking out of the window but he was conscious of a change in Bell. He gave him a sidelong look. The tip of Bell's thumb was caught between his teeth, his eyes were downcast. He asked:

"How long would she be away?"

"Probably a couple of months."

Bell gave a little embarrassed laugh. "Don't think me too inquisitive," he said, "but I can't help asking this. Someone—I think it was Mrs. Clapperton—told me that there is a sort of engagement between Adeline and her cousin. Is she—are they going over there as an engaged couple?"

"I think almost everyone in the family wishes they were but it isn't so. Adeline hasn't shown any preference for Maurice and they're too sensible to press her. Her father wouldn't allow any urging. He's in no hurry to give his daughter to a man who is to live three thousand miles away."

"Whoever marries her," said Bell, "will get a lovely wife."

"He will, and a high-spirited one. He'd need lots of character."

"It would be strange," Bell now turned his inviting blue eyes on Finch, "to live in the house with one woman—one whom you loved desperately—and no one else . . . I used to live in the house with five women. Of course, that was very different. If you lived alone with a woman you deeply loved, everything she said or did would be terrifically important. And all the time you'd be watching yourself, in fear you might say or do something that might hurt her. And if by any chance she gave you a hurt you'd have to hide it from her. You've been married. Isn't that so?"

"There are worse things than being hurt," said Finch. "There's suffocation."

"But not if you really loved her!"

"Well . . . you never know till you try it."

"I expect he'll marry her all right," said Bell, turning again to the thought of Maurice. "He's got money and good looks, the family behind him. He's got everything."

"Except Adeline's love. He hasn't that—yet."

"This journey together will do the trick. I can just see them in some picturesque old Irish mansion—the sort of place to captivate a girl." Bell forced a smile to his small sensitive mouth, as though the picture were a pleasant one.

Finch began to talk to him of Ireland, of old Dermot Court whose property had been inherited by Maurice. "Speaking of Ireland," he went on, "my wife was an Irishwoman, a forty-second cousin. We separated and we came together again."

"That was good, eh?"

"No. It didn't last."

Walking homeward Finch remembered his wife Sarah. Her dark form glided out of the pale muffled wood and stood on the rustic bridge waiting for him. He saw her sleek black head with its convolutions of plaits, her white hands gripping the snowy hand-rail of the bridge, as though to keep herself from running to meet him. He remembered the feel of those hands on his neck . . . and now she was dead, dead as that fallen ash tree, blown down by a gale in its prime. . . . Of her there was left only the memory of her sensual hold on him—his struggle to escape —but he could never be the same again. She had done something to him . . . Yet—had he ever been whole— sound? He doubted it. And here at Jalna was their son. Here was Dennis who was always so glad to have him at home. It touched him to see the little boy's pleasure in his return. But, when it came to being a father, he felt himself to be a failure as compared with Renny—Renny who had been a father to his brothers, to Eden's daughter, and now a better father than himself to Dennis.

What bright elegance was Sarah's! She was as finished as a china ornament. She was as ruthless as a storm. From her far-off grave in California she spoke to him in a moment's communion and he hesitated on the bridge to hear that icy whisper. He looked back at his own deep foot-prints in the snow, blue caverns sunk in its whiteness. There was an oak tree that had somehow contrived against all the gales to retain two brown leaves. Now, in the still air, one of them detached itself and fluttered slowly down-ward like a weary bird. . . . The sound of the dogs' barking came from the direction of the house. They barked angrily from the porch, wanting the door opened. In a moment it opened and the barking ceased. The door closed with a bang.

Finch pictured the warmth and light inside the house. Whiteoaks had lived here for all but a century. Perhaps would live here for a century—two centuries—more. Who knew? He felt the pull of the house—urging him to hasten to it—not to lose any of the cherished hours under its roof, the only roof beneath which he felt sheltered, safe. Sometimes when he was on a tour, was playing the piano in a distant city, he would remember the piano in this house, and his spirit would return to it and his fingers return to that keyboard, and all else would be blotted out and the next day the critics would say he had played his best.

When he stood inside the hall where the bob-tailed sheepdog, the bulldog and the Cairn terrier were humped by the stove pulling at the clots of snow between their toes, he stood warming his hands and listening to the voices of the two old uncles in the library, like the rustling of the two last oak-leaves on the tree in the ravine, he thought. Urgent and steady came the tick of the grandfather clock. Now the sound of the dogs licking their wet paws, and a growl from the little Cairn as the sheepdog lay down too close to him.

Cap in hand he stood in the doorway of the library.

"I'll not come in," he said. "I'm too snowy."

"Thank you, dear boy," said Uncle Ernest. "I am so very susceptible to cold."

"Where have you been?" asked Uncle Nicholas.

"A good walk. Then I dropped in on Humphrey Bell."

"Albino-looking fellow," remarked Nicholas.

"He served in the Air Force. A very nice young man," reproved Ernest.

"Didn't say he wasn't nice." Nicholas spoke testily. "Said he looked like an albino." Nicholas stretched till the chair creaked beneath him. "What a long day! I shall be glad when spring comes. Spring! It's March. Think of the primroses in England. Why, you could hardly put your foot down without treading on 'em. Shall never see them again." He voiced a "Ho-hum," that was something between a yawn and a grunt of resignation, for he was not unhappy.

"Your Uncle Nicholas has days," Ernest remarked, "when he will not listen to the radio. Says it tires him."

His brother's grey moustache bristled. "Didn't say it tired me. Said it made me tired. It makes me tired because there are too many stars. Stars used to be few and far between and they shone brightly. Now there's a regular Milky Way of radio stars. They make me tired. That's what I said. Too much of everything. That's what I say."

They heard Adeline's footsteps flying down the stairs. She brought palpable joy into the room. "What do you suppose?" she cried. "Mother and Daddy have said I may go to Ireland with Maurice! And they'd like you to go with me, Uncle Finch, to look after me. As though I needed looking after! Daddy says the rest will do you so

much good. Will you come, *please*? Because whether I
go or not depends a great deal on you."

Renny now followed his daughter into the room and
Finch asked of him,—"Why don't you take Adeline over
yourself? She'd rather have you than anyone else."

"I know. And I'd like tremendously to go, but for one
thing——"

"Now don't say it's the money," cried Adeline. "You
know you can afford it, darling."

"For one thing," he persisted, "it's the expense. For
another—and I won't say it doesn't count most—it's that
I'm afraid to leave home for fear of what Clapperton will
do. I've heard that he plans to build a factory of some sort
on the Black place."

"He couldn't!" cried Ernest. "My parents would turn
over in their graves."

"A lot he'd care. He's a business man. It would be a
paying venture. It would be two miles from his own
house."

Nicholas said,—"He'll never do it. I'm sure of that. It
would depreciate the value of his own property. All this
talk is to aggravate us. He knows it will and the horrid old
fellow enjoys it."

"I think you're right, Uncle Nick," said Finch.

Adeline caught his arm in her hands and rubbed her
cheek on his shoulder. She said,—"It's decided somebody's got to go with Mooey and me. Daddy won't. So
you must, Uncle Finch. It'll simply break my heart if I
can't go."

"Alayne ought to go," said Finch.

"Of course she should," agreed Renny. "It's years and
years since she was over there but she won't go. She's in
a rut and won't budge out of it."

Alayne in the doorway overheard this. In her heart she
knew that Adeline would prefer the companionship of
Renny or of Finch to hers. It was not a happy thought but
it was so and she herself was probably to blame, for though
she loved Adeline the child was not and never had been
congenial to her. And there was her son. Was he congenial to her? He had her father's lofty white forehead

and piercing blue eyes but so far he had shown, not her father's intellect or sweet, self-effacing nature, but an erratic mind and a profound egotism. She found herself not near to either of her children.

She said,—"I can't think of anyone who would enjoy the trip more than you, Finch. And I'm sure there is no one Adeline would rather have—with the exception of her father."

"Now then, Finch," said Renny, "it is up to you."

"Dear boy," Ernest stretched out his hand and took one of Finch's in it. "I think you should agree to go. Mooey very kindly invited me to accompany them and I think he intended to pay all expenses but the more I think it over the more certain I become that the effort would be too great for me. I am almost ninety-five. Can you believe that?" He raised his eyes rather pathetically to Finch's face, as though he asked for assurance that this was not so.

"There's a good fellow, Finch," said Nicholas. "There's a good fellow."

It was impossible to resist. Besides he wanted to go. The thought of the sea voyage, the thought of Ireland, elated him. The thought of a journey with Maurice and Adeline elated him. All his journeyings were by plane or train and solitary, with a concert looming at the end. The thought of seeing his brother Wakefield, now acting in a play in London, elated him.

As always when Finch was moved he lost control over his voice. Now it came loudly from his mouth. "I'll go with Adeline. I'd like to go. It's just what I'd like to do."

She threw both arms about him and he felt their strength. "Oh, splendid! Oh, heavenly!" She danced about the room weaving her way in and out among her elders.

"What's splendid? What's heavenly?" asked Dennis from the doorway, his eyes shining beneath his yellow fringe.

"Uncle Finch and I are going to Ireland."

"Can I go too?"

"You're too young."

"People go over when they're babies."

"They go with their mothers."

"I'll go with my father."

"No," said Finch. "You can't come."

"Why?"

"There are dozens of reasons."

"Tell me eleven." He tugged at Finch's sleeve.

Finch wanted to get away from Dennis. He ran up to his room on the top floor two steps at a time. But he heard Dennis pursuing him. He heard him coming step after step without panting. Finch turned and faced him.

"Well?" he asked.

"I want to go to Ireland."

"You're too young. Your turn will come."

"If we all took turns by age my turn would never come till I was old."

"I'll bring you something nice—whatever you want," Finch said comfortingly and had a recollection of Wakefield as a small boy begging to go places.

"M—m," murmured Dennis. He took Finch's hand and stroked it with his cheek. He pushed back Finch's sleeve and stroked the inside of his wrist. He stroked it as Sarah had been wont to do.

"Let me go," Finch said, breathless. "You must run along, Dennis. There's a good boy."

He got rid of him and shut the door behind him. He spread open and flexed the hand Dennis had caressed.

D

VIII

IN THE BASEMENT KITCHEN

RAGS THE houseman sat on the smaller of the kitchen tables smoking one of Renny's cigarettes. His wife was scraping the burnt top off a gingerbread. An aura of pale blue smoke was about her heated head and she sucked her underlip in exasperation.

"You always will have the oven too 'ot," he said, in his cool Cockney accent which he retained after nearly thirty years in this country.

"Mind your own business," she returned briefly in her Ontario voice.

"Are you suggesting that it ain't my business?" he asked. "When I take burnt gingerbread in on the tea-tray I'd like to know who'll get the glum looks—you or me."

"The old gentlemen never complain."

"Don't they? And 'ow do you know?"

"They never complain to me."

"That's it. All the complaints are reserved for yours truly. Whatever goes wrong. Now there's gas escaping! 'Aven't you got no sense of smell?" He sprang from the table, went to the stove and turned off the leaking faucet.

"In some ways," she remarked, "I liked me old coal range better."

"Then why don't you use it? It's standing there."

"Light a fire in it for me then. The boss likes it best too."

"He likes everything that gives more trouble. They all do."

"Tell him that."

"Oh, him and me get on all right. Don't you worry."

She banged the oven door shut and carried the ginger-bread into the pantry. "It'd take more than you to make me worry," she said.

When she came back she found old Noah Binns, a former farm labourer at Jalna but long since retired because of age and rheumatism, sitting in the kitchen. He frequently dropped in for a cup of tea and a chat for old times' sake.

"Howd'do, Mrs. Wragge," he said, in his pessimistic tones. "Tarrible weather, ain't it?"

"I haven't time to notice weather," she said. "It takes my husband here to do that."

"There ain't," said Noah Binns, "goin' to be no spring."

"No spring!" She stared.

"No spring whatever." He grinned, showing his one upper tooth. "We're goin' straight from the depths of winter straight into roastin' boilin' bakin' summer—the worst yet. All the signs pint to it."

"Well, I never."

"Nor did anyone never. It'll beat all."

Rags said,—"Don't go discouraging the wife. She's just burnt her gingerbread."

"I prefer it burnt," said Binns. "It tastes less like gingerbread."

"I guess I won't offer you a piece after that," said the cook.

"Whatever you bake is good, Mrs. Wragge," Binns hastened to say.

With her rolling gait she went into the pantry and returned with a plate of gingerbread cut into squares.

"I see the kettle is biling," said Binns.

"It's always boiling in this kitchen. Make us a cup of tea, wife, do." Rags now spoke affectionately.

Noah Binns continued with his gloomy weather predictions till they all sat about the table with their cups full of hot tea. The light came into the basement windows direct off snow mounded outside the windows. Rows of alumi-nium and even a few old copper utensils hung on the walls. There were shelves covered by packages and bottles of cleaning mixtures, so many that Alayne often wondered

how the Wragges could use them all. There was a large
rack in which stood platters from many bygone dinner
services, mostly having their enamel cracked by much
overheating. A table was crowded with brass and silver
objects waiting to be cleaned.

Rags nodded towards them. "Silver-cleaning day tomorrow. Like to come and give me a hand, Noah?"

Binns was for a moment speechless from gingerbread,
then he said,—"My working days are over. Nobody in
this neighbourhood has worked so long and hard as me.
And the way I've rung that bell."

The two Wragges winked simultaneously at each other.

"The church bell you mean, Noah," said Mrs. Wragge.

"I rung that bell," he said, his voice vibrating with
pride, "for fifty year. Nobody before or after has rung it
so loud. When I was in my prime the churchwardens
spoke to me for fear I'd bust it. I could put words into the
mouth of that bell. Whenever I seen Colonel Whiteoak
late for church I'd make that bell say—'Hurry up, you red-
headed son of a gun, dang you—dang you—dang you!'
And the bell would ring it clear."

The Wragges shook with laughter. "And would he
hurry?" she asked, making a picture of it in her mind.

"Hurry? Why, he'd come on the run. But the work got
too heavy for me. For a year I ain't been able to ring
the bell and I never seen so much lateness as there is
now."

"There's a new drug what cures rheumatism," said
Rags. "But it won't be ready for a year or two."

"I've no faith in drugs," said Noah. "I've took enough
drugs to make a atom bomb and they done me no good.
The only medicine I take now is senna. I started off with
senna and I'll end with senna."

A knock came on the outer door. Mrs. Wragge called
out—"Come in"—and Wright the head stableman
entered. He was ruddy-cheeked, square built, and had been
working at Jalna since he was eighteen, thirty years ago.
He made a clatter stamping off snow, then greeted them
with a cheerfully sarcastic.—"Lovely spring day, isn't
it?"

Noah Binns groaned. "It's all the spring we'll see. Straight from this we'll go into roastin' boilin' bakin' summer. All the signs pint to it."

"Well, I guess we can stand it after all we've been through," said Wright, drawing up a chair.

"We don't know what trouble is in this country," said Rags, "except what we make for ourselves."

"We don't make the bugs and the blight, do we?" Noah Binns demanded, his voice trembling with anger.

"The greatest trouble-maker about here," said Wright, "is old Clapperton."

Mrs. Wragge placed tea and gingerbread in front of him. "What's his latest?" she asked.

"Well, you know about the Black place?"

"Yes. He's bought it."

"That was a dirty trick," said Rags, "selling it to old Clapperton without giving Colonel Whiteoak a chance to buy it."

"Black knew where he could get the biggest price." Wright gloomily stirred his tea. "I've heard on good authority that there's going to be a factory built there."

Noah Binns tee-heed into his cup. "There'll be factories and service stations everywhere before I'm dead. There'll be one right here where we sit."

"Well, you are cheerful, aren't you?" exclaimed Rags.

And Wright added,—"I hope I'm underground before that day."

Mrs. Wragge thumped a fat fist on the table. "The Colonel'd never allow it! All them that owns property would be up in arms."

Noah Binns pushed his face close to hers. "Have you ever knowed property owners able to stop anything?"

"Colonel Whiteoak stopped him building bungalows," she declared.

"Raikes tells me," said Wright gloomily, "that they're going to dig the cellars for new ones as soon as the spring breaks."

Mrs. Wragge glared at them over her swelling bosom. "It won't be allowed," she said.

A polite knock now sounded on the outer door.

"I'll bet it's Tom Raikes," said Mrs. Wragge. "He always knocks that polite way. Come in!" she sang out and Raikes entered, bent a little as though bowing. He took off his hat as he came and a black gypsy lock fell over his large eyes.

He was made very welcome by Mrs. Wragge while the men looked at him a little doubtfully. Soon he had a cup of tea and a piece of gingerbread in front of him. As the cook placed them there his head touched her solid warm arm and he smiled gratefully up at her, his white teeth gleaming in his dark face.

Noah Binns whispered in Wright's ear,—"I don't like his looks."

"Ssh," Wright warned out of the side of his mouth.

Raikes was saying,—"What a backward spring we're having. As I came along the path the snow was up near to me knees."

"And more of it in the sky," said Wright.

"It's tarrible," said Noah, "how the days is lengthening. I don't know of a worse sight than a long day and no sign of spring."

"Have another cup of tea, Noah." Mrs. Wragge pushed it across the table to him without ceremony. "It'll make you feel better."

"This new bell-ringer they've got at the church," he said, "don't seem to have no knack with the bell. Every Sunday I stand by him both morning and evening and my hands itch to get ahold of that rope. He can't ring the bell proper and never will though I direct him at every pull of the rope."

"Lands sakes!" exclaimed Mrs. Wragge.

"I wrastle with that young man," he continued, "till the prespiration is apouring down both our faces. 'Faster!' I say, and then 'Not so fast! Put some muscle into it!' I say, and then I say, 'Don't writhe around as if you'd the stummickache." And he yells back and I can't hear him for the ringing of the bell. It's enough to drive me crazy."

"Land alive!" exclaimed Mrs. Wragge.

Raikes said on a deep reminiscent note,—"You should hear the bells where I come from, Mr. Binns."

"That'd be in Ireland, eh?" Noah asked in a disparaging tone.

"Yes. In Ireland. It's only a village church but we have six lovely bells and a ringer to each. You ought to hear the chimes on a special occasion."

"They'd be Catholic bells, eh?" said Noah in a still more disparaging tone.

"No. Protestant."

Wright said,—"I'll never forget my trip to Ireland. Old Mr. Court there, he'd sent for little Maurice to go over and stay with him and I took him. It was a big responsibility but I enjoyed it."

"Well do I remember the poor little feller comin' to tell us good-bye. My, he was cute," said Mrs. Wragge.

"And he's a grown-up young man now and going back to claim his property." Wright gave a sigh. "Lord, how time flies!"

"Flies!" exclaimed Noah. "Fifty year I rang that there church bell and did ever one of this here family say I done it well? No. Not one."

"Are you countin' me?" Mrs. Wragge asked.

"I was not. Do you want to be counted one of this family?"

"Well, Colonel Whiteoak often does."

"You're welcome to him." Noah stared straight at her.

"I suppose," Raikes said in his soothing tones, "that it's a fine property young Mr. Maurice owns over there."

"Beautiful," Wright agreed with pride. "A mansion there is—three times the size of this, with old armour in the hall and a grand stairway."

"I don't call this much of a house," said Noah.

"It's the finest in these parts," Wright said truculently.

"Shucks. Y'ought to see some of the houses them millionaires have built, down on the shore."

"I have seen 'em. They're welcome to 'em—with their swimming pools and rumpus rooms and bars. There isn't one with stables equal to ours." Wright pushed his cup and saucer from in front of him and folded his arms. "Them—with their three cars and a station waggon—bah! They don't know they're alive."

"I had a bit of an accident last night," said Raikes. All looked enquiringly at him.

"Aye. I was coming home—I was driving Mr. Clapperton's car and a truck bumped me right into a telegraph pole. The car was pretty well smashed."

"My, that was bad luck," said Mrs. Wragge. "It is hard on the nerves, these smashes. Have another cup of tea."

"Thanks. I will." He drank down half of it blazing hot.

"What'd Clapperton say?" grinned Wright.

"He was a bit upset. But he couldn't say much as it wasn't my fault. He allows me the use of that car. The other's just for the use of the family."

"How's the pigs?" asked Wright.

"Ah, the young ones are dead." A look of sadness softened Raikes' face.

"Better luck next litter," comforted Mrs. Wragge. "How's that D.P. gettin' on?"

"She's leaving tomorrow."

"Is it true she found a snake in her bedroom?"

"I'll bet it was Clapperton," grinned Wright.

Mrs. Wragge gave a yell of laughter which she quickly controlled. Rags uttered repeated giggles. Noah choked on his last mouthful of tea which he brought up. Only Raikes remained placid.

"It was no snake," he said, "only a harmless mouse. But it isn't for that she's leaving. She's not used to country life and she's not used to our ways. She's going with some friends of hers. We could make her stay on but we can manage without her. I'll help with the work."

"You!" laughed Mrs. Wragge. "I'll believe it when I see it."

"I'll help you in your own kitchen this minute if you say the word."

"I do most of the work here," said Rags.

Before she could make a retort Noah Binns raised his rasping voice. "It's a sinful crime," he said, "the way the government brings these furriners to take the bread out of our mouths. They're goin' to be a blight on the country and bring it down to ruin."

Steps were heard and a pair of pretty legs were seen

descending the stairs from the hall above. A gay plaid skirt came into view, then a green blouse, and lastly Adeline's smiling face. The men began to shuffle their feet under the table and push back their chairs but she called out:

"Don't move! Goodness, what a pretty picture you make! Hello, Noah, what do you think of this for April?"

"It's just what I foretold, Miss, away last fall. There'll be no spring, I says, and we'll go straight from the depths of snow into roastin' boilin' bakin' summer."

Adeline perched herself on the wide window-sill.

"You must pray for good weather for me, Noah," she said. "I'm going on an ocean voyage."

Noah Binns groaned. "That's bad," he said. "There's storms brewin' and German mines still floatin' about. Danged if I'd go on a ocean voyage—not if my way was paid on the *Queen Mary*—and they say she rolls like all possessed."

"Oh, Noah, don't be so discouraging!" But she laughed delightedly.

"I suppose you're going with Mr. Maurice, miss," said Wright. "I well remember when I took him over."

"Yes. And Uncle Finch is coming too." She eyed the gingerbread.

"Like a piece, Miss Adeline?" asked the cook.

"I shall be taking the tea upstairs directly," said Rags.

"Don't be so mean, Rags." Adeline jumped from the sill and came to the table. "Not on a plate, please, Mrs. Wragge. Just in my hand."

She returned to her perch eating the gingerbread. The April sun which had not before shown itself that day now burst out strong and made a brilliant halo about the girl's head. The five seated about the table stared at her in pleasure as they might without embarrassment stare at a young doe in its early grace and beauty. Their hands lay on the table relaxed or held the handles of their cups. Beneath the table their feet were disposed in characteristic attitudes. Mrs. Wragge's in red woollen slippers toed inward, the calves bulging sharply from the ankles; her husband's,

D*

neat in black shoes, were planted side by side; Noah Binns'
ankles were interlocked and his shabby overshoes seemed to
have absorbed moisture rather than cast it off; Wright's legs
were outstretched and ended in leather leggings and thick-
soled, well-oiled shoes; while Raikes' top-boots were drawn
back on either side of his chair, thus disposing of his long
legs. So characteristic were those nether parts that an
observer seeing them separate from the upper parts could
have linked them without difficulty.

"You'd never guess what she's goin' over for," Mrs.
Wragge said to the men.

They shook their heads smiling at Adeline.

"Why, she's goin' over to choose herself a husband.
She's goin' to look them over in Great Britain and Ireland
and pick out a prize one."

"You don't need to go that far, do you, miss?" said
Wright. "There's good men at home here, eh?"

"She's after a title," said Mrs. Wragge. "She aims to be
'my lady'—like her great-aunt."

Noah Binns spoke truculently. "No man living has a
right to a title, except the King. George—King of Canada
and Great Britain."

"What about Ireland?" asked Raikes.

"Ireland!" Noah gave a snort. "Ireland's a foreign
country now and will perish as such."

"When did you start talking biblical?" asked Wright.

"I'll bet you a dollar to a doughnut," declared Noah,
"that I'm the only one present who could say a piece
from the Bible by heart."

"I'll take you on," said Adeline. "At school we had to
memorize from the Bible as a punishment. I was always in
trouble so I know masses by heart."

"I was not including the ladies," returned Noah.

Mrs. Wragge interrupted,—"You're getting away from
the subject."

"Well, miss," said Raikes, "I hope you'll find a nice
young Irish gentleman to your liking."

Noah Binns said,—"There's men in this country, better
than any duke."

"What Miss Adeline'd like," put in Wright, "is a gentleman with a stable full of show horses or a string of race-horses."

Rags gave his insinuating smile. "She's got him picked out," he said. "I've heard his name—not many times, but once."

Adeline imperturbably finished her gingerbread. Through the window behind her the face of the bulldog appeared, and behind it the legs of a horse.

"It's the boss," exclaimed Wright. "I guess he'd like me to take his horse." He hurried out followed by Raikes and then by Binns, the last shuffling along with knees bent and an expression of pessimistic curiosity on his face.

"Thanks for the gingerbread, Mrs. Wragge," cried Adeline. "There's Daddy! The message I came down to give you was from Mummy. She says will you please make less gravy—no, put less grease in the gravy—no, I mean, don't burn the gravy! Goodness, I forget what it was!" She ran from the kitchen and joined the three men standing about the horse. The feeling of joy she always had when she saw her father on horseback was as sweet to her as the smell of the sharp pure air. There was no man living, she thought, who sat a horse as he did, whose legs and body so merged in the body of the horse, the lines of whose back and shoulders so flowed into the lines of the horse when he cantered. She drank in the sight—the man's bare head, the naked arching head of the horse, the look in their eyes of accepting restraint to only a certain point. She ran through the snow and put her hand on the beast's powerful neck, the flesh so hard, so muscular, tightly bound in that glossy chestnut hide. He swung his head towards her, mumbling his bit as though in dismay at finding it there in his mouth.

"Shall I take him to the stable, sir?" Wright asked. He took the bridle in his hand.

"Yes, thanks, Wright." Renny threw a leg across the horse and slid to the ground. The horse gave a petulant look at Wright and then minced delicately with him towards the stables, ready at any moment to misbehave.

Raikes smiled at Renny with a kind of intimacy. "A lovely horse, sir," he said. "Is he the one that took first prize at the show?"

"He is. He's perfect except that you can't always depend on him."

"I've seen hundreds of horses," said Noah, "and I never seen one that had any brains."

"Then where did the expression *horse sense* come from?" demanded Renny.

"I'll bet your grandfather made it up." Noah cackled in delight at his own wit. Afraid that he would not have the last word he clumped off through the snow, more of which had begun to fall.

"Lord, when will spring come!" exclaimed Renny, looking up into the heavy sky, as though he did in truth invoke the Deity.

Adeline put her arm about his waist. "It can't come too soon for me. What a spring to look forward to!"

"My daughter is going over to your country," Renny said to the Irishman.

"Ah, that's where she'll see a lovely spring." Raikes' eyes were clouded as though in nostalgia. "I hope you enjoy it, miss."

"Thanks. I'm sure to. I have a wonderful power of enjoyment." She spoke in Ernest's very manner.

"It's a grand thing to have, miss."

With his gravely polite bow Raikes took the path that led behind the stables and so to Vaughanlands. He could not help comparing the cheerful atmosphere of Jalna with that of Vaughanlands where so often the family seemed at cross-purposes, neither happy themselves nor able to make those they employed happy. Still he was far from dissatisfied. He would stay where he was and make the best of it. The litter of young pigs had been sold at a fair profit. There were other things. . . .

He kicked the snow from his boots and went into the kitchen. Tania was there stirring something on the stove, a look of distaste darkening her face.

"Where's the boss?" asked Raikes.

"Can't do. I go," she returned.

He came close, smiling into her face.

"Can't do," she said, raising the spoon as though to hit him. "You go."

IN THE BASEMENT KITCHEN 85

"You're a divil," he laughed. "Understand that?"
He left her and went into the hall. Eugene Clapperton was
there tying a muffler round his neck.

"Well," he said sharply, the memory of last night's
collision fresh in his mind, "has the car been taken away
for repairs?"

"It has that, sir. They're pretty busy and say it will
take three weeks before it's done."

"Hm . . . Well, in the meantime you'll have to walk.
No taking out of the Cadillac, mind you."

"No, sir. No indeed." Raikes hesitated, reluctant to go
on. "But . . ."

"But what? What's the trouble now?"

"It's the mare, sir. The one Colonel Whiteoak sold you,
for riding."

Eugene Clapperton had bought the mare half against his
own better judgment in the flush of a reconciliation with
Renny Whiteoak, with the feeling too that riding would be
good for his health. But he never had enjoyed it. The
thought that the mare should be exercised hung over him.
The fear of her, when he was mounted, never left him.
But he was proud of her. The thought of anything going
wrong with her filled him with dismay. He asked:

"Is she ailing?"

Raikes answered softly,—"Her health is fine, sir. I
wouldn't ask for better, but it's her eyes that's troublin'
her."

"Her *eyes*?"

"Yes, sir. She's gone quite blind in one eye and the
other is bad too. In a little while her sight will be quite
gone."

"Why didn't you tell me this before?"

"I hadn't the heart to tell you, sir. So many things had
gone amiss. At first it come to me as a big surprise her not
seeing so well. Then I made certain she had the same
trouble as two other horses I've known. One was a mare
in Ireland and it developed slow in her. The other was a
gelding out in this country and it developed fast in him.
But it's the same throuble. I've worked with horses all my
life and I couldn't be mistaken."

"We must have the vet to see her."

"If it'll make you more sure, sir—of course. But the vet at Stead is no good for this sort of thing. If you don't mind I'll take her to the one at Belton. It's quite a way but I'd sooner trust him."

"Let him come to see her."

"He'd do that but he's got some throuble in his back and he's only able to look after the animals that are brought to him. He'll be around again in a month, they tell me. Perhaps you wouldn't mind waiting."

"Better take her at once."

Raikes hesitated. "There is his fee, sir. He's a man who likes to be paid on the spot. Then there'll be my lunch at the hotel and some oats for the mare."

Eugene Clapperton handed him a ten-dollar bill. "Let's hope the vet can do something for her. Upon my word I'm sick and tired of the things that go wrong with the animals. They look so strong and yet . . ."

"Ah, they have their throubles, sir, the same as us."

Out on the hard-packed snow of the road Eugene Clapperton put back his shoulders and consciously set his lungs to work expelling the dry warm air of the house and inhaling the cold purity of the outdoor air. There was now a hint of moisture in it and the large flakes that were beginning to fall had a softness like feathers and clung gently to whatever they touched. He made up his mind not to let the mishaps of the farm depress him. He had enough in his own house to do that.

Gem was not the docile young wife he had expected. She had a will of her own. She was even critical of him. God knew, he was willing to spoil her, to give in to her when it was seemly to do so. What hurt him was her aloofness, her drawing into herself, the way she and Althea stopped talking when he came into the room. He wished there were some way of getting rid of Althea but he saw no such possibility. In fact the poor girl was not fit to go out into the world. She needed the shelter of his roof and the companionship of a sister. If only she would marry! But who would want to marry her? And whom could she be induced to marry? She was so shy that she fled at the sight of a stranger. He supposed he would go on to the end of his days with her hanging round his neck like a mill-stone.

When he came to the little gate that led into the Fox Farm he suddenly decided that he would drop in and have a chat with Humphrey Bell. He felt sorry for that young man. He was so misguided, so wrong in leading the life he did. Disaster might come of it. He was without doubt mentally ill. Eugene Clapperton waiting for an answer to his knock reproached himself for not having come to see Bell sooner, but the young man had seemed to shrink from him and he was not one to push in where he was not wanted. He had a desire to help Bell, to be Bell's bene-factor. The day might come when Bell would seek him out to thank him for what his advice had done for him. "All I am I owe to you, Mr. Clapperton"—and his insignificant little face would glow.

There was not a footprint on the snowy path that led to the door. Obviously Bell had not put his nose out that day. Yes—he had! There were footprints leading to a feeding table for birds built in the crotch of an old apple tree. A dozen small birds rose fluttering from it at his approach. There was a card by the door announcing that the bell was out of order. It would be out of order! Eugene Clapperton could not imagine anything in order in that house. And what a small insignificant house it was—a fit abode for Bell!

He opened the door at the peremptory knock and looked ready to shut it again in his consternation. He stammered:

"Oh—how d'you do? Mister—Mister——" He could not for the life of him remember Clapperton's name, often as he had spat it out in anger.

The friendly expression on the face of his visitor faded. He could not believe it possible for anyone to forget his name. It was done to make him look small, to make Bell feel important. But he was not going to take offence. He smiled and held out his hand.

"I thought I'd drop in and see how you are getting on," he said. "I am Eugene Clapperton."

Bell took his hand, looked at it, shook it, and said in his
low voice,—"Oh, yes, I remember. Won't you come in?"

He placed one of the two easy chairs for the visitor,
facing the stove, and himself sat down on a stiff-backed
chair against the wall.

Eugene Clapperton looked appraisingly about the room.
"You've made yourself quite comfortable here," he said.

"I like it," returned Bell defiantly.

"You must indeed—to have stood it so long." He saw
the small carvings on the mantelshelf and his face lighted.
"Ah, you've got a hobby. Good. I'm very pleased to see
that. In fact I was going to advise it. There's nothing better
than a hobby—for you."

"For me?"

"Yes. For your state of mind. Psychiatrists prescribe it.
Takes your mind off your frustrations and inhibitions. Who
advised you?"

"Nobody."

"You just thought it out for yourself?"

"Yes."

"Splendid. Now that's a real good sign. You look better
too. Your face shows that you're not quite so mentally ill
as you were."

"I'm not mentally ill."

"Come now. You can be frank with me. I've read a good
deal on this subject in the newspapers and magazines. I
know the strange states of mind people can get into. Do
you realize that a large percentage of the population is
mentally ill? Some realize it. The majority don't and they
just go on suffering and making other people suffer . . .
I've one of them in my own house."

Bell brightened.

"Yourself?" he asked.

Eugene Clapperton gave a loud laugh. "No. Not me!
My sister-in-law, Althea Griffith. Have you seen her?"

"Yes."

"She's a dear girl and I think a great deal of her, but . . ."
he shook his head expressing more than any words he
would have dared utter. An idea had come into his head.
If he could bring these two together, what might not come

of it! There was something about Bell that might appeal to Althea. As for Bell he must be terribly lonely. Any personable young woman would surely attract him. If only he could bring it about . . . but the difficulties were baffling. Both the young people disliked meeting strangers, both were possessed of natures that made them balk at any urging. But Eugene Clapperton was exhilarated by difficulties, he even was glad of them, for there was little in these days to be overcome. His life was rather one of endurance of ills beyond his control.

In spite of himself Humphrey Bell felt curious, also anything was better than talking about himself. He said:

"Someone told me she's very shy."

"Shy! That's putting it mildly. I believe she'd run away from her own shadow. That's just her state of mind. She's neurotic. She's supersensitive. But all that could be cured by proper handling."

"Why don't you set about curing her?" Bell asked, bitterly sarcastic.

"Ah, I might—but one symptom of her sickness is dislike of me. Just imagine. She avoids me whenever possible. However, I do my best to help her. I encourage her in her hobbies. One of them is painting. Now I don't find much in her paintings to admire but you might like them. I've offered to pay for lessons for her from a first-rate teacher but she'll not hear of it. I've offered to pay for treat-ment from a psychiatrist, but at the mention of it she went to her room and stayed there for two whole days. Now it seems to me that you two could do a great deal for each other—if you could just get together."

"Control yourself," Humphrey Bell was repeating inwardly. "Don't let him know how you'd like to bash his head in with that poker. Don't begin throwing things at him. Don't look as though you minded." With these thoughts in his head he sat on his hands like a child staring at Clapperton, his small pale face set, his pale hair standing erect as though in surprise.

"Of course, it's the war," said Clapperton. "Neither you nor Althea were what you now are before that. She lost her only brother. She thought the world of him. Just imagine what it would have done to your four sisters if you'd been killed. You have four sisters, haven't you?"

"Hm . . ." grunted Bell.

"Then there's yourself—I mean your experience as a prisoner of war." He looked piercingly at Bell. "It might do you good to talk of that to me. Just to pour out what's been bottled up in you for so long. It might be the keynote of your recovery."

Bell sat and stared.

In an encouraging voice Clapperton continued,—"You must have seen and suffered terrible things. Now I'd like to hear of your treatment at the hands of the Germans."

"They treated me fine," Bell said almost in a whisper.

"And you don't look back on that time with horror?"

"I liked it," Bell got out.

Eugene Clapperton rose. He came and put his hand on Bell's shoulder. "You are even more mentally sick than I had suspected. You must let me help you."

Bell rose also and the two stood facing one another.

One more question came. "*Will* you consult a psychiatrist?"

"No!" shouted Bell. "I've told you that before. I'm perfectly well. I have never been happier. All I ask is to be let alone."

"Come, come, don't get excited," soothed Clapperton. "I'm only trying to get you out of the rut you're in. I'll go now and leave you but I'll be back again. In the meantime work away at your hobby, feed the birds, get plenty of outdoor exercise. Above all, don't avoid people. Uproot all fear from your heart. Ninety per cent . . ."

Bell was gently urging him to the door. Now the door was open, the snow was blowing in. The cat drifted in. Eugene Clapperton inexorably took Bell's hand. He pressed it till it hurt.

"Good-bye," he said. "And don't let yourself be discouraged. We'll get this condition of yours under control—never fear. But—I must have your co-operation. Ninety per cent . . ."

Humphrey Bell closed the door. He returned to the room and threw himself on the sofa. He lay on his back

with his legs straight in the air like a man doing exercise.
He did not know what to do with himself to express his
relief at getting rid of Eugene Clapperton, his anger at
having been subjected to his presence. The cat leaped to
his chest. She put her face close to his and pressed her cold
lips and frosty whiskers against his cheek. Every hair on
her body stood out electric with cold. When she began to
purr it was not a comfortable purr but a hoarse, commanding purr right into his face.

IX

THIS WAY AND THAT

"IT'S JUST as I feared, sir," said Raikes. "It's all up with the poor mare's sight."

"That is what the vet said, eh?"

"That's what he said." Raikes' head drooped, his large sensitive mouth hung open a bit in his dejection.

"This is the limit. One sickening thing after another. The young pigs—the cow—the car—and this! Well, I suppose there's nothing we can do about it. I certainly won't ride her again."

"It wouldn't be safe for you, sir."

Mingled with his exasperation Clapperton felt relief from the obligation of riding. He could get all the exercise he needed on Shanks's mare. Yet he was regretful that he would no longer cut a fine figure on the handsome bay. The thought of buying another did not occur to him. He wondered if it were possible that Renny Whiteoak had known of the threat to the mare's sight—but no, three years had passed since the purchase.

"I have a friend, sir," Raikes was saying, "who has a small fruit farm. He's been wanting a horse for light work. He'd give the mare a good home and the best of care but he'd not be able to pay a high price, sir."

"How much?"

"Not more than fifty dollars, sir."

"Fifty dollars! Good heavens—I paid five hundred and fifty for her!"

"Ah, but she's not what she was. She'd get a good home with my friend, sir."

Eugene Clapperton considered. The price offered was an outrage yet what better could he do? He would like to be rid of the beast—never see her again—and he had been so proud of her! Raikes' contemplative gaze was on him. He gnawed his lip, not able to make up his mind.

"She'd be no use to you the way she's got this throuble with her eyes, sir, and my friend would give her a good home. He'd make a pet of her."

Eugene Clapperton heaved a sigh. "Very well," he said, "I'll do it."

"I'm sorry this has happened to the mare, sir," said Raikes. "I hope you don't think I'm to blame at all."

"No, no, no, you're not to blame."

"I do the best I can, sir."

"I know you do." He spoke with something approaching heartiness. He never had had a man he liked so well as Raikes. Raikes was the only one in a succession of men who showed sympathy in one's bad luck, the only one who was really human.

That same afternoon Raikes drove the D.P. to the railway station.

She sat beside him impassive in the car, clutching a large handbag and a bundle. Her cheekbones were so high that, when he glanced sideways at her, he saw only the tip of her nose. Her mouth expressed strong purpose mingled with distaste. A wisp of black hair blew across her face. Raikes drove in such a way that the discomfort of every rut on the road was felt in a bounce. He said:

"So you didn't like the work here?"

"Can't do," she snapped. "I go. Please."

"Where might you be goin' to?"

"You shut up. Please."

"By jingo, your English is coming on! Who did you get that one off of?"

She gave him a black look. After a silence he said:

"You're the first woman I'm not able to get on with."

"You shut up. I go."

Raikes showed his white teeth at her. "Aren't you goin' to kiss me good-bye, Tania?"

"Can't do."

"Why don't you like me? Sure I'm not so bad, am I?"

She sat inflexible. An especially rough bounce made her

set her jaw and give him a thunderous look. They were now at the little railway station. Suddenly dignified, Raikes lifted out her trunk, her suit-case, and set them on the platform. If he expected a smile of thanks he did not get it. Looking straight ahead of her she said:

"I know. Can't do. I go. Please. Shut up."

Raikes grinned cheerfully. "Givin' me the whole works, for a good-bye treat, aren't you? Fine. Bye-bye, Tania."

He left her standing on the platform, a stocky black figure against the whiteness of the snow. The scream of a locomotive sounded in the grey distance. She turned towards the oncoming train.

Raikes drove home pensively, carefully. He liked the Cadillac and only wished the boss would let him have full use of it. He flicked a bit of fluff from the seat the D.P. had occupied. Well, that was the last of her and he was not sorry. Her watchful eyes had seemed to be always on him. Now he would breathe freer, act freer. He put the car into the garage, stamped the snow from his boots, and went into the kitchen.

He could hear Gem Clapperton's sweet voice singing. She was in the pantry where there was a sink. He could hear the slosh of water as she washed the tea-things. He went to the door and looked in at her with his deferential comforting smile. She stopped singing.

"Excuse me, ma'am," he said, "but won't you let me do that for you? It's a shame to see you with your hands in the dishwater."

"I like it," she answered. "It's a treat to me to do housework. You know, I was an invalid—I was crippled all my girlhood. Even now I can't stand for very long at a time."

"You're tired now, I'm sure. Please let me fetch a chair for you." He brought a chair and she sat down, laughing to find the dishpan now too high for her. "How ridiculous!" she said and stood up again.

"Please let me," begged Raikes. With sudden male overbearingness he took the dishmop from her hand and her place by the sink.

"Then I shall dry," she said quietly. She polished the

china teapot, her eyes on his muscular hands wet with suds.

"There's so little work for me now," he said, "except for shovelling the paths and feeding the stock. I can do all the dishwashing and cleaning and peel the potatoes. Ah, we'll get along fine!"

"Well, that's very nice of you, Tom. Of course, my sister will help but it's my husband who has always been used to having maids. He can't understand how lonely it is for them in the country."

"Ah, it's hard to get maids to settle down in the country. But meself, I'm country bred and I've no use for the town except for the races."

She widened her eyes at this new light on him. "So you like horse-racing! I've never been to a race."

Raikes regarded her with pity. "Never been to a race, ma'am? Well, I never. You're just the one I should think would like racing."

"Why, Tom?"

"Ah, I can't just tell. But I'd think you'd like the excitement of it." He put into her hand half a dozen silver spoons.

"How clever of you! I love excitement—anything new and strange. I was brought up in Wales, you know, and it was very remote where we lived."

"Ah, Wales is a lovely country," he said, wringing the dishmop and hanging it up.

Her face glowed. "It's the most beautiful country in the world. It's my dream to go back there. But first I want to travel."

"Sure. Mr. Clapperton will take you travelling, now that it's more comfortable getting about."

Her face closed in. She hung up the towel and asked,— "Have you ever been to Wales?"

"Yes, indeed. I've crossed over from Ireland on a cattle-boat to look after the beasts."

"You've done so many things," she said, as though enviously.

"I've done a good few."

"And what did you enjoy most?"

"Working about horses, ma'am."

"It's a wonder you didn't go to Jalna to work. They are such people for horses there."

"I don't think I'd get on with Wright, ma'am, or with Colonel Whiteoak either. I like being where I am."

"I'm glad of that, because my husband and I are very well satisfied with you."

"Sure, I do the best I can."

How uncommunicative he was! She wished she might know all his past, be aware of his thoughts as he stood gently smiling at her. She said abruptly:

"It's odd you haven't married, Raikes."

"Ah, I never was much of a one for the girls."

"But they must have been after you," she laughed.

Imperturbably he replied,—"Well, look at Tania. She couldn't bear the sight of me."

"Tania hated everyone."

"It was the loneliness of the country that upset her, ma'am. She'll be better in the town."

It was obvious he did not want to talk about himself. She gave him a speculative look. "You're very dark for an Irishman," she said.

"I expect it's the Spanish in me, ma'am, from those fellows shipwrecked off the Armada, or so they say."

The room was almost dark. She looked about and said,— "I wonder what I ought to do next."

"If it's the evening meal you're thinking of, ma'am, don't worry. I'll be after getting that."

"Oh, you can't, Tom."

"Indeed and I can. You'd be surprised at all I can do."

"My sister has such a headache—I sent her to lie down."

"I'll carry up a tray to her," he said at once, eager to help.

"You *are* kind, Tom. I shall get it ready and you may carry it up."

She lingered a little watching him bring potatoes from the basement and set to peeling them. He did everything as though with a quiet enjoyment. It was almost touching to her to see him moving about the kitchen in his heavy boots trying to make no noise.

In the living-room she found her husband reading the
Reader's Digest. He laid it down.

"I've just been enjoying a splendid article," he said,
"on causes and cures for mental illness. Several books are
mentioned in it and I have a mind to get them. The trouble
is that the books become too long-winded and complicated.
On the whole I prefer condensed articles. D'you know,
Gem, if I were a young man today I'd go in for psychiatry
as a profession."

"Really?" she said indifferently.

"Well, don't you agree that there is nothing more interesting than the study of human nature? The real motives
behind people's actions, all the queer frustrations and
inhibitions that beset the weak? I feel that I am cut out for
this study, being absolutely free of all these disabilities."

Suddenly she looked at him hard, laughing.

"You'd never make so much money at that sort of
thing," she said.

He laughed too. "Oh, shouldn't I? I'd probably make
more. Those psychiatrists do pretty well. I'd make money!
You can trust your Tiddledy-winks for that, girlie."

"I believe you," she agreed.

"Well," he said seriously, "I've always thought out
what I wanted and gone straight for it." He stretched out
a hand and caught at her skirt. "You, for instance."

She avoided the hand, went to the window and looked
out. The house was built in a hollow and in that shelter the
trees grew thick and close to the house. The snow-laden air
lowered itself to their tops. She said:

"Darkness is coming fast, and more snow with it. Shall
we never have spring?"

"Spring will come, girlie. Nobody will be gladder of it
than me. I think I'll take you down to Atlantic City. How
would you like that?"

"It would be lovely," she said absently.

He regarded her with some irritation. "What's the matter
with you, girlie? You used to be so enthusiastic. Now
you've got so don't-care about things."

"It's the winter," she said. "It's so long."

"You weren't like that last spring."

"Wasn't I?"

"What you need is a change."

"What about Althea—could she come?"

"No." He spoke sharply. "One thing that is wrong with us is her being always on the spot. Love her as we may we need to get away by ourselves for a while. It's not right for married people to always have an outsider with them. After I've gone a little deeper into the subject I intend to make a close study of Althea and find out just what her particular emotional upset is. Now young Bell I understand. His neurosis is definitely the result of his imprisonment in Germany. I sometimes fear for his sanity. You'd never guess what he said to me. He said he *liked* the prison camp."

"Perhaps he didn't enjoy your probings."

Eugene Clapperton gave a smile of self-satisfaction. "He had no idea I was probing. It was all done so delicately. That's what we psychiatrists have to be so very careful about—to do it delicately."

It was out! He had called himself what he had been longing to! Gem turned away to hide the sardonic grin that bent her mouth down at the corners. She said:

"Well, you have two patients right at hand."

"Three, Gem!" he cried. "But the third is incurable. I wouldn't bother about him. I refer to Colonel Whiteoak. He's got a family estate fixation—a grandmother complex—and a fear neurosis—all inside that foxy red head of his."

"I find it hard to associate fear with him," Gem said coldly.

Her husband gave his loud, rather mirthless laugh. "Fear! He's one bundle of it. He's always afraid of what I'm going to do, when my ambition is to be a benefactor to the neighbourhood."

"You don't call those bungalows a benefit, do you?"

"I do. They're well built. They're pretty, in my opinion. I'm going to build a pretty little village here."

"What about the Blacks' farm?"

The skin about his mouth tightened. "I'm going to make a nice little pile of money out of that. If Colonel Whiteoak doesn't like what I build he can lump it." He gave a consciously nonchalant yawn and added,—"It might be a jam factory."

"But, Eugene," she cried, "you promised——"

He cut her off with an almost violent change to a tone of authority. "Don't remind me again of any half-promises I made."

"They weren't half-promises!"

"You said that bungalows on Vaughanlands would annoy you. This is a different matter. All Jalna lies between us and Black's farm."

"It would depreciate all the property in the neighbourhood."

He spoke with resignation to that possibility. "We needn't worry about that, girlie. We'll, in all probability, be far away."

"Eugene! What do you mean?"

"I mean that I'm getting tired of the old-fashioned Victorian atmosphere of this place. Ninety per cent of the neighbourhood are reactionaries and Colonel Whiteoak is the worst of them all . . . He'd threaten me, would he? Threaten he'd lay hands on me! We'll see. We'll see. He who laughs last, laughs . . ." So worked up was Eugene Clapperton that he could not recall the last word of the proverb but kept on repeating—"laughs—laughs . . ."

She was intimidated by his manner. She could only ask,—"Where would we go? Why, I thought you intended to spend the rest of your life here!"

"I did, and I still may, but, as I said, there is much against the place—against the whole country, for that matter. The winters are too cold, too long. Look at this for April! They say you live ten years longer if you go to California. There is a lot in that country to attract a man of my age and my temperament."

"Hollywood?" she asked.

"No. Not Hollywood." He was displeased and fixed her with a stern eye. "I don't quite know what you mean by that remark."

"Nothing. I was just wondering. It is the only place in California I've heard about."

"Well, your education leaves a good deal to be desired.

There are lots of interesting places there. There are lots of people that would be congenial to a man of enquiring mind who likes to look into the heart of things and try to find out what is beyond the materialism of our times." He was pleased by this speech. He looked searchingly at her to see what she thought of it. She looked impressed, he thought. He added:

"There's also a beautiful climate. What would you say to such a move, Gem?"

"What about Althea?"

"She would come, of course."

"And her Great Dane?"

"He could come too, if he wanted to." Eugene Clapperton felt exhilarated by the thought of going to California. He felt kind and generous.

"It is good of you to say that, Tiddledy-winks," she exclaimed. "And would you sell this property?"

"I think not. I think I'd like to keep a hold on all my property here. It would give me a good deal of interest to come back now and then and see how my factory and my little village were getting on."

"And this house?" she asked, her eyes shining. She could not help thinking what fun it would be to go away. She had seen so little of the world.

He pursed his lips. "Well, I think I'd probably let this house to the manager of the factory. I know the very man. A rough diamond but as honest as they make them. Oh, don't you worry, girlie. I'll fix everything so it will be watertight!"

Upstairs the Great Dane began to bark.

"He wants me to bring Althea's tray," Gem cried. "Poor dear, she's lying there neglected in the dark!"

"Raikes will carry it up for you, Gem. I hear him in the kitchen whistling. I must ask him not to whistle in the house. His is a particularly penetrating one."

"But so sweet." She bent her head to listen.

Left to himself Eugene Clapperton took the chair in which he was sitting by the arms and walked, dragging it after him, to face the oil painting of the shipwreck. He settled himself comfortably to gaze at it. At the first shadow of dusk he had turned on the electric light beneath it. Now, with almost ceremonial gravity, he raised his eyes to it. The thunderous clouds, the lurid lightning, the ship staggering towards the black menace of the rocks, enthralled him. How much longer had the ship lasted, he wondered. How many of the sailors clinging to the rigging had survived? Not many, he was sure of that. What a wonderful thing it was, he thought, to be able to lose oneself in that pictured struggle—to absorb the elemental grandeur of the scene! There were few business men who had the imagination to do it, few whose minds ever strayed from the mundane, the materialistic . . . And it never had done him any harm. Only good. Consciously he relaxed, letting his mind swim in the roaring terror of the scene, hearing the pounding of the waves, the reverberation of the thunder.

In the kitchen Raikes was still whistling. Gem had prepared a tray for Althea and he had carried it up for her. Now he leant against the sink watching the Great Dane eat its supper of dog biscuit. Earlier in the day it had had its meal of meat and vegetables. Now it was not very hungry and chewed the hard morsels as if only to oblige. Raikes watched it kindly while he awaited Gem's return. His thoughts moved forward to the hour when the Clappertons would be in bed—to the moment when he would gently open the door of the garage, take out the Cadillac and drive to the club.

X

GOOD-BYE

ON THE last day of April the onrush of spring was able to defeat even the iron will of that winter. With glittering force the sun pushed back the heavy vapours and gave his fervent attention to land and rivers and lakes. With equal fervour they sought to make up for the delay in their reunion. Lake steamers began to nose their way through the spongy ice. The first captain to make the trip was presented as always with a top-hat. The rivers, as though roaring with laughter in their freedom, piled up great blocks of broken ice, broke down bridges, overflowed their banks, brought floods, drowned people and cattle, showed themselves brown and menacing. In the woods catkins appeared, in the gardens crocus and scilla smiled gold and blue. The stems of the willows turned glossy yellow. Sap moved in the maples and came oozing down their trunks. Gnats, bugs and worms appeared as though from nowhere and sunned themselves according to their pleasure, observed by Noah Binns with gloomy forecast. Piers' cows, ewes and sows gave themselves up to the bliss of having young. Hens ran cackling from the streaming barnyard and flopped into their nests just in time to lay an egg there. Piers' little daughter Mary was given her first skipping-rope and spent long, panting hours in trying to achieve one successful hop over it. The grass that covered the graves of all the Whiteoaks in the churchyard turned a delicate green and the sound of the church bell came sweet on the air.

The windows at Jalna were thrown open and the sunshine discovered fresh worn spots and cracks in the furnishings. But the old house bore the inspection well. Behind the rosy leaf-buds of the Virginia creeper the rosy brick showed solid and strong. Woodwork and shutters had been freshly painted the year before and still looked fresh.

"You stand the racket pretty well, don't you?" said Renny Whiteoak, addressing himself to the house from where he stood on the gravel drive. "You'll soon be celebrating your centenary. Lord, what a party we'll have for you!"

In his mind he went over the list of those of the family who would come to the party. His sister Meg and her daughter, Roma and Dennis, Piers and Pheasant and their children—young Maurice must come over from Ireland. Finch and Wakefield certainly, whatever distance they might have to travel. Perhaps they might be married by then, Finch for the second time. The right sort of wife would be good for him—he'd had bad luck in his first marriage. And Wakefield, God knew, had had bad luck in his first love. Well, better luck for them both next time, he hoped . . . By that time Piers' two younger sons would be grown up. Nooky was already as tall as Piers, and Philip a strapping fellow at fifteen. Mentally he added up the total number of the family who would be present at that party. Eighteen, if the two old uncles survived so long. Would it be possible? He sincerely hoped so. His mind shied away from the thought of their death. He would not consider it. Their mother had lived to be over a hundred, why not they? He raised his eyes confidently to the house, sunning itself after the long winter. How almost knowing it looked! How benign! He would protect it against all encroachments. It would remain as a fortress guarding the traditions of his forebears. He thought of Clapperton and gave a wry smile. He'd always be up to some mischief. But he felt himself a match for Clapperton. The day would come when he would put Clapperton permanently in his place—keep him there.

He heard a quick step and Adeline appeared from the darkness of the evergreens and came to him. She hooked an arm about his shoulder and looked up into his face.

"Daddy," she said, "I want to ask you a very serious question."

Before he spoke he studied that youthful face, in a moment's delight, so warmly alive, so full of character as yet untried. Then he asked:

"Well, what is it?"

"It's this. Can you really afford this trip for me? I know it's terribly expensive."

"Now, look here," he spoke in some exasperation, "if I can't afford a sea voyage and a visit to Ireland and London for my only daughter, things have reached a pretty low level with me."

"That's all very well, Daddy, but everything costs so terribly nowadays. Why—when Maurice told me the cost of the mere passage there and back I was shocked to the marrow. That's to say nothing of the hotel bill in London!" Breathlessly she hurried on. "I know how the men's wages are twice what they used to be and that the horses we've sold haven't brought what we hoped they'd bring. I do think that perhaps I'd better give up the idea."

"Too late. Your passage is bought and paid for."

"Not really?"

"Yes, really. So stop worrying your head about cost."

Still she was not satisfied. "But, Daddy, why have you refused to come? If you can afford it why won't you come?"

"I have things to do at home."

"Nothing that Uncle Piers can't attend to, I'm very sure."

"He can't attend to Clapperton."

"Are you joking?"

"No."

"What a menace that man is!" she exclaimed.

"He is indeed . . . Well, by next year I hope to settle him. Then we shall go to Ireland together."

"I will hold you to that," she said sternly.

But whether Renny was to accompany her or not, her pleasure in her preparations for the voyage made her days and even her dreams at night joyful. She went about the house singing, in a good voice but never in tune for more than six bars. She had a remarkable gift for starting on one tune and ending on another. It was impossible to discover

why or on what note the change was made. For one thing
she never sang the words but tra-la-la-ed her way in happy
ignorance of her destination. This fascinated Finch.
"*Pomp and Circumstance!*" he would shout, and then, after
a few more bars,—"*Rule, Britannia!* How on earth do you
do it?"

"It's easy," she would answer. "We learned them at
school."

She would, had she been allowed, have done all her
shopping and packing in two days; but Alayne was fastidious as to buying and to the careful packing of the clothes
—"Though what your things will look like by the time you
return I can't imagine!"

"If only I could do as Uncle Finch does! Packing is
simple for him. Oh, I wish I were a boy!"

"Girls do practically everything today that boys do. They
wear their clothes, take up their professions, or business."

"It isn't the same. Even if a girl becomes a gangster
she never would be as dangerous a one."

"You're being really silly, Adeline."

"Of course I am," cried Adeline. "To tell the truth I
hardly know what I'm doing these days. I live in a delicious
haze. When I went to Ireland before, I was a child. It was
wonderful going with Daddy, but—I was too young to
appreciate travel as I can now. You remember how you
felt when you went to Italy, when you were a girl."

"Indeed I do . . . . It was another world then."

"Yes, I know. But even if travel and life and everything
have deteriorated—as I'm sure they have—still, life seems
pretty good to me."

There were certain things to be done before she sailed
and two of the most important of these were bidding
good-bye to her cousins and her brother who were at
boarding-school. To be sure she had seen them not long
ago in the Easter holidays but she had promised all four
that she would make a special journey, at the very last, to
their schools. What pleased her most about these good-
byes was that, in each case, Renny was to drive her to the
schools. That meant two whole days in his company. So
soon they would be far apart—the ocean rolling between.

E

They motored first to Roma's school. She was younger than Adeline, the daughter of Renny's brother Eden who had died when she was a baby. She was an odd child whom Alayne had always disliked and, because of something Roma had done, now almost hated. Adeline had not much love for her cousin, holding the same act against her, but Renny loved the girl, and she, in her cool fashion, was attached to Adeline.

As the car drew near the school Adeline leant forward in pleasurable anticipation. She savoured her freedom from rules and regulations. How hard she had found it to conform to them! The very core of her had rebelled at doing everything in unison with fifty others. Yet on the surface she had not been rebellious. She had a sense of duty implanted in her chiefly by her two great-uncles. Even when she was very small it had been—"You owe this to your father—you must behave in a way to please your mother—remember, you are a Whiteoak!" When she did disobey rules it had not been in little ways but in larger matters that had occasionally shaken the school. Roma, on the other hand, was constantly evading rules but in such a way that she was seldom found out. Yet Roma clung to the school, felt a little dread of the time when she must leave it.

Now Renny and the two girls were in the reception-room together, the head-mistress having given her greetings, exclaimed at Adeline's growth and exchanged a look with Renny in silent commentary on her beauty.

Roma's beauty, thought Renny, was her hair, of an odd shade of gold that had an almost greenish cast. It was Eden's hair, he thought, and he searched her face for a resemblance to Eden. But, if it were there, it was no more than a fleeting shadow in her smile. Her eyes and cheek-bones were those of her mother, Minny Ware.

Roma said,—"Aren't you a lucky thing! Going off on an ocean voyage and all of us here swotting away with never any fun."

"Your last letter," answered Adeline, "was full of the fun you'd been having."

"Oh, that was nothing. I've forgotten it."

Renny said,—"Your time will come, Roma."

She smiled at him. "Will it? When?"

"Well, perhaps next year or the year after—when I go across with Adeline."

Roma's narrow eyes were hard with jealousy. "She again—so soon?"

"He's just talking," put in Adeline, her spirit in arms against the thought of Roma's going with them. "Goodness knows when I shall travel again."

At that moment they looked like women.

Roma went on,—"Everybody says there'll be another war before long. Then I may never get across—excepting with some horrible women's auxiliary corps."

"Nonsense," said Renny.

"Anyway," Adeline exclaimed, "that's all in the future. We're in the present."

"I was born in Italy," said Roma. "I'm longing to see it. It makes you feel different when you've been born abroad."

Adeline considered this one of Roma's "uncomfortable" remarks. She said tersely,—"You can't remember anything about it."

"Oh, yes, I can. I remember a lot."

"What?" asked Renny. "You were only two when you came to Jalna."

"I remember cypress trees, and a dark woman and little donkeys, and falling on hard stones and cutting my knee."

"I wonder who was the dark woman," said Renny. "Certainly not your mother."

"I don't remember her name but I remember her."

Adeline said,—"I'll bet you wouldn't know her today if you met her."

"Oh, yes, I should. I'd know my father too."

"You've seen very good photographs of him," said Renny.

"Even if I hadn't seen them I'd know him. I'd know his voice."

"You've never heard his voice!" exclaimed Adeline.

"I've heard it in his poetry."

Adeline pressed back the hair from her forehead in a gesture of despair. Was Roma going to spend this short time for which they had come so far, in talking in this embarrassing fashion? She appealed to Renny: "Are we going to take Roma out to lunch?"

"Yes. Miss Ellis said we might." His eyes were on Roma's face. "I'm glad," he said gravely, "that you read Eden's poetry. It is supposed to be very good. It was a pity he died so young."

"Do you think so?" A faint smile lifted Roma's lip— "I don't."

His eyebrows shot up in his dismay. "What a thing to say, Roma! What do you mean?"

"I think it's good to die young—before you find out too much."

"Then he didn't die young enough."

"What a pity!"

Adeline sprang up. "I didn't come here," she cried, "to talk about death."

"It's the first time," said Renny, "that Roma has spoken to me of her father." He spoke soothingly, as though to a colt that had shied at something on the road.

"Daddy, she can talk to you about death all the holidays, if she wants."

Roma stood up. "All right," she said, "let's go. Will you come up with me, Adeline, while I get my hat and coat?"

The two girls went up the stairs together. From the class-rooms came the hum of voices. Somewhere scales were being practised on the piano. Clean spring air came in at an open window and a tree was seen rustling its half-open leaves in the May breeze. In the room shared by four girls Adeline surveyed the beds, carefully made by the girls themselves. She exclaimed:

"To think that I once slept here! How did I ever bear it!"

"You had fun and so do we. Last night we had a party. I mean just the four of us."

"I know—buns and chocolate bars and at midnight you crept down to the kitchen and made cocoa!"

"Yes . . . Adeline."

"Well?"

"What if . . . over there . . . you'd meet someone?"

"What sort of someone?"

"I mean, supposing you fell in love—over in Ireland."

"Don't you worry. I shan't do that."

"What's to stop you?"

"Roma, your hair's lovely."

"So's yours."

"Yours is like greeny gold—not like that pinkish blond stuff they make out of peroxide."

"Yours is like copper, Adeline . . . You know, I shan't be a bit surprised if you have an affair over there. There's Mooey's friend Pat Crawshay."

"And there's Mooey himself!" cried Adeline. "And a million other Irishmen." Then she spoke seriously: "Roma, there isn't a man living I'd leave Jalna for."

"You should have said—for whom I'd leave Jalna."

"Roma! Can't you ever forget you took first prize in English?"

"But seriously, Adeline, you might fall in love."

"No fear. I'm going to Ireland to enjoy myself."

"They say being in love is fun."

"Who said?"

"Well, perhaps not actually fun, but exciting."

"You may have that sort of excitement. Just living is excitement enough for me."

"I'm looking forward to the time when I——"

"Oh, for goodness' sake, shut up, and put your coat on!"

"Adeline, if it happens, will you write and tell me?"

"Yes."

"You swear that?"

"Yes. Come on!"

"Adeline, would you like to be famous?"

"I'd like to come out on top in an international horse show. For high jumping, I mean."

"What I mean is for poetry or writing a novel."

"Well . . . I've never thought about it."

"Won't you ever think romantic thoughts?"

"Never . . . I'd better go and tell Daddy you don't want to come out to lunch."

"But I do!" She put on her dark blue coat and little round hat.

They walked lightly, side by side, down the stairs.

In the country town hotel Renny looked at them with pride as they sat at table. They were a pretty pair, he thought. The blood of his family running strong in their young veins. Himself and Eden translated into feminine bodies. Eden's and his manliness submerged into foreign meaning. They sat up nicely, he noticed. They never had been allowed to slouch like some girls. They studied the menu with dignity and were very polite to the waiter. Yes, they were a pair to be proud of. He would have liked to keep Roma at Jalna, but Alayne so disliked the child that he had sent her to live with his sister Meg and the arrangement had turned out very well. Meggie was so kind, so affectionate, she was bound to make anyone under her roof happy.

After lunch Roma was taken back to the school, with a few extra dollars in her handbag and a box of chocolates. Renny and Adeline turned homeward. He always had disliked motoring and, considering the reckless nature of his driving, it seemed a miracle that he never had had an accident. Now he handed over the wheel to Adeline and relaxed with a cigarette.

Out of the sides of his eyes he saw her clear-cut profile, almost stern in her calm concentration. She drove well, he thought, and it was pleasant to go homeward through the early May afternoon with her at the wheel. He did not like the thought of parting with her, even for so short a time. Almost he wished he were going with her, but then he would miss his favourite season at Jalna. Had he a favourite season? Were they not all dear to him in their turn? As they neared the house he said:

"Take a good look at it. Pretty fine old house, isn't it? I don't mean that it's so handsome, but there's an air about it. A woman like my grandmother couldn't live there for nearly seventy years without leaving her mark on it. And there was my grandfather and my father. Men of character."

"And you, too!" she said eagerly.

"Yes. Me too . . . A lot has gone on under that roof.
It seems to me that the house knows all about it. Do you
think I'm hay-wire?"

"Oh, no. I feel the same about it." Always she tried
to feel what he did.

"Now when you see Maurice's place, you'll see a grander
house but to me it hasn't the same feeling. It's an old house,
built in an old land, by people who had lived there since
God knows when. But there was the first house built on
this thousand acres——"

"It's not a thousand acres now, is it?"

"No. Just five hundred. Half of it was sold off, at various
times, to get my uncles out of financial difficulties. Now
that's something I've never done and never shall do—sell
an acre of this land . . . As I was saying, this is the first
house built on it. The primeval forest was hewn down to
make way for it. Your great-grandmother came every day
to watch the building of it, and before it was quite finished
she took to her bed—that same painted leather bed you
sleep in—and gave birth to a son there."

"I wonder if I ever shall," she said.

"What?"

"Give birth to a son there."

He looked at her in a moment's astonishment. "Good
Lord, what put that idea into your head?"

"You did."

The car was at the door. Renny stared at her, then he
said—"Well, not for a good many years, I hope."

"Say when I'm forty?"

He laughed. "Even twenty-five is a long way off."
Then he added seriously,—"There's room enough at
Jalna for you and your husband and Archer and his wife—
when the time comes." Always he was convinced of the
elasticity of Jalna and its capacity to shelter all the family.

"It would need to be a castle to have room enough for
me and Archer's wife."

Renny looked at her inquiringly.

"I'd be bound to hate any woman Archer would choose.
He's conceited and she'd be bound to be conceited."

"He'll get over that."

"She wouldn't."

Finch came out of the house. He asked,—"Did you have a nice time, Adeline?"

"You can imagine it. We drove to the school, picked up Roma, took her out to lunch, took her back to the school."

"Well, it was a satisfaction, I suppose, to tell her good-bye."

"It always is," she returned cheerfully.

Renny said,—"Roma grows less like Eden in looks."

"Does she?" said Finch. "That's a pity."

"Still she has his hair and when she smiles there's a distinct look of him."

"Let's hope she inherits his talent."

The three went into the house where the uncles were waiting to be told all about the visit to Roma.

A visit to another school was in prospect. This was to say good-bye to Adeline's brother Archer and her cousins, the two young sons of Piers. She looked forward with much pleasure to this because she thought boys' schools were more interesting than girls' and because the older cousin, Nooky, was her favourite.

He was a gentle boy of eighteen, tall and fair, with hazel eyes. He would seldom have been in trouble at home or at school, had it not been for the influence of his wild young brother Philip. But this year he had grown fast. He was head boy of the school. He would matriculate at the end of term, bringing honour to the school, the Headmaster confidently expected. He felt that he had outgrown Philip. Yet Philip showed him no deference beyond what he was forced to show him as a prefect. At fifteen he was Nooky's superior in sports. He was so good at football and hockey, at running and jumping, that the sports-minded masters often ignored his escapades. The brothers were much attached to each other and, at home, shared the same room. They looked on Maurice as almost an outsider.

The youngest of the three Whiteoaks, Archer, bearing Alayne's maiden name, also bore a striking resemblance to her father who had been a professor in a New England university. He had a noble white forehead which sun never noticeably tanned, piercing blue eyes, and a mouth usually set in a sombre line as though the weight of the world was on his shoulders. Yet when he did consent to give a smile it was one of extraordinary sweetness. It was a disappointment and even a heartache to his mother that physical resemblance was so far all he seemed to bear to her father. She could not have told you what was wrong with Archer's nature but certainly it seemed to her that a good deal was wrong.

On this day he was one of those who were to be confirmed by the visiting Archbishop. Renny, Alayne and Adeline were coming for the occasion.

Archer, with the other small boys in his dormitory, had been waked by the early bell, had fallen asleep again. Then had come the slippered steps of Robertson, a prefect, his commanding roar, the leap out of bed and the rush to the lavatory. Archer stood in front of a basin and gingerly washed his face. Hughes, the boy at the next basin, was splashing water over its edge on to the floor and over Archer's bare feet.

"Stop it!" shouted Archer.

"He wants you to be nice and clean for the ceremony," said Elton.

Archer threw a handful of water at him. A water fight began. The matron put her head in at the door. Instantly there was order, except from little rosy-faced Elton who found it impossible to obey orders without persuasion. He thrust a wet hand down Archer's back. Archer writhed away, giving a gurgling yell.

"Come here, Elton," the matron said sternly.

He went to her, his rosy face shining with wet.

"You are to be confirmed today, aren't you?"

"Yes, Miss Macqueen."

"Well, I think you ought to behave properly this morning, don't you?"

"Yes, Miss Macqueen."

"If I have any more disturbance from any of you there'll be trouble, do you hear?"

They all heard and looked at her meekly out of bright mischievous eyes. But the door was scarcely shut behind

E*

her when there was a hubbub. The morning was lovely. It was a whole holiday. They could not bring themselves to behave. Archer sprang on Elton and brought him to the floor. They rolled together in the wet. Hughes put his thumb under a tap and sent a spray of water into the face of Trotter, a plump boy, the only child of very rich parents who pampered him. Trotter was always brought to school in a limousine, driven by a chauffeur, instead of coming by train with the mob. Everything he owned was too expensive. Each week a package of fruit, sweets and cake, such as not supplied by the school, arrived by post for him. Trotter was lucky if he got one orange out of the package. Usually it was fallen upon before ever he saw it, opened, and the contents distributed. After holidays he returned from home with his pockets full of money. Then, while it lasted, he had friends of a sort, but his air was so strutting, he was so conscious of his own superiority, that soon he was alone again. His loving parents little realized when they read his letters, so full of his happy doings at school, how miserable he really was.

Now, with the water squirting full in his face, he gasped, ran, stumbled, and one of his fine kid slippers fell off. Instantly it was pounced on, struggled over, hurled into the air, flung down the room, and finally kicked out of the window. Trotter was really roused. He took off his remaining slipper and began to beat Elton with it. The scene was riotous when the door opened and the Head Boy looked in.

The effect was far more startling than if the matron had reappeared. Seldom did the Head Boy condescend to look into the room. Struck motionless the small boys stared questioningly at him.

"Elton and Trotter," he said, "both of you will go to the prefects' study after breakfast."

He left, closing the door quietly behind him.

"It's a caning for you!" exclaimed Archer. He did a hand-stand, waving his wet pink feet in the air.

"It will be my forty-second since September!" cried Elton boasting. He kept strict account of his canings and no other boy could rival him in this respect. No boy was

better liked by the other boys, the prefects and the masters.
No boy in the school was happier, but he was incorrigible.
Rules, for him, were made to be broken. Impositions,
being kept in, lectures on behaviour or kindly talks, had
no effect whatever on him, rosy-cheeked rascal that he
was.

"It will be my first," mourned Trotter.

All scampered back to their dormitory which was in an
incredible state of disordered bedding and clothes strewn
on beds and floor. An observer might well wonder how
the boys were able to find their own garments and get into
them with such speed. A lover of beauty might well have
admired the swift movements of their naked white bodies,
from which summer tan was gone and which still retained
the charming contours of childhood.

Now more than a hundred boys were gathered for
breakfast, standing with bent heads while grace was said.
This grace was punctuated by quiet shuffling of feet and
low coughs, for colds were plentiful. In this school the
boys ranged in age from seven to nineteen—from tender
small ones to six-footers. They set about eating their por-
ridge; Elton with gusto, Trotter languidly, Archer Whiteoak
not at all, for he disliked anything milky. Alayne had
arranged for extra milk for him to drink at recess. This he
was able to sell for a few cents a glass to boys who liked it.

After breakfast the Head gave a few instructions about
the proceedings of the day. He asked the boys to remember
that the day was a serious one when certain of them were
to take part in an important spiritual ceremony.

Returning to the prefects' room Nook had remarked to
the group there: "I've got Trotter. He is coming for a
caning."

"Trotter!" There was a general show of interest.

There was not one among them who had not wished
for this moment, who had not thought that a caning was
badly needed by Trotter.

"What is it for?" asked Robertson.

"Fighting in the wash-room."

"Who with?"

"Elton. He's coming too."

A groan was drawn from the prefects.

"Elton," groaned Robertson. "I'm worn out with beating that boy!"

"You don't have to do it," said Nook. "Nichol will."

Nichol, a tall dark youth, with a lazy smile, got to his feet with zest. "When are they coming?" he asked.

"Now. They're at the door."

A timid knock sounded. At the door's opening the two small boys came in. Elton looked resigned, almost cheerful, but Trotter very apprehensive.

The prefects turned away, as though occupied with more important affairs. All but Nichol who said:

"Now then, Trotter. Touch your toes."

Elton spoke up. "Would you mind doing me first, Nichol?" he asked. "I've got my pets to feed and I'm late with their breakfast already. And I've a trap set in the woods."

"A trap! You're not allowed to set traps."

"Oh, but this isn't the sort that injures the animal. I want to catch a squirrel and make a pet of it."

"All right," Nichol said obligingly, "you touch your toes."

Archer Whiteoak, as soon as he was free after breakfast, ran to the lake. There it lay, with its gentle green shores protected by woods and fields. The sky was a clear blue and the round white clouds, barely moved by the breeze, were reflected with dreamy splendour in the lake. Archer squatted by the brink, dabbling his hands in the wet coolness. Now and again he would pounce on some tiny fish swimming in the shelter of reeds and capture one. He would hold it in his hand till its wriggling ceased, then he would return it to the lake, just in time to save its life. From the wharf he could see the largest of the three sailing-boats move out on to the lake. Nooky, Robertson and Nichol were manning it. So they had finished with Elton and Trotter! He saw Elton, running after his brother who was in the fifth form. Their mother was dead and he had promised their father to have a kindly eye on this small boy. Now the second sailing-boat moved out on to the lake. Now the third. Now a canoe with two half-naked boys in it. It was the first warm day.

After a while Archer left the lake. He went at an easy jog trot towards the little wood and the fields. As he passed the playing field he saw some sort of game in progress, heard the sports master shouting directions. In the wood one of the little boys was playing alone. He was very small but quite sufficient unto himself. He was in fact a train. Moving his arms as wheels, making chugging noises in his throat, he passed rigidly along the rails of his fancy. He came to a certain tree, halted and called out, in a shrill little voice,—"Belleville!" Farther on it was—"Port Hope!" Then—"Kingston!" Clumps of sweet-smelling hepaticas were about him, coming up through the moist dead leaves of last year. The delicate white petals of trilliums were about to unfold, but he saw nothing of them. He was machinery, pure and simple, or the minion of machinery. He gave not the slightest attention to Archer who stood regarding his activities with the deepest pessimism. Archer had no recollection of ever having indulged in such futilities.

He jogged on till suddenly he spied a snake. It was a small green one, sunning itself on the path. In a moment he had it by the tail. He examined it with a coldly critical eye, then jogged on, through the wood, into the field. Now the sun was almost hot. The sound of a bugle came to him from where a cadet was practising.

Two of the younger masters were lying on a grassy knoll in the field. They had gone there to talk and to be away from the boys. Lying there luxuriously they saw Archer approach.

"It's Whiteoak three," said one, "with a snake."

"Oh, Lord," said the other. "You won't get away from that kid."

Archer gave his sweet smile. "Please, sir," he said, "would you mind looking after my snake for a few minutes?" He placed the tip of the snake's tail between the reluctant finger and thumb of the master and ran off.

After a while he returned with a snake in either hand—harmless snakes, but the young master did not want to touch one. He rolled on to his side and turned his face away. Archer said:

"The first of these snakes may be a *Thamnophis Sirtalis*, the other may be a *Natrix Sipedon*. But they're both very unusual specimens. I must show them to Mr. Wickens. So will you please help me carry them to him?"

"Don't you think he'll be too busy this morning to look at them?" asked one of the young men.

"He is never too busy," returned Archer severely, "to look at specimens."

Soon the three went, in Indian file, down the little path, Archer leading the way, each of the masters holding gingerly, at arm's length, a snake. They entered the little wood where the very small boy was still chugging along imaginary railway lines and did not turn his head to look at them. The sunshine was suddenly much brighter, the air very warm. The three snakes, heads down, writhed and stretched.

Having deposited them with the science master Archer turned his steps towards the tuck-shop, which was in charge of a fifth form boy named Yuell. As Archer went in he met three small boys coming out each carrying a bottle of ginger ale and a chocolate bar. Inside, on an upturned box, sat Archer's cousin, Philip Whiteoak, drinking a "coke". He was a strongly built handsome boy, with bright blue eyes and yellow hair. His cadet uniform was very becoming to him. From his shoulder was suspended his bugle. It was he whom Archer had heard sounding the Reveille. He had just mastered it and was so fascinated he could scarcely keep the bugle from his lips.

Yuell, rearranging his wares, turned to Archer.

"Want something?" he asked.

"Yes," answered Archer, "but I haven't any money."

"Then you'd better clear out."

Philip set down the empty bottle. "Give him a coke on me," he said.

Yuell did and Philip picked up his bugle. He sounded the Reveille with vigour, his eyes growing prominent from the effort and his cheeks pink. Archer, the bottle to his lips, looked at him with respect.

"Pretty good," said Yuell. "Almost perfect."

"*Almost?*" Philip stared, not pleased.

"Well, what do *you* think?"

"Oh, I guess it could have been better."

"I think it was pretty good," said Archer.

It was cheek for him to offer an opinion.

"A lot you know about bugling," said Philip. He put the bugle to his lips and again sounded the Reveille.

The spring air was shattered like fine glass by the ringing notes.

"How's that?" asked Philip.

Yuell answered,—"Fine."

Archer was silent.

"Have you anything to say against it?" Philip demanded.

"Keep practising," said Archer, "and you'll do it right." He set down his empty bottle and stalked out. He was so remarkably straight that his neck had a look of arrogant stiffness.

He went to the lake and there found a canoe not in use. He arranged himself in it and took up the paddle. Dipping it gently he moved out across the shining surface of the lake. He saw the raised head of a snake as it swam towards the reedy shore. He envied it its freedom. To be a water snake, free to do as it liked on land or in water, at no one's bidding. He liked snakes better than he liked most people. He never wanted to beat them with sticks—to kill them, as some of the boys did.

His mind moved to his coming confirmation and he wondered what it would do to him. It would admit him to the taking of the Communion; but what would it do to him inside? He remembered the boys who were confirmed last year. What had it changed in them? Nothing. He was sure of that. They could not be changed. They were too stupid. But he would be changed. He pictured to himself how the masters and boys would look at him in wonder and whisper to each other,—"How greatly Whiteoak three has changed!" He plied his paddle and swept out to the breezy middle of the lake.

Archbishop and parents were arriving before lunch and the ceremony was to take place soon after. Everywhere was the bustle of preparation. Archer was late in coming to the dormitory to dress. Elton was the only boy there and he was putting the last touch to his tie. He said,— "Better hurry up. You've just five minutes. I saw your mother and father and sister coming in."

Archer began to pull off his jacket and shirt. Then, with his shirt over his head, he remembered that he had not given his blue Sunday suit to the housemaid to be sent to the cleaners. He had forgotten this as he forgot everything that did not interest him.

"Hurry up!" shouted Elton and ran out of the room and down the passage.

Archer emerged from the shirt and looked about the room. It had been in order when the boys had come in to dress, with each boy's clean Sunday suit stretched on his bed. All but Archer's. Now all were gone but Trotter's which lay in readiness. But where was Trotter? Archer had no time to waste. He got out his Sunday suit and looked with dismay at its spotty front. He pictured his mother's fastidious turning away, his father's frown, Adeline's grin. He laid his suit on Trotter's bed, spotty side down, and took Trotter's suit in its stead. He must hurry or Trotter would catch him in the act. He put on a clean white shirt.

The suit was a little large, for Trotter was a plumper boy than Archer, but it looked very nice. He put on his collar and tie with satisfaction—his clean socks and best shoes. He was just tying the laces when Trotter came running in. He was red in the face and Archer could see that he had been crying.

"Get a move on," said Archer. "You're late."

"I know," murmured Trotter. "Gee, I bet I get into more trouble! Whiteoak, will you help me with my tie?"

"No time. There goes the bell!"

He ran down the stairs. The clamour in the passage subsided into an orderly entrance into the dining-room. The Headmaster said the Latin grace and everybody sat down. Archer stared at the Headmaster's table where he could see his mother sitting beside the Archbishop. He could see his father's head and shoulders, Adeline's profile set off by her copper-coloured hair. Archer did not want his lunch. He felt apprehensive, as he had felt before his tonsil operation. Elton was eating hungrily, enjoying rhubarb pie, first of the season. Trotter was eating too, in a distraught sort of way. He looked ready to burst out of Archer's spotty suit but his collar was nice and clean. The hum of voices was subdued. It was strange to hear the sound of women's voices from the Head's table.

Alayne's eyes roved over the boys, trying to find her son. She discovered Nooky, manly and self-contained. Always he had been a favourite of hers. He had been such a shy sensitive little boy; now he was developing into just the sort of man she had hoped for. He had a look of Pheasant though he was fair. . . . Then she found Philip, whom Renny called "the spit of Piers"—with his bold mouth and handsome head . . . But, where was her darling?

She whispered to Renny,—"Do you see Archer?"

"Why, yes, at the second table from the end, the fourth boy—looking very spruce and nice."

She looked and her heart quickened its beat. There he was, his pale rather stiff hair up from his high forehead! So intent was her gaze that it caught his and his face lighted with a smile—a smile so fleeting it made her feel sad. She had felt anxious and hurt by his not being on hand to meet her when she arrived. She wondered what had kept him from her. She pointed him out to the Archbishop who showed a gracious interest in discovering him.

After lunch there was time for a brief reunion before they went to the chapel. On the sunny lawn Alayne threw an arm about Archer's shoulders. "Do you mind if I kiss you?" she asked.

He raised his forehead and she kissed it. Renny patted his back, while Adeline regarded him with detached curiosity.

"You seem to have shrunken," she said.

"Why, Archer," cried Alayne, "you *are* thinner! Do you eat enough?"

Here was too good a chance to let slip. "There's never anything I like," he said. "Trotter has a hamper sent to him every week."

"Nonsense," said Renny. "The food is good."

"Oh, but I must arrange for him to have more milk," exclaimed Alayne. "His suit is *loose* on him."

They could see the Trotter family taking a large hamper from their large car. The parents beamed as their son staggered with it into the school, followed by a horde of other small boys, gathering like locusts about the prize. Archer's eyes followed them contemplatively, knowing how short a while the contents of the hamper would last and how small a share would be Trotter's.

Mrs. Trotter came and spoke to Alayne. "It's disgraceful," she said, "the lack of care that's given to the boys' clothes. Here is my boy going to be confirmed today in a suit covered with spots."

Certainly, thought Alayne, remembering her glimpse of the son, he was not a very prepossessing boy, his hair untidy, his eyelids pink and his suit a size too small for him. She said:

"It is all so difficult. One never knows. One is practically helpless. My boy looks thin to me."

"He is a charming boy," said Mrs. Trotter. "Such nice manners and so well-groomed. I'm just ashamed of Herbie. But he's so happy it makes up for a great deal."

The boys had now gone into the chapel. The parents followed, strolling across the grass beneath the trees, reluctant to leave the sunshine and the breeze that blew in from the lake. The little boy who had been a train, now shunted, huffing and puffing, last of all the boys.

Inside, the organ began to peal. Alayne, Renny and Adeline were led to a seat near the chancel. Seated there in two pews were the boys who were to be confirmed. To Alayne Archer's face stood out with startling clearness, the silvery fair hair, the pallor, the look of complete composure. He sat between Trotter and Elton. Trotter's eyes were fixed on the Archbishop, in his magnificent robes. Elton's eyes roved, the dimples at the corners of his mouth could not be restrained. Even so solemn an occasion as this could not make him solemn.

The school chaplain, in a surplice that seemed to swing of its own volition, jauntily proceeded with the service. A psalm was read by Nooky Whiteoak from his place

among the sixth form boys. The great moment arrived
when those to be confirmed came one by one and knelt at
the Archbishop's feet. How small they looked! How
weak and defenceless! Alayne's throat was constricted
as Archer took his place. The Archbishop laid his hand on
the child's head. "Defend, O Lord, this thy child with
thy heavenly grace, that he may continue thine for ever;
and daily increase in thy Holy Spirit more and more, until
he come to thy everlasting kingdom. Amen."

Alayne was an agnostic. She had been brought up in the
Unitarian faith of her earnest parents. This ceremony held
no early associations for her, but because of her child,
because of the benign beauty of the Archbishop's face, she
was moved. Renny sat, with his intent dark gaze on his son,
wondering what sort of life he would have, what sort of
world he would grow up in—very different from the world
he himself had grown up in. He liked the sermon the
Archbishop preached to the boys—easy to understand—
not too long. But he was not sorry when it was over. He
must remember to give Archer a little money before he
left.

All was a dream to Adeline, seen through the shining
prospect of her voyage to Ireland. It was as though part
of her were already on the way. Before the moment of
saying good-bye arrived she had already said it in imagination. Nooky drew her aside. "Think of me," he said,
"swatting at exams while you and Maurice disport yourselves on the ould sod."

"Oh, Nook, I wish you were coming!"

"Why has Maurice all the good luck?" he exclaimed.
"He inherits a fine place in Ireland and money to keep
it up, and when he goes over to claim it he has you for
company."

"You'd have hated to leave home as he was made to
when he was a small boy."

"I shouldn't have minded."

"Nooky, you would have howled your head off. You
were such a clinging little boy."

"I'm still clinging," he said, giving her a warm look.

"Well, you've plenty to cling to."

"Not you."

They laughed, a little embarrassed.

The visitors were moving into the Headmaster's large living-room where tea was served. With them were allowed to go those boys whose relatives they were. Nook brought tea to Adeline and a scone.

"What's the matter with Archer?" she asked. "He looks funny."

"Somebody else's suit."

"I thought so," she chuckled. "Mummy thinks he's lost weight—poor little fellow!"

Archer passed, carrying a perfectly balanced cup of tea.

"I've always wondered," said Nook, "what Archer will be. Now I know. He's a born waiter. Give him a tray. Put a napkin over his arm. He's perfect. He's got the wooden expression and his hand would be always out for the tip."

"Oh, Nooky, I think he's a born professor. Look at the armful of prizes he gets every term. And he's always near the head of his form."

"True. I guess I'll be the waiter . . . Will you write to me, Adeline?"

"Of course."

"Tell me all about everything. Promise."

"I promise."

"Don't go falling in love with some Irishman."

"Catch me falling in love!"

"I wish I could," he said teasingly, "with me."

XI

THREE ON A JOURNEY

ERNEST'S ninety-fifth birthday was celebrated with more flourish than usual. What was the reason for this no one could have told you, but excitement was in the air. Ernest himself felt it and referred to the day, as it approached, as a milestone to be noted. "Not that I ever shall attain the great age Mama did," he would say, a little wistfully. He was not particularly afraid of death but he had a great love of life and, in his own small corner of the world, felt that he had much to live for—a strongly individual family over whom he felt he had great influence, not realizing how much of that was affectionate tolerance.

A dinner party was given for him, to which all the family and a few old friends were invited. The dinner was really a spread, with Alayne arranging a quite elaborate menu to please him, and Nicholas providing the champagne. Candlelight shone on bare white shoulders and white shirt-fronts. Adeline took Nicholas' hair in hand and actually made it lie down, but before the first course was over, he had run his hand through it and again roused it into a plume. Nicholas was in a wicked mood and sought to bring a blush to his brother's cheek by recalling early escapades in London and Paris, but Ernest was only pleased by this, for he felt it put him in a gallant light in front of the younger members of the family.

Renny proposed his health. "Let's drink the health," he said, "of the gentleman—and gentle man he is, if ever there was one—who was the first baby to be born at Jalna. He drew his first breath under this roof. We're all proud of that. We're all proud of having him still with us, and hope, with all our hearts, that he'll live as long or longer than his magnificent Irish mother."

The health was drunk with gusto. But Alayne, smiling at Finch, saw there were tears in his eyes.

In the days that followed, Renny almost regretted that he had made up his mind not to go to Ireland. Adeline's joy in the prospect was so palpable, it so shone out of her eyes and so echoed in her laugh that he would have been glad to see its fulfilment. That there would be fulfilment he did not doubt. Ireland would suit Adeline, as it suited him. On his own part he would have liked a change. Since the war he had been almost nowhere, apart from trips to the New York Horse Show. His horses, shown there and in Canada, had taken prizes and some of them had been sold very well. The farm prospered. He could not complain. Yet, in some insidious way, the presence of Eugene Clapperton as a neighbour had poisoned the air for him. The plans for building which Clapperton had seemed to abandon after his marriage, once more menaced Jalna. All about the countryside ugly little houses, hideous service stations, were springing up, but Jalna and Vaughanlands remained untouched, except for the few bungalows Clapperton had already built.

Alayne had bought sensible but pretty clothes for Adeline. To Renny they were not fine enough. He would have liked to see his daughter elegantly turned out. He had to satisfy himself by buying her several pairs of expensive shoes. "She's got Gran's feet, you know, Alayne, and they must be shod to advantage." A week before the departure he gave Adeline extra money for her expenses. Having handled so little in her young life the amount seemed very large to her—more than she needed. She pressed back some of it into his hand. "No, no, Daddy. I couldn't take so much! I don't need it." Her face was flushed by excitement and the evidence of his generosity.

He refused to take back the bank-notes.

"You have your travellers' cheques," he said. "They are for the necessities. This cash is to enjoy yourself with —to buy things you fancy."

"But Uncle Nick and Uncle Ernest have both given me money," she objected.

"Don't worry. You'll find how fast it will go."

She threw both arms about him. "You are generous, Daddy. Thank you, thank you."

When three days had passed he insisted on adding another bank-note to her store. "I've been thinking over your needs," he said, "and I'm afraid you're going to find yourself short of funds, so I'm giving you this."

"No, no," she said, "you can't afford it! I won't take it."

"You'll do what I tell you to," he said sternly but his eyes were laughing. He held her two hands in one of his and pushed the bank-note inside her collar.

She raised his hand, which smelled of Windsor soap, to her lips. "All right, Daddy," she said, as though humbly. "If you say so."

And that was not the end. When they were saying good-bye he opened her handbag and thrust several rather crumpled notes inside, then snapped it shut.

"They're American bills," he said. "Buy yourself something in New York."

By this time Adeline was too much excited to make any objection to the gift. She took it in a dazed way. Ernest took her in his arms and, a little brokenly, said his good-bye. "God bless you, dear child. How I wish I were going with you! But I am afraid my travelling days are over."

"I wish you were coming, Uncle Ernest," she returned, scarcely knowing what she said. "Take good care of yourself while I'm away." She turned to Nicholas. "Both of you, take care of yourselves. I shall have so much to tell you when I come back."

Alayne, Pheasant, little Mary, Dennis, the old uncles and the Wragges stood about the car. To Pheasant's mind came the remembrance of the terrible day when Maurice had left for Ireland as a young boy. The pain of that parting had foreshadowed his final break. Never would he be hers again. But she smiled at him with fortitude.

"I'll be coming across to visit you," she said.

"You should be coming now," he answered, half-angrily, for it had been his dream to take his mother back with him.

"Who would look after Piers and the baby, and the boys when they come from school?"

Piers said,—"We've been over all this before. If you were set on going we could have managed."

"But I was not set on going," she smiled. "It's just fun to think about."

Piers looked at his watch. "There's no time to spare. Everybody set to go?" He laid his hands on the wheel. Finch began to scramble wildly out of the car.

"Good Lord!" he exclaimed. "I've left my wallet upstairs!" Dennis ran after him.

"I'll fetch it for you, sir!" cried Rags, and a little bent, not very agile, he began to hasten up the steps.

"I couldn't tell you where it is," cried Finch, already in the hall. He ran upstairs, two steps at a time. Up the two flights to his room he sped and, in the disorder there, looked wildly about. It was not on the top of the dressing-table. It was not in either of the top drawers. He could hear Rags panting up the final flight.

"This is an awful thing to 'appen, sir," said Rags. "It seems too bad you should mislay something so important at the very last." He began to pull out the contents of the chest of drawers and scatter them over the floor.

Wherever Finch was searching Dennis was there too, his small neat hands scrabbling among ties, handkerchiefs, note-books, concert programmes, the mass of odds and ends that Finch invariably collected. Finch shouted at him:

"Go away! I can't search with you here!"

"'E's always interferin', sir," said Rags. "'Is hands is into everythink."

Dennis moved to the doorway and stood there watching.

Renny's voice, with a vibration from the chest, came up the staircase. "Finch!"

Finch, brushing Dennis aside, came on to the landing. "Yes?" he called back.

"If you can't find that damned wallet come without it! You're going to miss your train."

"I can't go without it. All my money is in it and my tickets!"

"When did you last see it?"

"This morning . . . last night . . . I forget."

"Well—of all the duffers!"

Finch shouted,—"If you keep me here talking how can I search for it?"

"There's no time to search!"

"Tell them to go without me." He turned back into his room.

Maurice and Adeline came running up the stairs and into the littered room. They began systematically to turn over, shake, and still further disarrange every object in it. Their faces were pale, desperate. Outdoors Piers began to sound the horn insistently.

"Look here," cried Finch. "It's no use. You'll have to go without me."

Dennis spoke in his cool little voice. "Here is the wallet," he said, taking it from between two books on the bookshelves.

With something between a groan and a cry of joy Finch snatched it from him and tore down the stairs. Maurice and Adeline leaped after him. Dennis had expected a chorus of thanks but instead found himself alone with Rags. For a moment they stared blankly at each other, then hastened after the others.

When Rags, very much out of breath, reached the porch the car was already speeding down the road, the dogs were looking dejected as they always did after a departure, and the uncles, with resigned smiles, were turning back into the house.

"What a pity you could not have gone with Mooey," Alayne said to Pheasant.

Pheasant could not answer. Her voice was stifled by tears. Alayne would have liked to comfort her but could think of nothing to say. Her innate reserve kept her from putting her arm about Pheasant. It seemed stupid to say, —"Perhaps before long you will go." Pheasant's tears were for the permanent loss of her son to another country. In truth she knew that in the last five years, when he had been at home, a part of him had remained in Ireland.

The travellers, with the aid of Renny and Piers, had barely installed their hand luggage on the racks when the

train began to move. There was no time for good-byes,
but Piers delivered a parting shot.

"Hard luck on you, Adeline," he said, "to have these
two crackpots on your hands. Don't trust them with your
valuables."

He hurried after Renny. The train was moving. Renny
took him by the arm and helped him off, anxious because of
Piers' artificial leg.

Finch put his hat on the rack, leaned back and closed
his eyes. He was humiliated by the mislaying of the wallet,
he was angry with himself for his absent-mindedness. He
was angry with Piers for the stony silence he had preserved
during the drive in, though he had to acknowledge that
Piers' handling of the car at such speed had been masterly.
They were lucky not to have been stopped for breaking
traffic laws. Finch felt exhausted nervously. He hated the
vibration of the train. He felt that he had spent too much
time on trains, rattling from one city to another, from one
crowd of strangers to another. If Piers led the life he did,
perhaps he wouldn't always be so cocksure of where he had
put things. And what was it that Renny had said?
"I might have known you'd bungle things!" Well, a
remark like that was enough to make anyone laugh.
He who led an infinitely more complicated life than
Renny! Good Lord—the simplicity of Renny's life! The
saddle—in place of the piano seat! The reins—in place
of the keyboard! And what a contrast their marriages! Of
course, Renny and Alayne had had their difficulties but
they really were devoted to each other. A man was lucky
to have Alayne for a wife . . . so steadfast . . . so sympathetic . . . with a kind of nobility in her that was rare
. . . He could hear Maurice and Adeline talking together
in subdued tones, as though not to disturb him. He heard
Adeline give an excited school-girl giggle. Through a slit
of his eyelids he looked at her. She too had taken off her
hat, and her brown hair, with its overtone of auburn, lay
tumbled a little on her forehead. Her lips were parted in a
carefree, expectant smile. Maurice was looking at her with
a possessive air, as though having got her away from Jalna
a new relationship between them had come into being. In

some inexplicable way the boy looked older, more assured. Finch closed his eyes again and felt for his wallet to make certain it was safe. He relaxed his long limbs, let his body sink into the chair. After a while the roadbed of the train became smoother, the sound of the wheels less irritating and by degrees grew into a soothing hum. After all he was not at the beginning of a tour but was setting out on a journey of pure pleasure. He would see Ireland and England again. He would be once more with Wakefield.

They were a gay trio in the restaurant car. They went early to bed, and next morning breakfasted in New York. Not once had Adeline or Maurice made any reference to the mislaying of the wallet, but Finch could not put it out of his mind. Every so often would his hand steal to his pocket. He would recall to himself how many times he had gone to a concert hall leaving his music, his watch, his handkerchief in the hotel; how often he had left his gloves or his goloshes in the concert hall.

New York was glittering in springtime brightness. Adeline must buy herself a new necklace of costume jewellery out of Renny's parting gift. Finch bought her a scarf and Maurice a box of chocolates and a basket of fruit from a superb Fifth Avenue shop. The price of those so alarmed her that she was subdued for some time. "If that is the way you are going to throw your money about, young man," she said to Maurice, "it won't last long."

Finch's agent had lunch with them at their hotel. Maurice and Adeline were quite impressed by the conversation between the two men. It seemed strange to them that Finch's doings should be of such consequence to someone in New York and they were even more impressed when they went aboard the ship to find that reporters, on the look-out for celebrities, were eager to ask Finch questions about his plans and to photograph him. These manifestations in a foreign country were more significant to them than all they had previously heard or read of Finch's reputation.

Finch's desire was to escape from these gentlemen. If the ship had been one of the great liners, with movie stars aboard, he was sure they would not have troubled about interviewing him. He and Maurice shared a cabin. It had been possible to secure a small one for Adeline, not to be shared by a stranger. Setting this little place in order, placing her belongings to the best advantage, enthralled her for a short while, then shoutings and the throbbing of the engines told her that the ship was about to sail. She hurried to the deck, through the confusion of people, to the confusion of moving lights against the blackness. It was midnight.

Finch found her and tucked his hand in her arm.

"We're off," he said.

"Yes. Isn't it marvellous?" But she was rather disappointed by the slow movement of the ship, the confusion of lights. Would she never ride out into the open? All about her were the dark forms of other passengers. She wondered whether she would speak to any of them. Would one of those dark forms become perhaps a friend? She heard a group of people speaking Spanish. She heard a rough Irish brogue from a stout woman talking to a priest. She asked:

"How old were you, Uncle Finch, the first time you crossed?"

He answered, rather heavily,—"Twenty-one."

"Oh, I remember hearing about it. You had just come into Great-grandmother's money, hadn't you?"

"Yes."

"And you brought Uncle Nicholas and Uncle Ernest with you, for a treat."

"Yes."

"Goodness, that was funny. A boy off on the loose with two old gentlemen."

"We enjoyed it."

"It must be wonderful to inherit a fortune."

"Well . . . I don't know . . . It can be embarrassing."

"I'd love to try it . . . Maurice has done it too. Aren't you a lucky pair!"

"I didn't hang on to my money for long."

"*Really!* What became of it?"

"I don't know."

"You actually *don't know*?"

"No."

She laughed gaily. "Uncle Finch, you *are* funny!"

He gave a grunt of agreement.

"Your wife was rich too, wasn't she?" It was the first time Adeline had ever referred to his marriage to him, but the ship had loosed her tongue.

"She had a good deal of money," he said, "but her last husband managed to get hold of most of it. What is left will go to Dennis."

"Lucky dog! I never used to think about money but now I realize how important it is. I see Daddy with never enough of it."

New York lay behind them, pillars of lights, bridges of lights, clusters of lights, with no discernible support, against the dark blue sky. The white foam of the wake was spreading like an opening fan at the stern. The air was cold.

"I promised to look after you," said Finch. "Now I think you ought to go to bed. You look tired—at least as tired as you are able to look."

He remembered the exhausted young face that he had seen reflected from his looking-glass when he was her age.

"I am a little sleepy," conceded Adeline, "but I promise you it's the last time I shall go to bed early on this voyage."

"Early! It's one o'clock."

"Is that all? Where's Maurice?" Now she saw him coming towards them. "Oh, there you are, Mooey! Where have you been?"

"Isn't it cold?" he exclaimed. "Let's get inside."

The deck was emptying. The throb of the engines was becoming resolute as the ship increased her speed. Inside there was light and warmth and a restless movement of passengers. There was searching for mislaid luggage, opening of telegrams and boxes of flowers. Adeline was delighted when she was handed a telegram from Nook wishing her *bon voyage*.

"How sweet of him!" she cried. "And it was only the other day when he saw me."

Another telegram was handed to her. This was from Humphrey Bell. It read: "With sincere good wishes for a happy voyage and a safe return."

It amazed her and made her laugh. "To think of it!" she exclaimed. "That funny little man!" But she was pleased. She cherished both telegrams.

Maurice shrugged. "I'll bet a lot of thought went into the wording of that telegram," he said.

At that moment Humphrey Bell, stretched in his bed, with his cat at his feet, was wishing with all his might he had not sent it and by sending it lowered himself still further in her eyes.

"I've been talking to a man," Maurice said. "A nice fellow. An Irishman."

Adeline was at once interested.

"He's standing over there lighting a cigarette. I'll introduce him now if you like."

"Wait till tomorrow," said Finch. "Adeline's going to bed."

"Are you going to be a kill-joy, Uncle Finch?" asked Maurice.

"Well—I promised this child's mother——"

Adeline gave him a hoot of scorn. "Point out the Irishman to me," she said, "and if I like his looks I'll meet him tonight, if I have to do it over Uncle Finch's dead body."

"I did point him out," said Maurice. "He's just at the foot of the stairs. His first match went out. Now he's lighting another. There—don't you see him?"

Adeline glanced at him. "I like his looks," she said, "well enough—but I think I'll wait till tomorrow to meet him."

The flare of the match had illumined an intent dark face, topped by upstanding curly hair. He took the cigarette from his lips now and revealed a strongly marked mouth that was both humorous and sensuous. His curious glance took in the face of each person who passed him.

"What part of Ireland is he going to?" asked Finch.

Maurice replied,—"Quite near to me. He hasn't lived there long. He was in the Army in the East. Now he's bought a small place and apparently is settled down."

"What's his name?"

"Maitland Fitzturgis."

"Help!" said Adeline. "What a name!"

"It is rather a mouthful. You must meet him tomorrow."

"How old is he?"

"In his early thirties, I should say."

Suddenly Finch thought,—"I have left my thirties behind." And he felt it strange.

The ship was rather crowded. It was easy to meet people and then lose sight of them again. Next morning there was a strong breeze and the dark blue sea was rough, carrying the ship jauntily beneath quickly moving white clouds. Up on the sports deck the breeze was almost a gale. Maurice and Adeline soon had enough of deck tennis. They wandered to a sheltered part where, over-shadowed by lifeboats and funnels, a number of people were stretched out in the sun. In a corner by themselves they almost stumbled over Finch and the Irishman, Fitzturgis.

"Don't get up," cried Adeline, and dropped to the deck beside Finch. "Do you mind if Maurice and I sit here too?"

He put an arm about her. "Adeline, this is Mr. Fitzturgis."

They were soon all four talking together with ease. Adeline was eager to tell how this was not her first visit to Ireland and that she had visited New York once before. She did not say that she had been only four years old at the time and Finch and Maurice kept silent on that point. The heat of the sun combined with the crisp coldness of the air was exhilarating. The four were soon on friendly terms. Finch knew America as well as one who merely tours a country filling engagements can know it but he was looked on as an authority by the other three. Fitzturgis felt that he had seen a good deal of New York, had tasted its promises and foretasted its disappointments. After a time Finch and Maurice wandered away and Adeline and the Irishman were alone together.

"I'm really only half Irish," he said. "My mother is English and I was sent to an English school."

"That's why I'm disappointed in you," she returned. "I expected you to talk Irish."

"Not really!" he laughed. "Well, if you want me to, I certainly shall." And, assuming a rich brogue, he began to rave over the beauty of sky and sea.

Adeline lay on her back looking up at him, her teeth white between her parted lips, her dark eyes laughing beneath the shade of their thick lashes.

"That's lovely," she said, "but you mustn't do it any more because it's not real. It is like my great-grandmother who used to go all Irish when her feelings were hurt."

"Do you remember her?"

"Oh, no. But in our house they don't let her memory die. We never seem to forget anything in our house."

"Do you like that?" he asked quickly.

"Yes, because if you let things die that belong to your family, your life has no meaning."

He looked at her in astonishment.

"What a strange thing for a young girl to say!"

"Don't you feel that?"

He closed his eyes for a moment before he answered. "No. I like to forget."

"Do you? Of course, I haven't much—not really anything to forget—yet. But there's been handed down to me a lot to remember."

"All pleasant, I'll wager."

"No, indeed. Some of it very sad."

He frowned down at her, as though angry that there should be anything to cloud her happiness. "And you actually want to hold in your memory what was sad?"

"Yes, because it's a part of me, though I wasn't there to see."

"Do you know," he said, "I tremble for you. I think you have a great power of suffering. . . . What are you going to do when things happen to you—bad things, I mean?"

"Bear them, I suppose, like other people do."

"No, not like other people," he objected. "You'll never do anything—just like other people."

She gave a little laugh. "You seem to know a great deal about me, considering that we've just met."

"I don't feel as though we'd just met."

"That's funny. I feel as though I'd known you quite a

long while. I guess the truth is we don't know anything about each other."

"Sometimes," he said, rather dictatorially, "one finds out a great deal in the first meeting."

"I suppose that means I'm easy to see through!"

He answered quickly,—"No, not at all. I think it means that there's a good deal in you to see, to know, and you're so unaffected. I've met girls—since the war especially—who spend their time leading you on and when you arrive—there's nothing there."

There was silence for a time, then Adeline asked abruptly, —"Won't you tell me about your life in Ireland? To judge from what my cousin says, there are only two sorts of people—the rich ones who do nothing and the poor ones who do nothing."

"I'm neither." Fitzturgis spoke rather sombrely. "I raise Kerry cattle. That is, I'm beginning in a small way. I've a rather nice house, with a lot of rhododendrons round it. Very secluded. Mountains all about—I suppose you'd just call them very high hills."

"It sounds nice but—rather lonely, for a young man."

He laughed. "I thought you'd look on me as almost middle-aged."

She drew back from that idea. "Oh, no. You see, I live in the house with my two great-uncles who are past ninety. I call them old. I don't call a man middle-aged till he's sixty. That's what my father is."

She went on to talk of all her uncles, telling their ages and what she considered their dispositions to be. She told him proudly of Finch's achievements as a pianist, of Wakefield, as an actor, of Eden's great talent as a poet. She was obviously surprised and a little hurt that he had not heard of one of them. She thought the less of him for that.

"But, you see," he explained, "I was away in the East for years and since I came back I've been buried in a rustic spot in Ireland."

"Have you no one to look after you?"

"I've a woman who comes in daily. She looks after me very well." Abruptly he changed the subject to say,— "Tell me about yourself. Have you any special talent?"

F

"Me? Oh, yes—if you call riding a talent. You should see the rows of cups and ribbons I've won. I've inherited that from my father. There's no better horseman in the Dominion. As for high-jumping! I don't suppose there's a bone in his body that hasn't been broken at one time or another."

"Well . . ."

"I'll tell you what I'll do, if you like! I'll go to my cabin and bring up a photograph of him on horseback to show you."

"It's too far."

"No, no, I'd love to. I can't sit still for very long. Just a minute!" Before he could answer she was gone.

He lay on his back on the deck, watching from narrowed eyes the black streamer of smoke that spread, at first dense, from the funnel, then wavered and was lost in the blue.

Considering the flights of steps she must have descended and mounted she was back in an incredibly short time. Her breath came quickly. A brightness, as of the morning at sea, shone from her. She proudly put the photograph in his hands. Now he was standing beside her.

"What a fine-looking man," he exclaimed, "and what a lovely horse!"

"Isn't she? Don't you think I'm like my father?"

It was plain that she wanted to be told that she was the image of this hard-featured, bony, weather-beaten parent. She—so lovely and with such a tender curve to her cheek! But, if she wanted it, she must have it.

"I see a striking resemblance," said Fitzturgis.

She smiled happily. "Oh, yes, it's there. And the funny thing is that he is the image of his grandmother. He and she and I all have red hair. His has never turned grey and I hope it never will."

"Have you ever cared for any person outside your family?" he asked abruptly.

She gave this serious thought and then answered,—"No, I don't think I have. There were school friends, of course, but I forgot them as soon as I was away from them. I don't exchange reams of letters with other girls."

"Your mother," he said, as they leant against the rail, looking down at the tumbling jade-green waves, "tell me about your mother."

"She is beautiful and clever. I can't compare with her in either way."

"And you're an only child?"

"I have a small brother. He's thirteen and he is clever too, but—well, I can't explain Archer. You'd have to know him to believe in him. He's cold and hard and yet he is sort of clinging. Now tell me about you. Are you an only child?"

At once he withdrew behind the barrier of the years between them. He could not pour out descriptions of his family as she did. In fact he shrank from talking of himself. All he could say was:

"I have a sister, married and living in America. I've just been over for a short visit. Three weeks. I hadn't seen her since before the war."

"All those years," she said, "and you stayed only three weeks!"

"It is impossible for me to be away for long," he said, a little stiffly.

"I suppose it is the livestock," she said sympathetically.

"Yes. The livestock."

That set her to talking about the livestock at Jalna, the horses in particular. Never before had she met anyone in whom she had wanted to confide, for, as the days of the voyage went on and they saw more of each other, she told him of her thoughts, of her unsophisticated ideas about life, in conversations that were absorbing to them both; to her because of this new experience of having a man friend—a man, not just a boy like Maurice; to Fitzturgis because of the pleasure, half-tender, half-sensual, of watching her vivid face, of glimpsing the woman who was coming into being. There was something in the Irishman's intense face that captivated Adeline's fancy. When she was alone in her cabin, his face would come before her, when she woke in the night to the sound of the waves, she saw him— now looking at her with those intent eyes—now gazing tranquilly out to sea.

Finch and Maurice liked him too. They invited him to
share their table. The four played deck tennis together, sat
together at the horse races; Maurice and Adeline danced
together, for the other two did not dance. Dancing with
her, Maurice remarked:

"You've got very friendly with Mait, haven't you?"

By now they called him by this abbreviation of his
Christian name. There was a note of jealousy in his voice.

"Well, haven't you? You were the first to call him *Mait*."

"One has to call him something and his name is rather
a jawbreaker."

"But you do like him, don't you, Mooey?"

"Yes. But you're usually standoffish with men. Humphrey Bell feels it, I know."

"He makes me shy, he's so shy himself."

Maurice steered her among a group of Irish-Americans
bouncing through the dance. "Remember," he said, "that
you're in my charge."

"The dickens I am! Uncle Finch is looking after me."

"I'm the one your doings most concern, Adeline."

"I don't need anyone to look after me," she laughed.

Into the minds of both there came simultaneously the
memory of a summer's night three years before, when
Adeline was no more than a child. Maurice had taken her
to the theatre to see *Othello* and with them had gone a man
named Swift who was at that time tutoring Maurice for his
matriculation examinations. Swift had volunteered to take
Adeline up the long driveway of Jalna to the house, while
Maurice went on to his home. In the darkness of the
hemlocks Swift had suddenly made amorous advances to
the young girl, taking her in his arms and violently kissing
her. She had fought herself free and Renny, waiting for
his daughter, had come upon them and knocked Swift
down. Maurice had got into trouble with Renny and with
his own father, for he had taken her to the play without
permission. It had been a humiliating remembrance to
him and now he wondered if Adeline ever gave it a thought.
He doubted it, for he looked on her as much less sensitive
than himself.

It had, in truth, made a wound on her spirit that was

still not perfectly healed. The scar was there and the scar was tender. Even the most tentative advance by a man had caused her to withdraw. In dancing she did not abandon herself to the music as it was in her nature to do. She was guarded in her acquaintance, even with boys of her own age. She had felt both curiosity and fear towards older men.

But with Fitzturgis it was different. She was conscious of a guardedness in him. Though he watched her so intently, listened to her so eagerly, sought her out at every opportunity, there was always a reticence on his side that gave her a feeling of safety. There was exhilaration in his companionship. It made her happy just to stand beside him looking at the sea. She was glad to think he lived not far from Maurice.

"And do you live all alone?" she asked, towards the end of the voyage.

He hesitated and then answered,—"Sometimes my mother comes to stay with me. She's there now."

"And she looks after things while you are away?"

"Yes."

"I'd like to meet her."

"You must," he answered without enthusiasm.

A feeling of sadness came to her. He does not mind if he never sees me again, she thought. She could not contain her sadness at this thought and her eyes filled with tears.

The shadow of a gull passed across the sunny deck. "Look," exclaimed Fitzturgis, as though in relief, "a message from the land!" But she stood gazing at the place where the gull's shadow had passed. Her eyes were clouded; the feeling of confidence she had had in this new and exciting friendship was shaken. She became conscious of the difference in their ages and of the accumulation of experiences he had passed through and—she had known so little of life!

But when night came it was different. It was the last night aboard for those who were disembarking at Cobh. They were a mixed lot—Irish-Americans of the peasant class returning for their first visit to the Old Land since the war, a group of nuns, a few priests, an Irish countess, an Englishman who owned land in Ireland, the three Canadians

and Fitzturgis. He and Adeline sat in deck-chairs in a
sheltered corner. They were wrapped in rugs, for the night
was cold. There was a gentle movement to the ship, as
though she swayed to the sound of the music from within.
A few dark figures could be made out standing by the rail
at the bow, as though to get the feel of Ireland before it
came into sight, Adeline, snug inside her wrapping, felt
the excitement a butterfly might feel, still folded in its
cocoon, but intending the very next morning to go forth
into the world. Little ripples of excitement ran, now and
again, through her nerves, but sometimes she lay just
expectant, giving herself up to the pleasure of the gentle
movement of the ship, the muted sound of the music. She
wore her travelling jacket and skirt.

She wondered if Fitzturgis was feeling the same or com-
parably the same sensations as she. She put out her hand
and just touched him.

"What were you thinking?" she asked.

His voice came muffled, as though his hand were against
his mouth. "Of you, my darling."

The word *darling* was not bandied among the Whiteoaks.
When they said it they meant it. Now Adeline could
scarcely believe her ears. She thought she must have
misheard.

"Did you mean that, Mait?" she whispered.

Now his hand came through the folds of the rug. He
caught hers and held it.

"Yes," he said low.

She gave a little laugh of ravishment. "Oh, I'm glad,"
she breathed. "I was thinking of you too—darling."

She was so inexperienced, knew so little what to say,
that the best she could do was to repeat what he had
said. But though it was imitation it went through him like
fire.

"I think of nothing but of you," he said to the pale disc
that was her face.

"I'm just the same—I think of nothing but you."

He threw back the rug and put both arms about her.

"Oh, Adeline," he cried, "if you knew how I'm longing to pour out my love to you."

"You don't need to," she whispered. "I can feel it through your arms."

His arms tightened on her. He gave a deep sigh which the waves caught and magnified, drew out till it was almost a moan.

She laid her head against his. "Oh, Mait, I'm so happy. I knew this was going to be a wonderful voyage but I never dreamed it would be as wonderful as this."

"Adeline—I loved you the moment I saw you."

"Tell me all about your feelings and then I'll tell you all about mine."

He threw apart his rug and emerged from its cocoon, not as a butterfly but as a moth in the dark salt air.

"I can't talk about it," he said. "I can't."

"We don't need words," she acquiesced. "I know what you are thinking."

"What am I thinking?" he demanded.

"Of me . . . and of all the lovely times that lie ahead of us."

"Adeline," he said, almost roughly, "you can have no idea what is in my mind."

She reached out and caught his hand and laid her cheek on it. "Darling Mait," she whispered against it.

A figure detached itself from the darkness and came to them. It was Maurice and he said in an icy voice,—"I'm going to turn in. You had better too, Adeline."

She felt angry. Why should Mooey come barging in like that? She felt like telling him to run off to bed if he wanted to, but to leave her and the man she loved alone. But the habit of obedience was still on her. She wished Maitland would say that they two loved each other. She would stand up there beside him and look Maurice in the eyes—tell him she would stay on deck all night if she wished.

The deck steward had folded and stacked away all the chairs but theirs. He lingered ostentatiously in the near distance. Now he came closer and picked up the rug Fitzturgis had dropped and began to fold it even as he asked,—"Finished with this, sir?"

Maurice, with an air of cold proprietorship, unwrapped Adeline and tossed her rug on the chair's end.

"Good night, Fitzturgis," he said, though he had been calling him "Mait" for three days.

Adeline stood irresolute, not knowing what to do. Fitzturgis went to the rail and looked down on the seething milk-white foam. The deck steward was briskly dragging away the chairs, as though his life depended on getting them stacked within the minute.

Adeline went to Fitzturgis' side. "Good night," she said. "See you in the morning, Mait." He turned to her.

His answer was inaudible, though his lips moved. The look in his eyes was an embrace. With a happy step she went down the deck with Maurice, through the heavy door and along the narrow passage to her cabin.

There, with her hand on the door, she turned and faced him.

"Whatever is the matter with you?" she asked. "Why did you come glowering at me the way you did?"

"Glowering!" he repeated, angrily. "Glowering!"

"Yes. You came down the deck like a thundercloud."

"What were you doing?" he demanded.

"Well, what was I doing?"

"Snuggling up to that fellow!"

"Why not—if I want to?"

"Adeline—what's come over you?"

"You sound like an outraged parent."

Maurice went pale. Then he asked quietly,—"Do you imagine you love this Fitzturgis?"

"I don't imagine it. I know it."

With a sob in his throat he broke out,—"You know how much I've cared for you, Adeline."

"That isn't what I call love."

"Not on your part, perhaps," he retorted hotly. "On mine it is."

She gave a little laugh. "Oh, Mooey, you don't know what love is. You're just a boy."

As though he had been struck he drew back. He wheeled and left her, almost running into the stewardess carrying a tray. "Sorry," he muttered, and hurried on to the cabin he shared with Finch.

Finch was propped up in bed reading a crime novel. His mousy-fair hair hung untidy over his forehead.

"Got all your packing done?" he asked.

"Yes."

"Did you find Adeline?"

"Yes."

"What's the matter?" Finch put down his book and stared at Maurice.

"I found her with Fitzturgis. His arms were about her and she was snuggling up to him. She tells me she loves him."

No one was more satisfactory than Finch for the receiving of shocking news. Shock struck him through and through.

"My God!" he said loudly. "Her father will blame me for this!"

"We both were supposed to look after her but she's been too much for us."

"What did he say?"

"He didn't say anything."

"Where is she?"

"In her cabin."

Finch looked at his watch. "It's too late for me to go to her." Relief came to his distraught expression. "Well, we shall land in the morning and that will put an end to it. She may never see him again."

Maurice said grimly:

"Fitzturgis lives less than fifty miles from Glengorman."

"Probably it's just a shipboard affair," Finch said hopefully.

"Adeline isn't like that. If you'd seen her face you'd realize she is in earnest. You know, Finch" (of late Maurice had dropped the "Uncle") "you know, I've always thought a great deal of Adeline. I've made plans. All the family has liked the idea. This is pretty hard on me."

"I know it is, Mooey, and I'm terribly sorry."

Maurice took off his jacket and hung it up so that he might turn his back to Finch.

Finch went on in a high complaining voice,—"This affair is just plain ridiculous. The girl can't be in love with him. She just imagines she is."

F*

"I tell you she's in earnest. I've never known anyone who knows their own mind better than Adeline. Besides —he's a very attractive fellow."

"He's years older than she is."

"That's one thing that attracts her. She looks on me as a boy—and despises me for it."

"Nonsense. It simply is that the affair has the glamour of shipboard. She'll soon forget it."

"I wish I thought so."

"Has Fitzturgis talked of himself to you, Mooey? Is he well off?"

"He's talked of his Army life. Not much about his private doings. I gather that he's not very well off."

"This is the last time I shall ever undertake to look after her. . . . Lord, what will Renny say!"

"He ought to understand her—she's enough like him."

The lights turned out, they lay in silence with the moonlight coming in at the portholes, and the ship gently rising and falling on the dark waves. Each lay occupied with his own thoughts—Maurice jealous and hurt—Finch recalling the coming of his love for Sarah and wishing he might protect Adeline from that emotion.

XII

BACK AT VAUGHANLANDS

RAIKES stood at the end of the kitchen table, his knuckles resting on it, a melancholy droop to his mouth. Facing him were Eugene Clapperton, his wife and his sister-in-law, their three pairs of eyes fixed on the plaster that was crossed over the bridge of Raikes' nose. He was saying:

"I know I done wrong to take out the Cadillac but this was the way of it; I'd gone to the club on me bicycle as usual, and when I was nearly home I remembered I'd left me wallet in the room where I'd been playin' Bingo. I thought how much quicker I could fetch it if I took the car, but I'd been told not to, so I rode all the way back at top speed and it's lucky I was to find the wallet in a dark corner, safe and sound. I was on the way back home when a thruck come of a sudden out o' the dark and knocked me clean into a ditch. The driver gave me no heed at all, but went on his way, leavin' me for dead. That's the way me nose was broke."

"Oh," gasped Gem Clapperton, "the brute!"

Raikes turned his eyes gently on her. "He was that," he agreed.

"Was your bicycle smashed?" asked Althea.

"No, miss. It's a quare thing but the bicycle was not hurt. Just the bridge of me nose broke."

"What next?" demanded Eugene Clapperton, his eyes boring into Raikes.

"Well, sir, I didn't feel able for the bicycle ride to the doctor's, the way I was bleeding. Me head was hurt and me back."

"You should have called me."

"Ah, I didn't like to wake you out of a sleep and me the sight I was. So"—Raikes' long back curved in apology

—"I took the Cadillac and drove to the doctor and he fixed me up. Then, coming back, as I told you, a thruck ran into the car and smashed her. I had a word with the driver and he was drunk if ever a man was."

"I'll get my hat," said Clapperton, "and have a look at the car."

He left the kitchen. The two young women stood gazing at Raikes. He raised his bloodshot eyes to Gem's face and his expression became even more melancholy. She turned to her sister.

"Are you going to telephone the grocer or shall I?" she asked.

Althea gave her an angry look. She drew herself together as though for an outburst, but instead muttered:

"I'll telephone." She almost ran from the room.

Gem moved a step nearer to Raikes. "Don't feel too badly," she said, in a sweet comforting voice,—"accidents will happen. The papers are full of them."

"They are indeed," returned Raikes, almost resigned. The shadow of a forlorn smile flickered across his lips. He put up his hand and gently felt the plaster on his nose.

Eugene Clapperton returned and the two men went out through the back door to the garage, where stood the Cadillac with its side stove in.

Eugene Clapperton stood staring at it in shock, then he exclaimed.—"Good God, is that my Cadillac!"

"It is indeed, sir," returned Raikes heavily.

"It's a wonder you were able to get home in it."

"It is that. But I don't think the engine is too badly damaged."

"When will my other car be repaired?"

"Well, ye see, sir, they're having throuble in getting the parts."

Clapperton turned away in disgust. "Well," he said grimly, "I shall have to leg it wherever I go for some time."

What bad luck was his, he thought. His animals ailing or dying . . . his cars smashed . . . his marriage . . . well, he'd put the disappointment over his marriage out of his mind . . . he wouldn't let it get him down . . . he wouldn't let any of his worries get him down . . . happiness and balanced living could only be achieved by an effort . . . keep the balance within, and the outer adjustments will inevitably take place. He would not let himself be angry with anyone—least of all with Raikes, the only decent man he had ever had. He took a good walk through the moist spring day and felt the better for it.

He ended by stopping at the door of the Fox Farm. He felt it his duty to do what he could to get Humphrey Bell out of the rut he was in. But Bell had seen him coming and he knocked in vain. The cat knew that the door should be opened and meowed again and again. Eugene Clapperton could hear her and he called out in a childlike way,—"Puss—Puss, let me in!"

Evidently the cat liked him, for it rubbed itself against the door, but Humphrey Bell remained flattened against the wall in a corner. Clapperton gnawed his lip in annoyance. He hated to be frustrated in his plans for good. Now he took out a pocket note-book and resting it against the wall he wrote,—"Enter the new day courageous and unafraid. Relax and get rid of the tension that is tightening your nerves and ruining your health." He did not sign it. The young man would know. He tore out the leaf and slipped it under the door. His heart felt lighter.

When the cat saw the paper appear beneath the door she curved a graceful paw and played with it. There Bell found her and the message.

"Relax!" he cried. "Relax! How the hell can I relax with that old fool eternally after me!" He took the poker in his hand and beat on a log of pine in the woodbox, as though for once he had Eugene Clapperton at his mercy. The cat sharpened her claws on his best chair.

At Vaughanlands Althea followed Gem into her bedroom. Speaking as though after running she said:

"Gem, I don't like the way you look at that man."

Gem was making her husband's bed, drawing the bottom sheet tight. "What man?" she asked, tapping the the sheet with her rapid fingers, "*This* man?"

"You know what man I mean," gasped Althea. "I mean Raikes."

Gem laughed. "Ho, him! What don't you like about the way I look at him?"

"Well—I can tell you it's almost tender."

"He'd hurt himself. I'd be sorry for Eugene if he broke his nose, shouldn't I?"

"They shouldn't be mentioned in the same breath—not by you."

"Why?"

"Eugene is your husband. After all, look what he's done for you."

Gem put her hands on her hips and stared at her sister across the bed. "I've repaid him," she said boldly. "I've repaid him twice over. Don't worry about him."

"You haven't made him happy. He's not as happy as he was when we first met him."

"It's all the worry he's had in this place."

"That's not so and you know it."

"What has come over you, Althea?"

"I have a sense of justice, that's all."

Gem continued with the bed-making and Althea bent to help her.

"Just compare the two men," said Gem. "If a woman's human she'll notice the difference."

Althea gently put the pillow in place. "The head that lies on this belongs to a good man," she said. "He may be boring——"

"You're telling me!" laughed Gem.

"How common you're becoming!"

"Yes. Stronger and stronger, and commoner and commoner. More like Raikes and his sort."

"I tell you, he's absolutely worthless!" cried Althea. "I've been sure of that for some time."

"You said to me not long ago you'd like to paint his portrait."

"Yes, as a gypsy-looking fellow, picturesque but no good to anyone. The kind silly women fall for."

Gem's face flamed. "Next thing," she said, "you'll be warning Eugene."

"Never. You may do what you like."

"Thank you."

Althea went up to her room. Gem finished her work and
then sought Raikes. He had just returned after taking the
damaged car to the nearest town for repairs.

"You are back quickly," she said.

"I had a lift right to the gate. 'Twas Colonel Whiteoak
took me into his car."

"I'm glad. You must feel tired."

"I do that. But it's no matter. I'm going to mow the
lawn now. It'll be grown hay if I don't get at it soon." He
moved towards the shed where the mower was kept. It
was as though he wanted to hear no more of car smashes
or bone-breakings. He took the handle of the mowing
machine and trundled it to the lawn. He bent to adjust the
knives, then went up and down the length of the lawn in
long swinging strides, grass blades flying from the wheels in
a tender green shower. Gem stood in the shelter of a lilac
tree, heavy with bloom; the sunlight falling through its
leaves dappled the skin of her face and neck, her white
bare arms. She reached up and drew one of the heavy
white blooms down to her. A scented shower of drops,
stored from an early morning rain, fell over her. She felt
it as a kind of blessing and smiled up into it.

Some weeks passed and the smaller of the two cars
was back in the garage again. The plaster was gone from
Raikes' nose and he looked himself. Eugene Clapperton
was cheerful once more. He would not allow himself to
be long otherwise, indeed considered he had much to be
cheerful about. He had rented the arable land of his
property to a farmer. He kept a cow, fifty laying hens and
a few pigs which Raikes looked after. Three new bungalows
were in process of building. The sound of that sawing and
hammering, so distasteful to Renny Whiteoak, had a cheery
ring to him in the summer air. The small property he had
bought from the farmer, Black, he was holding till he had
a suitable offer from a factory builder. He realized that
these projects were going to spoil the already damaged
seclusion of those parts but he did not care. He had made
up his mind to move to California where the salubrious
climate, the interesting variety of places, people and
religions would, he thought, suit him well. He thought

rather in the fashion of a travel booklet and his imaginings
were like its bright-coloured illustrations. But he would
like to have Raikes with him wherever he went. The
sooner he made this certain the better. He found the
Irishman cutting asparagus in the garden. Kneeling he
held a bundle of the fine robust stalks in his hand. He
wore a thoughtful, even meditative look, as though living
were for him a serious affair.

Eugene Clapperton strode across the asparagus bed to
him, taking care not to step on the tender green tips that
thrust up through the earth. Without preface he said:

"Tom, if I moved to a better climate, say to California,
would you come with me?"

Still kneeling Raikes gave his polite little bow. "Indeed,
sir," he said, in a voice that comforted, "I hope to work
for you many more years. I'll go with you anywhere."

XIII

ARRIVAL

ALL PASSENGERS who were disembarking in Ireland were up early in the morning. It was fresh and fair and so chill that Adeline shivered in her light coat. As usual everyone had been roused far earlier than was necessary. They stood about in determinedly cheerful groups or sat resignedly in the lounge, waiting for the summons to show their passports. Fitzturgis joined the three Whiteoaks, casting a swift look at each in turn. Maurice tried to look friendly, to conceal his shock, his chagrin of the night before. Finch's eyes, with their accusing glance, contradicted his cheerful "Good morning." He fervently wished they had never become acquainted with Fitzturgis, though up to this time he had liked him very much. But Adeline had been given into his charge and what would he say to Renny if his daughter became entangled in some silly love affair? He thought of himself at her age and of his lovelorn thoughts of a girl whom he used often to see but never met and never did meet. He realized that Adeline was different.

Fitzturgis met their looks coldly. Then he let his eyes rest for an instant on Adeline. He knew that both men were watching him and he gave her a tranquil smile. The lighting of her face and the happy sparkle in her eyes were proof enough of her feeling for him. She was too unskilled in deception, too ardent in nature to attempt concealment.

After the long time of waiting, the passengers filed into the room where the passports were to be examined. Finch and Maurice stood close to Adeline like two guards, giving her no chance to speak to Fitzturgis. She looked past them, smiling at him, not caring. There was plenty of time ahead. Feeling important, a traveller, she held her passport firmly. She opened it then and saw the stern young face pictured inside. Maurice glanced at her coldly, accusingly. He felt that she had spoilt his return to Glengorman. How often he had pictured their arrival, their first days, when he would lead her through all the dim old rooms, revisit with her all the hills and valleys, the cottages of the peasants he remembered so well.

The tender came alongside and they went aboard. Everyone was anxious about his own luggage. Irish-American voices called out loudly. Adeline had never seen so many suit-cases and trunks in such a muddle. She said, with a tremble in her voice,—"I shall lose all my best things! I know I shall."

Finch and Maurice began anxiously to scan the disorderly mass of luggage. Though it was May the wind blew icy. A stout man in uniform put his hand on Adeline's arm.

"It's too cowld here for ye," he said. "Get ye into the war-rm." Gently he pushed her towards the saloon. Finch and Maurice she had got rid of. Fitzturgis was just ahead. She pressed forward till she was beside him. She touched his arm and said,—"Hello, Mait."

He turned sharply and looked into her eyes.

"I felt you coming," he said. His low voice went through her like the sound of a bugle and all her nerves sprang to attention.

"Isn't it glorious?" she said, and held up her face to the wind.

They saw people crowding into the saloon, stout women, men in stiff suits, nuns, a priest or two. They pushed their way along the narrow passage, through another smaller saloon, past people clutching bundles, out on to the foredeck. A thousand waves were playing about the ferry, as though wondering what they would do with her. Seagulls cried out, then winged swiftly, as though in a race, or sailed with wings as still as marble.

Fitzturgis put his body between Adeline and the wind. He said,—"We're almost at our journey's end. It's been . . ." he hesitated and then went on quickly, —"one of the happiest times in my life."

"And *my* happiest."

"No, no, don't say that."

"Why not?"

"It couldn't be . . . except for one reason."

The warm colour flooded her face. "And that *is* the reason, Mait."

Finch came out of the saloon towards them, his brows drawn together in a frown, his sensitive mouth embarrassed. "I've located your luggage, Adeline," he said.

"Oh, thanks, Uncle Finch."

"I suppose you've been worrying about it," he said grimly.

"Oh, yes—I mean, oh, no—I knew you'd find it. Thanks so much."

Fitzturgis said, in his tranquil voice,—"Quite a crowd on board. Two hundred they say."

"Yes." Finch put his arm about Adeline. "If you're determined to stay out here, I must try to keep you warm."

"We shall soon be there," said Fitzturgis.

"We are to be met by a car. What about you?" asked Finch.

"I go by train from Cork."

Adeline put in,—"Can't you come with us in the car?"

Well, that was forward of her, thought Finch. If she were going to behave like this he wished she'd been in charge of someone else.

"There'll be lots of room. It's a big car, Maurice says."

"Of course, it's Maurice's car." Finch looked hard at her.

Fitzturgis said,—"I have business in Cork. And, in any case, I'm not convenient to Glengorman."

"I thought you were quite near," she cried, disappointed.

"No, not very near," he returned, as though indifferently.

She gave him a mischievous look. ("He is not going to let Uncle Finch see what there is between us.") She could not discover from Finch's expression whether Maurice had told him anything. They stood looking at the approaching island, clothed in the pastel freshness of spring.

Maurice now joined them saying—"We're about to land." He gave an accusing look at all three, as though they made a conspiracy among them against him. There was a general movement towards the stairs.

Adeline's fingers touched Fitzturgis. His hand grasped them a moment and held them fiercely.

"Mait," she whispered, "we'll stay together as long as we can."

"Yes. As long as we can."

Soon they were in the confusion of the Customs sheds. The letter W was far from the letter F, yet they soon discovered that the porters were not slaves to initial letters. As some of them could not read they set down the luggage where it was convenient and left the distraught passengers to discover it. So it turned out for Adeline, pressing through the crowd in search of the immense brown suitcase which Ernest had lent her ("I would gladly give it you, my child, but I may need it myself, at any time." As though he, poor old dear, would ever take another journey!) She searched most diligently in the vicinity of the letter F, and there by the counter that ran the length of the shed, she espied Fitzturgis standing with his belongings opened up in front of a Customs officer.

She heard him speak and the sound of his voice drew her like a magnet. She stood beside him, looking eagerly into his face. "Oh, Mait. Uncle Ernest's suit-case is lost. Have you seen it?"

"No, but I'll help you search. Where are the others?"

"At the far end. They've lost things too."

The officer was chalking something on the cases. Fitzturgis set them on the floor and took Adeline by the arm. "We'll soon find them," he said.

They pushed their way among the baffled throng, dodged porters pushing barrows of luggage or carrying loads too heavy for them. One was very old for such work, one was very young and thin and ragged, but everyone was so good-humoured it made Adeline happy. The group of nuns had been met by a small, very efficient Mother Superior. She marched here and there giving orders to porters like a diminutive sergeant-major. The youngest nun was small

too and extraordinarily pretty. It was plain that she had
never been away before. She clung to the hand of one of
the other nuns with the look, half-frightened, half-pleased,
and wholly trusting, of a little child. When the older nun
moved she led her so, a pace behind, glancing down at
her with a proud protective look, like a mother with her
little one.

"That little nun," thought Adeline, "knows nothing
of the happiness I feel or how amazing it is to be me."
The cold draught that swept through the shed was beautiful to her. She thought no more about the suit-case but
gave herself up to watching Fitzturgis as he intently examined one heap of luggage after another. She wanted to
impress his every feature on her memory—the way his
crisp curly mouse-brown hair grew on his forehead, his
deep-set eyes, high cheek-bones and full-lipped mouth.
She had no plans, no feeling that could be called desire,
only a wild wish to live and to exult in living.

At last the suit-case was found. Again Finch and Maurice
joined them. Maurice was too much concerned about his
trunks to give a thought to Adeline. One by one the trunks
were swung up by a derrick and of them all his were the
last. Before he had recovered them Fitzturgis said good-
bye. There was regret in his eyes as he shook hands. He
was conscious that their attitude to him was not as friendly
as it had been. However, Finch said vaguely,——

"I suppose we shall see you before long. You don't
live too far away, do you?"

"About fifty miles. That's quite a way in Ireland."

They hesitated, looking doubtfully at each other. Finch
raised an enquiring eyebrow at Maurice. (Adeline was
willing,—"Oh, Mooey, please, please, please ask him to
come to Glengorman.")

"There's my smallest trunk!" cried Maurice, and
pressed to the platform's edge.

The stout man in uniform who had driven them back
from his narrow platform half-a-dozen times again complained,—"It's not allowed. Ye must get into the shed.
Come, now, young lady——" and he took a pinch of
Adeline's sleeve and himself led her back. How willingly

she went! Anything to be separated from her two guardians.

Fitzturgis and Adeline stood alone together in the crowd.

"Good-bye, Mait," she said and gave him her hand.

He took it and held it. "I will come," he said.

"How soon can you come?"

"I'll let you know." He paused irresolute, as though he tried to say something, then repeated his good-bye and turned away.

But she would not yet part with him. A space had cleared ahead of them. Suiting her step to his she walked beside him towards the main door.

"How soon?" she asked.

"Very soon."

"We've said good-bye, haven't we?" she said when they reached the door.

"Yes."

A porter had engaged a car for him and it stood waiting, his suit-cases inside.

"My darling one," said Firtzturgis quietly, "I must leave you now."

She held up her face to be kissed. He put his arms about her and their lips met. Then he sprang into the car and was gone.

She was in a daze till she found herself in Maurice's old Armstrong-Siddeley, driven by the same Patsy who had come to meet him when he was a small boy.

"You're not a bit changed, Patsy," exclaimed Maurice. "Och, I'm the same ould Patsy," he agreed, showing a number of black teeth under a shaggy grey moustache, "but the place is not the same—with the masther dead and gone and you away off in Canada. It's glad I am ye've come home, and everything clane and tidy for your welcome, though me missus says the curtains is like to fall down and the cairpets to break under yer feet, what with the moth and the rot."

Adeline whispered to Finch,—"Listen to him—calling this 'home' to Mooey."

"And so it will be, from now on. What a pity his mother could not have come to see him in it!"

"Yes," she agreed, then added happily, "but we're here to enjoy it and we shall tell her all about it . . . Look, Uncle Finch, a cart with a darling little donkey! I remember them so well. You know, the time when I was in Ireland before doesn't seem very long ago, but what a difference! Now I'm grown up." She added to herself,—"grown up —a woman—deeply in love!"

She mused on herself, at the change in herself . . .

When they reached Cork the streets were busy. But women with black shawls over their heads moved slowly in an ancient leisure. Over all hung the canopy of a clear blue sky and bright pale sunshine. They went into a restaurant and had buns and hot coffee to warm them. Adeline talked of everything she saw, yet her eyes were in constant search of that one figure. The family at Jalna were proud of their well-shaped bodies. They noticed, more than they should, the proportions, the carriage of other men. So Adeline had noted with admiration that Fitzturgis, though not tall, was admirably proportioned. Now where was he? Hastening along the road towards his home or somewhere in Cork? What would she not have given for just one more glimpse of him!

Maurice avoided her eyes. He would not be friends with her—not yet. Perhaps never again would their relations be the same. And yet, what was this little infatuation for Fitzturgis? Nothing more, in all probability, than a shipboard affair that would be forgotten after a week on land. But try as he would to be philosophic about it Maurice was much disturbed. Never before had Adeline shown a preference for any man. The callow love passages of most girls were not for her.

As the car moved along the country road towards Glengorman Maurice ceased to make response to Patsy's recital of all that had taken place during his absence and gave himself up to the disappointment of his return.

"She has spoilt it all," he thought, remembering how he had lain awake most of the night. "Last night—the night before landing—and today—the day I have so long looked forward to—she has spoilt them both. I'll never forgive her for this." He was conscious, in every fibre, of her sitting in the seat behind. He could hear her voice and imagined how, the evening before, that same voice had said loving things to Fitzturgis.

Perhaps too easily he felt himself living in the midst of uncertainty, felt himself slighted. He who should have been the proud eldest son, like his uncle Renny, was the son his father liked least. Nothing he could do, he felt, was congenial to his father. Even his mother, whose love for him was so palpable, had let him be sent away to Ireland when he was a small boy, to live with an old man she had never seen. She had, not long ago, confessed to him that it had nearly broken her heart—she had been persuaded by others to give him up. Maurice had not forgiven her. Even though the visit had brought forth the planned-for fruit and he had inherited Glengorman he had not forgiven her. Even though his years in Ireland had been the happiest of his life he would never forgive her. She should not have let him go.

Finch was remembering his last visit to Ireland and his reconciliation with his wife from whom he had been separated. She had sought him out, not he her. She had rekindled the dark fire of his passion for her. Dennis had been conceived. When Dennis was born her love had been transferred to him. She had thrown off her infatuation for Finch as a snake sloughs its skin. How different she had been from the traditional Irishwoman! She had been reserved, with a strange stillness in that white face of hers. Never could she have been called laughter-loving or gay. The very jet-black convolutions of her hair, worn long when other women wore theirs short, had a classic coldness. And how rigid had been her movements! Before they had parted for the last time the sight of her crossing a room had called forth an antagonism from him, yet with all this coldness, this rigidity, there had been the hooded passion of her secret nature. . . . And now she was dead and buried. How long had she been dead? Was it four years? Sarah dead. . . . He pictured her grave in the Californian cemetery and, for a moment's abhorrence, what lay in the grave. . . . The country they were passing through was indistinct before his eyes. Dim curtains of colour opened, closed, melted into each other. Patsy's voice came from the front seat but no intelligible words.

Now he saw the bare hills in their rocky greenness, the wooded valley where a stream ran, an empty mansion, with its roof burned off.

At last they reached Glengorman, passed through the stone gateway, along the drive to the house. Adeline was satisfied with the gargoyles above the door. That was as it should be. But she was disappointed because there was no line of bowing domestics to welcome Maurice, only Patsy's wife, Kathleen, a wisp of a woman, not nearly so impressive as Mrs. Wragge. And what did she do but throw both arms about him and kiss him. "Just for ould times' sake, when you were a darlin' boy!"

Later Patsy said to his wife,—"There's no nature in him. Hardly a word did he spake and him with all this waitin' for him."

"I'd respect him less if he chattered," returned Kathleen. "He's mourning for the ould master, and right and proper it is. You must remember too that he's part English."

Lunch was waiting and, when they sat down at table, Maurice was in the heavy carved chair where once old Cousin Dermot had sat, Adeline on his right, Finch on his left. Beyond them the table stretched empty. Maurice was embarrassed, shy, proud, all at once. Here he was very much "somebody", instead of a young unimportant member of a large family. Adeline was elated by the changes of scene, her eyes bright, as though poised to receive all that came to her. Finch's dark thoughts had slid away from him, like seaweed from a swimmer, and he was ready to strike out boldly, to enjoy this freedom from the stress of life.

Maurice looking at Adeline thought,—"I'm a fool to let myself be troubled by that fellow. She'll forget him in no time here." His spirits lifted. Thoughts of his new free life crowded in on him. There were so many things he would do. He was freed from his father's critical gaze that always both angered and took the pith out of him. He looked forward to the day when Piers would visit him at Glengorman, see him as master there.

"This house makes Jalna seem small, doesn't it, Adeline?" he asked.

"Small? No. Jalna's big enough. This is too big."

"You think so?"

"Well, we have more land. You have only two hundred acres. We have five."

"Children, children——" grinned Finch.

"What I mean is," she said, "it is the land that counts. It's rather silly for one boy to live alone in a house this size."

"I shan't always be alone."

"Good luck to you, Mooey, whoever you choose."

"All this means nothing to you, does it?" he exclaimed angrily, as though they two were alone.

"Everything concerning you means a lot to us, doesn't it, Uncle Finch?"

"We've got to be very civil to Mooey," said Finch. "He has us at his mercy."

"Adeline loves to deflate one," Maurice complained.

"So did Gran," said Finch.

Adeline preened herself, tossing back her russet locks.

"It's been a great mistake," declared Maurice, "this telling Adeline how much she resembles Gran. She might have been a nicer girl . . ."

"Wait till I'm a hundred and you'll see how nice I shall be!" she cried.

"I shall not be here to see. I'll die long before you."

"Of course you will. You'll give up the ghost at the first creak in your joints."

"And you'll hang on, I suppose, till everyone is tired of you."

"No one was tired of Gran."

"People could endure more in those days."

They were always on the verge of a quarrel.

Patsy came in carrying a bottle of wine. He said:

"This is a bottle of rare good wine, sir. I managed to save it when the executors locked up the cellar and all. It's been waitin' on ye all these years and ye couldn't find a betther, if ye scraped Ireland with a small tooth-comb." His little eyes glistened under his coarse grey brows.

Amity reblossomed. Maurice's health was drunk and his future happiness at Glengorman.

He had left his dog, a fawn-coloured Labrador bitch, behind him when he returned to Canada. After lunch she appeared with her son, as large as she. She sprang on Maurice and made much of him.

"She remembers me!" Maurice cried delighted.

At first shyly, then a little closer, gambolled the son, his muscular body brimming with careless vitality. His mother and he locked jaws and pushed one another this way and that. Their life was one long-drawn amiable wrestling.

Now Maurice set out to show his property to cousin and uncle. They climbed a long flight of moss-grown stone steps between high walls in the garden. Rhododendrons heavy with bloom pressed close to the walls, hung over them. The dogs took the steps in bounds and stood waiting at the top where, on level ground, were the stables, their only occupants a cow and several hens and geese with their broods.

Adeline went from stall to stall. "Splendid!" she declared. "What a fine place for horses!" She caught her cousin by the arm. "Mooey, will you let me fill these stalls with horses for you? Wouldn't you like to spend some of your money on your stables?"

"Not a penny," he returned curtly. "I'm quite satisfied to keep chickens. I like them."

The tiny chickens ran about the stable yard. The gander thrust out his neck and hissed.

Maurice led the others through the formal gardens to a knoll where an ancient beech spread its mossy limbs and where Adeline was afraid to step for fear she should tread on a primrose. Their clusters grew thick, creamy-gold, arranged as though to pattern the knoll. Maurice raised his arm and pointed. "There is the sea!"

"May we go to the shore now?" she asked.

"I'd rather show you the house first—if you don't mind."

"Yes, show us the house first," said Finch.

"Oh, yes, we'd love to see the house," agreed Adeline, and thought,—"The shore can wait. I'd like to go there all by myself." She took a hand of each and linked together they returned to the house.

It had the chill of a place long shut up. Now all the windows stood open and the mild sunshine entered. It sought out dim mirrors and tarnished gilt frames, the rosewood of cabinets and the china figures inside. It gleamed on the smooth stone flags of a passage and on the glass door-knobs of the bedrooms. Maurice pointed out a group of little pictures—portraits of fighting-cocks, made from feathers.

"Look!" he cried. "I remember admiring those the very first day I was here. Aren't they clever?"

Adeline read the words beneath one of the cocks.

"'The Bronze Cyclone who was known to kill two other cocks in five minutes.' Whew!" she gasped. "He was a little terror, wasn't he?"

"I never looked at the words," said Maurice, drawing back, "only at the bird."

"He's lovely," breathed Adeline, her eyes held by his spurs. "You're lucky to own such interesting things."

"Now I feel I'm really at home," he said. "Everything had grown a little dim. And yet, in a way, it's unreal with Cousin Dermot gone . . . I called him Grandfather, you know."

"Yes, I know . . . But it won't seem unreal for long—not with me here. Will it, Mooey?"

XIV

LOVE'S PROGRESS

ADELINE chose a path that led from a corner of the garden half-hidden by rhododendrons and then on through a plantation of specimen trees brought from foreign parts by some former Court. These had, through the long years, grown to enormous size and a great silence reigned among them. Some had such strange leaves that she paused to examine them; some were cloaked in grey moss; the branches of some, when they drooped to the earth, found succour there and sent down new roots and up rose a new tree; some had bark with such deep crevices that she could lay her hand in them. Wherever there was an open space where sunshine fell, a rhododendron presented its mass of pink or coral-coloured or mauve flowers. Never still, the two Labradors moved swiftly through the long grass, noses to earth, their golden backs smooth as snakes, their long tails waving against the bluebells.

To be alone, that was what she had been longing for. This was her second day at Glengorman and always Finch or Maurice had been by her side, calling her to come and see this or come and do that. She craved solitude by the sea and in that solitude to savour the joy of this new emotion that possessed her, that ran through her like a quick fire in the grass.

She crossed steep hillsides, their only growth grey boulders, and now she saw the glistening blue floor of the inlet, and beyond it the bare, mountainous, grey-green land. Calling the dogs she ran down the hillside to the rocky shore. On a little grassy point among the rocks she threw herself down, her cheek on the grass, her eyes seeing no more than that small space, the clumps of sea-pinks, the smooth shoulder of rock, the scrap of sky. It was enough. She could not have borne more. Deep down among the rocks, the small waves came and went, repeating without one weary note the first song they had learned.

She was conscious of all her being; of her feet that had run so gladly down the hillside and now lay side by side, the toes pressing the earth; of her knees, strong and supple, that so often had clasped a horse's sides; her loins, her sides, her breast rising and falling with the weight of the salt air. One hand curved about a clump of sea-pinks to protect them in case she made a sudden movement. She did not know what she might do next. She felt as inconsequent as the two dogs who came and sniffed her and then ran off again, satisfied to know she was there.

She closed her eyes and swam in the crimson and gold world behind their lids. She drew long slow happy breaths of the salt air. She tried to think, to realize that she was here, to be entirely conscious of her inner self. What came to her was the image of Fitzturgis, surrounded by a scarlet and gold aura, like the image of a saint. That image stood high above all the world and she held it a moment, in breathless worship . . . What had he done to her in those few days? Her spirit melted in pity for herself and her eyes filled with tears.

She opened them and the translucent spring world formed itself and the sound of the wavelets in the crevice below came to her . . .

Her hand was still curved about the cluster of sea-pinks. She touched them with her fingers, then sat up and looked about her, as though for the first time. A little freighter, foreign-looking, was moving past in the direction of Cork. The hills and woods on the opposite shore were brighter. Set in a park she could make out a large white mansion and, here and there, a farm-house.

The Labrador bitch came and nuzzled her coaxingly, then planted a large paw on the sea-pink cluster.

"Oh, naughty Bridget!" cried Adeline and heaved up the paw. In distress she examined the flowers. They were not broken. One by one the little heads would rise again. Down to the very water's edge grew their fellows. A scrap

of earth no bigger than a thimble made a cradle for their
young.

Now, with the two dogs, she scrambled up the steep
and ran along the stony path up to a barren hilltop. There
the wide sea stretched before her, lustrous in the sunshine
like a damascened shield. There was wind here and it
pressed her thin skirt against her thighs, caught at her
breath and blew out the bright waves of her hair. She
threw up her arms and stood on her toes, straining upward
as though on wings. "Oh, Maitland Fitzturgis," she sang,
"I do love you!"

She laughed at herself, but sang it out again and again,
running over the hilltop, not knowing what to do with
herself for joy. The dogs leaped about her and about each
other, carrying on their endless loving combat. Rolling
over and over, gnawing, making as though to swallow one
another. The son was the more persistent, the mother in
the last event the stronger.

So they progressed, over the hill, down into a valley,
in whose shelter rhododendrons had sprung up, and bluebells. She saw the figure of a man standing, fishing-rod in
hand, on a jutting rock. She saw his arm rise and in a
sweeping movement throw out the line. She saw the glitter
of the fly as it danced above the pool. Again and again he
cast and at last, swimming brightly into the air, came a
fish. Detaching it from the hook he laid it in a fishing basket
and she saw that there were others there.

The man, who was young, became aware that he was
watched. Still squatting beside the basket he raised his
face and looked up at her. They stared motionless, taking
each other in, appraising each other; she, moved to admire
the tweed-clad figure bent, with that air of solicitude, above
the basket; he, startled to pleasurable surprise by the windblown figure of the girl, a dog on her either side . . .
Why, he thought, those are the dogs from Glengorman!
And the girl must be Maurice's cousin, Adeline Whiteoak.
So—Maurice had arrived.

He slapped the lid on the basket, and, with it and the
rod in his hands, began to clamber over the rocks and come
towards Adeline. She waited, amused. It had not taken

much to cause him to give up his sport. Just the sudden
appearance of a strange girl. But perhaps she was no longer
on Mooey's land. Perhaps the man was coming to order
her off for trespassing. That was the reason, she decided,
and awaited him, with more than a little truculence in her
air.

He came steadily upward, with the certainty in his
movements of one who knows every inch of the way.
The dogs, after one perfunctory bark, ran to meet him
with tails waving.

"Hullo, Bridget," he said. "Hullo, Bruce!" Then to
Adeline,—"I think you must be Miss Whiteoak. I'm
Maurice's friend——"

"Don't tell me!" she interrupted. "Let me guess."

He stood smiling, his sanguine fair face flushed, waiting
to be named.

She would have said,—"You're Pat Crawshay," but he
had been so ceremonious with his *Miss* Whiteoak, that she
said with dignity,—"I guess you are Sir Patrick Crawshay."

"Do you really remember me?" he exclaimed, pleased.

"I know you are Maurice's neighbour."

"But you don't remember me?"

"Yes, I do. I met you at the Hunt when I was over here
as a child."

"Good. I shall never forget you—and our parting after
the Hunt. Do you remember our parting?"

She did indeed. He had asked her to kiss him good-bye
and she had tried to prove her strength by the hug she
gave him. She laughed at the recollection. They both
laughed.

"How long are you staying?" he asked.

"All the summer."

"Splendid. There'll be no hunting for you but there'll
be other things."

"May I see your fish?" she asked.

He opened the basket and she saw the firm shapes, the
iridescent scales, the last quick tumble of life in that small
space.

"Oh, lovely!" she breathed, in admiration.

"Do you like fishing?"

"I don't know. I've not had much opportunity. I'd like to cast, the way you do."

"I'll teach you."

"Thanks, but not now. They'll be wondering what has become of me."

"I'll walk back with you, if you'll let me."

She watched him as they walked together and thought how different he was from all the boys she knew. She tried to think what the difference was. First, but least important, there was his complexion, ruddy against white, as though sun had never tanned him or dry hot winds sucked the moisture from his skin. Then there was that look of innocent careless strength about him, as though he had never been disciplined, never been tried. He was like an innocent healthy young animal. He looked, she thought, as though he'd always had just what he wanted, and what he wanted had never been wrong.

As they walked she kept turning over in her mind how she might bring the conversation round to Fitzturgis. He was never out of her thoughts. But, try as she would, it could not be manœuvred. At last she asked out plain:

"Have you ever heard of a man named Maitland Fitzturgis?"

"Maitland Fitzturgis," he repeated, in his liquid Irish voice. "No, I haven't."

"Never heard of him?" It seemed impossible. "Does he live nearby?"

"I—don't know. At least—I guess it's quite a long way off. I met him on shipboard."

"Oh, I see . . . What was he like? A young man?"

"Quite a lot older than you. He was in the war."

"He would be that. An Irishman, you say."

"With that name, of course."

"Names get mixed up between the two countries."

"His mother was English."

"Ah, I see."

"I suppose you wondered why an Irishman would go to the war."

"They did—lots of them—Montgomery for one."

They were nearing the house She halted and faced him.

G

She said, with her colour rising,—"I'd rather—please——"
She could not get the words out.

"Yes?" he encouraged.

"Please don't say that I asked about Maitland Fitzturgis.
. . . Maurice didn't like him."

She felt that she had given herself away. She was swept
by shame and, to hide it, she stalked proudly and coldly
into the hall where Maurice and Finch were waiting.

"It's about time," exclaimed Maurice. "We were just
organizing a search party——" Then, seeing young Crawshay, he ran to greet him. "Hullo, Pat! This explains it
all. How splendid! Uncle Finch, this is my friend Pat
Crawshay."

He stayed to lunch. Finch watched Maurice with
pleasure, seeing him expand in giving hospitality, seeing a
new and confident Maurice. Piers had been bad for him,
no doubt of that. And what a pity Pheasant was not here
to see her boy!

They were a gay laughing party at lunch. Afterwards
Finch and Adeline went to write letters, leaving the two
youths alone. It was not long before Maurice asked:

"Is there a fellow named Fitzturgis anywhere in the
neighbourhood?"

"Dozens of them—for all I know."

"This fellow was on board ship with us. He'd heard of
you."

"What was he like?"

Maurice gave a little shrug. "I didn't take to him."

"Did your cousin?"

"Adeline? Oh, she liked him well enough."

"Why are you interested in him?"

"I'm not particularly. It's just that—well, there's
something a bit odd about him."

"Did he tell you what village he's near?"

"No."

"What does he do? Has he money?"

"He does a little farming. I think he has a small income.
I believe he has a pension. He was badly wounded in the
East."

"Good looking?"

Maurice laughed. "What a question from you, Pat! As though you'd care!"

"Somebody else might."

"Who?"

"Your cousin."

"Has she asked you about him?" Maurice demanded, with an edge to his voice.

"Well, now—as though she would! Why, I've barely met her."

"She did! She did—the little fool!"

"For heaven's sake, don't let her know you caught me out."

"You couldn't lie to me, Pat." The friends sat close together on a deep window-seat. They lighted fresh cigarettes.

"It's splendid having you back," exclaimed Pat Crawshay. "I've had no other friend to take your place. But I wager you made lots of friends over there."

"Not one. Pleasant acquaintances. Not one friend."

They smoked in silence for a space, then Maurice demanded abruptly,—"How did she come to ask you about him?"

"I don't remember. I think just out of the blue."

"Good Lord!"

"But it's nothing. Any girl . . ."

"Adeline isn't just any girl. She's never shown any preference——"

"She's got to begin some time. Let her begin on him."

"You don't understand."

"I think I understand that you're pretty fond of her yourself, Maurice."

"It doesn't matter what my feelings are," said Maurice bitterly. "What matters is that she must be kept away from this fellow."

"I'll find out about him."

"Do, Pat, like a good friend, but don't mention him to her."

"You did like him at the first, didn't you?"

"Very much."

"Then it is just jealousy," thought Pat Crawshay. He

himself felt a twinge of jealousy towards the unknown
Fitzturgis.

Three days passed before he had news of him for
Maurice. In the meantime he had spent many hours at
Glengorman and the three Whiteoaks had dined with him
and his mother. On this afternoon he drew Maurice into
a chill little room off the hall, where stood a desk, with the
telephone on it, and the walls were lined with old books.

"I've heard something about the villain," he said
lightly, as though it were a matter of small import to either
of them.

Maurice, trying to smile also, asked,—"Well, what
about him?"

"His father was Irish, his mother English. He went to
school in England and to Oxford University. From there
into the Army and went through the Burma campaign.
After the war he and his mother came to Ireland and
bought the small place where they live. He and I both live
with our mothers. There the resemblance ends. My mother
is a dear but I gather that his is not. He has a married sister
in America—that was the reason for his trip over. I'm
told they keep strictly to themselves. There is something
wrong about them—I mean they have made no friends."

Maurice drummed with his fingers on the window-sill.
"Thanks," he said thoughtfully. "I guess we've seen the
last of him." Then he added,—"Mind you, I have
nothing against the fellow. I liked him, till I found he'd
been making up to Adeline on the sly. It was a shame
because she's only a kid and I'm supposed to look after
her."

Pat chuckled. "I'm afraid you're a failure as a baby-
sitter, Maurice."

"I'm not worrying," said Maurice, his young forehead
tied into knots. "They won't meet again. I'll see to that."

When the morning post came it was handed to him and
almost tremblingly he watched for a letter bearing an Irish
stamp and addressed to Adeline. He did not ask himself
what he would do with it if one came, but he had confused
imaginings of throwing it in the fire—of striding to her
with an accusing scowl and demanding that she should

open it and read the contents to him—of carrying it to
Finch and asking his advice. Never did he attribute his
anger to jealousy. No, he was righteously angry because
Adeline, before the ship had even reached the shores of
Ireland, had given her first love to a stranger. He did not
quite look on Fitzturgis as a villain but as next door to
one. When her guardians, her uncle and her cousin, had
barely turned their backs, he had made love to a foolish
young girl.

Adeline herself watched eagerly for a letter, though in
those first days she was too full of the happiness of her love
for Fitzturgis to feel more than a moment's disappointment that a letter did not come. The days passed in dream-
like happiness. Over and over again she relived those
moments on the dim deck, the night before they reached
Cobh.

Then suddenly her mood changed. A night of wind
whipped the sea into wildness. The cold rain slanted in
stinging darts out of the black sky. It hissed against the
pane and she could not sleep. Always she had been a poor
sleeper. As a small child this wakefulness of hers had been
a torment to Alayne. The child's cot had been in her room.
Adeline's chatter, her singing and laughter, as though it
had been noonday, instead of late at night, had been an
almost unbearable trial.

Now, in those night hours at Glengorman, her love for
Fitzturgis had drawn sleep from her pillow. She lay awake
recalling his every feature, recalling all they had said to
each other, having imaginary conversations with him,
saying things so witty to him that she laughed aloud at the
thought of them; he saying such beautiful things to her
that they brought tears to her eyes.

But this night of storm had changed her mood. She
tossed on the bed in a sudden panic of misgiving. Why did
he not write to her? Oh, why did he not write?

Then she remembered his telling her that he was no
good at letter writing. Once he started he could do it, but
the hard thing was to start. A great sense of relief flooded
her mind. That explained everything. He did not want to
write. Nothing would satisfy him but to see her. And there

had been so much for him to do, after an absence. He would come tomorrow. When the rain had ceased they two would walk together by the sea.

She was quiet for a while, then she thought,—"If he really loved me, nothing would keep him away. Nothing. He would throw aside everything to come to me. He does not love me!" She threw herself to the other side of the bed. She put out one foot from under the bedclothes to feel the cool air on it. She threw aside her pillows and lay with her burning cheek against the sheet. But she could not endure any position for long. At last she rose and walked about the room. She went to the open window and let the wet wind flutter her nightdress. She could hear the roaring of the sea, and the voices of the land where branches strained as though they would be torn from the tree and the wind whistled through the crevices, rattled shutters and shook the garden gate.

"Oh, where are you sleeping, my dear love?" she said aloud, and then pictured him not asleep but standing by a window, looking out into the blackness, as she was. That comforted her and she put out her hands, felt for the bedpost, crept back between the sheets shivering. Yet it was long before she slept.

The next day was aglitter with sunshine. The stones and roof of the house shone as though polished. So did the leaves of the laurels, and petals of rhododendrons lay scattered everywhere. The succulent stems of the bluebells could not stand up under the weight of the flowers but let them droop to the grass. The wind had fallen and the air was warm.

Patrick Crawshay had bought a new sailing-boat and Finch and Maurice went to inspect it. Adeline had said she wanted to explore the shore. They left without her. She had made up her mind to find Fitzturgis. She could not face another such night as the last. She told Patsy she was going to take out the car.

"Wisha, young lady," he said, "ye'll be into the ditch as sure as fate. Ye know we drive different in this country."

"I know, and I can do it. Don't worry about me. If my

cousin comes home before me, tell him I shall be back by evening."

Prophesying disaster the old man brought round the car. He gave Adeline a flood of directions which she did not understand and stood mournfully shaking his head as she drove off. She was glad the road was so quiet, for in truth the car had a different gear from that she was used to. However, she met no one in the first miles but a boy with a load of gravel drawn by a thin horse, and a woman with a cartful of children drawn by a shaggy donkey. Adeline felt proud with purpose, pleased with herself. Why had she not thought of doing this before! Still, even if she had thought of it, there had always been Finch and Maurice about. Today was her first chance and she was making good use of it.

She passed through a village where all the shop-windows looked dingy but the one where spirits were sold, and that shone invitingly. She came to a small town and enquired there for the hamlet of which Fitzturgis had spoken. Carefully she was directed, so carefully, with so many ins and outs, and ups and downs, that it was all she could do to keep the half of it in her head. She set out again, feeling suddenly hungry, wishing she had bought a chocolate bar in the shop. There had been a mistake in the supposed distance. She had already driven twenty miles. She took a wrong turning and found herself in the squelching ruts of a lane, face to face with a team of horses dragging a great oak whose trunk was wreathed in ivy. The labourers came to the car giving her directions that she could not follow because she did not understand half of what they said.

A little discouraged she backed out of the lane. She looked at her watch. It was a quarter to four. She was on the road again. She would find him. She would. Her thoughts reached out like hands drawing him to her.

"Oh, Mait, tell me where you are—please tell me where you are," she kept saying over and over.

Along the road a little way she overtook a Protestant clergyman riding a bicycle. She stopped the car and spoke to him. He put his feet to the ground and looked at her out of guileless eyes in a ruddy face.

"Fitzturgis," he repeated. "Maitland Fitzturgis. Yes—I've heard the name. Let me think. Yes, I remember. He bought Mr. Brady's house, some time ago. His grandfather used to own quite a large property, but in his father's time it passed into other hands."

"He lives alone with his mother," Adeline said, eager to show that they were not strangers to her.

"His mother, yes. And I think there's a sister."

"But she's in New York."

"Oh, is she?" He looked doubtful, then he brightened. "Well, now, I'll tell you how to find his house. Take the third turning to the left, then straight on, over a hump-backed bridge, then the second turn to the left—still to the left, mind you—and you'll come to the ruin of a small church. If you have the time it'd be well worth your while to go in and have a look at it, for it has some finely moulded trefoil-headed windows and some very interesting carved tombs."

"I'm afraid I haven't time today. Could you tell me where I go after I pass the church?"

"Well, let me see. You pass the church and take the second turn to the right and down in a meadow you'll see the ruin of an ancient castle. If you had the time to spare it would be well worth your while——"

"I'm terribly sorry," interrupted Adeline in desperation, glancing surreptitiously at her watch, "but I have no time to spare. I must hurry on. When I have passed the ruins of the castle, which way shall I turn?"

"What a pity you are in a hurry! Perhaps another time you will return."

"Oh, I hope I shall."

With his hands indolently holding the handlebars of his bicycle he continued,—"Now about this road—to tell the truth, I am afraid I can't direct you clearly after you reach the castle, but you'll surely meet someone who can. I'm so sorry . . ."

Adeline thanked him and drove on. She saw that the afternoon was past its prime and she had not yet found the hump-backed bridge. But she had made up her mind. Nothing would hinder her, not if she searched till

nightfall. It would be impossible, she told herself, to turn
back.

At last she came quite suddenly upon the bridge and,
standing in fishing-boots, in the stream below, was a young
man with a rod. She got out of the car, leaned against the
railing of the bridge and called out,—"I'm sorry to trouble
you but can you please direct me to where a Mr. Maitland
Fitzturgis lives?"

The young man looked up. For a moment he seemed
transfixed by the figure on the bridge, then he came out of
the water, clambered up the bank to her side and demanded
in a high querulous voice:

"Who is it you want to find?"

When she told him he said,—"It's not an aisy place to
find but I'm going that way myself and if you'll give me a
lift I'll direct you to the very gate."

Gladly she opened the door of the car to him and shyly
he seated himself beside her. All the directions he gave,
and they were so intricate she wondered how she would
ever find her way back again, he gave in that same high sad-
sounding voice.

"It's very much farther than I thought," she said.

"Ah, we're very inaccurate about distance," he answered,
"and you'll find that few will tell you the way correctly."

"Do you know Mr. Fitzturgis?" she could not help
asking.

"I do not. But my father knew his father. He was a
well off man once."

They passed among the bare green hills and in the valleys
below saw rich greenness and fields with stone walls about
them, and white farm-houses. There was a man in one of
the fields swinging a scythe.

"How peaceful it is!" Adeline exclaimed.

"Yes, it's peaceful enough. Haven't you peace where
you come from?"

"Ah," she spoke in Ernest's very tone, "the country's
not what it used to be. It's mechanized. The young men
want to go to the cities. They've no love for the land. . . .
Did you say you'd never seen Mr. Fitzturgis?"

"I've never set eyes on him, but I've heard that he's a

nice young man. Here we are at his gate. You'll see himself."

He got out of the car, bowed politely and sauntered down the road, soon disappearing between high hedges, for here was a place of richer soil, where flowery hedges grew, and the house in front of her was hidden by rhododendrons massed with white and coral-pink blooms. She could only glimpse the white stucco house, half-hidden in wistaria, with a glass vestibule and a small conservatory and a smooth-shorn lawn in front.

For some reason she could not have explained, she was disappointed in the house. It was not the sort of house she had expected him to live in. And suddenly she was very shy. How could she drive up to the door and ask for him? If only she would see him walking down the road—smiling with delight to discover her! Instead of him she saw coming a herd of cattle, ambling on and off the road, driven by two barefoot boys who waved sticks at them, shouted at them, but to whom they paid little attention. She would be surrounded by them. In panic she drove through the gateway and stopped the car just inside. A buxom girl was walking down the drive. Adeline alighted from the car and went to meet her.

"Can you tell me if Mr. Fitzturgis lives here?" she asked.

"Indeed he does," answered the girl, in a hearty voice, "but he's off."

"He's not at home?"

"No, miss."

It was too bad to believe. She had not counted on this. She stood staring forlornly at the girl.

"I'll tell you what," said the girl, "you'll find him at ould Tim Rafferty's, for he said he was goin' there. It's across the road and down a bit."

"May I leave my car here?"

"Sure you may, and it's myself will show you the way to Tim Rafferty's."

They went through the gate and into the midst of the cattle. The boys hallooed and whacked them with their sticks. A small low cloud threw down a spatter of rain. The girls had to move into the squelchy ditch and Adeline gave a wild hop to avoid stepping on a beaming rosette of primroses.

A short way along the road, its thatched roof just visible as it perched on the steep hillside, was a whitewashed cottage.

"Are you sure he's here?" Adeline asked nervously.

"I saw him pass through the gate itself. Ould Tim was worritin' about somethin' and Mr. Fitzturgis went to pacify him."

"I see. Thank you very much." She watched the girl go down the road, then opened the wicket gate and, escorted by half-a-dozen hens, crossed the little yard to the door of the cabin.

It stood wide open and on a bench by the fire she saw Maitland Fitzturgis sitting beside a sturdy rosy-cheeked old man, with a grey moustache and thick grey hair growing low above his forehead. One glance showed her that, then her eyes, in joyful wonder, were fixed on Fitzturgis. It seemed to her so long since she had seen him that she half expected him to be changed. But no—there he was, just as when they had parted at Cobh, excepting that now his face was lighted by astonishment, by incredulity, as though he saw a vision.

XV

FITZTURGIS AT HOME

"Hello, Mait, I thought I'd look you up," Adeline said, her voice trembling, a pulse in her throat throbbing.

"Adeline," he gasped, coming to her with hands outstretched. "Is it possible?"

She could not answer. The trembling of her voice now had become the trembling of her whole being. So had her love swept through her at the sight of him standing there, his intent eyes fixed on her, his troubled smile, the beautifully moulded structure of his face, his curly hair that seemed to have no colour of its own, but, where the firelight touched it, was edged by bronze.

"Who brought you?" he demanded.

"I came alone." She could no more than whisper the words.

"Alone," he echoed. He raised his arms as though to take her into them, then let them fall.

His uncertainty gave her strength. "Yes," she said boldly, "and no one knows I came."

Now her strength was coming back to her. They stood looking into each other's eyes, seeing there the sea at night and the two of them alone on the deck, feeling how the circling of their blood had joined and, as in a miracle, flowed together.

"No one knows you came," he repeated, under his breath, and she saw the colour mount to his forehead, as though he were embarrassed that she had to seek him out, instead of his going in search of her.

The old man sat on the bench, his bright eyes full of curiosity. In his left hand he held an egg which he had been eating from the shell, and in his right a spoon which he raised as though in salute. His bare feet were planted side by side on the earth floor.

"This," said Fitzturgis, "is Tim Rafferty. Tim—this young lady comes all the way from Canada."

Rafferty spoke in a voice so hearty that it was almost a roar. "Welcome to this country and welcome under my roof," he roared, "and I wish I might stand up to welcome you proper but I've the rheumatics so bad from bein' in the wather so much that 'tis all I can do to get from me bed to me bench here, wid the help of me niece."

"I'm so sorry," said Adeline, holding out her hand, but it was clear that he did not ask for pity. He beamed benignly up at her, laid down his spoon on the seat beside him and clasped her hand in his warm grasp.

The slatternly middle-aged woman came forward, smiling sadly, and shook hands also.

"I must tell you," said Fitzturgis, "that Tim has been a great fisherman in his day. There isn't a stream hereabout that he doesn't know by heart——"

"And all the fish in it," roared Rafferty. "Never did I cast me line in vain and 'twas fishin' be day and night that gave me the rheumatics."

He made room for Adeline on the bench beside him, his niece first dusting it with her soiled apron. Fitzturgis seated himself opposite, the fire burning low on the hearth between. The stone fireplace filled one end of the little room. The hens picked for breadcrumbs.

"Do please finish your egg," Adeline said anxiously.

"Och, it can wait. It's not often we have a visitor as foine as you, my lady." With his spoon he pointed proudly to Fitzturgis. "This gentleman's father I worked for, and his grandfather, and he owning all the land about and as fine a man as ye'd meet in a lifetime. Go into the bedroom, Katie, and bring his picture to show the young lady."

Adeline saw then that the niece was barefoot too. Her black hair hung in strings about her face. She came back carrying a large framed photograph of a man of forty, wearing a large cravat and sidewhiskers. It too she polished with her apron.

"He's very nice," said Adeline to Fitzturgis, across the picture of his grandfather. "Do you remember him?"

"No. I wish I did."

Rafferty began a long story about the grandfather, his brogue so enriched as he talked that Adeline could not follow it. She wanted to go, to be alone with Fitzturgis. Why did he sit there smiling as though they had hours to spare, when in truth the day was nearly done? A sense of foreboding crept into her mind. At last she said:

"I think I must be going." She stood up.

"Yes. Of course." He stood up too. "Perhaps Miss Whiteoak will come again, Tim. Then you can finish your story."

"And there's your egg to be finished," said Adeline. "It will be quite cold."

Rafferty made a grand gesture with the egg. "Sure it will kape," he declared, "but if ye must be going, I'll wish ye God speed, and may God bless ye, young lady, and give ye the foine husband ye deserve."

"Would ye like to see the bedroom then?" asked the niece.

Adeline said she would and was led into the one other room. The niece returned the picture to its place on the wall. She remarked,—"The beds is not made yet, miss, because of the wakeness that comes over me in the marnins. I've hardly the strenth to move at all." She looked at the two tumbled beds that almost filled the room, as though she longed to creep into one. She began to pour out the details of an operation she had undergone. In the other room the old man was roaring jovially at Fitzturgis.

When at last he and she stood on the road together the sun was sliding down through misty clouds towards the mountain. On a little river far below, the wild swans moved among the rushes. Fitzturgis asked, in an almost matter-of-fact tone,—"Where is your car?"

She answered, in a small voice,—"In the driveway of your house. A maid was coming out and she told me where you were. You see," she hurried on, "I had the car out and I knew this was your direction and—I thought I'd just drop in and see you." She was faint for food, her heart was beating heavily. Suddenly a gulf had come between her and Fitzturgis. He was almost a stranger. She turned her head to look at him and their eyes met but only for an instant. Then they looked away again as though even a glance of intimacy was unbearable. "What is the matter?" she thought. "What has spoilt everything?" Even the earth beneath her feet felt less secure, and she who walked as lightly as a young doe stumbled. He caught her arm, and her name came from his lips in solicitude.

"Come in here and sit down," he said and he led her through the gate, past the car, and to a seat beneath a grim grey-green cork tree. It was twilight in here and there was a smell of damp. He picked up a mossy twig from the mossy ground and tried to break it but it only bent.

"Adeline," he began.

"Yes?" she encouraged, her eyes, her whole being waiting.

"I want to talk to you," he said, "to explain why I've acted as I have—though nothing I say can make it right."

"Not *right*," she repeated, the sense of duty that had been implanted in her raising its head.

"I had no right," he went on, in a low voice, "to make love to you—I mean, to say those words of love to you."

A light broke on her. "You mean you're already engaged?"

"No."

"Married?"

"No." He had managed to break the twig. He threw it to the ground and now his hands hung limp between his knees. "Not married—but I am not free. I'm irrevocably tied. You asked me if I lived alone and I told you my mother came to stay with me sometimes. The truth is that she lives with me. She's dependent on me because my father lost everything he had—drank himself to death."

"Is *that* all!" she exclaimed, relieved.

"I wish it were. But my sister also is dependent on me. She lives here too."

"I thought she lived in New York."

"That's the married one. This one is younger. She's twenty-eight. She was married to a friend of mine. He was

in the Air Force. She was going to have a baby. He came
to London on a few days' leave. She loved this chap with
all her heart. There was an air-raid and she saw him killed
—horribly. She was splashed with his blood. Then the
baby was born dead and she nearly died. It unhinged her
and she was in a mental home for several years. Then the
war was over and I was back in London. The mental homes
were crowded and my sister was said to be almost well.
She was brought back to my mother, and now—the two
of them—they've no one but me. They're quite incapable
of looking after themselves—as you will see."

"Do you want me to meet them?"

"Of course. But now you see why I had no right to
say one word of love to you. I'm not a free man. And I'm
a poor man. It's all I can do to keep this place going."

"It's a terribly sad story, Mait. I wish you'd told me
before."

"It was such a happy time I hadn't the heart to tell you.
Everything would have been changed."

"Nothing is changed in me." She spoke in a low but
confident voice. In truth she could not discover what all
this had to do with their love. Their love was like the hills
beyond the valley. Though clouds hung over them the
hills were not changed.

"I did wrong," he persisted, "to rouse any feeling in
you of love for me." And he spoke like a man who knew
his power.

"You could not help it," she said. "Just to be near
you made me——" She could not continue. Her voice
trembled. She pressed her hands together between her
knees.

From the far end of the bench his deep-set eyes were
fixed on her in pity and longing.

"It's very hard on you," she said.

He gave a short laugh. "I hadn't thought of being sorry
for myself, not till you came on the scene. Now I confess
I am."

"Can't anything be done?"

"Wait till you meet my mother and sister. That will be
answer enough."

A shadow, darker than the tree, closed over them. Raindrops fell on the leaves. His hand moved along the bench and closed over her two hands pressed together. She turned her face towards him. Her eyes, eager and loving, were raised to his but her lips were firm in her innate dignity.

"It's beginning to rain," she said.

He bent his head above her hands and kissed them.

"I must go," she said, and gently withdrew her hands.

"Go!" he repeated blankly, and straightened. "You can't go without coming into the house, meeting my family. However did you find your way here?"

"I asked."

"And they—Finch and Maurice—let you come alone?"

"I've told you—they don't know."

"Good God—what will they think?"

She smiled. "I can't imagine."

"Did you have lunch?"

"No."

"Nor tea?"

"No."

"Why, my darling—" he exclaimed in consternation, "you must be starved."

"I am rather hungry. No—I think I'm past being hungry."

He looked at his watch. "It is five o'clock. I must take you straight to the house and my mother will give you tea."

She said reluctantly,—"Do you think your mother will want to meet me?"

"She'll be delighted. Make no mistake about that."

"And your sister?" The word he had used about her—*unhinged*—came to Adeline's mind and she found she was afraid of the sister.

"Oh, she's very quiet," he answered in a matter-of-fact tone.

They stood up. The tree let down a veil of rain in front of them.

"We must run for it," he said. "Give me your hand."

She put her hand in his. They bent beneath the branches and then ran along the drive to the house. The front door

stood open. On a table in the hall there was a bowl of tulips.
He led her past it into a long low room where a table set
with tea-things stood beside a small fire of greenish wood
that gave off more smoke than flame. At the table sat a
woman in her fifties, with a round pale face, rather puffy
eyes and a mass of hair that was dyed a rich henna. She
wore a green knitted pullover, a necklet of heavy beads and
long earrings to match. A stare of astonishment widened
her eyes. Fitzturgis said:

"Mother, this is Miss Adeline Whiteoak. We met on
board ship. She comes from Canada."

Mrs. Fitzturgis took Adeline's hand in a warm soft clasp
and held it. "Ah, yes," she said, "how very nice! I'm
so glad you've looked us up. We are so few in this be-
nighted spot that we're glad of a call from literally anyone.
I mean we are a great many people but they're all the
wrong sort. I mean that to a woman like myself who has
been accustomed to pick and choose it's simply ghastly
to live in so isolated a way. Upon my word, if ever I'd
known I should come to such a point I'd have gone stark
staring—no, of course, I don't mean anything so drastic
as *mad*—certainly not. But I'd have resented it deeply."

"Yes, Mother," put in Fitzturgis. "And will you please
give us tea? Miss Whiteoak is starving."

Mrs. Fitzturgis at once sprang to her feet and snatched
up the teapot. So precariously did she balance it that a
driblet of tea ran from its spout to the carpet. Fitzturgis
put out his hand to the pot. "Mother, see what you're
doing!" he exclaimed.

She was unperturbed. "That old carpet," she said
scornfully. "I'm sure Miss Whiteoak will see that nothing
can make it look worse." She now shifted the teapot so
that its dribbling pointed towards Adeline.

"Mother!" cried Fitzturgis, and again righted it.

"Don't be so fussy, Maitland. You've completely put
out of my head what I was saying." She put a hand to
her forehead. "You know, Miss Whiteoak, but indeed
you cannot know, for you are far too young to realize,
how trouble and continual anxiety can destroy one's
memory, not that I ever had a particularly good memory,

for my own mother used to say to me, 'Alicia, your head is no more than a sieve'. But you know what young girls are, my dear, being one yourself—and an extremely pretty one. I must take the time to tell you, even though my son is glowering at me so, that your hair is exactly what mine was, not so many years ago. Do you remember, Mait?"

"Yes," he frowned. "Let me make the tea, Mother."

"Indeed I shall not. I am very, very exact about tea-making, as you well know."

"Don't you think there may still be enough in the pot?" asked Adeline.

"It has lost all its goodness and must be quite cold. We waited for my son till we could not wait any longer. He seems to make a point of being late for tea. Only yesterday —no, it was not yesterday but the day before."

A low clear voice spoke from a settee in a dim corner.

"For goodness sake, make the tea, if you're going to."

Adeline started and turned to see a young woman in tweed jacket and skirt sitting there and smoking a cigarette.

"Oh, Sylvia," said Fitzturgis, "I didn't see you." And with a strained smile he introduced the two girls. "My sister, Sylvia Fleming, Adeline Whiteoak."

The resemblance between brother and sister was notice-able. Her face had the same modelling, too strongly marked for her extreme thinness to bear with advantage. She had the same crisp curly hair but that hers was fair, and her eyes were large and blue instead of narrow and grey. A feeling of relief came over Adeline. The sister was not so odd as she had expected. She was, in truth, attractive, and when she rose and crossed to the tea-table her walk was singularly graceful.

"I'll bring some more bread and butter," she said and picked up the plate.

"No, please, no, Sylvia," said Mrs. Fitzturgis anxiously. "It only fusses me to see you handling a knife. You're so——"

Fitzturgis interrupted,—"You stay and talk to Adeline, Sylvia, I'll get the bread and butter. We shall need lots of it." He followed his mother who left driblets of tea behind her as she crossed the room.

Adeline might feel relieved by Sylvia's appearance of normality but she did not want to be left alone with her. She had a child's shrinking from the strange. She tried to speak lightly. "I can't imagine what my uncle and cousin will think of me being away so long. They didn't even know I left."

"You came to look up Mait, did you?"

Adeline flushed. "Oh, no. I was driving in this direction and I lost my way and where I enquired he was there. It's just a chance meeting."

Sylvia stubbed out her cigarette. "You're lucky," she said, "to have a car to go about in. We can't afford one and, even if we could—well, they'd not trust me with it. You saw what my mother was like about cutting the bread. They've got it into their heads that I'm . . . very nervous or something . . . while the truth is it's they who are nervous. They behave sometimes as though they were nutty." She lighted another cigarette.

Adeline tried to sympathize, to talk naturally and lightly, but she watched with apprehension both Sylvia and the increasing wind and rain beyond the windows.

"It's turning into a hell of a night," remarked Sylvia. "I love it, don't you?"

"I might—if I hadn't to go out into it in a strange car, on a strange road."

"Better stay the night here."

"Oh, I couldn't."

Sylvia regarded her thoughtfully. "My advice to you is—don't start off your life by taking things hard."

"Do you?" Adeline asked, and then, in panic, tried to recall the question and could not.

"I used to. . . . Not now. I've discovered that nothing is worth tearing yourself to bits for."

"I suppose that's sensible."

"Yes. I've worked out a philosophy to suit myself. The worst is *they* don't agree."

"Whew," thought Adeline, "I wish Mait would come back."

Very soon he and his mother did return. This time he carried the teapot and she a tray on which was a plate of bread and butter, a dish of jam and a square fruit cake.

"Plenty of fresh tea," he said. "*And* plenty of butter on the bread." He brought a small table and placed it beside Adeline. Mrs. Fitzturgis asked her many questions about her home and her family. She repeated her disappointment that her son had been forced to settle down in Ireland with no prospects to speak of.

"He was doing so well, my dear," she said, "in a promising job on a rubber plantation in Malaya. Now, of course, that's out of the question and we decided that the best thing for us to do was to come back to Ireland where this scrap of land is all that's left of the property my husband inherited. He was one of those unfortunate men, though some people think he was to blame, and indeed everything would be very different now if he had been different, but then you may say that things would be still more different if all of us were different, but I say we're all the creatures of circumstances which we can no more control than we can control that rainstorm outside though it's obvious that all my husband needed was a little self-control. Don't you agree?"

Adeline fervently said she did agree. She was so very hungry, the bread and jam and tea were so delicious, that she forgot her anxiety about the return journey and thought only of her pleasure in the nearness of Fitzturgis. When their eyes met, her heart gave several quick beats, and involuntarily her lips parted in a smile. Sylvia did not speak again but sat smoking, her eyes fixed on the wildly blowing rain beyond the windows.

When tea was over Adeline and Fitzturgis went to the front door which still stood open, with the edge of the storm wetting the stone floor.

"Do you think it will soon stop?" she asked.

"No. And if it did, it is impossible for you to go back to Glengorman tonight. You must stay with us. My mother says so."

"But I can't! They'd be wild if I didn't come."

"You can telephone them."

"Oh," she gave a gasp of relief. "You have a telephone!"

"Yes. It's necessary for us to be able to call a doctor if he's needed."

"I see." She had a momentary vision of a doctor coming at post haste in the middle of the night to that house. She said,—"I think I'd better telephone right away. They'll be sure I've had an accident."

He led the way to a small room at the back of the hall. A telephone, a kitchen chair and a large glossy calendar advertising an Irish whiskey were the only furnishings. He turned on an unshaded electric bulb. Under its light they saw each other's faces, pale and intimately revealed.

"Shall I call them for you?" he asked.

"Please."

He looked up the number in the directory, asked for it, then put the receiver into her hand. He left her, closing the door behind him. Maurice himself answered. Even with his first word she was conscious of strain in his voice.

"Hello," she called.

"Is that you, Adeline?"

"Yes."

"For God's sake tell me what's happened!"

"Nothing. I'm all right. I'll be back in the morning."

"Where are you?"

She was thankful for the distance between them, thankful that she was not face to face with him. She said haltingly:

"I'm spending the night with Mrs. Fitzturgis."

She spoke so indistinctly that Maurice did not hear the prefix Mrs.—only the surname.

"Fitzturgis!" he almost screamed. "Are you quite mad?"

"I don't see anything wrong in it," she answered hotly.

"*Wrong!*" he repeated. "*Wrong!* Where is his house?"

"I don't know the way well enough to explain. Don't worry. I shall be back in the morning."

"Send that man to the telephone," Maurice ordered.

"Very well. He's right here."

She opened the door and said,—"Could you speak to Mooey, please, Mait? He's in an awful rage."

Fitzturgis stared. "A rage? At you?"

"At both of us, I guess."

He strode to the telephone, put the receiver to his ear.
"Oh, hullo, Maurice," he said.

Adeline could hear her cousin's accusatory voice hollow
in the telephone. She could hear the rain beating on a
skylight in a passage behind the hall. Fitzturgis said:

"There's no sense in talking that way. Adeline's quite
safe here."

He listened to another outburst and then exclaimed,—
"Good Lord—we're not alone! My mother and sister are
here . . . Adeline did tell you . . . I'm sure she did . . .
Look here, Maurice, what sort of blackguard do you take
me for? . . . Well, I hope you will come and see for
yourself . . . About what time? . . . All right. We shall
expect you."

He turned and smiled at Adeline. "He thought I lived
alone," he said. "In any case, he seems to have a low
opinion of me."

"I told him I was staying at your mother's!" she cried.
"Really, Mooey is impossible to explain things to. He
simply doesn't listen."

They stood close together in the tiny room. He looked
at her intently. He said, in a low voice,—"Now you have
seen them, do you understand?"

"You mean do I understand why you didn't come to
see me or write?"

"Yes."

"Well—I don't."

"Adeline—" he spoke almost angrily—"surely you
can understand my predicament. I had no right to show
you that I love you . . ."

She interrupted joyfully,—"Then you still do?"

"You have never been out of my thoughts since we left
the ship."

"And never have you been out of mine!"

He turned his head away as though he could not bear
to see that happy face. "My darling," he said, "you and
I have nothing to look forward to—that is, together."

"Aren't we going to get married, Mait?"

"How can we?" he exclaimed in exasperation. "I have
nothing to offer you. You see what my life is. In the first

place I'm poor, but I could soon remedy that—if I were free. I'm not free. My mother and sister are completely dependent on me. You see how unpractical my mother is —though she does her share of the work, make no mistake about that. My sister . . . well, there are times when I am the only person who can control her."

"She doesn't seem—terribly different. I quite like her."

"She was one of the most attractive girls I've ever known. Gay—high-spirited—but now—well, now there are days when she's sunk in melancholy, and other days when, as I said, I'm the only one who can control her."

"Isn't she going to get better?"

"She possibly may. She may get worse."

"In that case," Adeline tried to make her voice impersonal, "you'd have to put her in a mental home, wouldn't you?"

"That would be the end of her."

"But they treat people in those places, so that they recover."

"We have had the best advice. It is—give her a country life and as little restraint as possible. The local doctor is very good and gets on well with her."

"She'll get better," cried Adeline. "She *must*!"

"It will be a long time."

"Years?"

"Yes, years."

"And we can't be engaged?"

"No."

"I'm willing to be."

"Oh, you reckless child—you don't realize what you're saying."

"You don't realize how I love you . . . You know, Mait, all my family say I am my great-grandmother over again. I'm named for her. She had many little loves in her life but only one great love. I will be the same, and you are my great love."

He turned to her. His face was ugly with pain.

"You're making this terribly hard for me," he said.

"It needn't be."

"Adeline—you don't know what you say. You will

look back on me, some time in the future, as one of your little loves——"

"I will not!" she cried, and broke into sobs.

In consternation he shut the door of the little room. He heard voices beyond the hall. He reached up and turned off the light. He took her in his arms and pressed his lips to hers, murmuring soothing words, then, as her sobs ceased, words of passionate endearment.

The mother's voice came to them insistingly calling his name. He put Adeline gently to one side, turned on the light, opened the door. He crossed the hall and said, in a repressive tone, "I was helping Miss Whiteoak telephone to her cousin. I told her you said she must spend the night with us and she has accepted. He's coming for her in the morning."

Adeline then appeared and Mrs. Fitzturgis warmly welcomed her as a guest for the night. "It will seem like old times," she said, "to have a young person staying in the house. We used to have so many visitors and, of course, when my daughter has recovered, we shall have many more. We are not accustomed, you know, to living like this. I well remember times when . . ."

She ran on in this vein while Fitzturgis crossed into the drawing-room and began to mend the fire. Sylvia was pacing the length of the long narrow room, her hands clasped behind her back.

"I feel restless tonight," she said. "This weather stirs me. I wish I were a fish out there in the sea, with all that heaving salty space about me and the stormy sky overhead."

"Well," he said cheerfully, "you happen to be snug in your own house, with a good fire burning and a nice visitor. I must ask her to tell you about Jalna, her own home. It will amuse you. She's mad about horses and takes prizes for riding at the big shows over there."

"I wish I had a saddle horse," said his sister. "If only I could gallop for miles and miles, I could get rid of this confused feeling in my head. I'm sure violent exercise would help me. Do you think you might get me a horse, Maitland? I'm cooped up too much with Mother."

"Yes, after a while, when you're stronger," he said soothingly, while he strained to hear what was passing between his mother and Adeline.

They came into the room and he was startled by Adeline's pallor which so accentuated the luminous darkness of her eyes.

"I've been telling my sister," he said, "of your riding. She'd love to hear about your horses and the life at Jalna. Tell her of the feud between your father and that man Clapperton."

"Imagine your remembering that," she exclaimed, her eyes caressing him.

"Oh, do tell us," cried Mrs. Fitzturgis, pleased as a child by the prospect of diversion. "We'll sit cosily about the fire and you shall tell us about life in Canada."

"I'd like to go there," said her daughter.

"Why, my dear, we can scarcely persuade you to go into the village!"

"That's different," said the girl gloomily.

They were seated about the fire and Fitzturgis drew on Adeline to talk.

"I'm sure," said Mrs. Fitzturgis, "that everything over there is very much better than here in Ireland. It must be so or the Irish wouldn't have emigrated the way they have."

"Oh, no," said Adeline. "Lots of things here are far nicer than there. But we have some better things. A few, I mean."

"What, for instance?" asked Mrs. Fitzturgis, happily clasping her hands on her stomach.

Adeline looked at the quietly flickering fire. She said— "Firewood, for instance. You should see the fire of birch logs my great-uncles sit in front of. It's silver birch, very white and pretty, and the flames leap and crackle in it. It throws a terrific heat."

"How lovely!" cried Mrs. Fitzturgis. "And have you central heating?"

"Oh, yes. My great-uncles can't bear the slightest draught. My uncle Ernest knows when the thermometer falls one degree below 75. He just *knows*. He feels it all through him." She looked proudly about the little circle.

"And my great-uncle Nicholas is a wonderful old man. He can play the piano though he's ninety-six. Not new pieces, of course, just bits of the ones he learned long ago. We're hoping they'll live to be a hundred like my great-grandmother did." Fitzturgis led her on to talk of Jalna, of horses and riding. He sat watching her face, now happily animated, now serious, one elbow on an arm of his chair, his hand shielding the telltale lips that could not hide his longing for her. The mild firelight played over the features of the group—the man, his mother, his sister, and the girl he loved, drawing them into a pensive intimacy, as though they had known each other for years.

When it was time to prepare the dinner Mrs. Fitzturgis rose with dignity. "I do all my own cooking, Miss Whiteoak," she said, "and since you have asked me to call you by your Christian name, I will, though I don't approve of using Christian names too early in acquaintance, but you are so young and so friendly that I'd like to call you Adeline—you pronounce it *Adeleen*, don't you?—as I say I do all my own work with the exception of what little my son can do to help, for he is busy all the day with his farm—well, not exactly *busy* all the day because I often think he's inclined to indolence like his poor father was, though when his father became really interested in anything, I've never known anyone who could be more absorbed, unless it is my son. As I say I shall go now and prepare the dinner. Fortunately I have a chicken stewing—well, not exactly a chicken, for to tell the truth it isn't very young but it's been simmering so long that I'm sure it will be tender, though perhaps not so actually *tender*, as possibly eatable. Mike, the man who works for my son, always peels the potatoes for me, for the sake of my hands, no—frankly for *my* sake, he's so very obliging, and I don't allow Sylvia to do anything with a knife, she's so nervous. So, if you will come and give me a hand, Maitland, we'll soon have dinner ready, though it can scarcely be dignified by the name of dinner as there are only two simple courses and one of them uncertain to say the least of it." Mrs. Fitzturgis smiled jauntily at Adeline, the firelight gleaming on her earrings.

Adeline thought,—"She smiles but her eyes look as though she'd cried a lot." She said,—"Please let me help. I'd love to." She feared to be left alone with Sylvia, who, as though aware of this, said, in her cool musical voice, —"Yes, do let her help you, Mother. I'm in no mood to be companionable." As though to settle it she picked up a book from the sofa and buried her nose in it.

This unexpected pleasure of helping to prepare the meal in the old-world kitchen with Fitzturgis by her side, touching her, as they passed, recklessly snatching a kiss from her, for in this moment he ceased to restrain his love, filled her with a wild exhilaration. Her mood affected Mrs. Fitzturgis, making her happy, and all three were for the time like people with no troubles.

Adeline kept her mind from the thought of tomorrow. Her gaiety affected them all. Even Sylvia laughed outright at some nonsense passing between the lovers at table. At the sound of her daughter's laughter Mrs. Fitzturgis sprang up, ran round the table to Sylvia's side and embraced her, then returned to her seat smiling, with tears in her eyes.

"Oh, how happy you've made us!" she exclaimed. She gave Adeline and Fitzturgis no opportunity to be alone together. This was not from any desire to separate them but because she herself so enjoyed the girl's company, was so eager to pour out the trivialities of her pent-up talk, so anxious that she should enjoy her dinner, so determined that she should be comfortable in her bedroom. Adeline had hoped that mother and daughter might go early to bed, leaving her and Maitland to sit together by the fire. All through the evening she pictured the two of them sitting together by the fire.

But that was not to be. Mrs. Fitzturgis all but put her to bed. She brought a nightdress of Sylvia's for her and a little crocheted jacket of wool to wear over it because of the chill of the bedroom. The bedroom, thought Adeline, left alone in it, felt as though it had not been occupied in a lifetime. Everything she touched had a clammy chill on it. Outside the rain still whipped the heavy foliage of the rhododendrons . . . She heard the clock in the passage give a rattling wheeze, as though this were its last effort, then sound the strokes of twelve. She fell asleep.

Though she did not hear it the clock had just struck one when she was woken by the sound of voices. They were raised as though in anger. Adeline sat up alert and shivering in apprehension. She heard Sylvia say:

"Let me go! I tell you I will go! Neither you nor anyone else can stop me."

Then came the voice of Fitzturgis but she could not tell what he said. Sylvia's voice was raised still more fiercely.

"You can't stop me! I've got to go outdoors."

There was the sound of a scuffle and a thud on the bedroom door. A girl less impulsive or of a more timid nature would have covered her head with the bedclothes in fear, but Adeline sprang out of bed and threw open the door, standing there in her nightdress staring with startled eyes at the brother and sister.

They stood, locked in each other's arms, like two wrestlers.

Fitzturgis was facing her. He tried to smile reassuringly. He said,—"Don't be frightened. Sylvia is feeling nervous. That's all." He released his sister and she wheeled and faced Adeline. She wore a loose coat over her nightclothes but her feet were bare. Her face was pale and distorted by emotion. She raised her hands in a beseeching gesture towards Adeline.

"Make him let me go," she said. "You can understand that I must be out of this house . . . out in the open . . . in the rain. You love Mait. I can see that. Make him let me go or—I swear I'll do something desperate."

"Come, come, Sylvia." Fitzturgis took her gently by the arm but she violently tore herself away.

"Will you tell me," asked Adeline, trying to think what Renny would have done at such a time, "why you want to go out? It's an awful night, you know. You'd get as wet as a rat."

"What should I care!" Sylvia cried wildly. "It's what I'd like. I'm suffocating in the house."

"I guess you'd a bad dream," said Adeline quietly, though she felt her heart beating uncomfortably in her throat.

"Yes, that's what I woke from." Sylvia passed her hand across her forehead and Adeline could see the beads of sweat there. "A terrible dream. My baby—my poor little baby—was in bed with me. It was living and it was feeling for my breast—the way a baby would—but my heart was breaking and I knew the milk in my breast had turned to blood. Then the window opened—not the door, mind you, but the window—and Dick, my husband, crawled in over the sill. He said,—'I've come for the baby—all the way through this storm'—and I said—'You can't take it out. It will kill it!' And he laughed, as though it was a huge joke, and said,—'*Kill* it! Why, it's dead as a door-nail already.' And I felt for the baby and it was an ice-cold nail—driven into my heart!"

"That's the way she goes on," said Fitzturgis, quietly, as though deadly tired.

Sylvia laid her forearm against the wall and hid her face on it. She was shaking as though from cold.

"Go back to bed, like a good girl," said Fitzturgis.

"No!"

"But you must." He spoke authoritatively. "You know very well that I shall not let you go out."

Adeline laid a firm, comforting hand on the shaking shoulder. She said,—"Will you let me go with you to your room—for company I mean? We could talk."

Sylvia raised her face, her blue eyes wet with tears. She gave Adeline a penetrating look, then,—"Yes," she breathed.

They went into Sylvia's room together. Fitzturgis stood hesitating in the doorway, anxious for Adeline.

"May I speak to you for a moment?" he asked.

His sister broke in,—"To talk about me! That's what you want."

"Nonsense. It's something—just between us."

"All right. Talk then." Sylvia sank to her bed as though exhausted.

Adeline followed him into the passage. "I think she'll be quiet now," he said, in a muffled voice, "but it's a shame you should lose your sleep like this. I hope you weren't too badly frightened."

"Oh, no."

"I shall leave the light on, in the passage, and when she's quiet you will go back to your room. If you have any trouble . . . well, I shall be listening."

She smiled rather wanly at him. She was so tired she wanted terribly to yawn. All emotion had left her.

"You must be sorry you looked me up," he said.

Still with the pale smile on her face she said,—"No. How could I be sorry . . . except for you?"

She went back into Sylvia's room, closing the door behind her. Sylvia had thrown her coat over a chair and got into bed.

"Shall I put out the light?" asked Adeline.

"Yes. I don't mind the dark, now that you're here."

Adeline felt her way to the bed and crept in beside Sylvia. She put her arm about her. How thin that body was, compared with the firm, rounded slenderness of her own!

"Talk to me," Sylvia said, "talk steadily. Tell me about your horses and dogs and your old uncles. Anything you can think of. Only talk. It's the silence that's so horrible."

Adeline held her firmly. She told her of the foal that had been dropped the very day she had left for New York, of its markings, of its sire's pedigree, of the prizes its dam had won. Purposely she went into details of the achievements of all the horses she could remember. When that came to an end she told her of Mr. Clapperton and the threat of his bungalows, of Tom Raikes and the name he was getting for drinking and car-smashing and generally cheating his employer. On and on she talked, till her voice grew husky, but if she stopped, Sylvia would say, like an insatiable child,—"Tell me more."

The image of everyone at Jalna was, in turn, conjured up and an oddly frank biography of them related, but when, at last, she reached the 'cute' sayings of baby Mary, Sylvia said,—"Go on, tell me more."

Now Adeline turned to Maurice and Finch. She told how Maurice had come to live with Cousin Dermot when he was a small boy, of his life with the old man and of how he had inherited his property. Within ten minutes she had exhausted the adventures and possibilities of Maurice's life. But Sylvia still said, "Tell me more."

Finch only was left. Adeline, with a supreme effort, tore from her memory all she knew about Finch. She was glad she had saved him till the last, for Sylvia showed a new sort of interest. She no longer just listened but asked questions, made comments, was in arms on Finch's side. Adeline remembered little of Sarah, Finch's wife, but she ruthlessly repeated all she could recall of what she had heard Renny, Piers and the great-uncles say of her. And, listening to this recital, Sylvia forgot about herself, and her being expanded towards the life of another. Her limbs relaxed, her body, beneath Adeline's arm, rose and fell in regular breathing. At last she slept . . . Now there was only one thing left for Adeline to do—to say her prayers. These she mumbled in a husky whisper, even thanked God that she had been able to keep awake, and had scarcely said Amen when oblivion came to her also.

XVI

WORDS WITH MAURICE

IT WAS nine o'clock when Adeline woke to find Sylvia dressing in the room and glittering after-storm sunshine pouring in at the window. For a moment she was confused. Where was she and who was the slim white-skinned girl with the curling fair hair and large blue eyes? Sylvia smiled at her.

"Have a good night?" she asked, as if that sort of night were nothing out of the ordinary.

"Oh, yes," Adeline answered, remembering all. "Is it late?"

"Not really late but later than I have slept for a long while. It's a lovely morning."

Adeline stretched, luxuriating in comfort, then suddenly remembered the meeting with Maurice, and drew up her knees and pulled the bedclothes over her head.

"What's the matter?" asked Sylvia.

"My cousin." Her voice came muffled. "He is coming for me and he'll be furious with me."

"Why?"

"I shouldn't have brought his car here—I mean so far—without telling him. Of course, it's not actually the car he's angry about. It's me."

"I see. Has he a temper?"

"I—really don't know."

Sylvia laughed. "Well, it'll be fun to find out."

Adeline sat up on the side of the bed. "I hope so but I doubt it."

"You seem afraid of him."

"Oh, I can look after myself." She sprang up and began to dress.

This morning she found nothing strange about Sylvia. Perhaps,—she thought, with a certain self-congratulation, —she had done her good. Or perhaps her malady came only in spells. Whatever the truth, never did she want to face another such night as the last. Like a healthy young animal she pushed the thought of it away from her. Her thoughts also turned away from the meeting with Maurice. Their focus was the man to whom her first love had turned.

"What hair you have," she heard Sylvia say, "and what eyes! I didn't realize last night what a beauty you are."

"I've been thinking the same about you."

"Oh, *me*!" Sylvia gave a contemptuous shrug. "I've lost any looks I had."

"I admire you very much," said Adeline, and added reflectively, "You look very much like your brother."

"Oh, *him*!" exclaimed Sylvia, in the same tone in which she had said,—"Oh, *me*!"

"What's the matter with him?" Adeline demanded hotly.

"He's just a lazy Irishman," Sylvia said emphatically. "He'd rather go fishing or sit talking in Tim Rafferty's cabin than get down to real work. He does a little farming. What does it amount to? He had a future ahead of him. Now he has none. My mother and I could get on without him but he won't let us try." Her face grew tense. She took up a lipstick and applied it with trembling hand to her pale mouth.

"I don't think he's lazy." Adeline spoke with equal heat. "Perhaps your mother persuaded him to stay."

"I suppose you're thinking of last night. But I can tell you his being here only unnerves me the more. I was far better when he was in America. No—I am just his excuse for staying at home."

No use in arguing with her, thought Adeline, better go into the bathroom and stay there for a little. She did and, when she returned, began to talk of something else. Soon they went down to breakfast. Fitzturgis had already eaten his and gone out. The disappointment of discovering this made it difficult for Adeline to show a cheerfulness equal to that of Mrs. Fitzturgis. She apparently had slept well and all through the meal she talked with animation if not always with clarity. She wore a different pair of earrings, more suitable for the morning, but though they were not so long, they still were long enough to play in lively fashion about the lobes of her ears. The bacon and eggs, in spite of all, tasted good to Adeline.

The round white clouds hung motionless above the shining world their predecessors had created. Tulips lay with their heads on the wet earth. Rhododendrons had cast down half their flowers. But the fuchsias looked none the worse for the storm, and the wallflowers springing from crevices in the stone wall gave out a delicious scent. "A heavenly morning," thought Adeline, standing alone in front of the house, "and what a pity I can't enjoy it, because of the things I have hanging over me."

Fitzturgis came round the side of the house. Seeing her, he took three strides and was at her side.

"Let us go where we can be alone," he said, after no more than a terse "Good morning."

"Where?"

He led the way through the shrubbery into a grove of gnarled old trees, their trunks rising out of the long grass, their boughs drooping down to it. Drenched bluebells grew thickly here and the curling fronds of bracken pushed upward through the grass.

"You're going to get your feet soaking wet," he said ruefully.

"It doesn't matter." She smiled at him, happy that this moment was granted to them.

He did not smile in return but took her hand and raised it to his lips. "Oh, Adeline," he said, "you see how it is with me. You see why I have no right——"

"I don't care," she interrupted. "I love you and I'm not afraid to say so."

"But you mustn't. I'm not in a position . . ."

"This can't go on for ever. Your sister will get better."

"I doubt it," he said bitterly. "Sometimes I think a tragedy hangs over us."

"Oh, no, don't say that!" she cried, frightened. "Sylvia slept quietly all night."

"What a trump you were to stay with her! We must seem a strange family to you."

"Not strange. Just suffering because of the war." They were silent for a space, then she asked,—"Do you want us to be engaged, Mait?"

He gave a short laugh. "What a question! It seems to me that I've shown you that it is the one thing on earth that I do want."

"You've never asked me," she said boldly. "And if you did ask me I'd say yes."

"Adeline," he was in an anguish of exasperation, "you torture me. You're not too young to understand that a man must have a certain freedom if he's to marry."

"I didn't say marry! I said be engaged. I don't want to marry—not yet."

"I have no right to ask you to be engaged. What would your parents say if you went home and told them you were engaged to a penniless Irishman with a mother and an invalid sister to support?"

She gave a mischievous smile. "I could add to that what your sister says of you."

"What?"

"That you're lazy."

He flushed. "She said that, did she?"

"What she really said was that you're not needed here—that she and your mother would be all right by themselves."

"Oh, she's accused me of being lazy before this," he said bitterly. "It's nothing new. And perhaps I am. I hadn't much ambition left when you came on the scene. But I can tell you there's nothing I so much want now as to work and——" he halted, his face became downcast.

"Be engaged!" she prompted, with animation.

"Oh, my darling," he said, "if only I could!"

"All you have to do is to ask me." She smiled in invitation of a contract.

"I *will not* ask you," he returned, almost harshly. "Enough has been said against me. I refuse to have it said that I engaged myself to a young girl whom I have no prospect of marrying."

"Do you really believe there is no prospect?"

"You saw what my sister was like last night?"

"When you were in New York she and your mother managed somehow to——"

He interrupted. "When I came back my mother was exhausted. In all that three weeks she had not had a proper night's rest. They both were at breaking point. Sylvia may say what she will of me but she leans on me with all her might. If I'm not here—well, no one knows what might happen. If I hadn't been here last night she'd have gone out into the storm. Mother can't stop her. It's best for Mother to keep out of the way."

"I was pretty good with Sylvia, wasn't I, Mait?"

"You were splendid. Better than I."

"Well, then," the words poured eagerly from her, "why couldn't I come and stay for a bit? I'd give her something different to think about. I'm so sorry for her. I—I like her. It would be for her own sake I want to help her—as well as—oh, don't you think I could? Why—I might even cure her. What do you think of that for an idea, Mait?"

"It cannot be," he said stubbornly.

"What is the matter with you?" she cried suddenly angry. "Here I make a perfectly sound suggestion and you only turn it down, as though I were——"

"You are a darling," he said gently, "and I love you with all my heart, but we cannot have people saying——"

"What people?"

"Your people."

"Saying what?"

"That I took an unfair advantage of your generosity—that I tried to trap you."

"They couldn't say that. I wouldn't let them."

"You're very brave," he said, "and very young. You cannot stop people from saying or doing things. You'll find that out."

"Well, I can do what I—know is right."

"It is not right and it can't be thought of."

"You mean that you don't *want* me to?" Her quick colour rose. "You don't *want* me to come here and help to nurse Sylvia and make her better?"

He demanded abruptly,—"Would you like to live here for years as a sort of nurse to Sylvia?"

"It might happen quite soon. Her getting better, I mean."

"It may never happen. Think what you'd be giving up. All the life you love."

"You'd be here."

"My darling, you'd hate me—hate all three of us— before six months had passed." He broke a tough twig from the tree beneath which they stood and sniffed it as though it were a flower. "I'll tell you what," he said, "if Sylvia recovers—if I have prospects—I'll come to Canada and ask you what your feelings are then—I'll lay what I have to offer at your feet."

He spoke almost lightly and it was a mistake. She drew back from him in hurt. She did not notice that the hand which held the twig shook.

"I hear a motor horn. It's Mooey," she said.

He caught her arm and drew her to him. "One kiss before you go," he said.

She struggled away. "No," she cried, "I'll not kiss you," and ran through the long wet grass.

Finch and Maurice were standing beside a station wagon. Mrs. Fitzturgis had come out of the house to greet them. She was effusive in expressing pleasure in having Adeline spend the night with her. Finch smiled but threw an anxious glance towards the two coming out of the grove, at Adeline's flushed cheeks and wet shoes. He shook hands with Fitzturgis, whose cheekbones seemed to have become higher, his eyes more deeply set in the past quarter-hour. Maurice bowed, with only a faint pretence of friendliness. He asked of Adeline:

"Where is the car?"

Fitzturgis answered,—"In the garage. I'll bring it round."

"I'll go with you," said Finch, as though to escape from something.

They went together.

Maurice said to Mrs. Fitzturgis,—"It was very kind of you to take my cousin in."

"Ah, but we were only too delighted to have her. We

have so little company nowadays. My daughter's health
has not been good, you know. I do hope that, now the ice
is broken, we shall see quite a lot of her and of you too.
You can't imagine how dull we find living in Ireland. I
wonder that a young man like you—though to be sure,
youth is never dull. I well remember how gay I used to be,
though now I come to think of it I always wanted to have
some excitement—not exactly *excitement*, you know, but
just to be aware of the fact that one was *living*, which is more
than one is, here, though you'd be surprised at the things
that do happen. For instance——"

The car was moving towards them along the drive.

Mrs. Fitzturgis begged the three Whiteoaks to stay for
lunch, or if not for lunch, at least for a glass of sherry.
When the invitation was declined with grave politeness by
Maurice, with a obvious desire to be gone by Finch, and
with desperate submissiveness by Adeline, she exclaimed,
—"How very sorry my daughter will be to miss you!
But surely you will come again! Dear me, who is Sylvia?
I mean—*where* is Sylvia? I do get so easily confused in
these days, which is something quite new to me for I used
to have an abnormally good memory—in fact my husband
used to say that I never could forget anything, though
that remark was not made in the sense to which I refer.
Maitland, do you know where your sister is?"

Sylvia, at that moment, came out of the house, to the
obvious surprise of her mother and brother. They exchanged a glance, as though to say—"Whatever will she
do next?" But the girl herself looked both cool and
friendly. She chatted so naturally to Maurice and Finch
that Adeline wondered for an instant if last night's experience had been a dream. But no, it had not been a dream.
Maitland's expression, as his eyes rested on his sister,
showed that. His lips wore the strained smile of one who
is watchful and uncertain.

In spite of Mrs. Fitzturgis' loving clinging to the visitors
the good-byes were at last said. Adeline wanted to make
the return journey with Finch and whispered her wish
to him, but Maurice pressed forward and jumped into the
station wagon beside her. Finch followed in the car.

Adeline glanced at Maurice's profile as they sped along the road in silence. She held her two hands tightly together, harbouring in her right palm the clasp of Maitland's hand. She knew she had been wrong in going off by herself as she had, but she felt resentment that Maurice should so express his resentment. She said, when she could no longer bear the silence:

"You look like all the kill-joys in the world rolled into one."

"Thanks," he returned, his lips scarcely moving, "it's nice to know what you think of me."

"I only think what the way you behave makes me think."

"How clearly you put it!"

"Is all this because I took your car without asking?"

He turned to look at her.

"Be careful," she cried, "you nearly ran over that hen." The hen flew squawking to safety.

"Are you so callous, Adeline," he said, speaking each word very clearly, "so callous that you can't see how you have hurt me?"

"You have no right to use such a word about what I did."

"What about calling me a kill-joy? But I suppose it's true and you were having a joyous time."

"I was not! I was having——" She could not go on. Her voice died in a sob.

Maurice broke out,—"What do you suppose I felt when we came back yesterday and found you gone and hours passed before we had news of you, then that fellow cool as a cucumber—saying you were there? I'd been telephoning the police—the hospital—to find out if there'd been an accident. I was nearly crazy, I tell you."

She could not bring herself to say she was sorry but sat frowning, with underlip thrust forward.

"Then I'm informed," he continued, "that you'd gone in search of Fitzturgis. Do you realize what that looks like? What do you think your father would say?"

"Well—he'd have a right to say it."

"And I haven't!"

"No."

He drove on in silence, his body drooping over the wheel. Their familiarity since infancy which made every expression of the face, every gesture, of the one, something instantly recognizable to the other, now was disrupted. They drew back from each other as from strangers whom they suspected and feared.

They passed on through the rising and falling-away of the barren hills, some of which were pale in sunlight, others dim beneath the clouds. Adeline's mind flew back to Fitzturgis and she relived the scene in the grove. In imagination she fitted it with different endings, one of which curved her lips in the smile of one who dreams, and another which filled her eyes with stinging tears. Maurice spoke twice before his voice came to her.

Then,—"What did you say?" she asked.

"I said I should like to know what you are going to do."

"I don't know," she answered simply.

"Are you engaged to this man?"

"That's my own affair."

"It won't be yours alone—for long."

"Does that mean you will write home and tell?"

"You have a low opinion of me."

"Well—you could scarcely have acted meaner to me than you have since I came here."

He stopped the machine with a jerk.

"How dare you say that to me, Adeline?" he cried. "You know that for years I've looked forward to this time more than to anything on earth."

"Yes! And why? You wanted me to come and see all your grand belongings. You wanted to show off in front of me. You wanted me to do just what you chose. And because I refuse to say how wonderful you are and how proud I am to have your attentions you behave as though——"

He interrupted,—"I love you, Adeline."

"You have a strange way of showing it."

"What do you want me to do?"

"I don't care what you do."

"I'd better get some lessons in love-making from that brute . . ."

"If you mean Mait, he could show you a thing or two."

They glared at each other with blazing eyes. The engine throbbed. Behind them Finch sounded his horn.

"I'm going back with Uncle Finch," said Adeline. She began to open the door.

Maurice put his arm across her and held the handle fast.

"Let me go," she cried. "I will not be stopped."

"You will listen to me."

With her closed fist she beat his forearm.

"Very well," he said quietly. "Go. To the devil if you like."

In a moment she was in the road. In another she was sitting beside Finch and the two cars again in movement.

Finch said,—"There's no use in getting upset."

She bit her lip to keep back the sobs. "Oh, Uncle Finch, I wish I hadn't come in the car with Mooey!"

"Did you quarrel?"

"The last thing he said was to tell me to go to the devil."

"That's nothing."

"It may be nothing to you but I'm not used to it."

"I meant he's just letting off steam."

Adeline moved closer to Finch. She said, in a trembling voice: "I realize I did wrong and I'm *terribly* sorry, but if you knew what my feelings have been these past days——"

"Don't worry," Finch said comfortingly. "Maurice will get over this——"

"Do you mean he'll get over wanting me?"

"I don't know about that, but he'll get over this affair of Fitzturgis."

"He may, but I shan't!" she cried.

Finch said soothingly,—"Well, well, we'll see. You gave us a fright, you know. "

"I had no idea how long it would take me to find Mait's house."

"Adeline, what was your object in going there?"

She turned her candid eyes on him. "I wanted to find out if he still loved me and why he hadn't come."

"And did you?"

"Oh, he loves me with all his heart, but——"

"But what?" Finch encouraged gently.

That was enough. Like a stream in springtime flood Adeline poured out the incoherent story of her stay in that house. Every picturesque and passionate word she had garnered in her short life she now flung at Finch in a vehement desire to convince him of the reality of her love for Fitzturgis and of his for her.

Finch was so satisfactory to confide in. He neither blamed nor offered a solution of the problem, but she was sure he understood; sympathy emanated from him. Now and again he would take his hand from the wheel and give her a pat or he would murmur,—"It'll all come right——" just as though he knew from experience that it would.

At Glengorman Maurice made a great effort to be friendly, to behave as though nothing had happened, but his unhappiness was so palpable, his attitude towards Adeline so silently accusatory that, after two days of this atmosphere, Finch suggested that he and Adeline should set out on the tour of Ireland he had already planned. At first she drew back from this. In her absence a letter might come from Fitzturgis. Yet she longed to put miles between her and Maurice. It ended by her writing this note, in her surprisingly firm and well formed handwriting:

"My dear Maitland,—

"(In my heart I begin this letter with the word *darling* but as you have not written to me I shall not use it.) This is to tell you that I am going away for a while with Uncle Finch who is the dearest uncle a girl ever had. When I come back I shall hope to see you—that is if you want to see me.

"Again I say I am like my great-grandmother. She was a woman who was true to one love in her life—and so shall be I.

"Adeline."

The next day she and Finch set out.

XVII

MOUNTING ANGER AND LOVE

It was almost what Noah Binns had prophesied months ago. Backward spring had burst into sudden summer, not actually "roastin' bilin'" hot, as Binns had foretold, but hot enough for discomfort. Because of lack of rain the foliage of the trees began to take on the look of August before July was well on the way. The grass crops suffered from drought, the small dry kernels of wheat and oats rasped faintly together in the hot dry wind. A man might stamp on the ground with his heavy boot and leave no impression. The pasture became so poor that the udders of the cows no longer bulged with milk, while about the eyes and nostrils of the poor beasts a horde of buzzing flies tormented.

The only ones who enjoyed the extreme heat were Noah Binns who rejoiced in the fulfilment of his prophecy, and the two old uncles, Nicholas and Ernest, whose spirits flowered in the heat as the dry flowers of the everlasting. The prolonging of winter had been very hard on them, but now they felt stronger than they had in a long while. It did them good to feel their flesh warmed through and through, their dry old palms moist with heat. They chaffed each other and laughed in a way that did Renny's heart good.

All the happenings of the farm or stables he related to them to keep their interest alive, nor did he spare them the unpleasant things, such as the doings of Eugene Clapperton. In truth Alayne sometimes wondered if it were good for them to be worked up into such rages. "Rascally old interloper!" Nicholas would growl, thumping his fist on the arm of his chair. "Despicable old rascal!" Ernest would sneer. Seldom did they anathematize him without reference to his age, though he was at least thirty-five years younger than they.

All pretence of friendliness between the two houses had vanished. There was instead open antagonism. In all this Alayne could feel only a reflected warmth of anger. She would have wished above all to hear no more of their hateful neighbour's doings. The very name of Clapperton bored and almost sickened her. It was a shame, she thought, that the last years of the two old men should be poisoned by the hate and fear of Clapperton. At the same time she was aware that, in a sense, they were revitalized by the irritation. There was always this subject for animated speculation. Now it was certain that a factory was to be built on the land bought from the Blacks. The deal would be completed within a fortnight, it was said, and in a matter of months a hideous structure would rise within a stone's throw of Jalna.

For some reason it seemed to outrage Renny's feelings less than the bungalows just beyond his stables. The factory would be hidden from them by woods, but the sight of them insulted him in all his activities, for they all led sooner or later in the direction of the stables. Two more had been added in as many months. It seemed impossible that they could be well built, yet Eugene Clapperton insisted that this was so. Every day he inspected the progress of the building, made friends with the families of those that were already occupied, enjoyed the smell of the clean planks that were piled on the ground, the wholesome sound of saw and hammer. In the stir of these schemes he found outlet for his energy which was still abundant, and he felt something amounting to glee in completely overcoming the opposition of Renny Whiteoak. Renny had worked hard to rouse the feelings of property owners of the neighbourhood, had originated petitions with their signatures and presented them to the authorities without avail. "The time is coming," he told himself, "when we shall be driven to sell Jalna, but—not while I live and have fight in me."

One noonday, when the temperature was well past

ninety degrees, he came out of the comparative coolness of the stables into the blazing light of the sun and walked, as he had a habit of doing, to a point where he had a clear view of the bungalows. He was alone, for, when he had left the house, his sheepdog, peering out of its woolly coat, had told him as plain as words could speak that this was a day unfit for venturing forth and had thrown itself with a thud on the floor of the hall. The bulldog and the Cairn terrier had followed him, side by side, half-way to a field where Piers was cutting hay, then the little Cairn, after giving Renny a long reproachful look, had turned and resolutely trotted back to the house. The bulldog had sturdily jogged on, had stood slavering while the brothers had talked, and then panting heavily had returned with Renny. When they reached the branching of the path he had halted and looked with yearning eyes towards the house, but he would not return without permission, yet was ashamed of asking for it.

Renny gave him a pat. "Go back, old boy," he said. "I agree that it's as hot as hell."

The bulldog nuzzled his hand in gratitude, then lumbered back. He could not get into the house but he found a shady spot in the garden where among the geraniums he dug himself into the cool earth, leaving broken stalks and scattered blooms for Alayne to discover.

"I don't remember a time," thought Renny, "when all those three deserted me. It really must be hot."

He himself was one of those men who never seem to look either very hot or very cold. His high-coloured, weathered complexion remained the same, his dark red hair, which in this bright sunshine showed a light sprinkling of white, never lay limp with sweat but covered his hard-sculptured head crisply. He walked to a point in the paddock behind the stables where he could look down on the five bungalows built on the edge of the hollow in which Vaughanlands lay. This was a form of self-torture in which he indulged at least once a day. In resentment he had watched their claptrap progress from foundations till the day when washing fluttered on the clothesline in the little yard. He pictured them spreading like a rash of ugly

pimples over a well-known face, till the face of Vaughanlands was changed, and at the thought he made a grimace
expressing helpless anger and chagrin at his helplessness.

It was the hour when the three workmen had found a
shady spot and were eating their lunch. They were drinking
cold liquids from Thermos bottles. Their muddy old Ford
stood in the lane. Mrs. Barker was so sociable she could
not keep away from the men.

"My goodness," she remarked to one of them, "it must
be awful hot up on that there roof shinglin'."

"You bet it is," he answered, "square in the sun."

"When will it be finished?"

"By the end of the week."

"Say, you boys work fast."

He laughed. "We got to work with that guy Clapperton
always pokin' round, watchin' us."

"There he goes now," said another. "Why don't he
stay indoors and keep cool?"

"He'd sooner die of sunstroke than lose a nickel."

"Don't you go talking against him," said Mrs. Barker.
"He's been awful kind to me. He's given me a lot of good
advice."

"About what?" sneered the man.

"Human nature, if you want to know. He makes a study
of it."

"Ho, ho, ho," laughed the man. "He'd better make a
study of Tom Raikes. He could learn a lot there."

Mrs. Barker's attention was turned to the new bungalow.

"Look who's on the roof," she exclaimed.

"Darned if it isn't Colonel Whiteoak! And he's ripping
off the shingles I just put on, as fast as he can."

They stared stupefied, bottles half-way to mouths, at the
sight of the Master of Jalna sitting astride the ridge-beam,
prizing off, with the prongs of a hammer, shingle after
shingle. At the same moment Eugene Clapperton appeared
from the direction of his house and was frozen, high as was
the temperature, by the sight that met him. He could for a
moment scarcely believe his eyes; then he strode nearer
and shouted:

"How dare you do that?"

"It comes apart damned easy," returned Renny, "even easier than I expected."

"Come down off that roof," almost screamed Eugene Clapperton, "or I'll call in the police."

Down flew a shingle almost in his face. He turned to the workmen. "Bring that man down," he ordered.

They presented uniformly sheepish smiles.

"Better call the police," said one.

"Do you mean to say," fumed Clapperton, "that the three of you are afraid to bring him down?"

"I'd hate to tackle him," said another.

"I wouldn't do it," said the third. "Not on that roof."

Mrs. Barker soothingly spoke. "Never mind, Mr. Clapperton. The men will put the shingles on again."

Eugene Clapperton gave her a furious look and strode to the bungalow. Children from the other bungalows gathered about, openmouthed. Shingle after shingle came frolicking down the roof.

"I'm going straight in," cried Eugene Clapperton, his voice cracking with fury, "to telephone the police."

Renny Whiteoak tossed up the hammer and caught it. Then he threw a leg over the ridge and slid down the roof to the top of the ladder. He descended the ladder and strolled across the gravel to face Clapperton. He, with his spirit on its way to California, had bought himself a suit of a light material, pale buff in colour, and a tie with gaudy figures on it. He wore no waistcoat.

Renny looked him over in astonishment. "So," he said, "you've come to this."

"Get off my land."

"Yes, gladly. As soon as I've had a good look at you." He gently took the end of the tie in his fingers. "Expensive," he said, "but what a design! I wonder your wife allows it."

Eugene Clapperton drew back as though from the touch of a viper. "You have not heard the last of this," he said.

"And you've not seen the last of me. I'll come every day and take down what your men have built. I think I can keep up with them."

"Put Colonel Whiteoak off my property," Clapperton
ordered his men. They sniggered but did not move.

Clapperton now spoke more quietly. "You will be
summoned to-morrow, sir, for trespass and damage to
property."

"Spoken like a man," said Renny. "But I still don't
like your tie."

He returned the way he had come. On the lawn he could
see the figures of his uncles, half reclining in comfortable
chairs in the shade. Indoors he found Alayne, his sister
Meg, and her daughter Patience, sitting with blinds drawn,
enervated by the heat.

"Why, Meggie," he exclaimed, pleased as always to
see her, "*and* Patience! What brought you out in the
heat?"

She put a plump arm about his neck and for a moment
held him close.

"Oh," she moaned, "that little house of ours! It's
simply unendurable in this weather. So I just staggered
to the car and Patience drove me over. Alayne has kindly
asked us to stay to lunch."

As their arrival had been timed to coincide with that
meal there really had been no alternative for Alayne.

"No one," went on Meg, "feels the heat as I do."

"No one," said her brother, "is as fat as you are."

"Fat!" she cried. "Fat! I don't weigh a pound more
than a hundred and thirty-nine."

"I dare you," he teased, "to come out to the barn and
let me weigh you."

She ignored this remark. "What makes me feel the heat
so terribly is having to do my own housework and eating
so little."

"I thought Patience did all the work."

"I refuse to be teased. It's too hot."

Wrinkling his forehead, he remarked,—"I suppose I'll
find it nice and cool in gaol."

Three puzzled feminine faces were turned to him.

"Explain," said his wife.

"Gaol!" echoed his sister on a note of apprehension.

"Now what have you been up to?" laughed his niece.

"Clapperton," he returned, "is going to have a summons served on me for pulling down one of his bungalows and tweaking his tie."

Alayne made a sound of exasperation. "It's much too hot to be funny," she said, "if that is what you are trying to be."

"I was never more serious," he returned. "I haven't actually razed the bungalow to the ground, but I ripped off part of the roof, and I didn't injure his tie though it was the most obscenely ugly object I've ever laid eyes on and I've been through two wars."

Alayne pressed her hand to her forehead. "All this," she said, "is going to lead to very real trouble."

Patience hugged her own body and laughed inwardly. "I'd have given worlds to see that show," she murmured. "Not that I think Uncle Renny did right."

"Right," cried Alayne. "It was madness, and it's going to bring us a most unpleasant publicity."

Meg raised her hand. "There," she said, "there goes the gong. How glad I'll be of a little nourishment, for I declare I haven't eaten enough during this heat to keep a dickybird alive."

At table the two uncles were told by Renny of the encounter with all details added. They were enormously pleased. Nicholas demanded to hear it all twice repeated. Ernest struck his slender fist on the table and exclaimed:

"Good for you, Renny. You've taught that old fellow a lesson." Though what was the lesson he did not say.

"I've this to say about Clapperton," Renny looked about the table as though he challenged anyone to deny it, "I've this to say. I don't believe he knows what it is to have one generous impulse. He's a coward too, for he winced when I took a step towards him."

"And a spiteful coward," added Ernest. "Vindictiveness sticks out all over him."

The object of this criticism was indeed feeling quite shaky in the legs after his encounter with Renny, and deeply revengeful in spirit. Over and over again he pictured that man ripping the shingles from the roof of the bungalow, grinning in derision at the one whose property he was mutilating. He recalled the foolish faces of the workmen as they sniggered at the scene. He recalled the figure of the woman standing with arms akimbo. He had a mind to put them all, with finality, off his property.

The coolness of the living-room was balm to his disarranged being. It was dim too, after the glare outside. He could just make out the shapes in his beloved picture of the shipwreck. He sat down in front of it trying to relax. The ornate clock on the mantelshelf chimed the half-hour. The door softly opened and his sister-in-law came in, closing it after her. She drew close, looking down on him.

"Well?" he enquired in irritable surprise.

"Eugene," she said in a low voice, "I've something to tell you."

Now what? he wondered, instantly suspicious.

"It's about the mare," she went on rapidly. "The one you sold because of its eyes. Well—there's nothing wrong with its eyes. I found that out this morning. I was in the woods at Jalna painting a group of those lovely silver birches and . . ."

"Go on," he urged harshly.

"And that man Wright came along and he began to talk about the trees . . ."

"What the devil have trees to do with the mare?"

"He says there's nothing—absolutely *nothing*—wrong with her eyes. He saw her yesterday at the farmer's who bought her from Raikes. The farmer said there never had been anything wrong with her sight. And not only that. She's in foal. She was when he bought her and, of course, Raikes charged a great deal extra for that. Wright thought you should know. But I beg of you—don't, don't tell Gem I told you."

"Why?" he got out, through his rage.

"Oh, she thinks Raikes is perfect, just as you do. No—not as you do."

"*Not* as I do," he gasped. "*Not* as I do. In some other way. Is that what you're telling me?"

"No. No," she cried and ran from the room.

He put his hand on the mantelpiece to steady himself. He felt dizzy. He had had suspicions that Raikes was not quite so reliable as he seemed, but he had put them from him. He stubbornly had wanted to think well of the man. He was honestly fond of him. Raikes had a soothing effect on him and he knew this was a benefit to his health. But what black suspicion Althea had planted in his brain! Not Raikes and the mare alone but Raikes and his wife. A thousand only half-noticed incidents crowded into his heated brain. Why had he not forced Althea to be explicit? She was very clear-headed beneath her oddities.

He paced up and down the room calming himself. "I shall cease trying to manipulate thoughts," he muttered. "I relax from nervous tension. I am at peace." But he started with a nervous jerk of the neck when Gem looked in at the door.

"Tom wants to know," she said, "if the men are to put on more shingles."

"My God," he said furiously, "what a question! Certainly they are. Tell Raikes to tell them—and then to come to me here. At once."

"What's the matter, Tiddledy-winks?" she asked.

"I've a headache."

"Oh, what a shame! Your lunch will make you feel better. It's ready."

"I don't want any."

"Oh, Tiddledy-winks——" She moved towards him.

"Tell Raikes," he snapped.

He kept moistening his lips with his tongue, taking deep breaths, saying to himself,—"I relax from nervous tension. I am at peace. All this will be finally adjusted."

Raikes stood in the doorway.

Eugene Clapperton saw him for the first time as a male, attractive to women—noticed the smooth brown contours of his throat, set off by the open neck of his shirt. He said harshly:

"I have just heard how you lied to me about the mare. I know that her eyes are perfect, that she's in foal. I know everything, so there's no use your lying any more."

Eugene Clapperton held himself erect. He looked at that moment impressive, an accusing figure. Yet in his heart he hoped that Raikes would deny all, even be able to prove his innocence. He had almost the feeling of a father who accuses his son.

But Raikes made no denial. After opening his eyes wide in astonishment, he lowered them and hung his head, like a bad son.

Clapperton braced himself. He said,—"I could have you arrested but I'm not going to. I shall pay you a month's wages and you will leave this place tomorrow morning. Never set foot on it again."

"I've worked hard here," said Raikes.

"Worked to injure me."

"You'll not get a man that'll work harder."

"Get out before I throw you out!"

Raikes smiled at that.

He returned to the kitchen. Looking into the dining-room he saw Gem sitting alone at table with a plate of salad in front of her. He came to the door.

"Where is Miss Althea?" he asked.

"She doesn't want her lunch. Neither does Mr. Clapperton. I don't know what is the matter with this family." She spoke in a tone of complete familiarity.

Raikes came in on tiptoe. His face was lighted by a loving smile. He bent and touched her hair with his lips.

"It's good-bye for us," he said low.

"What?"

"He's fired me."

She drew back staring up at him.

"He couldn't—he wouldn't—he——"

"He has."

"Oh, Tom." Her jaw dropped in tragic consternation. "But why?"

"It's some talk he's heard."

"About you and me?"

"Lord, no."

"I won't let him."

"It's done."

She covered her face with her hands. "Oh, Tom, I'd follow you to the ends of the earth."

He looked down at her as something desirable but not for him.

"He's fired me right enough," he said. "I'm to go tomorrow."

"Tomorrow!" The word meant doom the way she said it.

He put his fingers inside her collar, against the creamy warmth of her flesh. He tried to think of something to say to comfort and yet to break off, but he could not. The tumult of their minds broke like waves against the rock of Eugene Clapperton's decision. For Gem an empty life lay ahead. For Raikes a new job.

The sound of an opening door came to them. In an instant Raikes was out of the room. With heavy steps the husband advanced along the hall and came to the table.

"Have you made coffee?" he asked.

"Yes."

"I think I'd like some." He dropped into a chair, limp, as though the strength were gone out of him.

She poured him a cup of coffee and he dropped four lumps of sugar into it. There was energy in sugar.

"I've sacked Tom Raikes," he said, his eyes piercing her.

"Oh?" she returned coolly.

"Do you mind?"

"There are other men to be found."

"I had thought we'd take him with us to California."

"What changed your mind?" She looked at him as cool as the slices of cucumber on her plate.

"Oh, things I've heard." He carefully stirred the sugar in his cup.

"Tell me."

"You want to know?"

"Sure I want to know."

There was something new about her, a deliberate commonness that was insulting to him and that made her, for some perverse reason, yet more desirable.

His gorge rose. He swigged down his coffee and stood up. "I'm going to lie down," he said. "We'll talk when this terrible heat lets up."

She sat like a statue watching him go, only her eyes living in her pale face.

He went upstairs to the bathroom and took three sleeping

tablets. He then lay down on the bed in the guest-room. Shut in this unused room he felt cut off from the rest of the house and all in it. He lay waiting for the tablets to work. They took a long while about it. He had known one tablet to be more efficacious than those three. Still he lay quiet, determinedly relaxed. He pushed away the dreadful thought that his marriage was a failure, that he would have been far better alone. A spasmodic jerk went through his whole body. He rolled over. Then the benign drug began to drowse him. He was still sleeping when Gem went to bed.

Raikes had kept out of the way, not wanting a scene with either husband or wife. This chapter in his life was over. To get his wages and leave peaceably, that was his idea. He would take out the car that night, go to his club and tell his friends good-bye, have a last game and a last drink with them.

When the house was in darkness he drove the car quietly out along the little road that led past the bungalows. The night was sweltering. Fireflies drew lines of brightness on the dark. A myriad crickets played their feverish tune.

XVIII

JULY BLAZE

IT WAS good luck rather than a steady head that brought Raikes safely back to Vaughanlands that night. From side to side of the road the car zigzagged. It just escaped being struck by a truck. It just missed running into a ditch. But he came back without mishap till he reached the door of the garage which he thought he had left open. But a wind had risen and blown it shut and he drove the car against it. He heard the splinter of wood. The jar threw him forward against the wheel. This sobered him a little. He alighted from the car and ruefully looked at the damage done. Well, in the morning he would push the car into the garage, shut the broken door, and they'd not discover it till after he was gone. What the hell did he care anyhow? He lurched across the gravel towards the house. On the grass plot by the kitchen door he grew dizzy and staggered. As he fell he caught hold of a feathery young shrub, but it had no strength to support him and he ripped it from the earth as he came down. He lay sprawling on the grass, the shrub gripped in his hand like a woman's hair. There he lay, glad to be at rest, not trying to drive a car, not trying to walk.

It had been midnight when he fell. It was three in the morning when he opened his eyes and looked about. Hordes of stars were staring down at him. All about fireflies darted, as though weaving him in a mesh. The crickets, the locusts, wove a tenuous mesh of sound about him. He lay still for a bit, feeling sorry for himself—a lonely man, to whom something bad had happened, he forgot what.

He felt stiff and decided he wanted to go to bed. Very

cautiously he got to his feet and stumbled to the kitchen door. Inside, he found he wanted a cup of tea. That would make him feel better, but instinct told him he was not capable of handling a kettle of boiling water. He did not want to get scalded. He rested against the edge of the kitchen table, feeling sorry for himself, wanting no more than a cup of tea yet afraid to make it . . . Well, he would have a cigarette. That would be a little comfort. With dazed deliberation he took one from a packet, lit it, blew out the match, threw it on the floor. Let her pick it up and be damned to her!

The cigarette smoked, he went quite steadily to his room. It was stifling hot. He pulled off his shirt and threw himself on the bed . . .

All energy in the house was suspended, with one minute exception. In the attic Althea slept naked on the sheet. Her Great Dane panted on the floor, his muzzle dry in the heat. The tortoise dozed inside his cool shell. The exception was the cigarette-end that Raikes had dropped on the kitchen table. It lay beneath a pile of old newspapers on the shelf above. Only a faint spark showed that it was not quite out, till a gust of hot wind came in at the window and blew one of the newspapers down on the table. The tiny spark fastened on the paper as though its life depended on it. After a little, a creeping flame appeared. Then, in an instant, the paper was ablaze. Then the whole heap of papers. Then the window-curtains. Then the window-frames. The fire had the kitchen to itself.

Before long the smoke from it poured into the hall. The acrid smell disturbed Gem Clapperton. She sprang up and ran into the passage, into the room where her husband was sleeping.

"Eugene!" she screamed, shaking him. "The house is on fire! The house is on fire!"

He was on his feet in an instant. He might have thought she was unduly terrified had he not smelled that horrible smell of smoke. She left him and ran out screaming her sister's name. He heard Althea coming, heard the dog bark. He ran down the stairs and saw the smoke pouring through the cracks about the door that led to the kitchen. He saw a brightness in there and heard the crackling of flames. He knew better than to open that door.

One thing he would save and that was the painting of the shipwreck. But first the fire department! Keeping good control of himself he telephoned to their office at Stead. The two girls came down the stairs, Althea, wearing a white coat, holding the Great Dane by the collar. They looked distraught.

"Get right outdoors," he ordered. "I've phoned for the firemen."

"It's horrible. Oh, I'm so frightened," came from his wife's white lips. Suddenly she remembered Raikes and ran towards the back of the hall. But she heard the crackling of fire and saw the smoke coming thick from under the door.

Althea was struggling with the lock of the front door.

"You fool," shouted Clapperton, letting himself go, giving voice to what he had always thought her to be. "We can't have a draught here." He herded them ahead of him into the living-room and slammed that door behind them.

In here was a different world scarcely yet threatened, with only a faint smell of smoke as compared to the hall.

"Tom! Tom!" screamed Gem, and ran and scrambled through the open window after pushing out the screen.

Eugene Clapperton was taking down the painting of the shipwreck. "I'll save my pictures," he said.

"Hand them out to me," said Althea. She too climbed over the sill and took the painting into her hands.

"Will the house be destroyed?" she asked.

"It's an inferno at the back."

"Will the fire-reels soon be here?"

"How the hell do I know?"

"Tom will be burned in his bed."

"The devil looks after his own."

With all speed he took the pictures from the wall and handed them out to her. She was bent double under their weight. They worked together like people of one mind to save the paintings which she loathed, and each despised the other.

Gem ran to Raikes' window. The room was thick with smoke. She could make out the pale shape of the bed.

"Tom!" she screamed, putting her face close to the screen, holding her breath. "Tom!"

He woke, rolled over, coughed.

"Tom!" She beat on the window screen but could not get it out.

He was up now. He came to the window, thrust out the screen, threw a leg over the sill. Red flames were rushing into the room.

"Oh, Tom, darling," she cried, and put her arm about his sleek torso. "Thank God, I've got you out!"

"Is the house afire?" he asked, dazed.

"Blazing."

"Och, 'tis cruel the way the smoke has got into my lungs. Every breath's a knife." He pressed his hand to his breast.

"Take deep breaths of the pure air, Tom."

The sound of men's voices shouting came to them. A woman in one of the bungalows, up with an ailing child, had seen the red smoke issuing from the roof. She had roused her husband and he had run from door to door, knocking loudly and calling out,—"Clapperton's is on fire!"

The alarm spread to the farmhands and stablemen at Jalna, then to the house. Now there was life everywhere. Lights came on, the pale dawn appeared in the east, the sirens of the fire-reels could be heard. The bright red reels turned in at the gate. The firemen fixed their helmets more firmly. The hook and ladder were ready to go to work—the men with the fire-extinguishing chemicals were there.

Raikes, as soon as he was able, went to Eugene Clapperton and said,—"We could carry a lot of this valuable stuff out, sir, you and me." He spoke in his normal polite voice.

"Get to work on the silver in the dining-room. It's not too bad in there."

They went into the room together and swept the sideboard clear of silver. They put the dining-room chairs through the window. Grimy sweat poured down Eugene

Clapperton's face but he was oddly exhilarated. The sense of struggle with disaster, of overcoming material loss, gave him a feeling of power that he had not lately experienced.

Now the fire chief came and spoke to him.

"A bad blaze," he said genially. "Everything's as dry as tinder. Everyone out of the house?"

"Everyone."

"Fine. No need for the ladders. But I don't think we'll save the building."

"It looks like that."

The fire was spreading fast, yet still was confined to the back of the house. While Raikes and the men from the bungalows and the farm labourers from Jalna were dragging out furniture and rugs, the firemen produced a hose and soon a stream of water was drenching the living-room. As fire and water struggled together it was soon seen which was the stronger.

Althea came running to Gem. She had tied up the Great Dane in safety but now her face was wild.

"The tortoise!" she cried. "I forgot him. I'll never forgive myself. I must go to him."

Before Gem could stop her, she flew round the house towards a side door that opened on to a passage. From this passage led a short stairway to a landing and from the landing another stairway to the top floor. The fire was on the other side of the house.

It was physically impossible for Gem to run with comparable speed. Already her back felt weak and strained. She called to the men to stop Althea, but the shouting, the giving of orders, the rush of water, the crackling of fire, smothered her voice . . . But now she saw her husband trotting, with sagging knees, in the direction Althea had gone.

"Eugene!" she shrieked. "Bring back Althea—she's in there."

He looked over his shoulder at her, put forth his strength in an automaton-like spurt, and ran into the house. . . .

He had not, in fact, heard the words that Gem had so frantically called out to him. He thought she was imploring him to keep out of danger, and in the turmoil of his mind

he felt a thrill of happiness at her solicitude for him . . .
In the midst of the confusion he had suddenly remembered
a handsome silver tea service that had been presented to
him by his employees at the time of his first marriage. He
greatly valued this and it was kept in a locked cupboard
in that same short passage.

The smoke was thickening here and the heat was almost
unbearable. He fumbled for the key of the cupboard where
it hung on a nail at the back. He unlocked the cupboard and
threw open the door. A volume of smoke poured out. He
held his breath, lifted out the tray, on it set the handsome
teapot, sugar-bowl and cream-jug. He held the tray in
front of him and moved resolutely forward, embowered
in ruddy smoke, like some grotesque picture of a grim
butler. The opening of the cupboard door had let the fire
through. Now it raged to get out of the cupboard.

Eugene Clapperton forgot the little step in the passage,
he stumbled, he fell with a crash of silver.

Renny Whiteoak had just sprung out of his car and stood
a moment appalled by the scene in front of him. Then he
saw Gem Clapperton standing, helpless, wringing her
hands. He ran to her.

"My sister," she moaned. "She's in there . . . And
Eugene too . . . He went to save her!"

Barker and Raikes came running. Gem repeated wildly,
—"My sister—my husband—he went to save her."

"I saw him go in," said Barker. "And I said to myself—
that's risky."

The three men went to the open door from which a
black cloud of smoke shot with flame issued. It would
have been madness to venture inside.

Renny came to Gem and put his arm about her shoulders.
"Don't look," he said. "Don't look."

But she ran from him to where she saw Althea emerging
from the shrubbery. Althea wailed,—"I daren't go in.
It was too terrible. I had to let him die. I'll never forgive
myself." It was for the tortoise she wailed.

"Althea!" screamed Gem, in frantic joy. "You're safe."
She clasped her sister to her.

Firemen came running with the hose and turned the

stream into the doorway, but drought had made the pressure of water feeble. For a moment the fire was subdued, but only for a moment. Then the flames, like thirsty tongues, lapped up the water. Everyone now crowded outside the fatal doorway. Everyone knew that Eugene Clapperton was somewhere inside . . . but not living . . . no one could survive in that fiery trap.

Piers and his sons joined Renny. Piers said,—"They tell me Clapperton's dead in there. An awful end."

Renny flung up his arm in tragic salute. "A hero's end," he said. "Clapperton went in to save Althea Griffith."

"But she's over there. She's with her sister."

"He thought she was in the house. His wife told me."

"God! I wouldn't have believed he had it in him."

The women from the bungalows were about Gem, crying, condoling with her. Then someone shouted that the nearest bungalow was on fire, and they left her and ran screaming towards their homes. The roof of the garage too had caught fire. Raikes was pushing the smaller car along the drive to safety. Then, at risk of his life he brought out the Cadillac and had them both safe.

The firemen ran towards the bungalows with a second hose but there was nothing to attach it to. The women's husbands, the farm workers and stablemen from Jalna, fought this new fire with buckets filled with water from taps.

Now the large house was fireswept from end to end. There was no saving it. What furniture had been saved stood forlornly on the trampled lawn. A group of stalwart old pines that grew just beyond the lawn, a young one rising tall in their midst, now claimed the attention of the fire. A single bright spark sped towards the nearest. It alighted on the full plumy needles. There was no delay, no hesitation. That pine was a bouquet of fire. All its needles shone red-hot against the sky. A red spark sped to the next pine.

"The trees," shouted Piers to the firemen. "Bring that thingamabob! That extinguisher!"

They came, their faces red beneath their red helmets.

Another pine was gone. Then another and another. The
firemen drenched them with the chemical. Some trees
stood, one side turned red from the fire, the other still
green. The young pine remained untouched. It shone
green in the light of the rising sun.

Renny's obsession was that he must get Eugene Clapperton's body out of that furnace. Twice he was prevented
by Piers and the firemen from entering the passage. Now
he stood waiting with impatience for the unrestrained
moment.

Piers' son Philip stayed close to him, held by the grue-
some thought of the body in there. The healthy boy had
been here, there, everywhere, exhilarated by the spectacle.
But now that the flames were dying down, that the house
was a ruin, he remained close to this last excitement,
peering into the smoking passage.

"When do you think you dare go in, Uncle Renny?"

"Now—in a minute. Everything is drenched with
water. It's safe enough."

"They say the roof's going to cave in."

"I want to get him out first."

"Can I come with you?"

"No. Stay where you are."

He stepped in on the wet charred floor. The bitter air
cut his nostrils, his eyeballs. He did not know how far
into the house Eugene Clapperton had ventured. Now,
after only half-a-dozen paces he stumbled over his body.
He drew back in astonishment. There he was, so near to
safety, yet overtaken! Renny bent down, took hold of the
blackened body and, walking backward, dragged it into
the morning light. He had one look—young Philip had
one look. The boy turned green.

"Why——" he stammered, "I saw him yesterday."

Renny took off his jacket and laid it over the blackened,
hairless head, the blackened naked shoulders. Piers saw
what he had done and hastened to his side, followed by
the firemen. There was nothing more for them to do.

"You've got him out," exclaimed Piers. "You shouldn't
have gone in there."

"It was nothing. He was in the passage, near the door."

"The smoke overcame him," said the fire chief. "Too bad. Too bad."

Renny turned to the men with a dramatic gesture. "Take off your helmets," he said. "This is the body of a hero. He gave his life trying to save a life."

Awkwardly the men pulled off their helmets and bent their heads. The ruddy sunrise blazed on the desolate scene, turned the smoke that rose from the roof to gold.

Now Noah Binns, his face sagging in disappointment, came panting towards the group. "Lands sakes," he mourned, "I wouldn't'a missed that blaze fer a year of my life! Oh, what a sight! Oh, what a conflaggeration! That big house nothing but a roon. What's that there on the ground? *Him*, hey? *Him* that owned it all! Didn't I foretell this was to be a roastin' *blazin'* summer? Folks *laughed* at me. Now they know." He bent and lifted a corner of the jacket. "Here's a sight!" He looked without flinching. "Here's a roon! Here's what boastful Man can come to in an hour! Was anybody else burned?"

They shook their heads.

"Well, well, nobody else, eh? Danged if ever I seen a conceiteder man. *He* knew it *all!* and now—danged if he don't know it all."

XIX

WHAT CAME AFTER

ALAYNE opened the door to Renny when, an hour later, he returned to Jalna. She wore a dressing-gown and her face was tense with excitement. She put out her hands and then drew back. "What a state you're in!" she exclaimed. "Why, you reek of smoke."

"Yes . . . Do the uncles know?"

"They are still sleeping. They haven't rung for their breakfast."

"God, how am I to tell them?"

"Is the house—burned down?"

He led the way into the library and closed the door behind them.

"Yes. Just before I left the roof fell in."

"Oh, Renny . . . Where are the family?"

"Clapperton himself is dead."

She turned white. He put out his hands to steady her, then withdrew them. "I mustn't touch you," he said.

"Eugene Clapperton is dead," she breathed. "How—what happened?"

"This is the way he died," answered Renny. "His wife told him that her sister had gone back into the house. It was full of smoke then and the rear part burning. He went in to rescue Althea and—the smoke overcame him. I brought out his body myself."

"And Althea?"

"Safe and sound. She'd never gone back. So he gave his life for nothing, you might say. But he died a hero."

"How tragic!"

"I was never so mistaken in anyone, Alayne. You can't know what's in people till they are put to the test."

"Poor man! . . . Where is his wife?"

A smile flickered across Renny's face that was made ugly by a mingling of soot and sweat. He said,—"She and Althea are in the newest bungalow—the one I ripped the shingles off. Lord, was that only yesterday? Alayne— the bungalows caught fire. Three of them are burned. There's only the one where the Barkers live and the new one left. I begged the girls to come here but I couldn't persuade them."

She tried to conceal her relief. "And they are in a place without furniture?"

"Oh, they've plenty of furniture. Raikes and Barker are carrying in some of what was saved. Enough to go on with."

"Is Mrs. Clapperton terribly upset?"

"Alayne, I've never felt so sorry for a man. There he lies—dead. And his wife—as soon as she knew her sister was safe—showed no more grief."

Alayne gave a little smile. "Everyone knows she didn't love him."

Renny broke out,—"I hated him—yes, *hated*! But now—I revere him, as a very brave man—a noble fellow. Alayne—don't you think we should have his funeral from here?"

"No," she cried. "I refuse."

"Why?"

"It would be horrible. Everyone knows how we felt about him."

"All the greater reason."

"Where is his body?"

"At the undertaker's."

"Then let the funeral be from the undertaker's. I cannot and will not endure to have him brought here."

Renny saw that he must capitulate. "Very well," he said reluctantly.

They were interrupted by Archer's throwing open the door. He stood facing them, his white forehead glistening, his expression one of accusation.

"Why didn't anybody call me?" he demanded. "Why wasn't I there?"

"It was no place for a child," answered Alayne.

"I'm going straight over now."

"*No*, Archer."

He clasped his arms about his middle and bent double in an agony of frustration. "Oh, oh, I can't bear it," he moaned. "Oh, I never do *anything* I want to."

"I'll take you with me when I go back," said Renny.

"When will you go?" asked Alayne. "Is it safe for Archer, even with you?"

"There's no danger," he returned, absent-mindedly. "I must go now and break the news to the uncles."

"I've done that," said Archer.

His parents stared at him in consternation.

"You!" cried Alayne. "Oh, that was very wrong."

"The shock might have been the end of them," said Renny. "If I had the time I'd give you a hiding you'd never forget. How did they take it?"

Archer, with a benign air, answered,—"Oh, they took it very well. I think they were glad it was me told them."

"I must go straight up to them," said Renny.

"Can I come?" asked Archer.

Alayne interposed her body between that of her husband and her son. She said to Renny,—"Hadn't you better have a bath first?"

"Oh, they'll like to see him this way," said Archer.

Renny went up the stairs.

As he ascended, a deep thankfulness rose through all his being that Jalna was safe. In the early morning sunshine the old house stood serene, all its rooms knowing him, its timbers, as it were, his bones. His first breath he had drawn under that roof. There he would draw his last. The door of Ernest's bedroom stood open, disclosing Ernest sitting up in bed and Nicholas in the armchair at his side. Both looked dishevelled, distressed, yet somehow drawn from the acquiescence of very old age by the disastrous news.

Ernest greeted Renny with,—"I'm waiting for a cup of hot tea. I think it will brace me. What a terrible thing this is!"

Renny said,—"It's a shame you had the news told you by that boy."

Nicholas gave a grim laugh. "Well, we had to have it and Archer gave us the dose quickly. He just opened my door and said,—'Clapperton's house is on fire. Clapperton's dead.'"

"He did the very same for me," added Ernest. "He opened my door and said the same words. Oh, what a shock!"

"Let me get you some brandy."

"No, thank you. I've sent for tea."

"Uncle Nick?"

"I've had some."

Ernest could not control his voice. It shook painfully as he said,—"You must tell us all about it, Renny. Wragge was quite incoherent when he answered the bell . . . Why, your hands, they're black . . ."

"What made them black?" asked Nicholas, in a tone of foreboding, as though he guessed without asking.

Renny looked at his hands, then put them behind his back. He said,—"I remarked of Eugene Clapperton yesterday that I didn't believe he'd ever known a generous impulse—and that he was a coward. Now I take back those words, with all the power that's in me. He died a hero's death. He lost his life in an attempt to save Althea Griffith."

"Is she dead too?" quavered both the old men.

"No, no, she had not gone into the house, as he thought she had . . . Did you hear me say that I take back all I've said against him?"

"Yes, dear boy," agreed Ernest. "You are quite right. It was a noble act he did and I too retract all I've ever said—or thought—against him."

Nicholas drew the end of his grey moustache between his teeth and gnawed it. "Never liked him," he growled. "Can't think of him as a hero. Shan't try."

XX

VARIOUS SCENES

A SHARP thunderstorm blew in from the lake that day, and heavy, though brief, rain. It left only a furtive smouldering in the more remote parts of the burned house, beneath the caved-in roof. All the rest was wet charred beams and bricks and broken glass. The scorched trees showed all the redder for being wet. The living trees, and more especially the young pine, in the midst of its dead companions, all the greener. Men had brought tarpaulins and spread them over what furniture had been salvaged, though some of it had been carried to the newest bungalow where the two sisters had taken refuge.

No one had worked so hard as Raikes. From the moment when Gem's voice had woken him he had laboured, doing the work of two. Smudged, blackened, dripping with sweat, then dripping with rain, he had delved into the ruins rescuing all he could. He had the two cars safe and locked against theft. He had collected basketfuls of blackened cutlery and china and put them away to be cleaned. He had heaved beams aside to get at what was pinned beneath.

"Lands sakes," said Mrs. Barker, as he sat at the early evening meal with her and her husband, "you sure look tired out. You ought to take a little rest."

Through a mouthful of fried potatoes Raikes replied,— "There'll be no rest for me till all the mess is cleared away." He had made no mention to anyone that he had been discharged.

"It's lucky for them two girls that they have you," said Barker. "They're an awful helpless pair. I wonder what they'll do."

"No need for them to worry," said his wife. "Think of the money they've got."

"Wait till you hear what the will says. Wills can be tricky things."

"You'll see he's left his wife every penny. He was crazy about her, wasn't he, Tom?"

"Well," said Raikes, "I wouldn't say that."

"How *did* they get on?"

"Pretty snappy at times."

"She looks like she's a temper," Barker put in.

"She's a swate girl."

"And you're the one that knows it, hey?" laughed Mrs. Barker.

"Come, now," admonished Raikes, "the man's not cold yet."

Mrs. Barker giggled unfeelingly.

"What's funny?" asked her husband.

"Oh, I was just thinking."

The men laid down their knives and forks to stare at her.

"Don't look at me like that," she gasped, now laughing hysterically.

"Out with it," said Raikes. "We can bear it."

"Oh, I was just thinking what you said about *him* not bein' *cold* yet! He was pretty *hot*, wasn't he?"

The men looked at each other.

"Women ain't got no heart," said Barker.

Now she was indignant. "It was us women that did the crying, wasn't it?"

"You ladies are temperamental," Raikes said, politely. "That's what makes you so lovable."

Barker cleaned his plate with a piece of bread, then put it solemnly into his mouth. "Mr. Clapperton," he said, "was a hero."

"He was that," agreed Raikes, with equal solemnity.

"I'm not a Catholic," continued Barker, "but I'm not ashamed to say—God rest his soul."

"Yes, indeed," said Raikes. "May his soul rest in peace."

Barker rose. "I'd like," he said, "for us to drink a

glass in his honour." He went to the cupboard and returned with a half-bottle of whiskey.

They filled their tumblers with whiskey and water.

"May we all," said Barker, "live as good and die as noble."

"I want to join in that," said Mrs. Barker. She picked up Raikes' glass and took a sip from it. She threw a provocative glance at the Irishman which he appeared not to notice.

"We're lucky," said Barker, "that our bungalow was saved. I thought it would burn for sure. And the new one. It's lucky it was there for the girls to move into."

"Now Mrs. Clapperton'll be on to everything you do," said his wife.

"I should worry," he replied. "She'll be too busy to notice me. It's Tom that'll have to be careful."

Raikes gave a smile that was both mischievous and sheepish. He emptied his glass.

"I must be getting along," he said.

"You haven't had your pie," she said.

"I couldn't. I'd such a late lunch."

He went out and his eyes swept the scene of devastation. The sullen ruin of the house and its outbuildings, the separate remains of the three bungalows, the scorched trees, the trampled vegetable garden, his pride, all stared him in the face, unrecognizable and as though reproachful. The origin of the fire was a mystery, except to Gem and Althea who had their suspicions, but Gem was ready to say, if there were an inquiry, that she herself had smoked a cigarette late that night in the kitchen. She was ready to say anything to protect Raikes.

He now came to the door of the new bungalow and quietly tapped. The Great Dane sent forth a tremendous barking. Raikes could hear him panting against the door. "Now, now, Toby," he soothed. "Quit that barkin'. It's me, Toby." The dog whined in recognition. The door opened and Gem's weary figure was revealed, her hair unbrushed, her eyes heavy. They met his only for a moment. A shyness rose between them.

"What can I do to help now?" he asked.

"Nothing. We're getting on all right. We're resting. They sent a hamper of food from Jalna."

"I know. After a bit I'll go out in the car and do a bit of shopping for you. 'Tis lucky I saved the two cars, isn't it?"

She gave a faint smile. Their eyes met, then they looked away again. After a moment she said,—"Mr. Clapperton's cousin, the one who married my youngest sister, is coming, and my sister too."

"And will he—see to the funeral—and all that?"

"Yes . . . Mr. Clapperton owned a plot in a large cemetery in the city. He'll be buried there, beside his first wife."

"I see." Raikes spoke with great solemnity. Then he added, on the same note,—"Well, 'twas a quick end. He didn't suffer much."

She gave a shudder, in spite of the heat.

"We all have to die," he said. "Some one way. Some another."

"Yes." A strange light of excitement swept the weariness from her face. The musical tone of her voice came out strongly. "I want to live," she said, "to be very old. I haven't *lived* yet."

A smile came into his eyes, rippled across his face, not touching his lips which remained serious. "Now you've the chance to live," he said. "You're free."

"Don't." . . . Yet she did not turn away.

The families from the three burned bungalows had been disposed of. Two families had gone to relations. The third had been given shelter at the Rectory. The noise of the radios, the cries of children had ceased. The poultry which Raikes had driven from the burning poultry-house were, with much confusion, with flying up and falling off and flying up again, finding perches among the trees. The parked cars of those who had come to see the ruin of one of the landmarks of the district were moving away.

But another car had just arrived and from it alighted Ernest and Renny, Ernest leaning heavily on his nephew's arm. He had said he could not rest till he had visited the scene of the fire. It was on his nerves, he said. Nothing

of reality, he said, could be half so dreadful as what he
pictured. Nicholas, on the other hand, wanted to remember
Vaughanlands as it was. "I'll take that remembrance of
it," he said, "to my grave. I'm too old to see familiar
things shattered. I've seen enough changes, and most
of them horrid."

Now Ernest stopped stock still on the drive, almost
overcome by the spectacle of the roofless walls, the gaping
apertures where windows had been, the charred front door
hanging on its hinges. At first he could not speak. He
just stood and stared. Then a sob broke from him and
tears ran down his cheeks.

"I told you not to come." Renny's voice was harsh
with concern. "I should not have let you come."

With a great effort Ernest controlled himself. He took
out his pocket-handkerchief, blew his nose and wiped
his eyes.

"It's all right," he said. "I shan't give way again. But—
of all sights I've ever seen—this is the most desolate."

"It is indeed," Renny agreed grimly.

Ernest moved close to the ruin. His light-blue eyes
widened to take in every detail of the destruction. He
pointed with his stick. "In that room to the left, my
parents slept while Jalna was being built. I remember
hearing my father tell how he would put his head out of the
window to smoke his last cigar because Mrs. Vaughan could
not bear smoking in the house. But what kind people they
were! True gentlefolk. Very different from that Mr.
Clapperton—even though he had so heroic an end, poor
man. And there, in the room on the right, our Eden died.
Bless me, there's little left standing on that side of the
house. Why—there on the poor wrecked door is the brass
knocker they brought with them from England. It's a
lion's head with the mouth open roaring. Bless me, it's no
wonder he roars."

Right round the house Ernest insisted on going, through
rubble, over fallen masonry, and all the way he recon-
structed the house, lifted it up again out of the ruins, filled
it with the people who had been dear to him. Near the
back door they came on an oil painting in an ornate gilt

I*

frame, leaning in drunken fashion against a scorched tree.

"It's a shipwreck," exclaimed Ernest. "God bless me, they shouldn't have left it out in the weather. Why, it was Eugene Clapperton's favourite picture. Really, Renny, I think we should put it in safety somewhere."

"I'll see to it," said Renny.

Ernest took out his handkerchief and mopped his brow. "What heat!" he said. "What a day! When I took my rest this afternoon I could not sleep. I tossed about the bed till I could endure it no more and got up. I shall sleep tonight, I can tell you. I'll go to bed as soon as we reach home."

"You're too tired, Uncle Ernest."

"No. Not too tired. Just—a little wrought up. No matter how long one lives, there are always unexpected things—things that can stir one to the depths—I suppose that's what makes life so interesting. You know, Renny, old age has not made me self-centred . . . I thank God for that." He paused, gathered himself together and added,—"Renny, I was conceived under that roof . . . of beautiful young parents . . . young." He turned away weeping.

XXI

ERNEST SLEEPS

THAT NIGHT there was another electric storm, this one accompanied by a wild wind. At Jalna the shutters rattled and banged. At Vaughanlands ashes were whipped into glowing red eyes. The air was full of disorder and fresh green leaves were blown from the trees and whirled like messages between the two houses.

Renny was roused by the gale. The air that blew across him was suddenly cold. He drew it into his lungs, breathing deeply. The heat wave was over, he thought. Then he remembered Ernest's susceptibility to draughts. He must go and close his windows. As he went along the passage the events of the day before crowded in on him. The clock struck four. That had been the hour when the fire had started the night before.

He met Alayne in her nightdress. He could see her by the pale moonlight.

"Why are you up?" he asked.

"I've been to Archer's room. He was almost blown out of the bed, and not a stitch on him. Where are you going?"

"To shut Uncle Ernest's windows."

"Oh." She stood in the passage waiting while he went into the bedroom. She heard the windows gently closed. Then there was silence. Then the light was turned on. Still silence. The old man had not woken. He had been very tired.

Now Renny came from the room, all the light at his back. He put his hand across his eyes, then drew it down over his face and gripped his mouth.

"What has happened?" she gasped.

"He is dead," came through the gripping hand that all but smothered the words.

"Oh, no—surely not!"

"Sh—you'll wake Uncle Nick. Oh, Alayne . . ."

"You're mistaken," she said, though she knew he was not. "He's just sleeping heavily."

"Do I know a dead man when I see one? Come and look."

He drew her into the room.

It was neat as was always Ernest's room, his clothes carefully folded or hung up, the bed smooth. Ernest himself lay on his side, one arm out on the sheet, the other curved, its palm cradling his cheek, the light from the bedside lamp full on his face.

"Am I mistaken?" Renny asked, his voice coming hoarsely from his throat.

"No . . . How serene he looks!"

"I've felt his pulse—his heart . . . Oh, Alayne, I never should have taken him to see that sight. It was terrible to him . . . He was quite broken up."

She spoke calmly. "It's been the strain and excitement of yesterday. It never stopped. He was very wrought up. I could see that. But—he's gone so peacefully."

Renny laid his hand on Ernest's shoulder, as though he comforted him in his aloneness. "I can't believe it," he said. "I've been coming into this room to talk with him— as long as I can remember and—in all that time—I never had a harsh word from him."

"And to me he was always so sweet." Her calm deserted her and she began to cry. "To think this would happen . . . poor Uncle Ernest . . . poor Uncle Nicholas."

"You're cold," he said. "You must go back to bed."

"No, no—I can't. Look—it's daylight. I'll go and dress . . . However can you tell Uncle Nicholas?"

"It will kill him . . . his only brother . . . seldom in all their lives were they separated."

She wiped her eyes on the sleeve of his pyjamas. She said,—"It won't kill him. Only the other day he said to me that they must soon be separated and that that separation must be faced . . . If you like, I'll tell him."

"Will you? Do you think we should have the doctor here?"

"Yes . . . I'm getting so chilled. What a change!"

"Go and dress, Alayne. I want to be alone with him for a bit." He touched Ernest's face. "It must have happened just a little while ago . . . I can't believe it . . . no, I can't believe it."

After a while he followed her to her room. She was nearly dressed. The house was deeply silent but the lively singing of birds came through the open windows. "You say you are cold," he remarked, "yet you leave your windows open."

"I wanted the air."

He noticed that she had put on a black and white cotton dress with a narrow red belt. "Haven't you a black belt?" he asked.

"Oh, Renny—as though it mattered!"

"It matters to me."

She took off the belt and found a black one.

"Is that better?" she asked, with a faint smile.

"Yes . . . I have telephoned Piers."

"At this hour!"

"I have sent a cable to Finch." She knew it comforted him to do these things.

"They must come home," he said.

"*They? Who?*"

"Finch and Adeline."

She turned on him aghast, even angry.

"Renny—how could you?"

"They must be here."

"It is *so* unnecessary. To cross the ocean—in the middle of a holiday—at a moment's notice—for a great-uncle's funeral! It's madness. Besides, they could not reach Jalna in time for the funeral."

"I told them to fly."

She sat down on the side of her bed, feeling weak from shock and nervous exasperation.

"Uncle Ernest is no ordinary great-uncle," he added. "He's lived at Jalna as long as they can remember."

"Renny, he would not ask it of them, if he were here."

"He is here—till he's taken to the churchyard."

She saw that Renny was not to be moved. The line between nostril and lip was sharply cut. He would have his own way. He said:

"I shall go down to the kitchen and tell the Wragges. Uncle Nicholas must have his breakfast before you break the news to him."

Alayne drew down his head and kissed him between the brows. "I know how badly you feel about this," she said.

"I do indeed."

"But it was bound to happen soon."

He turned away and went to the basement. He knocked on the Wragges' bedroom door. The snoring ceased and the little grey man appeared. His thin hair stood on end. His sharp-featured face was an interrogation mark.

"It's bad news," Renny said. "My uncle has died in the night."

Rags opened and shut his mouth without uttering a sound.

His wife called from the bed,—"Which uncle, sir?"

"My Uncle Ernest."

She gave a groan, clutched the sheet and rolled over.

Rags got out, through shaking jaws,—"This will be 'ard on Mr. Nicholas, sir. They was that attached to one another, you can't think of them separated."

"I'm going to get you a drink, Rags," said Renny.

"Thank you, sir. My nerves ain't wot they used to be."

He had got into his clothes when Renny came back to him, with whisky in a glass. "Bring a pot of tea for me and coffee for Mrs. Whiteoak to the dining-room," he said. "When Mr. Nicholas rings take him his breakfast as though nothing had happened."

"I'll try to look natural, sir, but it'll be 'ard."

Renny went out through the kitchen door, as he heard Piers' car on the drive. Piers was alighting from it. He came towards Renny saying:

"Just one thing on top of another, eh?"

"Yes. It's hard to believe on a morning like this." His eyes swept the blueness above, the rain-freshened greenness of the earth.

"Has Uncle Nick been told?"

"No. Alayne has promised to do that."

Archer stuck his head out of his high-up bedroom window. He called out:

"Hullo! Why are you up so early?"

"Don't make a noise. When you're dressed, come straight to me."

"Has something happened?"

"Yes."

"I'll be right down," he cried, as though his presence would smooth all difficulties.

When he was told the news his first remark was,—"I'd better break it to Uncle Nicholas."

"Go near his room," said Renny, "and I'll skin you alive."

"Then may I see Uncle Ernest? I didn't see Mr. Clapperton. Philip did and he said——"

Renny took him by the collar. "You will not," he said, "go up those stairs without my leave."

Alayne joined them, walking swiftly across the grass. Her son ran to meet her. His arms tightly clasped about her waist, he raised his eyes to hers with an expression of exaggerated sympathy.

"I want to help," he pleaded.

She laid her hand on his forehead. "Nothing will help us so much as——" She hesitated, anxious not to hurt his feelings.

"Making yourself scarce," supplied Piers.

"Yes," agreed Renny. "Go to Mrs. Wragge and ask her to give you breakfast. We want ours in peace."

Reluctantly Archer moved away. He went beneath Ernest's window and gazed up at it, as though expecting some ghostly apparition there.

Seated at the breakfast table, the three discussed what must be done. An ironic smile flickered across Piers' face when Renny told him that he had sent for Finch and Adeline. Piers said:

"From what I'm told, they've just arrived in London."

"That can't be helped." Renny turned sombre dark eyes on him. "They must be here for the funeral."

"A good thing," said Piers, "it's turned so cool."

Renny sat, elbow on table, the tips of his fingers pressed to his forehead. There was silence. Alayne could see Archer peering in at them through the window. How bad for him all this excitement was!

"To think," exclaimed Renny, "that we shall never again see Uncle Ernest sitting in his place at this table!" He made a tragic gesture towards Ernest's chair.

"It's hard to believe," said Piers. "But he had a good life."

"He wanted to live to be a hundred like Gran. He'd have done it too, if it hadn't been for the fire. Now the shock of his death will be the end of Uncle Nick."

"You must not look on the black side of things," said Alayne. "Uncle Nicholas will be brave."

"Today," put in Piers, "is the day of Eugene Clapperton's funeral."

Renny sprang up. "My God, I'd forgotten," he exclaimed. "That brave man. Why, I have a thousand things to see to." He walked in a circle round the room.

Archer came into the room from the hall. He held in his hand a rather faded white geranium blossom which he presented to Alayne. "I thought this would cheer you up," he said. "It was one of Uncle Ernest's favourite flowers."

Nicholas rang for his breakfast early that morning, for he was conscious of disturbance in the house. An over-solicitous Rags brought it to him, his hands shaking as he placed the tray. . . .

"Has my brother rung yet?" asked Nicholas.

"No, sir, 'e 'asn't rung," quavered Rags.

"Good. He's having a long sleep and he needs it."

"Yes, sir."

"Let me know when he rings."

"I will, sir." His nerves unable to bear any more, Rags hastened out.

XXII

OFF TO LONDON

FOR A MONTH Finch and Adeline drifted in desultory fashion about Ireland. If, when they went to a place for a day, they liked it, a week might well pass before they moved on. They were congenial companions. The same sort of things elated or moved them to mirth. Both disliked crowds. Finch had not known such relaxation in years. He threw aside all plans for his future and gave himself up to the pleasure of living, as he thought Adeline did, in the moment. He could not believe that behind her happy youthful face there was a mind linked by thoughts of Fitzturgis to longing and sometimes almost despair. He asked her nothing and she kept these thoughts to herself. When Finch had been her age no effort of will had been strong enough to keep his emotions from showing in his sensitive face, but Adeline's firmly modelled features, her clear-cut lips and brows, did her will and masked her when she chose.

The truth was that Fitzturgis was seldom out of her thoughts. When she was at her happiest, she pictured him standing beside her making her pleasure entire. When she felt helpless and cut off from him for ever, as she sometimes did, she drew on her strength and showed a front no less than composed. Never a mail but she looked for a letter from him. None came. When at last they turned southward she burned to be at Glengorman again with the chance of seeing him.

Maurice greeted her with affection but still with distrust. He hoped with all his heart that she had got over her infatuation, as he called it. He took the first opportunity of finding himself alone with Finch to ask:

"Is Adeline normal again, do you think?"

"That's a funny way of putting it," laughed Finch.

"It's just what I mean."

"Is anyone ever normal?"

"Adeline certainly was normal till she met that fellow."
Suddenly Finch felt defensive for Adeline. "Remember,"
he said, "how much we both liked him at the first."

"Not for long. There's something wrong in him. I feel
that. I'm not the only one. Pat feels it too."

"Perhaps because you and Pat are both in love with
Adeline."

Maurice stared. "Not Pat. He's as heart-whole as a
gannet."

"I daresay *they* are lovers in their season."

"Pat has only one idea in his head at the moment—his
new sailing-boat—and he's often said to me his mother is
sweetheart enough for him."

"How nice!" exclaimed Finch enviously. Always he had
hungered for the love and companionship of a mother.

Maurice went on,—"People who know the Fitzturgis
family say there's a taint in them. The grandfather died
half mad. At the last he tried to give away all his posses-
sions. His son drank himself to death after losing everything he'd inherited. Sylvia, Mait's sister, is unbalanced."

"I saw nothing strange in her," said Finch.

"They say she's been found wandering on the roads
alone in the middle of the night."

"They say—they say! Don't believe everything you
hear, Maurice."

Maurice stared. "Then you are in sympathy with
Adeline's feeling for Mait?"

"How you twist things, Mooey! You're unreasonable.
But I don't think we need worry about Adeline. All the
while we've been away together she's appeared a happy
girl."

"I'm glad to hear that," said Maurice moodily.

Finch was sorry for the youth. The return to Ireland was
so different from what he had looked forward to. Yet he
was irritated by Maurice for continuing to wear the mien
of disappointed lover. He was sure that was not the way

to attract Adeline. She on her part had come back to Glen-gorman with the intention of playing the charming cousin to her young host, of taking up their old relationship once more. But it was impossible. What right had Mooey to look at her as he did, to criticize her silently for her be-haviour, as though he held a microscope to her every act. She wanted to take long walks alone, when she might dwell with clinging thoughts on her recollections of Fitz-turgis. She had known him so short a while that sometimes a fear would come to her that his image would grow less clear. At other times she felt that his face was clearer to her than the face of anyone she knew, except her father's.

Each time the clump of the postman's boots was heard on the drive she ran without shame to the door and without shame she let the blankness come into her face when the letter was only from Roma. One morning there was a letter for her, addressed in a masculine hand and having an Irish stamp. Maurice appeared in the hall at the same moment. The postman had laid the letters on a small table by the door. Maurice was there first and picked them up— almost snatched them up.

"That's for me," she cried, reaching to take her letter from him.

He held it out of reach, but only for a moment; she was almost as tall as he.

"Give it to me," she demanded.

"What urgency!" he exclaimed, in what she called his superior voice.

She caught his wrist. They struggled together, their faces flushed with the anger they could not conceal. The letter was torn in half.

"Beast!" she hissed between her clenched teeth.

"Spitfire!" he returned, putting his half of the letter into her hand.

As she ran up the stairs with it he called after her,— "Sorry. I didn't know you'd take a little teasing that way."

She did not answer. In her room she stood motionless a moment, the mutilated letter pressed to her breast, her breath coming hard. Then she took the two halves from the torn envelope and looked at the first words. She read,—

"Dear Miss Whiteoak,

"I wonder if you remember me. I am the boy from
Chicago you danced with on the boat. I have never forgotten you and I'd certainly love to meet——"

She crushed the letter in her hand.

She walked up and down the room still crushing it
between her two hands. She went to the window and laid
her forehead against the cool pane. The garden lay below
in the high bright tones of summer. Pigeons were perching
on the damp stone walls. They made her think of home.
For an instant the thought of home rose before her. But
the day was only breaking there, the pigeons only fluttering down from their high night perches. She tried to
think of home but the image was broken by the feel of the
letter in her hand, by her disappointment that lay like a
stone on her heart. Why had he not written to her? Sent
no message?

Her shame that she had so struggled for a worthless
letter resolved itself into anger at Maurice. If he had not
shown himself so unfriendly to Maitland, Maitland would
have come to see her. All her being cried out for some
reassurance from him—that, or a complete cutting away.
She could bear the uncertainty no more.

She saw Finch and Maurice mounting the steep stone
steps beyond the garden, the two Labradors bounding ahead
of them. She would run downstairs now and telephone to
Mait. Why had she not thought of doing that before? She
would hear his voice and ask him straight if he loved her.

Down the stairs she ran and along the passage to where
the telephone was. She found his name, the number of
his telephone in the book. It was so easy. She pictured
the tiny room where his telephone was, the unshaded
bulb, the glossy calendar advertising whiskey on the wall.
She asked for the number and after a little a voice came
on the wire. It was a woman's voice with a thick brogue.
Adeline could not understand what she said.

"Could I speak to Mr. Fitzturgis?" she repeated.

"Misthress Fitzturgis," came thickly over the wire, and
more as though in a foreign language.

"It's *Mister* Fitzturgis I want," she said, with desperate distinctness.

"Och, the masther," said the voice. Then silence.

At last she heard steps. His voice, with a shock of reality, as though it were the only reality in the world, spoke to her.

"Oh, Mait, is it you?" she exclaimed, in a low voice, tremulous with feeling.

"Adeline!"

"Yes. I had to speak to you."

"Where are you?"

"At Glengorman. Soon I shall be going to England."

"Oh."

"Don't you care?"

"You know what I feel."

"Yet you've never written—not one line. You didn't even answer my letter."

"You know why."

"And we're never to meet again?"

"Oh, Adeline—you make it hard for me."

"But I *want* to see you. Is that clear?"

"I'll come."

"When? Let it be soon."

"Today. I'll be there at three. Where can we meet? No—it's not to be secret. I'll come straight to the house."

"Oh, Maitland—how shall I live till then?"

She gave a laugh of happy anticipation, and it was echoed briefly by him, as though he too would be happy but dared not let himself.

She chose one of her prettiest dresses for lunch that day. Finch surveyed her with a half-humorous admiration. He touched the ruffled elbow sleeve, ran his fingers along the delicately rounded arm, saying:

"I hope this dressing-up is for me."

Taken aback, she found nothing to say.

"Who for, then?" he asked.

"Do I looked so dressed-up?" she hedged.

"She's expecting Mr. Fitzturgis," put in Maurice.

She turned her eyes full on him. "What if I am?"

Neither Maurice nor Finch found anything but the

defiance of words in this. Neither for a moment believed that Fitzturgis would be so openly prepared for, were he indeed expected. Under the luminous darkness of her gaze Maurice's heart melted towards her. He smiled almost tenderly.

"You look sweet, Adeline," he said.

Her friendliness always ready, she smiled and leant towards him. "Thanks, Mooey."

Finch said,—"You should have seen how people stared at us in the hotels. They thought we were on our honeymoon, and what an ill-assorted couple! Whatever did she see in that old codger, they asked each other."

"Oh, it was fun," cried Adeline, thankful to have the talk turned into a different channel. "But people didn't think as Uncle Finch says. They thought, whatever did that distinguished-looking man see in that empty-headed girl? She'll lead him a dance."

"And so you would," said Maurice.

The meal proceeded amiably. Not long before three o'clock the two men set out to inspect a cottage that had been newly thatched. Adeline was left alone.

She paced the lime-shaded drive between gate and house. She thought of her situation as romantic. Who wouldn't? A beautiful young woman—for, when alone, she acknowledged herself as beautiful—waiting in a mossy tunnel, with fuchsias and brier roses all about, for her lover. She wished the two handsome dogs were with her to complete the picture but they had followed the men. She tried not to look at her wrist-watch oftener than every five minutes. She would bend and hold communion with some small flower whose name she did not know, while all the time her ears were strained for the sound of his car. There were so few cars, his would be the one.

It was half-past three when she heard it and her whole being froze to attention. If he did not come she would lie down here, in the cool shade, and die. Yes, die, and they would find her body and be sorry. She pictured herself stretched out on the earth, the little nameless flower in her hand. The dogs would discover her and run whimpering to tell the news.

The car had turned into the drive. It had stopped. Fitzturgis was out and coming towards her. He looked pale
and intent. She noticed the line of his shoulder and the
easy movement of his walk.

She could not speak but went to him holding out both
hands. He took them and she looked into his eyes. They
were so close to her, they became two worlds, mysterious,
that she could not look into without fear. What was their
colour? The colour of the sea on a cloudy day. "Yes,"
she thought, "if I drew him to me, so close that our fore-
heads touched, still would his eyes be strange to me."

"Am I late?" he asked. "A fellow stopped me on the
road and talked to me. I couldn't get away."

Adeline thought,—"If I were going to you, a whole
army would not stop me."

"I really couldn't," he reiterated. "You don't know
what that fellow is. He started some rigmarole about a will
he's contesting and it was impossible to stop him. I started
out in time, I——"

"Oh, Mait," she interrupted, "you're here. That's all
that matters."

He laughed, out of sheer joy of looking at her, hearing
her voice. "What shall we do?" he asked, as though they
had a long while ahead of them and a choice of places to
go.

"Uncle Finch and Maurice are out. We could sit on the
bank here and talk."

"They'll be back soon?"

"Oh, yes. But they needn't see us."

He opened his eyes wide and looked at her as though in
defiance. "I refuse to have them saying," he spoke in
heat, "that I have met you in secret. I refuse to be the sort
of fellow that every decent man would like to kick on
sight."

"What do you want to do?" she broke out. "Go and
sit in two straight-backed chairs in the hall, with our eyes
fixed on the front door, waiting for them to come
back?"

"Oh, my darling—you will not put yourself in my
place," he said. "You're too young."

"I've grown a lot older in these last weeks," she returned. "I'm no longer a carefree girl—if that's what you're thinking."

"I curse myself," he said, "for every moment of unhappiness I've given you."

"I had to grow up."

They sat down on the bank and he began,—"Am I the first man you've——"

She interrupted,—"I've told you already. The first and the last—for ever."

He looked at her in wonder. "What am I to deserve this?" he asked, taking her, as he spoke, into his arms. Through her thin dress she felt the pounding of his heart. She put both arms about his neck.

"You're just the one man for me," she answered.

"I daren't let myself kiss you." He hid his face against her hair. "If I kiss you I'm lost."

"Lost—to what?" she breathed.

"To you. It's not to be, my darling. You're to go back to your father, free of any promise. You may tell him, if you choose, that you met an Irishman you rather like and, when you come back to visit Maurice, if I am here and things are different with me . . ."

She interrupted,—"Do you know what I call you?"

"No."

"The half-hearted lover."

"*Half-hearted?*"

"Kiss me then. Just one little kiss, Mait, and I shan't feel so lonely."

He put his hand beneath her chin, raised her face to his, and their lips met and the wild leaping of their pulses met and the yearning of their two beings urged them on. Incoherent phrases were spoken, as though they were learning a new language, as though they were foreigners with the necessity of understanding one another in some grave matter.

"Is this a parting?" she asked, as she leant back against a tree wreathed in ivy, as though in weakness.

"If I had my way," he said, "we should never be parted again."

She put all her longing into the wish,—"If only I might take you back to Jalna."

He gave his short laugh. "What a picture! What a prize! Oh, my darling . . ."

She cast herself from the support of the tree, against his shoulder. She clung to him, as though she would never let him go. "You must not say such cruel things about yourself, Mait. It hurts me, because you're so splendid, so . . ."

He silenced her with a kiss, then put her from him. She saw how pale he was. Shyly she put her hand on his mouse-coloured hair. "I've always wanted to touch it," she said. "And your eyelashes are curly, too." And then added,— "My, but you're beautiful."

That made him laugh outright. "What distortions love can make!" he exclaimed. "I wager I'd look a satyr to your dad."

Before she could answer, her quick ear caught the sound of voices. "They're coming," she cried. "I won't move! I will sit here with both my arms about your neck."

But before she could touch him he was on his feet, facing the direction from where the voices came. Now Finch and Maurice were appearing round the bend in the drive. Adeline exclaimed, on a despairing note:

"Oh, why did we stay here—to be found! I know the loveliest spot by the sea where we might have been. I'd say good-bye properly and sweetly, Mait, if you'd come there tomorrow. Do say you will."

He scarcely heard her. His frowning defensive gaze was on the advancing figures. Maurice's eyes were on him: Finch's, in concern, rested on Adeline's emotion-swept face.

Maurice broke out,—"So you did come, Fitzturgis."

"Yes. To say good-bye to Adeline." He turned to Finch. "You don't mind, I hope."

"That depends," returned Finch.

"On what?"

"On how you say it."

"We said it with a kiss," Adeline's voice came clearly. "There's nothing wrong in a kiss, is there, when you love a man?"

Maurice said to Fitzturgis,—"You know what my uncle and I think of this."

"I can't prevent my feeling towards Adeline," returned Fitzturgis. "Having those feelings, I came to bid her good-bye. But good-bye it is. I shall not see her again—not till I'm able to offer her marriage."

The word marriage was to Maurice a challenge from an opponent, a coming into the open with a drawn sword. To Finch it was solidifying feelings that had been mercifully fluid. Now there was no escape, except to get Adeline out of Ireland as soon as possible, return her to the authority of her father.

To Adeline the word gave her a new status. She could face those male relations, shoulder to shoulder with Fitzturgis. She rose and stood beside him. A line from a history book came into her mind: "Don't shoot till you see the whites of their eyes". She stiffened her spine, looking into Maurice's eyes.

Finch said to Fitzturgis,—"I'm glad to hear you speak as you do. You see, Adeline is in my care. I'm accountable to her parents."

"Eighteen is of age in a girl," put in Adeline. "Not that I intend to be defiant to you, Uncle Finch, for no uncle could have been sweeter to me than you, but I know what is in my heart and I don't see any use in hiding it."

"That's a good girl," said Finch, trying to cajole her back into childhood.

"There's nothing more to be said," added Maurice.

Fitzturgis looked from one to the other. "I may as well be going," he said.

"Much better," agreed Maurice.

A flush crept up from the Irishman's neck and suffused his face. He turned away, as though he could not trust himself to speak. Finch held out his hand to him. He said,—"Good-bye, and I hope that, when we next meet, the atmosphere will be more serene. Please don't think I haven't enjoyed meeting you. It's just . . ."

"I understand," Fitzturgis returned coolly. "I was all right so long as I kept my distance."

"Just that," agreed Maurice.

Adeline turned fiercely on her cousin. "You are enough, Mooey," she said, "to make me throw myself right at Mait's head."

"I don't doubt it."

"You're horrible."

"Thanks." He turned away and strode towards the house.

Finch stood irresolute. Should he leave Adeline and Fitzturgis alone, for a last good-bye? It would be only kind. Yet he was responsible for her. What if she ran off with her lover? She had Gran's wild blood. It might lead her to some passionate exploit for which Renny would never forgive him.

Fitzturgis was regarding him with an ironic smile.

"I'll settle it for you," he said.

He came to Adeline and put his hand on her shoulder. "Good-bye, Adeline." He took her hand and raised it to his lips.

"Write to me."

Her eyes were large and dark in her pale face.

"No," he answered. "It will be better not."

"But you can't leave me like this," she cried.

"Yes, I can—and must."

"If I write, won't you answer my letter?"

Fitzturgis looked at Finch.

"I think you might answer," said Finch. "I certainly think you might."

"Thanks." A light came into Fitzturgis' eyes. "Then I will." He went quickly to his car.

Finch put his arm about Adeline. She stood rigid while Fitzturgis backed his car and turned it. He waved his hand from the window.

Adeline broke from Finch. She ran a few yards after the car, called out "Good-bye, Mait," in a strangled voice, then halted. She watched the car pass through the gate, then, with a dazed look in her eyes, came back to Finch.

"That was kind of you, Uncle Finch," she said quietly.

Finch expecting a despairing outburst from her, was grateful for her self-control. "Good girl," he said. He

stopped himself from adding,—"You'll get over this."
Instead he asked,—"Should you like to go for a walk?"

"Yes," she answered. "But—do you mind if I go
alone? I want to think."

Finch was relieved. "Of course. It would be better.
Take the dogs with you."

"Uncle Finch."

"Yes?"

"I want to leave."

"Well, we are leaving in a week."

"I want us to go now. Tomorrow. I can't bear being
here any longer."

Finch was willing. To go to London, to have the
excitement of meeting Wakefield, of the theatres, the
crowds, would do Adeline good.

"Very well," he said, "we'll leave as soon as I can get
passages for us. But there's one thing you must promise.
You must make friends with Mooey before we leave."

"I promise."

They walked side by side along the drive, Adeline with
dignity refusing the weakness of another backward glance.
In front of the house Maurice was playing with the Labradors, ostentatiously at ease. He flung a stick for them and
they hurled their muscular fawn-coloured bodies after it
in an abandon of pursuit. The mother secured it but her
son gave her no peace. He rollicked beside her, jostling
her, growling and at last caught the stick in his mouth also,
and so united they galloped gracefully to their master's
feet.

Maurice did not look at Adeline but again threw the stick.
This time the son captured it and Bridget, the mother, as
though disgruntled, lowered her tail and slipped out of
sight among the rhododendrons. When Adeline reached
the path that led to the sea Bridget was there beside her,
trotting through the bracken, its unfolding fronds tickling
her sides.

They moved on together, trees close on their right, and
on their left the path falling away to the black rocks below.
The tide was moving in, pressing with resonance through
glistening clefts, rippling, muttering, plashing with faint

but inexorable urging against seaweed and sand. Now and
again Adeline paused to look down on it, then walked
swiftly on. She must be out on the stony headland, alone.
In a tiny cove she saw two boys draw in their boat. They
had been gathering sea-gulls' eggs from the cliffs. She saw
the great basketful of them and for a moment pictured the
young gulls that never would be hatched. She saw the
bare brown feet of the boys and their long windblown
hair.

She gained the open. The path led to a low stone wall
and beyond it wound among grey boulders upward to the
headland. She looked about her. There was no one in sight,
no living creature but Bridget at her side. She climbed the
stile over the wall. With a leap Bridget passed over it and
seemed to move with a new grace and a new meaning, as
though an invisible leash had been taken off her.

Adeline walked steadily along the path, among the
boulders. No one could hear her now and she cast off all
restraint and cried openly. At first the painful tears stung
her eyes, then they came more freely. She cried out loud,
hearing her own voice, now hoarse, tearing at her throat,
now high and clear like a weeping child's. Bridget gave her
one look askance, then no more.

Where the path ended at the cliff's edge, she stood looking
out on the open sea where no sail was to be seen, only
endlessly moving waves. She grew calmer and, at last, she
sat down on the brink, quiet except for the heavy rise and
fall of her breast. She picked up a small stone and cast
it over the brink. She heard the faint noise of its falling but
it made no sound when it disappeared into the sea. "I
shall disappear out of his life like that little stone that's
been swallowed up by the sea." She felt her helplessness
in the immense movement of the world. She was used
to thinking of herself as a strong character, in contrast
to Roma whom she thought of as weak. She had had no
experience of life to prepare her for the emotions that had
stirred her since the birth of her love for Fitzturgis. She
found herself battling in a world she could not comprehend. Now she was alone, her heart aching with the
love she could not tear from it, and with the consciousness

that Fitzturgis was master of himself, hardened by life, able to face with fortitude what he had to face. She felt a kind of anger at him for his strength. If he would have sat down and wept with her, she could have borne it. But this loneliness, this desolation. . . .

She threw herself on the hard ground, and again crying aloud, she clutched at the harsh dry grass and tore it. She rolled to the very brink of the cliff and lay looking down at the tide grappling at its base. As she lay watching the insurge of the waves, she grew quieter. She lay still for a while, watching the dim sun lose itself in the dim horizon.

At last she sat up and looked about for the Labrador. Bridget had left her to explore the cliffside, trotting among the grey boulders, discovering in that barrenness scents that woke instincts long forgotten. She was lost to view among these prehistoric forms for a time. Now Adeline saw her returning as though in fear. As she drew nearer her fear grew. The hair along her spine stood upright, her mouth hung open, and her eyes rolled in terror.

"Bridget! Come!" called Adeline, and the dog all but flung itself on her for protection. It looked back towards the more distant boulders, watchful for the source of its panic. Adeline too was afraid. She rose and went towards the spot where Bridget had been. But when she was there she discovered nothing on the hillside but the stark boulders. Now she saw in them grotesque resemblances to idiotic or distorted human heads. Bridget had refused to follow her but sat with pricked ears, statuesque and watchful against the sky.

Adeline found nothing but the emptiness of the stony land, the emptiness of the sky and the emptiness of the sea. The wind dried the tears on her cheeks. She returned to Bridget and they went homeward along the path. All the way, Bridget kept close behind her. Every now and again Adeline would feel the touch of the sensitive muzzle against her leg.

She had made up her mind to be friendly with Maurice. It was easier when she found Pat Crawshay having a drink with him and Finch. The three men looked at her with concern. It was plain that she had been crying. Blades of grass clung to her hair. One of her stockings was twisted. Addressing Pat Crawshay rather than the others she poured out the story of Bridget's fright.

Pat heard it with gravity. "No one can tell what she saw," he said. "Queer things have happened among those hills."

"Why, surely," exclaimed Finch, "you don't believe Bridget actually *saw something*?"

"She may not have seen it as we see. Perhaps she just felt it. It's not the first time I've heard of strange frights on that bit of land."

"Oh," said Adeline, drawing a long breath, "no wonder I was afraid."

"You did well to run home," said Pat, "or we might never have seen you again."

"Don't frighten her," said Maurice, on a protective note.

"I'm just warning her." His eyes embraced her, from her twisted stocking to her rumpled hair.

She moved to stand beside him, as though to show her confidence in him.

Maurice brought her a glass of sherry. "This will steady you," he said.

"Thanks." Their hands touched and she gave him a little smile.

Two days later, she and Finch were on the packet on their way across the Irish Sea.

It was a nice new packet glistening with fresh paint. They sat, side by side, in the lounge, unnoticed by the group of Irish people, mostly women, who sat solidly and wholesomely in the middle of the room, discussing in loud practical voices the affairs of their village. The women held their baskets and bundles on their knees as though they would not risk parting with them, even for a moment. On their own knees the men laid their hard-worked hands that looked large and resigned.

Finch was glad to take Adeline away from Ireland. The last thing he had expected when they had set out on their voyage from Canada was such complications as had arisen from her meeting with Fitzturgis. Looking back, he blamed himself for not having discovered the way the wind was blowing and seen to it that Adeline and Fitzturgis were not left alone together. But how he would have hated to interfere. It was not in his nature to dominate or even to guide others. He had found the circuitous turnings of his own spiritual path quite enough. Now he looked at her sitting composedly beside him, her eager eyes absorbing the oddities of the group before them, and he wondered how deep the wound had been.

They took a turn on the little deck before they went to bed. It was a starless night and dark sky and dark sea were one.

"The second part of our voyage," he said.

"Yes. How different from the first part! This is so dark and quiet." Her words implied not only the exterior darkness and quiet but that of her spirit.

Finch answered cheerfully,—"The Irish Sea can be very choppy."

"Yes. I remember."

Still more cheerfully he continued,—"This is a new boat, you know. They've got some sort of contraption on her that keeps her steady."

"Yes. So the steward told me."

There was silence between them for a space, then she asked,—"Uncle Finch, was your wife your first love?"

"Good Lord, no. I'd half a dozen of them. It is really the best way. You get something out of your system."

"Did it get something out of your system?"

"To tell the truth, no. I can't even remember their names."

"Then—you married your first real love?"

"Yes."

"How lucky you were!"

"Lucky—" he broke out—"lucky! If I had known what that marriage was to bring me I'd have run to the ends of the earth to avoid it."

He could just make out the pale disc of her face, but he saw the widening darkness of her eyes.

"How terrible for you!" she breathed.

"Yes, it was rather."

"Were you happy for long?"

"No. Not for long."

"But I don't see," the words seemed to come painfully from her, "how that could be. Not if you really loved."

"We did, but she had a way of distorting love—hers and mine—that made a new picture. Something I wasn't prepared for."

"Was it as hard for her, do you think, as for you?"

"I don't think it was. She never was a defenceless sort of person. If things didn't go right one way, she'd try another. She was as complete as a——" He stopped.

"As a what?"

"I can't use that word about Sarah."

"If I guess right will you tell me?"

"No."

"Just the same, I don't think that you and Sarah ever loved each other as Mait and I do."

"People in love always feel that way."

"I never expected you to be cynical, Uncle Finch. You've been so understanding. If it hadn't been for you I couldn't have borne—all this." She looked back towards the land. "Isn't it strange," she said, "how a curtain seems to have fallen? It's like the end of a play. No—just the end of the first act."

Later she lay in her berth, feeling the movement of the ship beneath her, the throb of its engine like the beating of a lonely heart. She wondered at herself that she was able to lie there so quietly while each beat of the engine took her farther away from Maitland. She pictured him in the house with his mother and Sylvia. Was he lying awake thinking of her? Or was he sleeping with that aloof, tranquil air that made him unapproachable? She fell asleep and, as he receded from her, his face became clearer and his presence more actual, till she awoke, feeling herself in his arms. From then on she slept fitfully till early morning, but was in deep sleep when the steward knocked on her door.

What a contrast that same steward was, when he came to get her bags, to the spruce young man of the night before. Now his jacket hung open above his crumpled shirt. His hair stood on end. "Picture him, if you can," said Finch, "on a British ship."

At Fishguard, into the train and the long hours' journey though Wales, past the farms, the red fields, the woods, into England. Finch buried himself in a book. Adeline stared out of window, observed the other passengers in the railway carriage. Would this day of joggling on the train never end?

But end it did at Paddington and among the first of those waiting on the platform they espied Wakefield, tall, slim, his dark face eager.

XXIII

LONDON

Wakefield Whiteoak was, for once in his life, early for an appointment. Or was the train late? He fidgeted along the platform, stopping at a bookstall to pick up a book, open it, and lay it down without even noticing its title. Turning away he almost collided with a stout woman carrying two cups of tea. As it was, the start made her slop some of it and she gave him an angry look. "Thenks," she said sarcastically. "Thenks very much indeed."

Wakefield raised his hat. Speaking with a foreign accent, he replied,—"Madame, a thousand pardons. I am in a state of excitement. I wait to meet the Contessa di Piccadillo and I thought you were she. The resemblance is remarkable."

"Well," she said, softened, "anything I can do to 'elp. . . ."

"You are too kind. Ah, there is the Contessa at last," he exclaimed, as he saw Georgina Lennox, an actress and a friend of his, coming towards him. He hastened to meet her. Affectionately they embraced.

The stout woman looked after him with a pleased smile.

"Whatever has brought you here, Georgie?" he asked.

"I've been seeing off my aunt and uncle and their two Pekes. What a time I had finding a carriage to suit them all! My aunt wanted one where she could smoke. My uncle wanted no smoking and the Pekes wanted no outsiders in it."

"And did you get them settled?"

"Of course I did. And what about you? Why are you here?"

"To meet my older brother and my niece."

"Where from?"

"Ireland. Will you come into the restaurant and have a glass of sherry?"

"Is there time?"

"There's always time to spare—or none at all."

"Well, this time there's none at all, for here comes the train."

"Wait with me and meet them, won't you, Georgie?"

"I'd love to."

They moved along the platform towards Finch and Adeline. Before they saw him Wakefield had a good look at them. Finch was just the same, he thought; perhaps more tired, but with that look of being puzzled by life, confused by its strangeness, which he had worn as a boy. As for Adeline, she had grown up—and what a walk! He had seen the struggles of young actresses to achieve such a walk, and here she was doing it unconsciously along the platform at Paddington. If she had been plain as a pipe-stem that walk would have distinguished her.

He kissed her and clasped Finch by the hand.

"Wonderful to see you here," he said. "I never really believed you'd come."

"Why not?" said Adeline. "Don't I always do what I say I will?"

He possessively took her by the arm, then introduced her and Finch to Georgina Lennox. Soon the four were packed into a taxi on their way to the hotel. Adeline relapsed into childhood and made no attempt to take part in the conversation. She was fascinated by what she saw through the window of the cab. She was suspended midway between exhilaration at the prospect of what lay ahead and the pain of the parting with Fitzturgis.

"I have no right to be at this family reunion," said Georgina Lennox. "Let me out at Hyde Park Corner, Wakefield."

"No. You're to come and have tea with us."

"I've had tea."

She sank back, with a smile at Finch. He smiled back at her, his large grey-blue eyes blinking a little behind his glasses, for he was tired. Their knees touched and he sought to move his long legs out of the way.

"Don't move," she said. "I've plenty of room."

"Georgie's a most adaptable person," said Wakefield.

Georgina Lennox (her real surname was Panks) was the daughter of a prosperous Midland manufacturer of stockings. He had given her a good education at an expensive school, and when she had shown a desire for stage life he had sent her to the Royal Academy of Dramatic Art. She had an allowance sufficient for an attractive little apartment in town and had known nothing of the hand-to-mouth existence of most struggling young actresses. She had some experience of the screen and had taken a minor but striking part in a successful film.

During the drive from Paddington to the hotel she talked with animation to the men, with an occasional question to Adeline, this with the air of one who encourages a shy child. ("What does she think I am?" wondered Adeline. "I'm taller than she. I have feelings she has never known, for she's shallow—too full of her own importance.") Adeline sat aloof, in her corner, taking no part in the conversation.

Finch said to Wakefield,—"I'm told you have written a play."

Wakefield made a grimace of despair. "I have written a play. That is the easy part. The hard part is to get hold of a man who's willing to risk a loss on it."

"It's a lovely play," exclaimed Georgina Lennox, "and I'm dying to play the leading part."

"You'd look it certainly," he said.

"You think I couldn't act it?"

"I simply don't know."

The two began eagerly to discuss the part, as though it were not possible for them to keep their minds for long from the fascination of their profession. As Finch listened, he remembered how he once had had leanings towards the theatre. What would his life have been, he wondered, had he followed that bent. He did not envy actors the bickerings, the jealousies of their profession. What he did envy them was the warmth of companionship, the friendships they formed. In comparison his life was isolated, lonely.

Miss Lennox alighted at Hyde Park Corner, after expressing eager hopes of again meeting Finch and Adeline very soon.

"I'm glad she's gone," Adeline exclaimed.

"Don't you like her?" asked Wakefield, surprised.

"No."

"Well, that's flat. May I ask why?"

"I can't explain. I just—don't."

Wakefield turned to Finch. "She has rather a striking face, don't you agree?"

"I scarcely noticed it," returned Finch.

"Wonderful." Wakefield hugged himself. "This is almost like being at home."

"We didn't mean to be snooty," said Adeline. "We just wanted a private reunion."

"We shall have one, from now on," he returned, putting his arm about her. "And, speaking of faces, you have a sweet one of your own."

Finch was staring out of the window. As they passed through the streets he was conscious of that peculiar feeling of excitement which no city but London could give him. It reached out to him from the very pavements, from the crowds, from the sober, massive buildings. Perhaps it came from the remembrance of his first visit there when he was twenty-one and had brought his two old uncles with him. What a time they had had together and how terribly young and vulnerable he had been, even for twenty-one!

At Brown's Hotel the three mounted the red-carpeted stairs, following the porter to Adeline's room. She looked admiringly at the Victorian mahogany furniture. "I like this," she said. She passed through the french window on to the balcony, with its boxes of red geraniums. Lights were coming out in the surrounding buildings. She was conscious of the vastness and majesty of London. She heard Finch and Wakefield talking of Georgina Lennox and turned back into the room to say,—"I suppose she's been married half-a-dozen times."

"No," answered Wakefield. "Only once."

"I pity him," she said. "Who is he?"

"They're divorced."

"They would be! Who *was* he?"

"An Irishman. They married during the war. I believe he was a bad-tempered fellow. The poor girl had an unhappy time."

"An Irishman," repeated Adeline. "I like Irishmen. What was his name?"

Wakefield knitted his brow. "It was Fitz-something...."

Finch interrupted,—"Come along to my room, Wake. It's time for Adeline to dress."

Adeline looked Wakefield square in the eyes. "Fitz?" she repeated, toying with the syllable. "Can't you remember?"

"Not possibly. It was an unholy sort of name."

"*Turgis?*" suggested Adeline.

"That's it! Have you heard of him?"

"Yes. We met him." The hot colour surged into her face.

"You did? And what did you think of him?"

"We—liked him." She threw Finch a look of desperate warning.

"Yes," Finch agreed. "We sort of liked him."

"Now I call this an extraordinary coincidence," exclaimed Wakefield. "Georgie is the first person you meet in London and she was once married to a man you met in Ireland."

"That's nothing," said Finch, his eyes on Adeline. "In San Francisco I met a fellow who had lived half a mile from Jalna most of his life and we'd never met in all those years."

Wakefield was too much occupied by his own affairs and by the pleasure of having Finch and Adeline with him to be interested in an unknown Irishman. Finch led him off to his own room but after a little returned to Adeline.

She opened the door to his knock and, inside the room, they stood staring at each other.

"I came back," he said, "to tell you that I shan't mention—anything to Wake—about you and Fitzturgis."

"Thank you, Uncle Finch," she murmured. "Do you believe that he really was married to that woman?"

"I suppose it's possible."

"It couldn't be. He'd have told me."

"Men don't always tell everything in their past, you know."

"But he would have told *me*. I'm sure of that."

"Why?"

"Because he loves me."

"Probably the very reason why he didn't."

"Oh!" Adeline pressed the tips of her fingers to her forehead. "I'm tired," she said, "and a little hungry."

Finch remembered that she had eaten little on the journey. Lost her good appetite, he thought, because of that fellow she'd left behind.

"Of course you're hungry," he exclaimed. "And I am too."

"What shall I put on?" she asked. "A dinner dress?"

"No. Just something fresh. And wouldn't you like a hot bath?"

She nodded. She could not speak. Desperately she wanted to be alone. When he had gone she closed and locked the door. Apprehension, anger, hurt and resentment surged up in her. But she must not give way. She must appear steady and unhurt, not let Finch realize the turmoil within her. She dug her fingernails into her palms and set her teeth. Forcibly she pressed down the welling tears. What had come over her—she who scorned a girl who cried—who, many a time, had felt superior to Roma's emotionalism? . . . but this—this was so cruel—so unexpected! The intent face of Fitzturgis rose before her—clearer than life. If only she could meet him face to face, find out all the truth about him so that there should be left no surprises, none at all.

The days passed. Finch gave himself up to the pleasure of being in London again. There were old friends of the family to look up; pleasant acquaintances, though he never thought of them as friends, in musical circles. There was Adeline to be taken about. He and she went together to see the comedy in which Wakefield was acting. It was playing to fair houses, and Wakefield's part, though not one of the most important, seemed so to Adeline. She was full of pride in him and wished everyone in the audience could know he was her near relation. For the time being, he was financially secure.

Finch, regarding her laughing face at the play, and seeing her apparent pleasure in their sight-seeing, thought she had taken the revelation of Fitzturgis' marriage with admirable fortitude. If she was full of pride in Wakefield, Finch was even more filled with pride in her. He cherished the shadowy hope that her attachment to Fitzturgis was less deep than he had feared.

He could not know of the passionate letter she had written, demanding that Fitzturgis should explain his lack of candour. On the very day, when her letter reached Fitzturgis, a letter bearing the Irish stamp was indeed handed to her. But it was from Pat Crawshay, a letter telling her how much he missed her and even touching the fringe of an expression of love. At the first she was too disappointed to do more than impatiently scan it, but later in the day she read it, with a sense of comfort, and the image of his ingenuous, eager face blurred for a moment the picture of Fitzturgis.

In Ireland Fitzturgis had read her letter, at first with momentary consternation, and then with bitter resignation. This was no worse than he deserved, he reflected. He had not told Adeline anything of his past, not of the past that most affected her. Now she had learned it, with what embellishments he could only guess, and she was cut to the heart by what she must think of as his calculated deception. His nature, the circumstances of his life, had made it hard for him to be open and frank. For years he had lived among people who knew little of him. He had no desire to open his heart to them. He was sensitive, and inclined to melancholy.

He had not spent many hours with Adeline before his passionate and sensual emotions were aroused by her. He longed, as he had never before longed for anything, to offer her marriage. Yet he had nothing to offer her but a restricted, a poverty-stricken life, which he could not remedy because of his bondage to his sister and mother. What use was there, he had thought, in confiding to her the fact that he had made an unfortunate marriage? Of that, at least, he was free, and he wanted to put it out of his mind.

He had met Georgina Lennox during the war, when he was on leave. It had been at a house-party in the house of the backer of the play in which she was then appearing. She was the same age as himself but years older in experience. She was greatly attracted by the young Irish officer and he was elated by her flattery and captivated by her sophistication. During the week-end they spent all the time possible in each other's company. Before his leave was over she had given herself to him. After his return to the front a continual flow of passionate letters passed between them. On his next leave they were married.

Early in their acquaintance he had introduced her to his sister and her husband. They too had been charmed by the actress, and the four had spent many pleasurable hours together, either in Sylvia's flat or dancing after the theatre in the feverish nights of bombing.

When the war was ended Fitzturgis returned to England to find his sister a tragic widow, her mind precariously near the point of breakdown. She had been placed in a mental home. With his tendency to idealize women, he had cherished a conception of Georgina which did not exist, never had existed. Soon he was irritated by her egotism, by her vanity which nothing could subdue. He discovered that she had not been faithful to him, but was the mistress of a man who had influence in moving-pictures and had, through his influence, secured her first part on the screen. Violent scenes took place between them, as she strove to justify her defection and passionately reiterated her undying love for him. Half beside himself from the troubles heaped upon him, he threatened to kill her. Their brief married life had ended in divorce. He had removed his sister from the mental home and taken her and his mother to Ireland.

Adeline's letter came as a shock to him. Then he asked himself what could have been more reasonable than that Wakefield Whiteoak, hearing his name, should connect

it with that of Georgina Lennox, and inform Adeline of
his marriage and divorce. He cursed himself for having
deceived her. Yet he looked on her as so young, so innocent, that the recital of what he regarded as a sordid story
would have been almost impossible to him. Now he wanted,
above all things, to justify himself in her eyes. He longed,
with an almost despairing fervency, to see her once again
before she sailed for home. The brief moments when he
had held her in his arms were relived, dwelt upon, pro-
longed, in the wakeful hours of the night. In the morning
he went to his mother.

"Mother," he said, "I'm going to London. Something
has happened that makes it necessary."

She was running a carpet-sweeper over an old Turkish
rug with a worn spot in the middle. She heard him but
pretended she had not. She was always impressing on him
how hard she had to work. Now, panting with every
stroke of the carpet-sweeper, she drove it up and down
the rug, avoiding the worn spot. But the sweeper, already
too full of dust, began to spit it out again, in grey clots,
as though in protest. Fitzturgis stood watching her for a
moment without again speaking. He was seething with
mingled exasperation and pity. Why did she have to be
so inefficient? Why did she wrap her head in that ridiculous scarf, with her long earrings dangling beneath? How
hot and tired she looked! She pretended that she had just
discovered his presence, and ceased the sweeping.

"Oh, good morning, darling," she said. "You're late
this morning."

"Yes, I couldn't sleep and then—I slept. Listen,
Mother——"

"I understand. I'm just the same. Lie awake and lie
awake, thinking of all the queer things that have happened
and then—just when it's time to get up—fall into a heavy
sleep. And *dream*! What do you suppose I dreamed last
night? Well, I dreamed that you were a little boy again
and were in this very room which was odd because we were
never here when you were a little boy, and, as I say, we
were in this very room, only it wasn't the same because
where that sofa stands——"

He interrupted,—"I'm sorry, Mother—I can't wait to hear now——"

Her feelings hurt, she answered, a little sharply,— "Really, Maitland, you have an abrupt way of speaking. And after staying so late in bed I think another minute wasted wouldn't much matter. Though, to tell the truth, it would take me a good half-hour to tell all the intricacies of that dream. It was so muddled and yet so clear. I saw you, as clear as I see you now, only with a much sweeter expression, for as a child you had a very sweet face and so had Sylvia, yet now——"

"I know," he said, between his teeth, "I know——"

She stared at him hard, out of her clear blue eyes, and he noticed that her head kept moving a little.

"I'm going to fly to London today," he repeated.

"Fly," she cried. "Why, that costs a lot more."

"I know, but I must go."

"Is it to see Adeline Whiteoak?"

"No—" but he could not lie to her—"yes. Don't ask me, Mother."

"Your shirts!" she mourned. "I didn't get those buttons sewn on."

"Never mind. I must go."

"You must do what you think best, but—always remember there's Sylvia to be thought of."

"I'm not likely to forget," he answered harshly.

"It's very hard on you, having us two always on your mind." She drew a deep sigh.

He put both arms about her. "Mother dear, I won't have you talk like that." He bent with his cheek to hers, and her earring pressed into his flesh.

The Irish servant had cooked his bacon and eggs for him an hour ago and was keeping them hot in the oven. They were hard and unpalatable. He quickly despatched them, then sought Sylvia whom he found in a corner of the chill living-room. She was sitting with bent head, her hands dangling between her knees, her eyes fixed on the floor.

"I'm off to London," he said. "I've booked my seat in the plane by telephone." He spoke in a cheerful matter-of-fact tone, as though all was well in that house.

"I never want to see London again," she returned, without looking up.

"No. Of course not. I shouldn't go, but—it's important."

"There is nothing important in my life."

He ignored this. He had so often heard it. The sight of her sitting there, the remembrance of his mother with the carpet-sweeper, shook him into a moment of impatience. "There'd be something in your life," he said, "if you'd give Mother a hand with the work. You know what an inconvenient house this is. It's too much for her."

"She doesn't want my help. It only bothers her."

"Very well," he said. "Sit here and mope, if you must. But—don't forget that other people have had tragedies——" He broke off and came to her side and touched her fair curling hair with a caressing hand. "It makes me so anxious for you," he went on, "to go away and leave you looking forlorn. I don't need to tell you, do I, how much you mean to me?"

She caught his hand, kept it a moment, then pushed it roughly from her. "You're a fool, Mait," she said, "to trouble your head about me. Just leave me to mope. It's what I like now."

"I can't, and you know it. I want you to promise me that you'll make an effort—not just a little one but a big one—to keep Mother cheerful while I'm away."

Sylvia laughed. "She doesn't need me to keep her cheerful. Cheeriness is a part of her and a damned irritating part at times."

"You wouldn't think so if you'd been with her just now."

"She likes to work on your feelings."

"Nothing can make me believe," he said sternly, "that you are as callous as you pretend."

She turned on him fiercely. "For Christ's sake, get out," she stormed, "and let me be. Go and meet your darling and I hope you'll have better luck with her than you had with your last."

He flushed, glared at her in anger, then controlled himself. This was to be one of Sylvia's bad days. He knew he should not go away and leave his mother alone with her. But he could not help it. He must see Adeline. Whatever happened he must see Adeline.

"Very well," he said, "I'll go."

The desire to leave that house, to breathe the air of freedom, moved him to a kind of feverish haste in his preparations. He flung his belongings into a suit-case, said a hurried good-bye to his mother and sister, and flung himself into his car by the side of the odd-job man who was to drive it.

First the train, soot-smelling and slow. Then the plane, clean and swift. He did not look at his fellow passengers but rested his spirit on the sweep of sky and sea beyond the plane. The steady throb of the engine numbed his thoughts and after a time he became calm.

XXIV

MEETING

ADELINE did not go out with Finch that afternoon. She told him she had shopping to do, and, though he did not believe her, as he believed she had little need or money for buying, he left her to herself. He was always willing to be free and alone in London. It was a hot, bright morning. The shining river cut through the shadows of the stone walls, moved beneath its bridges, where people leant over the parapet to watch it, played with its barges, its tugs, its ships, in a gay youthful mood.

Adeline went down the short flights of red-carpeted stairs to the lounge which at this hour was almost deserted, and found a seat from where she could see the door. Through it, at this hour, the postman would appear and conceivably bring her a letter from Fitzturgis. If she had counted the hours, she would have realized that this was not possible, yet so intense was her desire to hear from him that it swept aside the limitations of time and space.

She sat, hands folded in lap, watching the entrance. Near it was the porter's desk where there was a constant coming and going of guests, enquiring about trains, buses, mail, leaving their keys, getting their keys. Close by stood two small pages, pink-cheeked, in their little liveries and pill-box caps. At the entrance another page opened and closed the swing door. His white-gloved hands looked too large for him. His expression varied between mild interest as he swung the door to admit someone, and mild expectancy if a guest were departing. Beyond the hall Adeline had a glimpse into the dining-room, with its vista of white-clothed tables and dark panelled walls. A single waiter moved about among them. The only other occupants of the lounge were a handsome woman with arthritical hands, and her husband. They looked at Adeline as though they wondered why she should have chosen a chair in such proximity to them and as though afraid she might speak to them. At the far end of the room a clergyman was doing the crossword puzzle in *The Times*.

People came to and went from the desk. The porter hung keys on hooks by pigeon-holes, took keys from hooks, searched through time-tables, all with an expression of good-humoured forbearance. The two little pages yawned, covering their mouths with their white gloves. One of them sat down on a high-backed chair and nodded. Adeline's eyes burned from watching the door.

The door swung open and disgorged two people simultaneously. One, a stout Belgian business man, went straight to the desk and demanded his key. The other . . . Adeline caught her breath, the other—his shoulders, his profile, she had seen before—seen on board ship—seen in Ireland. She was on her feet. She was at his side. At first her voice would not come, her throat was so constricted. Then she got out his name. He wheeled and looked into her face.

"Adeline."

He saw how deadly pale she was. Was she going to faint? She put her hand to her throat and swallowed. There was only dryness there and an aching constriction. He kissed her on the cheek and led her into the lounge. They found a secluded seat in a corner.

"You are surprised," he said.

"Yes," she whispered, shaken by the impact of his nearness.

"I had to come, after I got your letter."

"You must have come right away," she said.

"I flew."

"Oh!" She looked at his hands which lay, as though tranquilly, on his knees. "You say you flew?"

"Yes. We had a good trip."

"Not rough?"

"No. It couldn't have been better."

"That's good." A long sigh escaped her. Her breath came more easily. Her heart ceased leaping in her breast.

He put one of his hands on one of hers. "I can imagine," he said, "what you think of me."

"I'm not thinking. I'm just feeling—that you're here."

"I wish we might be alone," he said.

The eyes of the clergyman were raised from the cross-word puzzle. They rested reflectively on the linked hands of Adeline and Fitzturgis, then, without having noticed their faces, returned to the puzzle.

She now spoke in a controlled voice. "It's better the way it is."

"How can I try to make you understand here?"

"I don't think you could say anything—anywhere—that would make me understand."

"I suppose you think I set out deliberately to deceive you."

"Well—you know, Mait, I haven't had any experience."

"That's just why," he said eagerly, "I couldn't bear to tell you."

"I don't see why. There's no disgrace in having been married before."

"No. But I couldn't bring myself to talk of it to you. Meeting you—being with you on the deck, in the sun and wind—was such a fresh, beautiful experience to me that I couldn't bear to drag my rather ignoble past into it."

She considered this and then said stubbornly: "You should have told me."

He answered with some heat,—"I expected everything to end with our arrival in Ireland. It wasn't as though I'd asked you to join your life with mine."

She drew her hands away from him and folded her arms. "Why?" she asked, with accusation in her eyes. "You knew I loved you."

"You very well know why. I had nothing to offer you."

"But, the last time we met, you said you'd come to Canada some day and ask me—if you were able—oh, you know what I mean!"

She spoke with passion, raising her voice so that not

only the clergyman but the reserved couple in the far corner of the lounge heard her and looked at her in surprise.

"Ssh." Fitzturgis gripped her knee. "Those people are staring."

"I don't care," she answered, scarcely lowering her voice.

A hubbub broke out in the hall. A party was pouring in for a wedding reception, women in wide-brimmed hats, men in top-hats and buttonhole nosegays. Other people began to come into the lounge for tea. A waiter appeared, pushing a tea-wagon loaded with sandwiches, cakes and strawberry tarts. The place was transformed, the atmosphere changed to that of a social gathering. One could talk without being heard.

"Will you take tea?" Adeline asked coldly.

"Thanks." He stared at the crowd without seeing them.

A low table was placed in front of them and soon they were choosing something to eat. Adeline noticed that Fitzturgis' hand shook a little as he raised the cup of tea to his lips. But how calm his face was. She became conscious of her own face from forehead to lips and tried to make it into such a mask. Mechanically she put food into her mouth—but even the tarts had no flavour for her. She heard him say:

"Let's get out of here, into the air."

"Yes. I'd like that. I'll run up and put on my hat."

He followed her to the foot of the stairs and bent over the glass case in which Penguin books were displayed, reading the titles while he waited.

She was not gone for long. Now she stood on the last step looking at him, filled for a burning instant with wild joy at the sight of him standing there, looking so natural, looking as though all were well between them. He turned to her.

"Ready?" he asked, with a smile.

"Yes," she returned, with no answering one.

They went out through the swing doors into Albemarle Street. "We'll go to the Green Park," she said.

The late sunshine was still beating down on Piccadilly. Three street musicians were playing a martial air, while a fourth man held out a little box to the passers-by. The ingratiating smile never left his face. Unconsciously Adeline moved in time to the music. Then, as they were confronted by the little box, she said,—"Give them something, Mait."

He put his hand in his pocket and brought out a shilling. Adeline, eyeing it, exclaimed,—"It's no good. I mean it's no good to him. It's Irish."

The man kept his smile, his eyes fixed on Fitzturgis, who muttered, "Of course, of course." He fished in his pocket, while the crowd jostled, and brought out more silver. Adeline snatched an English half-crown from his palm and dropped it into the box. The man took off his hat and made her a bow.

They crossed the street and entered through the tall iron gates into the park.

Adeline asked,—"Did I give them too much?"

"Too much? I didn't notice."

"It's just that I'm feeling sorry for people who aren't happy."

"They probably are—as happy as any of us."

The park was emptying. Those who had been lounging on the grass or in the chairs, women with children, women with dogs, were moving towards the gates homeward. But a steady stream of people passed along the paved walks through the park towards Buckingham Palace Road. A smell of warm earth and grass rose to the nostrils, as Adeline and Fitzturgis sought a quiet spot. Here and there the grass was pressed down by the weight of human bodies, but by tomorrow the grass-blades would rise and the imprint have vanished. How lovely to walk on grass again, Adeline thought, pressing her toes against the ground, and making for the shade of an oak in which, high up, a song-thrush poured out his happy memories of the day.

She dropped to the grass, between light and shade, that side of her face nearest the tree pale and grave, while the other side, played on by the sunlight between the gently moving leaves, seemed almost to smile.

Fitzturgis dropped beside her, stretching out his legs and, for an instant, closing his eyes, as though he postponed

the moment of looking into hers. She contemplated him
with a feeling of more detachment than she had yet known.
From the hour of their first meeting her feeling towards
him had been intensely personal and instinctive. Now she
saw him almost as an outsider who had thrust his way into
her life, troubling it to its depths. Yet the delight of his
nearness, of seeing him stretched on the grass, was there
too, making conflict within her.

Now he looked up into her eyes. He said:

"You make me do everything I swore I wouldn't
do."

"Such as what?"

"Falling in love with you. Giving you a wrong idea of
myself. Following you here."

She considered these three aspects of him—the lover—
the deceiver—the follower. Then she said,—"You did all
these of your own accord."

He sat up. "I did not. I swear I was helpless."

"I can't imagine your being helpless, Mait. What is a
face for, if it doesn't show the character?"

He said between his teeth,—"If my face showed my
character I hate to think what a face it would be."

"Talk like that," she returned, in her great-uncle
Ernest's manner, "doesn't do any good. I want your
explanation."

"Of what?"

"Of why you married Georgina What's-her-name."

"I thought I loved her."

"Really *loved* her?"

"Well—I thought so."

"Did you feel the same about her as you now think you
feel about me?"

"It was entirely different."

"Why?"

"Because she is entirely different."

"You mean she is experienced?"

"It was partly that. Partly that the times were different.
Men on leave were reckless. They thought their time on
earth might be short. They snatched at pleasures."

"And Georgina was one of yours?"

"Not for long. . . I can tell you this, my darling, and I want you to believe me—any feeling I had for Georgina was . . ." He made a quick gesture, from the wrist only, and narrowed his eyes, frowning. He did not finish the sentence. In the proud, fitful imagination of first love Adeline magnified everything he said, or did not say, into something momentous. She leant towards him, with parted lips, to receive his words or thoughts half-way.

"Yes? Yes?" she encouraged.

He continued, his hand gently touching her shoe,— "Comparisons are silly. Isn't it enough that I love you with all that's in me? Georgina was in my past."

Adeline broke out,—"Oh, I wish I were older! Eighteen is so stupid to be. I have no past. I can't understand."

"Where you are concerned I have no past either. It's all present. It's all you."

"Have we no future?"

"You have."

"Not without you." Her lips quivered and she steadied herself with difficulty.

At some distance she saw another couple on the grass. They had escaped from some office or shop and come to the park to be together. The man lay flat on his back; the girl sat beside him. Fascinated, Adeline watched her wooing of him, her fondling of his sandy hair, caressing of his cheeks, tickling of his neck; his supine acceptance of these attentions. Adeline said,—"Let's walk along."

"Don't you like it here?"

"Those people . . ."

He sat up and looked without interest. "Very well," he said, "but we shall scarcely find a quieter spot."

They moved among the trees, the thrush's song following them. The sun was now lowering into a greater brightness rather than towards a sunset. The upper branches of the trees were enmeshed in a golden web. The noise of traffic came subdued. Again they dropped to the grass, this time side by side, their backs against a tree.

Adeline repeated, as though there had been no interruption:

"I have no future without you."

He replied, almost violently,—"If I were wiped off the face of the earth at this instant your life would go on. In a few years from now—with me in Ireland, you in Canada——"

She interrupted,—"You say how much you love me, yet you talk to me like this!"

"I want to make you realize that I am only an incident."

"Why did you come here?"

"To explain."

"You have explained nothing. I love you. You love me. I'm willing to wait for you. Isn't that clear?"

He looked at her as though he did not see her. "Terribly clear," he said. "You're offering up your youth as a sacrifice."

"Bother my youth," she exclaimed. "I'm sick of hearing of it. May not we have some pleasure out of it?"

He frowned at her. "What do you want to do?"

"I want to be somewhere alone with you. I'd like to drink wine and to pretend that it would go on for ever."

He took her hand and they sat so linked for a time, without speaking. The song-thrush, out of some waywardness of his own, had chosen to follow them, alight on the topmost twig of their tree and there carry on his song. This topmost twig and he were the last objects burnished by the sunlight. Far below, Adeline and Fitzturgis sat in deep shade. It was becoming cool.

He told her of his first meeting with Georgina Lennox, of their almost immediate and passionate attraction for each other, of their rushing into marriage. "There was no friendship," he said. "I simply wanted the excitement of it. I wanted something exciting enough to make me forget the war."

A pang of jealousy went through her. "And did you forget the war?" she asked.

"In a sort of way—as though someone blowing on a tin whistle in your ear might make you forget the blast of a trumpet outside your room."

Adeline laughed. "Compare me to something," she said.

"What shall I compare you to! The harp that once

through Tara's halls? That's it . . . that's the thing! Or perhaps a sword that's run me through."

"Oh, Mait—my great-grandmother would have loved you!"

"Would she now? That's interesting. How do you know?"

"I know because—in a strange sort of way—she lives in me. . . . But I'm different too. I've had a different sort of bringing up. I've had more gentleness."

He drew her on to talk of herself, of which he never tired. He lay, resting on his elbow, looking up into her face, seeing her eyes darken in the twilight, her hair darken to brown, and her skin take on a camellia-like pallor.

She would have remained there unmindful of time, had not Fitzturgis glanced at his watch and said,—"It's past seven o'clock. What about your uncles? Will they be expecting you?"

She answered tranquilly,—"Wake will be at the theatre. Uncle Finch—he'll be wondering."

"What do you want to do?"

"Whatever you say."

"I'd like to take you to dinner somewhere. Do you like Claridge's? No. I'm not dressed for it."

"Besides it costs too much. Mait, let's go to a restaurant I know in Soho. We can telephone to Uncle Finch that we're there."

Fitzturgis frowned at the thought of telephoning such a message to Finch. "Hadn't we better present ourselves at Brown's and ask him?"

"No! He might refuse. I want to go straight to Soho."

As they crossed the park beneath the dark trees they saw the mild light of evening showing through the leaves and the crowds moving quietly along the pavement.

Fitzturgis became matter-of-fact. He looked Adeline over and said,—"You're not very tidy. There's a bit of bark in your hair." He picked it off. He brushed blades of grass from her jacket, she standing straight and docile to have it done. A couple passed close beside them hand in hand. They walked on and came to the pair they had seen earlier. These two were in the same positions, only the girl more amorous, the man more flattened out.

Along Piccadilly a fresh evening breeze swept. In the distance was the sound of a band. Fitzturgis hailed a taxicab and they climbed in, as into a secret refuge. The back of the driver was as a shield, the four walls of the cab close about them, the traffic pouring past the windows, the smell of leather and cigarette smoke.

"I'm not going to mind about anything," Adeline exclaimed, out of her dark corner. "I mean I'm glad you're here, even though I don't like what brought you."

He put his arm about her. "I'm glad too. It's another hour snatched before parting."

"Don't talk of parting."

"No. We'll talk of being together always."

"Together always," she repeated. "Wonderful words. They're like wings you can fly away with, where nothing can hurt you."

"I found an old book," he said, "in the bookshelves at home and it gave the meanings of names. Adeline means 'noble maiden'."

"How lovely! I do like that."

"And it has a second meaning."

"What?"

"'Noble serpent'."

She drew back from him staring. "No!"

"Yes. 'Noble serpent'. The serpent that tempts me."

"Oh, I like that too." She gave a low, happy laugh and laid herself against his side.

Fitzturgis put both arms about her. He held her fiercely, as though he would defy temptation, and all that followed surrender to it, to harm them. His lips, in the moving light of the street lamps, sought hers, and he kissed her as he had not before. No more than broken phrases were exchanged between them till the cab stopped in front of the Italian restaurant and the head of the driver turned on his drooping shoulders.

Inside the restaurant it was so crowded that at first it seemed no table could be found for them. The black-coated, black-haired waiters, hastening among the white

tablecloths, seemed a multitude in themselves. Two of
them, carrying loaded trays, were climbing the stairs to the
restaurant on the floor above. The head waiter, with eyes
still interested, in spite of the flow of patrons, found at last
a small table just vacated. With an heroic smile of discovery
he led them to it. All the sounds, the lighting, the faces,
seemed foreign and delightful to Adeline. She put her
hands up to the little hat she had bought in New York and
placed it, as she thought, at a better angle. Fitzturgis,
calm and detached, studied the menu.

"Please order for me," she begged. "I never understand
these things."

She listened admiringly while he ordered the meal. No
wonder, she thought, that the waiter listens to him so
attentively. No wonder that a second waiter stands in
readiness . . . There sat Fitzturgis in his best suit, an
impecunious Irishman, behaving with the assurance of a
capitalist. When the hors d'œuvre was set in front of them
he smiled across the table at her. She threw aside all her
newly-acquired troubles and smiled back. She was hungry
and ate the Italian dishes with relish. She sipped her wine,
as though discussing its flavour. It exhilarated her. She
joined her voice and laughter to the rising note of that
about her.

But as they sat over their coffee Adeline became pensive.
She could think of nothing to say. Excepting that they were
lovers they were strangers to each other. They had no past
in common. They never had been about together. There
were no remembered incidents, no remembered little jokes
to recall. Fitzturgis was one of those who did not trouble
to talk unless it pleased him. Now he felt the shadow of
their parting stretch forward to envelop them. His eyes
rested on the Benedictine in his glass, his fingers turned the
glass's stem. He almost broke it at a sudden exclamation
from Adeline.

"Oh," she said, on a note of dismay. "Oh, Mait, you
forgot to telephone to Uncle Finch!"

Her consternation was reflected in his face.

"By the Lord, I did," he said. "It went right out of
my head. I'll go straight and do it."

She gave a little laugh. "Now," she said, "my name will be mud."

"It's all my fault. But will Finch be very angry or alarmed?"

Her wide-opened eyes rebuked him. "Well, wouldn't you be? If you'd brought your niece to London and she didn't show up for dinner or send any word, what would you feel?"

"I don't think I'd mind."

"Mait, I sometimes wonder if you have any natural affection in you."

"So do I."

"Does that mean you feel cold and hard inside?"

"Often I do—except towards you."

"Oh, Mait darling." She leant towards him, smiling.

With his love hot in his eyes he said,—"Supposing we don't go back."

"Not go back—ever?"

"I don't say *never*."

"But you mean *run away* and get married?"

The talk in the room became a deafening sound in her ears. She saw that his lips moved, that his face was pale, but she could not hear his words. She repeated her question. He stood up straight, looking down into her upturned face.

"I'm going to telephone," he said, and moved among the tables towards the door.

Adeline saw two people enter immediately after he went out. They came straight towards her, then were given a table at a little distance. As the theatres opened at seven, people were, at this hour, appearing after the play.

Adeline heard a voice say,—"There's Georgina Lennox."

She saw the actress, and with her Wakefield. She should have considered the possibility of meeting them here, for it was Wakefield who had introduced her to this restaurant, which was a favourite of his.

She all but cried out for Fitzturgis to come and protect her. But a wilder impulse came. The impulse to follow him, and so escape. She sat shielding her face with her hand, her knees trembling, too weak to support her. Her

elbow drew the cloth askew, slopping the liqueur from
Fitzturgis' glass. From nowhere a waiter appeared,
straightened the cloth and spread a clean napkin over the
stain. Adeline still shielded her face with her hand.

After a little Fitzturgis reappeared. He sat down with
his back to Wakefield and Georgina.

"Well?" asked Adeline, lowering her hand.

"It was just as I expected—only more so. He'd been
telephoning the hospitals."

"Goodness!"

"He told me what he thought of me."

"Goodness!"

"No. Badness."

"Mait?"

"Well?"

"Do you want me to run away with you?"

"No."

"Why?"

"I shouldn't know what to do with you."

"Do you mean there's no room in your life for me?"

"I suppose so."

"But look what you said a few minutes ago."

"I was out of my head."

"But you could take me home—to your home—for a
little. Then I'd take you back with me to Jalna. Daddy
would forgive us. You'd see."

"I have my honour," he said calmly. "I have told you
what I will do. When things are better with me—if ever
they are—I'll go to you and—if you want me——"

"I shall always want you."

He took her hand across the table. "You make me
ashamed," he said.

"But why?"

"Your youth. What you are."

Adeline now saw that Wakefield and Georgina Lennox
were looking at them.

"That actress you were married to is at a table behind
you, with Wake."

Turning his head he regarded Georgina's back without
surprise. "When did they come in?" he asked.

"While you were out. I want to go over to their table and speak to them."

"In God's name, why?"

"I can't explain. . . . Yes, I want them to know that we . . ." She could find no words, but a compelling smile curved her lips. "I want them to know," she repeated.

"I can't see that it matters. I can't see that it would be anything but—painful."

"Have you finished your drink? Then let's go over."

He rose with resignation and followed her to the other table. Wakefield was on his feet and, holding out a hand to Adeline, drew her to his side. "This is Maitland Fitzturgis," she said, with dignity.

"What a nice surprise!" said Wakefield.

"Hello, Mait." Georgina put out her hand towards Fitzturgis, in a gesture, half playful, half coaxing, as though to say,—"It's all over, so let's be friends."

He held the hand a moment, then returned it to her with a coolness which mystified Adeline. What did he feel? she wondered. If it were pain, he concealed it. Georgina, on her part, looked exhilarated. Wakefield's bright eyes moved from one face to another, in amused enquiry.

"Won't you sit down with us," he asked, "and have another drink? We'll have so much to talk about." He did not ask how Fitzturgis happened to be in London.

"We must go," said Adeline. "We only wanted to speak to you. Mait flew over from Ireland to see me."

Wakefield and Georgina exclaimed at this, as at something not exactly surprising, but quite interesting. Wakefield's thoughts could not remain long from his own affairs.

"I've had a letter from my New York agent," he said. "He's found a producer who is interested in my play."

"And now Wakefield's real troubles begin," added Georgina, showing off her eyelashes.

"The play I'm in is folding up," Wakefield went on. "I'll go straight over to New York."

"How splendid!" said Adeline. "Then you'll come to Jalna."

"Of course."

"Daddy *will* be glad to see you. You know you promised to read that play to me and you haven't."

"I'll read it to you tomorrow." He turned to Fitzturgis. "Will you be in London tomorrow?"

"Yes."

"Good. I'd like you two as an audience."

"It's a lovely play," breathed Georgina. "About frustrated love. It goes straight to your heart."

"What an achievement!" said Fitzturgis.

"I'm not being funny." Georgina pouted. "It really does."

"I'll read it to you tonight," exclaimed Wakefield, "if you will come to my lodgings."

"I'd love to," said Adeline, "but I must go back to Brown's. Uncle Finch will be worrying."

"For the love of Mike!" exclaimed Wakefield. "Don't tell me that Finch has descended to the role of the poor old worrying uncle."

"Well, I've given him a good deal to worry about." His lips set in a cold smile, Fitzturgis stood a little apart.

"Truly, Mait," said Georgina, "you'll adore the play. I know your tastes so well."

"My tastes have changed."

"But you still love art where it is good."

"Ah, yes."

Adeline exclaimed contritely,—"Your dinner is getting cold. Come, Maitland."

They said good night.

Now they were in a taxicab moving slowly through the press and glare of the streets. It had begun to rain, only a shower but enough to run down the windows of the cab. One drop would trickle half-way, hesitate, then would be joined by another. The two, accelerated, would hasten the rest of the way. The faces of the people on the 'islands' were blurred. Some looked anxiously upward, but most looked quietly enduring. A crop of umbrellas suddenly appeared, like mushrooms in damp weather.

The rain made a wall of intimacy about the two in the cab. But he could not forgive her for having forced the meeting between him and Georgina Lennox. It rankled with him that she had overridden him, for he looked on her as tender and tractable. He remembered how she had sat beside him on the grass in the park, her body half-folded, with her back against a tree. There had been the smell of warm grass. Now—it was stuffy in the cab and he opened a window wide and let in the smell of the rain. He kept the side of his shoulder to her and his face averted.

Now she felt the stronger of the two. "Angry, Maitland?" she enquired, in a caressing tone.

"Yes," he returned briefly, and he put out an angry hand and clasped hers.

"I couldn't help it. I wanted her to see us together."

"It doesn't matter."

"But you're angry."

"If you want the truth I think it was rather stupid."

"Well—that's forthright."

She tried to withdraw her hand but he held it close.

"I want to forget the past," he said.

"But—I've just heard about it."

"Well," he said, "you have seen me face to face with her. How do you feel?"

"I wonder what you ever found in her to love."

"So do I."

"Is she a good actress?"

"Very good—within her limits."

The taxicab was held up in the traffic. People surged past. Umbrellas bobbed. The rain, no longer a shower, came down in a silent grey curtain.

"Oh, it's lovely in here," exclaimed Adeline. "I wish it might go on and on."

"Shall I tell the man to drive round for a bit?"

"Just for a little while. But—do *you* want to?"

"Adeline, I don't quite know what I want." But he leant forward, tapped the glass and told the driver to go round the Park.

They passed the Marble Arch and went along the Bayswater Road, under the blurred lights, the trees thick and dark on their left.

"Are you bored?" asked Adeline, he was so quiet.

"By my life—yes."

"I never could be bored."

"You are lucky."

"But I can suffer. I can be unhappy. At this moment I'm happy and adventurous. Have you forgiven me for what I did?"

"No."

"Have you an unforgiving nature?"

"I think I have."

"Do you still wish we could go away somewhere together and not come back?"

"No."

"Oh, Mait." She sank back into her dark corner of the cab.

They were silent for a space. Pictures from his past stormed upon him. She had no past other than childhood. Never had they shared any experience. Never had they done anything together. A throng of figures crowded his mind—from his life in London, from his life in Malaya, from the war. In hers there were only the family.

But he began to talk in desultory fashion, of Georgina, of Sylvia and her dead husband. Some of the things he recalled were trifling but he had never talked of them before and it was a relief. Of some things, which were the important ones, he spoke only in broken sentences which he completed with an expressive gesture.

"Mait," she once interrupted him to say, "you are a little Frenchified. It's funny, but you are."

"I had a French grandmother."

"Do you remember her?"

"I do indeed."

The cab moved on. The rain had ceased but the pavements were running with water. Out of the darkness came a glimpse of the shabby wooden fence sprung up during the war to take the place of wrought iron. Now the dark trees were so heavy with rain that, at each gust of wind, they produced little individual showers of their own. The taxi-driver's back was a black hump of resignation. As Fitzturgis talked he became more tranquil. She stored away all he said, to ponder in the future which spread mysterious before her.

They passed over a little bridge, she saw the glint of water among the trees, they passed Hyde Park Corner, then went all the way round, for the third time. At last they were in Dover Street and he was paying the driver. They went along the quiet passage of the hotel and looked through the glass screen into the lounge. A few people were sitting there but not Finch.

"I think I should see him," said Fitzturgis, "and explain. Shall I ring up his room?"

"Yes." She surrendered herself to his care.

While they waited, she asked—"You'll stay in London for a few days, now you're here, won't you?"

He nodded, his eyes fixed on Finch coming towards them. He was pale and his hair looked as though he had run his hands through it. Without looking at Fitzturgis, he said,—"I've had a cable from Renny. Uncle Ernest died last night. We're to be back for the funeral. I've been able to get passage on a plane for tomorrow."

XXV

RETURN TO JALNA

RENNY WHITEOAK and his son Archer were waiting at the airport for the plane from Montreal. It was late and, as their eyes continually sought the sky for a sign of it, they moved restlessly across the grassy verge beyond the waiting-room, unable to settle down stoically as the others did. Physically there was no resemblance between them, but in common they wore grey suits and on the left sleeve of each was a black band of crepe. So unusual had this sign of mourning become that people turned to look at them, sometimes in curiosity, sometimes with a little amusement, as they would look at people who had not moved with the times.

Archer asked,—"May I break the news to Adeline?"

"Don't be silly," returned his father. "If she doesn't know, why is she coming?"

"I thought Uncle Finch was just bringing her."

"He'd have to tell her."

"If I were going to a university abroad and Uncle Nicholas died, would you send for me?"

"I suppose so."

"And if Auntie Meg died and Uncle Piers died and Auntie Pheasant died, would you keep right on sending for me?"

"I should probably be dead too."

Archer considered this and, as he turned over in his mind the enthralling possibilities of these flights, the gleaming plane appeared in the pale blue sky.

"There it is," he cried and ran forward.

Down the plane sank and reached the runway. From being a fabulous bird it became rather an undignified piece of mechanism as it trundled along, hesitated, stopped and disgorged. The passengers, from being helpless, strapped-in creatures, suddenly became active as ants, clutching their belongings, on the march, defensive. They did not cast a look behind but hastened forward to whatever pleasure or miseries awaited them.

Adeline caught Renny's arm. "Oh, Daddy, how glad I am to see you!"

"Uncle Ernest is dead," said Archer.

Adeline gave him a hug but he disengaged himself. He fixed his eyes on Finch. "The funeral," he said, "is tomorrow."

"So soon!" exclaimed Finch.

"It's not soon. He's been dead for days."

Renny drew Finch aside. "This has been a blow," he said, "on top of all that went before. I'm sorry I had to send for you, but—you understand."

"Yes. How is Uncle Nick?"

Renny's face lighted in pride. "He's bearing up wonderfully. Far better than I could have hoped."

"I'm glad to hear that," said Finch heavily. "Tell me how it happened."

"Well—he was determined to see the ruin——"

"*Ruin!* What ruin?"

"Ruin of Vaughanlands. It was burned down."

"Burned down!" almost shouted Finch.

"Yes. And Clapperton in it. Well, as I said, Uncle Ernest insisted——"

"But why didn't you tell me in the cable?"

"I told you all that mattered."

Finch looked about him, at the hurrying figures, at Archer stowing luggage in the car, as though at a picture too unreal for belief. He muttered,—"You were saying he was determined to go."

"Yes. He insisted and it was too much for him. He died in his sleep."

"That was merciful."

As Archer stowed away the luggage with unnecessary precision, he was saying to Adeline in his high detached voice, "The roof is fallen in. Everything is as black as

your boot, and Philip says Mr. Clapperton was too. In fact,
I know he was, for I saw him myself."

"How terrible!" For the moment, Uncle Ernest's
death was obliterated by this catastrophe.

"Yes," improvised Archer, his body rigid, "and I took
off my jacket and covered his face. It's the proper thing
to do, you know. I mean where his face *had been*."

Renny, coming up to them at this moment, noticed
Adeline's extreme pallor. She looked as though she might
faint. He took her arm and half lifted her into the car,
then slid under the wheel beside her.

"Don't feel so badly," he said. "After all, he was
pretty old and he went without pain."

"Yes," she breathed, and grasped his knee in her hand,
as though for support.

During the drive to Jalna he spoke of the arrangements
for the funeral, Finch leaning forward to hear, Archer,
in his eagerness, listening as though he would tear the
words from his father's mouth. The evening was descending in gentle gold and green. The rain had repainted the
greenness of the land. The sun moved in and out behind
little gilded clouds, casting its light now here, now there,
now touching a slope, now sending spears of brightness
into a dark wood. When they reached Jalna, all the windows
of the house were ablaze and, for an instant, the terror of
fire shocked Adeline's nerves. Now the gravel crunched
beneath the wheels and the car stopped at the side entrance.

Catching Adeline by the hand, Archer whispered,—
"Want to go round to the front and see the long black
streamer on the door?" He dragged on her hand, urging
her.

"I saw it."

Renny opened the door, with calculated caution. In the
hall there was dimness because of drawn blinds but it was
almost brutally broken by splashes of crimson and purple
from the stained-glass windows. There was a heavy scent
of flowers.

Piers came from the drawing-room to meet them, moving
with the decorous air with which he carried the alms-dish
along the aisle on a Sunday. He looked fresh and pink-

skinned and so natural that the two newcomers let their eyes rest on him in relief.

He took their hands. "You made it, eh?" he said. "Did you have a good trip?"

"Fine," answered Finch. "There was no trouble."

"Who is in there?" Renny asked, nodding towards a murmur of voices from the drawing-room.

Piers gave the names of some old friends of Ernest's.

"Lord," exclaimed Renny, in a whisper, "I haven't heard of them in years."

"I didn't know them, they'd aged so," said Piers.

"Don't take them up to Uncle Nick."

"Oh, no. They haven't suggested it. Alayne is with them."

Finch asked,—"May Adeline and I go upstairs?" Renny nodded and they tiptoed up the stairs.

In the passage they were met by Roma. "Oh, hello," she said, looking Adeline up and down, and holding a flower-pale cheek towards Finch. He bent and kissed it, then, in long silent strides, mounted to his own room. He closed the door after him and stood motionless in the safety of the room. How often, in his boyhood, had he come to its shelter, how often, in his manhood, returned to find it unchanged, waiting for him. The bed whose mattress knew every bone in his body, the washing-stand at which he had gone through the perfunctory ablutions of youth, the dressing-table with the mottled mirror into which he had peered in anxiety to tie his first evening tie, the window through which he had looked out at the night sky.

Still moving softly, as though he feared to wake someone, he went to the window and leant his forehead against the frame. Beyond the trees he could see the roofs of the stables and the last sunray touching the weather-vane. He could see the orchard and the fields heavy with growing grain. Over all there was a look of finality, as though all movement, all effort had come to an end with the passing of Ernest. Not that Ernest had made much effort in his life, except to enjoy it, in a pleasant and amiable way. Forty years ago he had begun his book on Shakespeare. He had written some chapters, born of books he had read on the subject. There were reminiscences of actors he had seen in the famous parts, and these were the only original bits in the manuscript. Ernest had cherished it, even to the last year, and promised himself that he would yet finish it, even though, a quarter of a century ago, his mother had twitted him for his inability to get on with it. Now the manuscript of his life had the final words added to it. His had been the first birth under this roof and he had spent the greater part of his life here.

"I did not want him to die," Finch said aloud. "I wanted him to be always here when I came home."

A sudden fear that he would be asked to look at Ernest swept through him. If he were forced to do that, he would not sleep tonight. He closed his eyes, seeing Ernest's face, disturbed by the fear of death. He could not, would not, go into that room!

A soft drumming came on the panel of the door. He knew at once to whom those small capable fingers belonged. A vision of Sarah, drumming on his door, came to him. He stood motionless, staring defensively at the door. The small fingers increased the tempo of their beat. A treble voice asked,—"May I come in?"

"Not now," answered Finch. "I'll be down."

"Soon?"

"Yes, soon."

"I'll be waiting at the bottom of the stairs."

"Good."

But there was no sound of footsteps leaving. Just silence. Finch listened for a little, then flung open the door. Dennis was standing there, pale, fair, with his hands clasped in front of him, as though to restrain them from drumming. Finch demanded:

"Why didn't you go when I told you to?"

"You didn't tell me."

"Yes, I did."

"How did you say it?"

"You told me you were going and I said 'Good'."

"Do I do any harm just waiting?"

"Well, not exactly. But when you say you're going to

do a thing, you should do it." Finch heard the dictatorial
tone in his own voice and was embarrassed. He patted
the little boy on the shoulder. "What I mean is," he went
on, "it's not proper to listen outside people's doors."

Dennis gave his small secret smile. "But I like to. I
like to imagine what they're doing. Did you bring me a
present from Ireland?"

"No. I'm sorry, Dennis."

"From England?"

"I left too suddenly. I intended to."

"What would it have been if you'd got it?"

"Will you go!" Finch exclaimed loudly. "This is no
time to talk of presents."

Dennis turned away. Two steps down the stairs he
looked over his shoulder. "We're supposed not to talk
loudly," he said.

Trembling with emotion and fatigue Finch poured water
into the basin and washed his face and hands. He brushed
his hair. He cleaned his nails, and the sharp point of the
knife penetrated the quick beneath the nail and it bled.
With an exclamation of pain he thrust the finger into his
mouth and sucked it. The pain seemed to go right up his
arm into his breast.

Now he felt more calm and went slowly down the stairs
into the library. Everyone was gathered there before the
evening meal. The sun was set but it was still light. The
room seemed full of people—Renny and Alayne, Piers
and Pheasant, Meg and her daughter Patience, Adeline,
Roma and Dennis. And there, yes, there he was, in an
armchair in a corner, his thick grey hair long to his collar,
his hand clasping his chin—Nicholas. Looking into his
face, Finch thought that there were traced all the experiences through which he had passed in his long life—the
bold, carefree youth of a boy born with a silver spoon
in his mouth, the storms and passions of middle life, the
rugged serenity of later years. Now indeed he had had a
great shock. The brother, so closely bound to him in
affection, if not in tastes, had closed his eyes on this world.
Nicholas had often regarded Ernest with amusement, but
always had been tolerant towards him. Though Ernest had

been of delicate physique, Nicholas had, for some reason, expected him to be the longer-lived. In truth Nicholas had not brooded on death. Now it had come so close to him that he felt the chill air of eternity on his forehead. His crest of grey hair rose as though in protest.

Finch put his hands on his shoulders, leant down and kissed him. "Uncle Nick," was all he could say.

Nicholas' voice came shaky but still deep-toned.

"Good of you—very good of you—to come. Ernest would be pleased. Very pleased."

Now Finch was enfolded in his sister's arms. "Oh, Finch, dear, what a frightful time we have been through! It's been hard for everyone, but—for *me*! Just imagine what it's been for *me*. I went to Vaughanlands as a bride and now it's burned down!"

"You got a good price for it," put in Piers.

She threw him a reproachful look. "If that isn't like you, Piers, to think of money at such at time!"

"I'm always thinking of it," he rejoined. "I'm forced to."

The folding doors into the dining-room were opened at that moment by Wragge, immensely important in a greenish black suit and large old-fashioned cravat. He announced the evening meal in a whisper.

"Where is Wakefield?" demanded Nicholas.

"He couldn't get away, Uncle Nick. He hopes to come before long."

Renny heaved the heavy old man to his feet and balanced him there. He stood, thus balanced, yet slightly moving, like an old oak, well-rooted still but rocked by the gale, and looked into the solicitous faces about him.

"I'm all right," he said, and holding to Renny's arm, stumped into the dining-room.

It was the first time he had entered it since Ernest's death. He stopped behind Ernest's chair. Renny said:

"Uncle Nick, we have set a place for Finch there, but if you'd rather the chair should be left vacant . . ."

"No, no, no," growled Nicholas. "Close in. Fill up the spaces."

"Quick march!" came in Dennis' high treble.

Renny turned on him, with a frown. "For that," he said, "you go straight upstairs to bed."

Astonishment on Dennis' face turned to concern.

"And go without my supper?"

"You may take some bread."

"I don't want it!" He ran from the room.

Finch thought,—"Why was I chosen to sit in this chair? I can't eat sitting here. It is still Uncle Ernest's place. Piers would not have minded." He saw Piers' eyes on him. He straightened himself and looked at the food on his plate. Suddenly he realized that he was hungry. Emotional strain always made him hungry.

He heard Renny say,—"Have some horseradish sauce with your beef, Uncle Nick."

"Thanks, I will. I always like horseradish but Ernest liked mustard best."

"He liked both. Both at once," said Renny, glad to hear Nicholas speak so naturally of Ernest.

"And yet," went on Nicholas, "he would have been better without either. He always had that weak digestion. I remember . . ." He forgot what he remembered and put a morsel of beef in his mouth.

When the meal was finished he decided he would go to bed. Renny helped him up the stairs, helped him to undress, sat by his bed till he fell asleep, under the soothing influence of a glass of whisky and water. He bent over him as he slept, watching how the puffed-out breath set the shaggy grey moustache aquiver, fearful, because of the way of Ernest's passing, that at any moment the breath might cease. But no—it went resolutely on, increasing in volume to a comfortable snore, and Renny tiptoed from the room.

In the passage he met Adeline. "I want you," he said, "to go into Uncle Nick's room every little while and see that he's all right. I have things to do."

She went and sat on the window-seat on the landing. The dark curtains were drawn there but she parted them, making a crack through which she could look out into the night. The new moon, clean-cut as a poised dagger, hung above the hooded trees. Adeline felt an exhaustion she never before had experienced. She had had no sleep on

the plane and her eyelids were as though weighted. An
unutterable sadness pressed on her heart. She felt that
she would never see Fitzturgis again. She recalled the
astonishment, the incredulity, on his face at the idea of
flying across the ocean for the funeral of an uncle. She
recalled Finch's brusque suggestion that they should say
good-bye, there, on the spot. They had complied without
protest. He had taken her in his arms, pressed his lips to
hers, murmured a few words she could not hear, and
left.

He was gone out of her life. Like Uncle Ernest's, her life
was over. It was done with. . . . The grandfather clock
on the landing gathered itself together to strike the hour.
It seemed to hum and haw over the striking, as though
reluctant. But from Ernest's bedroom the hour came, clear
and sweet, from his little glass travelling clock whose
visible works had always charmed her. Who would wind
it now, she wondered. She knew where the key was kept,
in the little drawer in the yew-tree desk in Ernest's room.
. . . With a start, she remembered her father's injunction
to look in on Nicholas. She hastened to his room, only
remembering to move quietly after she had reached the
door. It stood open and through it, like a persistent call
to life, sounded the old man's snoring. It rumbled in his
throat and shook his lips. Gentle moonlight just touched
the articles on the dressing-table. The rest of the room
was very dark. The light glimmered on the tumbler in
which had been the whisky and water. It touched the
yellowish ivory of the toilet articles, bottles with silver
stoppers, the glass of a framed photograph.

In the passage Alayne, coming up the stairs, met Adeline.
How quietly everyone moved! It was Adeline's first experience of death. She had a sudden desire to go to her mother
and hide herself in her for protection. The heavy scent of
flowers came up the stairway.

"We've had more people in," said Alayne, with an
exhausted smile. "I think that is the last of them."

"I wish I could help."

Alayne gave her a curious look. "What are you doing
here?" she asked.

"Daddy told me to keep an eye on Uncle Nicholas."

"Really, there is no need for that. Your father is over-careful. In any case, I shall be quite near in my own room. You must go to bed, Adeline. You look terribly tired."

"All right," Adeline answered in a choking voice. "I'll go." She put her arms about Alayne and they clung together, in the most loving embrace they ever had known.

"You must not feel so badly, darling," Alayne said, conscious of Adeline's tears. "Let us be thankful that Uncle Ernest had no suffering."

Adeline could not tell her that it was Fitzturgis for whom the tears came. . . .

When the last of the visitors were gone Renny and Piers stood outdoors in the cool of the night. The moon had long since disappeared. It was very dark. Piers took out his cigarette-lighter, the one Pheasant had given him on his last birthday, and held it to Renny's cigarette. The flame illumined the aquiline features, the long flat cheeks, the brown eyes, in which there were greenish lights.

Piers thought,—"Old Redhead wears well. No matter how much worry he has, he is able to take it."

The light from a window touched the leaves on the nearest trees. These few leaves stood out wetly bright, the rest were a dark mass. Finch came through the door and joined his brothers. It was characteristic of him that, on occasions of stress, he could look more grievously afflicted than anyone else. Now Renny and Piers regarded him with mingled tolerance and cynicism. Renny said:

"You'd better go to bed."

"I'm not going to bed."

"Then how would you like," asked Renny, "to stay in the room with Uncle Ernest?"

"I couldn't." Finch's voice came loudly. "I couldn't possibly."

Piers spoke soothingly. "Of course not. You're tired out. We're all tired out." And he added,—"I was just saying I'll be glad when all this is over."

"He can't forget his haying," said Renny.

"It's strange," Finch's voice was now low and husky,

"how the crops are gathered in and, in our turn, we're gathered in."

"Sort of jolly merry-go-round, isn't it?" said Piers.

Renny said,—"This is the first funeral at Jalna since Gran's."

"I'll never forget that day," said Piers. "The weather was perfect. The whole countryside turned out. There'll be no such crowd tomorrow!"

"I'm afraid not," agreed Renny. "Uncle Ernest had a retiring nature. He made no such impression. He didn't live to be a hundred."

Piers yawned. "I'm going home, fellows."

"Be here in good time tomorrow," adjured Renny.

Piers went to where his car was parked. In a moment he passed the others with a wave of the hand. The headlights of the car fell on a syringa bush in full bloom. The movement of air brought the sweet scent to the two standing in the darkness.

"You say you're not going to bed?" asked Renny.

"I couldn't sleep."

"Come in and we'll have a drink."

Standing in the dining-room by the sideboard they raised their glasses in silence. The portrait of their grandmother, in her yellow satin gown, smiled down on them, that of their grandfather, in his Hussar's uniform, wore a look of unquestioned and unquestioning wellbeing, not reflected on the faces of his descendants.

"They lived in better days," said Renny.

Finch nodded, feeling the glow of the spirits through all his nerves.

"It's a funny thing," continued Renny. "I've been through two wars. I've seen a lot of death. But . . ." He reached for the decanter and poured another drink. "But —I never grow . . ." he sought for a word, then added,— "less afraid. I have a horror of death. To tell you the truth, and you must never repeat this to Piers, I should like to hide in the woods till all this is over. It's a sort of instinctive animal feeling that I can't explain."

"Yet you are the one who attends to everything—insists that everything shall be properly done."

"Naturally."

Finch raised his voice a little. "And you are the one who suggested I should stay in that room tonight."

"Yes," he grinned.

Finch had swallowed his second drink far too quickly. His thoughts became confused, there was the roaring of a distant sea in his ears, Renny's face appeared to him hawk-like, the eyes gleaming, the grin cruel.

"It was a damn cruel thing to suggest," he muttered.

"I wanted to find out about you."

"Well, I didn't do it and I wouldn't do it for any man . . . Don't think I didn't love Uncle Ernest. I thought more of him than any of you did." He spoke incoherently.

"That's possible."

"What I mean is, Uncle Ernest understood me better than anyone else did."

"Ah, he had a kind heart."

"He had an understanding heart." Finch spoke angrily now, as though someone had denied this.

"True. Very true."

Finch took another drink, this time in stormy silence, his hand shaking, his heart beating heavily.

"If you go to bed now," said Renny, "you'll sleep like a log." He took Finch by the arm. "Come along," he urged.

"No!" But he allowed himself to be propelled towards the door.

In the hall Renny halted abruptly, his eyes caught by a thin line of light beneath the door of Adeline's room. This room had once been her grandmother's.

"Look," exclaimed Renny. "Adeline's light! Good God, that child shouldn't be sleeping down here alone."

"Adeline's a brave kid," muttered Finch.

Renny tapped on the door. There was no answer. He gently opened it. Adeline's clothes had been cast off in confusion over chairs and floor. She lay, in her white night-dress, without other covering, her white feet close together, one arm shielding her eyes.

"Why, she's grown!" exclaimed Renny. "How tall she is!" She uncovered her eyes and looked at them without surprise.

"You shouldn't be here alone," said Renny. "You should have gone to the spare room."

"I wanted my own room. Mummy said to go with her but I said I'd stay here."

"I can't leave you."

"I'll shtay with her," said Finch. "Lie on the floor outshide her door."

"No. She shall go upstairs." Renny put a hand beneath her head and raised her to a sitting position.

She looked up into his face. "Daddy, I want to see Uncle Ernest. Now. I can't sleep till I do."

"Very well, you shall."

"No, Adeline, don't do that," Finch said hoarsely. "Don't let her, Renny. It will be upsetting to her."

Without answering, Renny set her on her feet. She stood white-draped, large-eyed, a symbol of youthful sorrow. Renny, with Finch following, led her along the hall to the door of the room where Ernest lay. He opened it.

At first Adeline could see only the flowers, wreath upon wreath, cross after cross, lying on the tables, lying on the casket, roses and lilies sending out their amorous scent, weighted with a cloying sweetness. Renny, with his arm close about her, led her to the casket. Finch stood a little behind. Her first thought was, why had they made Uncle Ernest so tidy? To be sure, his hair always was smooth, his clothes in order, but this terrible sleekness, this iron immaculateness, was unreal. And he who always had a pink complexion was now a strange waxen white. He wore a faint secretive smile, unlike any smile she had ever seen on Uncle Ernest's face.

She looked at him quite calmly. This was not the dear old man over whose body she had romped as a child, who had been so eager for her to marry Maurice. This was a stranger. He was as unreal as the unreal flowers about him.

"It's extraordinary how natural he looks, isn't it?" said Renny.

"Yes," she breathed, and added after a moment,— "I'd like to go now."

"It's a beautiful old face," said Finch, and bent and kissed Ernest on the forehead.

"It is," agreed Renny, "and he had a beautiful nature. There never was another Whiteoak with such a gentle disposition."

They went into the dim hall, closing the door behind them.

"Now do you feel more natural?" Renny asked.

"Yes. I'll go to whatever room you say."

He led her up the stairs to the spare room, while Finch, with a muttered good night, mounted, rather unsteadily, the second flight of stairs.

Alayne, in a dressing-gown, appeared from her room.

"This child," said Renny, "has decided to sleep in the spare room after all."

"That is what I begged her to do but she refused." Alayne spoke in the impersonal tone of extreme weariness.

"Well—she sees now that you were right."

Adeline stood between them, docile, in her long white nightdress. She looked on while they turned down the covers, plumped the pillow and prepared a nest for her. When she was in it she looked up at them trustingly, lovingly, as when she was a child.

XXVI

THE BELL TOLLS FOR ERNEST

ALTHOUGH Noah Binns was now a man of seventy-eight, he insisted that he should not only toll the bell for Ernest but dig his grave for him also. From the moment when he learned of Ernest's death, these two acts loomed large in his mind, with himself as the central figure. A sparkling breeze tossed the leaves and it was pleasantly cool. He had made a good start with the grave on the day before, so this morning it was just a matter of digging it a little deeper and shaping it.

As he stood in the cool earth-smelling cavity he thought how remarkable it was that, in spite of all modern inventions, nothing better than a grave had been invented for the finish of a man. Noah made this remark to young Elmer Chalk who had succeeded him as sexton.

"There ain't nothing better," he said, "than a grave. It beats cremation hollow."

"Give me cremation every time," said Chalk.

"*Every time!*" repeated Noah, in derision. "There's only one time. Why do you want to be cremated?"

"It's cleaner."

"I call ashes dirty. Who wants to be a handful of ashes? Let me keep my shape as long as it will last."

"How long do you say it will last?"

Noah indicated, with a jerk of his earthy thumb, the graves enclosed in this plot. "If you was to open these up," he said, "you'd be surprised. You'd find Captain White-oak; the old lady, his wife; their son Philip and his two wives; Philip's son Eden, and them three babies—all with their clothes on."

In spite of himself young Chalk was impressed.

311

"Just the same," he said, "give me cremation. What about being buried alive?"

"I seen every one of these, except the babies, and if ever folks was dead they was." With an air of finality he drove the spade into the rich earth.

"My grandfather, the blacksmith, knew them all."

"And I dug *his* grave and it was a cheap coffin his folks gave him."

"They gave him the best they could afford."

"Hmph . . . Well, I have the money saved up in the bank to pay fer as fine a funeral for me as fer any danged Whiteoak."

Still nettled, the young man returned,—"There won't be so many to mourn for you, Mr. Binns."

"I don't want no mourning for me. But I've lived a danged sight better life than some of them that rests in this plot. That young feller, Eden, he was no good but you'd ha' thought he was a saint, the way they buried him."

"What did you expect them to do?"

"There's ways and ways. Folks like them are gettin' rare. Before long they'll be distinct."

"Extinct," corrected Chalk.

"Have it your own way. That's what young folks is like. They think they know it all. When I feel like givin' a young feller a kick in the pants, I remember I hadn't no sense when I was his age."

It was seldom that Noah Binns was so talkative, but grave-digging always exhilarated him. It had been hard indeed for him because of advancing years to give up this profitable pleasure.

Now the job was done and he leant on his spade tired out. Young Chalk had gone and the churchyard was silent except for the flutter of birds' wings as they hastened with food for their young, and the occasional passing of a motor car along the road below. Like some ancient robin, Noah drew an earthworm out from the side of the grave, examined it critically, then dropped it on the ground and drove the spade through it. He watched the agitation of the two halves for a moment, then planted his heavy boot on them.

There was now little enough time in which to go home, have some food, wash himself and return to toll the bell for the service. He tossed out his spade, laid his hands on the sides of the grave and prepared to heave himself out. But he could not. The grave was too deep and his arms were too tired. Again and again he heaved himself but each time his body seemed to grow heavier and his arms weaker. He began to feel exhausted, trapped. His voice, when he opened his mouth and called for young Chalk, came hollowly. His mouth hung open disclosing his one black tooth. He began desperately but weakly to call for help. At first the birds were frightened but they became used to the calling and a hen robin even dropped to the mound of earth beside the grave and began pecking in it for worms.

Noah felt ready to drop. In a panic he uttered a loud hoarse yell. "Help! Help!"

He heard steps, first on the gravel, then on the grass. He looked up, in mingled relief and chagrin, into the face of Renny Whiteoak. He had rather have been rescued by anyone else.

"Huh," he grunted, with a truculent look upward, as though he would deny his predicament.

"What's the matter?" demanded Renny.

"I've dug this here grave too deep. There ain't no call fer any grave to be this deep. I can't get out."

"The digging's too hard for you. You should have let Elmer do it."

"Don't you worry about me." Noah stretched his mouth in a malevolent grin. "I'll dig many a grave yet."

"Why, you were retired at our last churchwardens' meeting."

"I still dig for them as is over ninety. And I'd like to see anyone stop me!"

"My God," exclaimed Renny, "I've a mind to leave you down there."

"Then what'll you do with your uncle? There ain't room fer two?" Noah's grin became jocular.

Renny frowned. "Come now," he said, grasping Noah's arms, "out with you!"

Profoundly relieved, Noah sprawled a moment on the grass, then gathered up his spade and earth-stained coat. Without a thank-you he clumped down the steep path to the gate and along the roadside towards home. All the way there he grumbled over his ill-luck in being forced to call for help from a grave. Such a thing had never happened to him before.

By an odd coincidence the black coat which he wore to the funeral was an old one given to him by Ernest White-oak. He greatly fancied himself in it and, when he had washed, eaten, and donned it, he had a good look at himself in the little looking-glass in his kitchen. The weather was turning hot again. His coat was tight. He was as thankful as it was possible for him to be when he got a lift right from his own door to the church. He felt quite fresh as he climbed the steps. He took off his black hat and laid it on a bench in the vestibule. In there, it was quiet and cool. He examined the bell-rope with great exactness, as though he feared it might not be strong enough to withstand the fervour of his pulling. High up in the steeple he could see the brazen bell hanging in slumber, waiting for his sum-mons to toll.

The relations between Noah Binns and this bell were peculiar. He looked on it as having a proud, aloof and stubborn nature which only he could control. He could, as he thought, make it talk, be jubilant, or strike its iron bosom in mourning. There was no doubt that the bell, on its part, was moody. For several years it had had a tendency to ring a flat and toneless note for a wedding and a cheerful flippant one for early Communion or a funeral. As Noah gazed up into the dimness where it hung he wore a look of grim command. As he dropped the bell-rope from his hand a quiver ran along it, up to the brooding bell.

"Ninety-five strokes I'll give the old gentleman. Ninety-five—if it kills me.—One hundred and one I gave his old mother and had lumbago fer a week. Thirty-one to his nephew Eden. And so it goes—right back to a single ding fer a baby. A good thing it was that not all of them lived. There's a danged sight too many of 'em."

He straightened himself, spat on both palms, and grasped the rope. He pulled hard but, though the bell rocked in its high place, only a toneless grunt came from it. Noah bared his tooth in anger, put all the strength in him on to the rope. "Come now, get goin', you rascal. Get goin'."

He must have pulled too hard, for the bell now walloped in the steeple, its tongue, as though in its cheek, defying him. But, at last, he was able to bring forth the slow sonorous notes of the tolling, each one dying away over the summer fields before the next one struck. Noah counted them aloud, though his voice was inaudible, even to himself. So slow was the tolling that small birds, affrighted by a note, would fly from the roof of the church, circle, and alight again before the next one struck.

Young Chalk appeared in the vestibule, dressed in his Sunday clothes. "How're you getting on?" he shouted.

"Fine."

"Shall I take a hold too?"

"Shut up. Ye're makin' me lose count."

Chalk stepped into the church. It was peaceful and cool in there but the air coming in at the windows was hot.

Before half the number of strokes had been counted, people began to appear, pass through the door and take seats quietly in the body of the church. Quite a number were already gathered when the hearse and the cars bearing the mourners appeared. Renny, Piers, Finch and Nooky shouldered the coffin and carried it up the steep path. Slowly they approached the church, the bell knelling their progress.

In the vestibule, Renny turned his head to look at Noah who, straining on the bell-rope, increased the velocity of the strokes, in an exhausting attempt to achieve the ninety-fifth. His jaw dropped in dismay at Renny's peremptory nod to desist. A final clang broke from the bell as the procession entered the church.

It passed the font which had been built for Ernest's christening. Almost a century ago his weak infant body had lain in the arms of the Rector while water was sprinkled upon his face, he having already, through his godparents, renounced the devil and all his works, the vain pomp and glory of the world and the carnal lusts of the flesh. Now, meekly he lay in his coffin before the chancel steps.

Mr. Fennel looked old and fragile, but his voice rang out clear and strong, saying:

"'I am the resurrection and the life, saith the Lord: he that believeth in me, though he were dead, yet shall he live, and whosoever liveth and believeth in me shall never die!'"

Nicholas had walked very slowly along the aisle, leaning on the strong arm of Piers' son Philip. He had let himself down into the pew cautiously, then rested his grey head on his hand, the light touching the heavy signet ring which he always wore. Alayne, sitting beside him, laid her hand on his arm, and, after a little, he took her hand in his.

Ernest lay, among his flowers, unable to hear the words that were spoken, or to smell the summer scents that filled the air. His favourite hymn, "Lead, Kindly Light," did not penetrate his fastness. By ones and twos the people came forward to look in his face. Nicholas had taken his last look before they had left the house but now he strained upward in his seat to glimpse his brother's profile once again.

The pallbearers raised the heavy coffin and the service proceeded by the grave.

Scarcely had the last of the congregation left the church-yard when young Chalk threw off his jacket and began to fill in the unsightly cavity with earth. As that mound diminished so the grave was filled, the grave was made and well shaped, it was covered by flowers. Chalk was joined by Noah Binns and the two looked down admiringly at their work.

XXVII

IN THE KITCHEN ONCE MORE

The summer was over and had been, as Noah Binns prophesied, a hot one. Now the ground was dry and the grass harsh for lack of moisture. The pasture was so poor that cattle must be given a deal of extra feed to supplement it. The kernels of the grain were small, the apples were smaller than usual, but, on the whole, crops were good and because of the warmth and sunshine the young creatures of the farm flourished. Wright, having tea in the kitchen with the Wragges, was well pleased by the growth of the foals which had been produced that year.

"I've never seen a likelier bunch than the four of them," he said. "It'll be a surprise to me if the boss don't get the highest prices for them."

"They sure look promising," said Mrs. Wragge.

His cup half-way to his mouth, he stared at her in surprise.

"You been over to see them?" he asked.

"Why not? I can walk, can't I?"

"Well, you don't often leave the house."

"Miss Adeline dragged her over," put in Wragge, "or she'd never 'ave went."

"I wish I'd been there," said Wright. "I'd like to have shown you about. Did you see our lovely two-year-old?"

"Sure."

"She's to be trained for the King's Plate."

"That's the way the money goes."

"Nothing venture—nothing win."

Mrs. Wragge looked sceptical. "If the boss wants to breed show horses, let him," she said. "If he wants to

317

breed high jumpers, it's O.K. by me. But—racehorses—
never! That's for men of means."

"D'you mean to say," demanded Wright, "that you
wouldn't call him a man of means?"

"Not the way money's counted nowadays."

"Look at the hired help he keeps!"

"Yes. Look at us. That's what I say to my husband.
We could get higher wages elsewhere. So could you."

"I'm satisfied," said Wright staunchly.

Wragge spoke, as from a high intellectual level. "We
are creatures of 'abit," he declared. "My wife wouldn't
know what to do with herself in a modern kitchen. Could
I get along without the inconveniences I'm used to? No.
'Abit is everything." He winked at Wright. "Wot should
I do if I found myself in possession of a slim wife? Nothing.
I'd be dumbfounded."

The cook laughed across her double chin. "And serve
you right," she said.

A knock came on the outer door. At the same moment
it opened and the gargoyle head of Noah Binns appeared.
Hospitable Mrs. Wragge called out to him to enter, which
he did, clumping down the steps with ostentatious effort.

"Stairs—stairs—everywhere," he grumbled. "They say
there's golden stairs leadin' up to Heaven. Why don't they
have an escalator that'd take a feller up without no trouble?"
He dropped creaking into the nearest chair.

"That's the way they go to the other place," said Rags.
"Smooth and slippery. You just sit down on the seat of
your pants and you're there."

"That's supposed to be wit," Mrs. Wragge remarked
to Wright. She poured a cup of tea for Noah. "This is
the first time I've saw you since the funeral," she said.

Reaching for a slice of thick bread and butter he answered,
—"I ain't the man I was. Forty-nine times I tugged on
that rope and every time the bell acted contrary, like it had
spite in it."

"For goodness' sake," exclaimed Mrs. Wragge.

"I was just gettin' the best of it when Colonel Whiteoak
ordered me to quit. My, what an unchristian look that man
can give!"

"I don't want to hear anything against him," put in Wright.

Ignoring the interruption, Noah went on,—"So I quit, though I had it in me to toll the full number of his years."

"It'd probably 've killed you," said the cook. "Have some more tea."

He pushed his cup across the table to her and cast a lustful eye on her rich curves.

"Not me," he said, reaching for cake. "I get terrible tired but I eat wheat germ and raw carrot and I'm ready fer the next funeral."

"Raw carrot, with one tooth!" exclaimed Rags.

"I thought you'd retired," said Wright.

"I have—except for folk over ninety."

Mrs. Wragge patted her hair and swept some crumbs off the table with the flat of her hand. "I've asked Mr. Raikes to drop in," she said.

Her husband frowned. "I'd like to know why you asked him."

Looking boldly back, she said,—"Ah, wouldn't you!"

"I doubt if he'll come," said Wright. "He's getting above himself, that guy."

"For the love of Pete!" she exclaimed. "Why on earth?"

"Well, from what I hear, he spends most of his time in the bungalow with Mrs. Clapperton."

"Now, look here," she said, in defence, "don't be mean. He's working for her to clear away the rubble."

"*Him* working! Ha, ha, ha!"

"The trouble with you men is you're all jealous of his looks," she jeered.

"I may not be handsome," said Wright, "but I wouldn't change faces with that fellow."

"Womenfolk are all for looks," Rags said, and added jauntily,—"The missus married me fer mine."

"He proposed to me in the dark," she threw back.

Noah had been scraping the jam-pot. Now he said,— "I've got along without looks. Never had no use fer them. Except in females."

"They say," said Wright, "that Tom Raikes plans to step into Mr. Clapperton's shoes."

"I like his cheek," said Rags enviously.

"Then there'll be a mess of bungalows," declared Noah. "Bungalows—blight—and bugs. D'you know how many birch trees died from blight this year? Twenty thousand! Twenty thousand bungalows was built and twenty thousand tater bugs is attackin' the taters. Blight, bungalows and bugs. What's the cure?" He attacked a piece of fruit cake while he waited for the answer.

"What?" demanded Wright.

"The atom bomb. That's the cure. And I hope I'll be here to see."

"Cheerful, ain't you?" said Rags.

His mouth full, Noah managed to articulate,—"The world's agettin' ready fer doom. Capitalism brung this state on. Communism'll bust it up."

"He knows all the answers," Mrs. Wragge said admiringly.

A shadow fell across the window and the company looked up to see Raikes' legs. His gentle knock sounded on the door.

"Come in," sang out the cook and again patted her hair.

He said a pleasant good-day and seated himself at the table. Mrs. Wragge dropped an extra lump of sugar into his cup, not unnoticed by Noah who at once stretched out a gnarled hand and helped himself to another.

"And how is the old gentleman?" asked Raikes of Mrs. Wragge.

"He's gettin' on fine," she answered. "I thought the shock would've killed him but he takes his food and he sleeps and makes his little joke, almost as good as ever."

"Just the same," added Rags, "he misses Mr. Ernest. We all do. I never 'ad an impatient word from 'im."

"Clapperton and him are both gone," said Wright, "and if I don't miss my guess, Mr. Ernest went up and Clapperton below."

"Ah, I wouldn't say that," objected Raikes.

"Wouldn't say Clapperton went below?"

"No. We all have our faults."

Wright gave the table a thump. "That man," he said, "did more to upset the neighbourhood than anyone has ever done."

"Upset this house, you mean," said Raikes. "Nobody minded about those few bungalows but the people here. And I've a bit of news for you. Mrs. Clapperton has sold the Black farm—that wee farm, y'know—and the man who's bought it plans to build sixty little houses on it. All like as peas."

"The bloody scoundrel!" Wright set his jaw hard, then said,—"Pardon my language, Mrs. Wragge."

"That's nothing to what I hear," she smiled.

"Well, I like that," declared Rags.

"I use only one curse-word," said Noah. "It's served me fer nigh on eighty years."

"Sakes alive," screamed the cook. "You must've begun usin' it in the cradle."

"That I did. It was the first word I spoke and I guess it'll be my last. *Dang*."

Wright was brooding on building possibilities. He asked of Raikes,—"What's to become of Vaughanlands?"

"Mrs. Clapperton hasn't decided. She's had several offers."

"Another outcrop of bungalows, I'll bet."

"I shouldn't wonder."

"It'll ruin this property," said Wright, with a black frown.

Raikes thoughtfully stirred his tea. "I doubt if Mrs. Clapperton will want to build a big house on the property," he said, "though there's a lot of good material can be salvaged."

Mrs. Wragge asked,—"How does she like livin' in that little bungalow alongside the Barkers?"

"Ah, she likes it fine."

"And her sister?"

"I'm not so sure about her. She's a quare girl." An enigmatic smile played about his lips.

Dennis came slowly down the stairs that descended from the hall.

"Well, my man," the cook asked, "and what do you want?"

"Something to eat," he answered, in his clear voice.

"You'll be eating at the proper time." There was no encouragement in her tone.

"I'm hungry now."

"I'm too busy. Run along."

He sat down on a step.

Mrs. Wragge said, in an undertone,—"He's an awful one to hang about and listen. I can't seem to make him out."

Rags brought a plate of cake to the little boy. "'Ere, take a piece and be off," he said.

Dennis looked the cake over. "I don't like that sort."

"You just say that to give trouble."

"No. Honestly. I like chocolate cake."

Cook said loudly,—"There ain't none. So you go up and shut the door at the top."

"I wasn't listening."

"Ho—ho." She turned in her chair to look at him. "Now listen. You tell me one thing we said and I'll find a piece of chocolate cake for you."

He tapped the tips of his fingers together. "Then you'd say I was a liar, wouldn't you?"

A chuckle ran round the table. Wright said,—"You're not going to fall into any trap, are you, Dennis?"

Dennis went up the stairs on hands and feet and, at the top, slammed the door behind him.

"'E's got a sly way with 'im," observed Rags.

"I never did like children," said Noah, smacking his lips, then wiping them on his sleeve. "They've got to be. We can't stop it. But keep them out o' the way, I sez."

Raikes smiled gently. "I always like young things," he said.

After a little he rose, thanked Mrs. Wragge for his tea, and departed. He went straight to the bungalow where the two sisters lived. He could see Gem's face at the window. His own face lighted. He raised his hand in salute. She beckoned and opened the door to him.

"Althea's out for the next hour," Gem whispered against his cheek. Nevertheless he locked the door.

"What's that for?" she demanded, as though angry.

"I don't like her walking in on us."

"We won't be doing anything that matters. What will she think if she finds the door locked?"

"I don't care a damn what she thinks."

"*I* have to live with her!"

"Okay," he said, "I'll unlock the door." This he did, then came and sat down.

"You usen't to sit down while a lady was standing."

He gave her a look that tingled through all her nerves.

"You're not a lady now," he said.

"What am I then?"

"The woman I love best in all the worrld."

She came and stood close to him, languishing against him. He wrapped his arm about her and raised his eyes, as in worship, to her face.

"I do love this little room," she exclaimed. "Oh, you've no idea, Tom, what it is to me to feel free. Although this is such a tiny place I can breathe in it. I was suffocated in that big house. I'm glad it is burned." She left him and walked up and down the room filled with cumbersome furniture from the big house. The face of Eugene had come between them, and, for a moment, pity shook her. "Don't think I'm not sorry for him," she added hoarsely.

"Of course you are," he said, in a comforting voice, "and so am I. Indeed he was a fine man."

"And I'm grateful, too."

"Of course. And so am I. Ah, he had a kind way with him."

"He used to call me 'girlie'."

"Did he now?"

"And I called him—no, I can't say it."

"Go on, tell me."

"No," she answered sharply.

A mischievous smile lighted his dark face. "I'll bet I know."

"You'd never guess if you guessed all night. No. That name is buried with him."

"Poor man, he had his troubles."

"Well, I guess he's better dead. I couldn't have gone on living with him."

"He was an old stick," Raikes added composedly.

She gave a wild laugh, throwing off her sadness of the moment.

"What's funny in that?" he demanded.

"The way you put things . . . You're irresistible."

He took out a full packet of cigarettes, extracted one, lighted it and laid the burnt match carefully on a convenient ash-tray.

The feeble electric bell tinkled in the kitchen. Startled they stared at the outer door. Raikes rose to his feet and looked questioningly towards the kitchen.

"No." She framed the word with her lips.

Raikes dropped his cigarette and put his foot on it. He kicked it under a couch. He picked up his hat. Another ring sounded. Gem went to the door.

Finch Whiteoak stood there, bareheaded, tall against the little front yard with its pink petunias. It was not the first time they had met since Eugene Clapperton's death. Before this, they had encountered each other by the ruins of the house. He had briefly sympathized with her, and escaped, too conscious of the gossip about her. Now he entered with an air of purpose. Raikes deferentially waited for dismissal, hat in hand.

"I suppose you have met Tom," said Gem, after she had exchanged greetings with Finch. "He looks after the place for me."

"Yes. I know. It must be a job to get things in order."

"Ah, it's not so bad," said Raikes. "We have the land let to a very good farmer. The thing is to get the place tidied up." He spoke with gravity.

"Sit down, won't you?" Gem said to Finch. It was exciting to have a visitor in this tiny house. "I feel like a cottage woman," she laughed. "I ought to be dusting the seat of your chair with my apron."

Finch seated himself and looked about the room. He wondered how the sisters could live in such a small space with so much large furniture.

Following his glance Gem said,—"I'm going to sell all this stuff and buy things suitable for small rooms."

"Then you're staying on here?" he asked, in surprise.

"Yes, for a while. Then I want to travel—to go back to see Wales. But I shall keep this place. Ever since these bungalows were built I've wished I lived in one of them instead of in the big house."

How could she stay here, Finch wondered, so close to the scene of her husband's tragic death? He asked:

"Are you going to keep all the property?"

"I may keep the farm and this land where Eugene planned his model village, but I'll not have any more developing. I hate it."

"Then why," Finch asked accusingly, "did you sell the Blacks' place to a building contractor? That is quite a blow to us at Jalna, you know."

She turned quickly to Raikes, who was still standing, as though to ask him to speak for her.

This he did, in a conciliatory undertone.

"Mrs. Clapperton thought, sir, that the building on the Blacks' little farm wouldn't be any throuble to you, as there's several large fields and a thicket between Jalna and it."

Finch, ignoring Raikes, demanded of Gem,—"Why didn't you give my brother the first chance?"

Again her glance appealed to Raikes, who answered,— "Mrs. Clapperton wanted the cash, sir."

Finch's colour rose. Still looking at Gem, he asked,— "What made you think my brother could not have paid the cash?"

"I don't know," she answered lamely. Then, as though to cover her embarrassment, she said to Raikes,—"Sit down, Tom," and added to Finch,—"Tom Raikes has been a great help to me through all this."

Raikes gave a somewhat sheepish smile and seated himself on the edge of a straight-backed chair. He laid his hat on his knees.

Gem continued,—"It's very hard for a woman left alone to know what is best to do for herself. Althea has no head for business."

"Well," said Finch, "I have come on a matter of business and should have preferred to speak to you privately, but—of course, if you——" He hesitated.

"It's all right," she said, with one of her bold glances, "Tom understands everything."

"I have come," said Finch, "to see if I can buy what's left of the house, and all the land."

She showed her astonishment. "But what would you do with it?"

Finch gave his quick boyish laugh. "Oh, I should rent the farm, as you do. I'd have the walls of the house pulled down and the material used to build a new house."

"And would you live there?"

"Yes."

"But you're away most of the time."

"I want to be more at home, to have a place of my own where I can write music. I've had enough of playing in public."

"Good heavens," she cried, "how can you say that? I'd give my soul to have a talent—any sort of talent that would bring me the least little bit of fame. It seems hard to me that two of my sisters are talented—Molly an actress, and Althea a painter, and me—nothing! You'd never find me retiring. I'd enjoy all the publicity possible."

"Probably," said Finch, and added quickly,—"Don't think I haven't enjoyed my audiences. But a time comes when one wants to belong to oneself."

"Can one really?" she asked with eagerness.

"I'm going to try."

"And you'll live at Vaughanlands alone?"

"Yes."

She laughed gaily. "And Humphrey Bell in his little house alone! And me in my little house!"

Suddenly grave, Finch asked,—"Have you settled on a price for the property? I mean the entire property—the farm, the farmhouse, the bungalows and the house and gardens."

"I'll sell everything but this bungalow for——" She glanced at Raikes.

His lips, hardening, framed a figure in excess of what they had previously settled on.

This passage was not unseen by Finch.

"Forty thousand dollars," she said, almost aggressively. "If I paid cash would you accept thirty-five thousand?" Again her eyes sought Raikes. He nodded.

"Yes," she said.

In a few minutes the bargain was struck and Finch left the bungalow elated.

As the door closed behind him Raikes threw his hat up to the ceiling and caught it on his head. Standing with it jauntily over one eye, he smiled happily at Gem.

"Good work," he commended, as though patting them both on the back.

"Oh, Tom," she cried, flinging both arms about him in ecstasy. "What *masses* of money we have!"

"What I want to know is," he said, with sulkiness in his tone, "when we're going to be married."

"Not for a year."

"I'll wait no longer than next spring."

"What will people say?"

"They'll say no worse than if we waited a year. Come now, say you'll marry me in the spring."

Her kiss of agreement was fresh on his lips when they heard Althea and her dog coming up the path to the door. Raikes released Gem and glided out through the kitchen.

As the front door opened, she saw the young moon shining above Althea's shoulder. The Great Dane, in massive elegance, stalked past her, and with a loud bark demanded his supper.

"It's the most divine evening," Althea said. "I met Finch Whiteoak and he told me you'd sold him the property."

"Oh, did he? He might have left that for me to tell."

"Are you glad he is buying it?"

"Well, it's nice to think I'm doing something to please the Whiteoak family."

"What do you suppose they'll think when you marry Tom? You are going to, aren't you?"

Gem stiffened in astonishment. Althea so seldom mentioned Raikes' name, and when she did let it pass her lips, she spoke it in a constrained and tremulous voice. Now she put this question in a cold matter-of-fact tone.

It was Gem's voice that trembled. "What makes you think I am?" she asked.

"Well, if I thought enough of a man to have him in my room at night, I'd think enough of him to marry him."

Each looked at the other with a sudden cold dislike.

"How do you know I have him in my room?"

Althea gave a little smile. "Don't ask me to go into details," she said.

"There's one thing certain," Gem said fiercely. "He never entered my room till after Eugene's death."

"But he made love to you."

"I'm flesh and blood. I'd have gone mad if I hadn't had something to make me forget Eugene." And she added,— "I love him. You don't know what it is to love a man."

"Oh, don't I?"

Gem spoke in a softer tone. "I don't want to drive you away by this marriage, Althea. You must stay on here."

Althea opened wide her light blue eyes, as in horror.

"*Me* stay on?" she cried. "In the house with that man? Never."

The blood rushing to her face, Gem demanded,— "Where shall you go? You can't earn your living."

"I soon shall be able to. I'm going to New York to live with Molly. I shall keep house for her in her apartment and go to a school of designing. It's all arranged."

"Have you told Molly all you know?"

"Yes."

"What a filthy trick!"

"I don't look at it that way," Althea said calmly. "I had to be prepared."

After a pause Gem asked,—"What does Molly think?"

"She says nothing you do will surprise her."

The Great Dane, which had gone into the kitchen, now came to the doorway, looked at Althea, and uttered a demanding bark.

"What about him?" asked Gem.

"Finch Whiteoak is going to keep him for me."

"What! Did you arrange that today—in those few minutes?"

"Oh, no, it's all been arranged for a month."

She went into the kitchen and began to prepare the dog's supper, he barking his approval.

Gem darted through the front door and round to where the car was parked. She had sold the larger of the two. Raikes was lounging against the car, smoking. "Oh, Tom," she panted, breathless,—"Althea is going. She's going to our sister Molly in New York. Isn't it wonderful? We shall be alone!"

XXVIII

FINCH AND HIS PLANS

IN SPITE of his sorrow over Ernest's death, and even perhaps because of it, Finch now experienced a fresh urge in life. Autumn, his favourite season of the year, was on the way. He had made no concert engagements till the winter. He was to own Vaughanlands, to be next door to Jalna. Soon he would have builders at work to build him a house, a design like the old house which now stood in ruins, to retain the character of the place. Months of freedom lay ahead of him. For a time he was his own man.

The afterglow of sunset blazed in the west. He turned his steps towards the ruin, no longer a ruin to him but the foundation of a new design in his life. A row of poplars stood between the bungalows and the grounds of the house. These were uninjured by the fire but, the first trees to shed their foliage, were already sending down showers of yellow heart-shaped leaves. Finch scuffed his way through these and drew a deep breath, inhaling the new scent now added to the air. A rabbit in his path was transfixed into incredible stillness. Then, as Finch took one step farther, it leaped in an electrified arc out of sight among the weeds. Already weeds were taking possession of the garden. Goldenrod, which above all wild growing things Eugene Clapperton had hated, now blazed in insolence. Ragweed was gone to seed. The pale down of milkweed floated in the air. On the unkempt lawns a late blooming of dandelions showed their sprightly heads. Even among the rubble there were delicate green growths. Seeds dropped by birds had taken root and were hastening to grow, as though with the urgency of spring rather than the lassitude of summer's dying.

Standing in front of the ruin Finch discovered the contemplative figure of Humphrey Bell. He had not met Bell since his return from England. Several times he had been on the point of calling at the Fox Farm but something always had intervened. Now he found himself glad to see him. He strode forward and they shook hands.

Bell said, half-apologetically,—"I thought I'd come over and see what the place is like. I hadn't been here since the night of the fire."

"A complete ruin, isn't it?"

"Yes. It made a terrific blaze. Strange how peaceful a ruin is. Much more peaceful than when there were people about."

"I suppose that depends on the people," said Finch, thinking of Ernest.

"Yes. There couldn't be peace where Mr. Clapperton was." Bell stared at the ground for a moment, then he raised his eyes to Finch's face and added, in his gentle voice,—"I used to think I'd like to kill that man."

"I can't picture your wanting to kill anyone."

"You've no idea what a temper I have. I've had murderous thoughts after a call from Mr. Clapperton. Now—looking at this—I'm sorry." Bell gave his peculiarly charming smile. "I'm sorry, but—I still hate the thought of him."

Finch had listened but vaguely. Now he said,—"I'm buying the entire property, with the exception of the bungalow where Mrs. Clapperton lives."

"You?" Bell cried, in incredulous pleasure. "Why—it's too good to be true."

"It's true enough. I've just come from making the agreement." On a sudden impulse Bell grasped Finch's hand. "To think I'll have you for a neighbour, instead of—but what will you live in?"

"The basement of the house is intact. I shall build a new one on it."

"And will you give up concert work?"

"Not entirely. But I shall be here the greater part of my time."

"I think," said Bell, his pale eyelashes flickering, "I think I know the real reason why you're buying this place."

"Why?" Finch demanded in astonishment.

"To stop the developing. Your eldest brother hates it so. I think you've done this for his sake."

"You're altogether too clever, Humphrey." It was the first time Finch had used Bell's Christian name. This, combined with the almost affectionate tone in which he spoke, brought from Bell what was an outburst.

"It seems too good to be true," he repeated. "It is splendid. And another lucky thing has happened to me. I've sold a story."

"Good! I *am* glad."

"It's the first one I have sold, and I've written I won't say how many. The fly in the ointment is that it's the poorest thing I've written and I hate the women's magazine I've sold it to. I hate all women's magazines."

"Never mind," said Finch, "it's a beginning." He added,—"I believe you hate all women."

"No, no, no—not all! Nevertheless, it is a pleasant thought to me that you'll be a single man in this house you're going to build. But perhaps you'll not be single for long."

"Oh, yes, I shall."

"You'll have your small boy with you?"

"Y—yes, I suppose so."

"He's a nice little chap. Comes to see me sometimes."

"Don't let him bother you."

"He's no bother. He's very advanced for his age."

"You think so? He strikes me as babyish. They've spoilt him at Jalna."

The two walked about the ruin, discussing the difficulties of demolishing it, the plans for the house to be built. Only darkness separated them. As they were parting, Bell asked:

"How is your niece?"

"Adeline? Oh, she's well." Finch hesitated, then added,—"In confidence, I'll tell you that the poor girl has had rather an unfortunate love affair. A penniless

Irishman we met on board ship. Of course, it can't come to anything, but I'm afraid it's hurt her."

"Oh, Lord!" said Bell, as though in pain.

"Yes," agreed Finch.

"I mean——" Bell's tongue refused to move, but clove to the roof of his mouth.

"She'll get over it," Finch reassured him.

"I can't imagine her falling in love." The words now came quickly from Bell's pale lips. "She's so . . . aloof."

Finch gave a short laugh. "You wouldn't have thought so if—but she'll get over it."

Bell turned away. "I won't," he muttered to himself.

He turned and almost flung himself along the path, in the direction of the Fox Farm. His small slight figure, his pale colourless hair were visible for only a few moments, then disappeared in the dark.

As Finch neared Jalna he heard a clear penetrating whistle and saw his eldest brother standing in the beam of light from a window. The notes of 'A Hundred Pipers and a'' sounded with a certain melancholy, as though the whistler, in pensive mood, were unconscious that he whistled. Finch strode towards him, coming on him from behind and laying his hand on his shoulder.

"I've been making a deal," he said.

Renny wheeled to face him. He said,—"I didn't hear you coming . . . What is the deal?" Nothing very interesting, he was sure.

"I've just come from Mrs. Clapperton's. I've bought Vaughanlands—lock, stock and barrel."

If ever the Master of Jalna could have been said to make a squeaking noise he did now. He squeaked in surprise.

"What?" he demanded. "Say that again!"

"I have bought Vaughanlands."

"How could you?"

"How could I?"

"Yes. Well . . . what are you paying for it?"

"It's to be thirty-five thousand dollars—cash."

Again the Master of Jalna squeaked. "Cash! Where the devil would you get that much cash?"

Now it was Finch's turn to make incoherent sounds. He got out,—"What do you suppose I've been working for all these years?"

Renny's brow wrinkled in amazement. "But from *music*! From playing the piano!" he exclaimed. "It beats me how you've done it."

"Well—I have—and I've bought Vaughanlands."

"You!" Renny looked Finch over in mingled astonishment and delight. "By Judas, you couldn't have done a better thing with your money! How much have you left?"

Guardedly, Finch said he wasn't sure.

Renny threw an arm about him and hugged him. "I can't tell you how glad I am," he said. "But you should never have made any such deal without consulting me. Why, you might have been horribly done. As it stands you've got a good bargain. Vaughanlands is worth considerably more than that. Was a lawyer present?"

"No. Just Tom Raikes."

"Why was he there?"

"You've heard the gossip."

"That scallawag! He'll make ducks and drakes of her fortune. Now tomorrow I'll have my lawyer out and we'll make things watertight."

"Gem Clapperton wants to keep the bungalow she lives in."

Renny knit his brows. "Well . . . we may let her do that."

Finch thought,—"Upon my word, he's taking the affair out of my hands already."

Again Renny regarded him in happy astonishment. "All that money," he exclaimed, "tucked away—ready to put your hand on when you wanted it! And you couldn't possibly do a better thing with it. Come—let's go in and tell the uncles." He put his hand to his head. "I mean tell Uncle Nick. He'll be almost as pleased as I."

Renny took Finch's arm and guided him, as though he were one to be cherished but one whose footsteps might falter, into the house. In the drawing-room they found the old man sitting by a bright fire and Alayne reading aloud to him. The two made a picture that caused the brothers to hesitate a moment in the doorway. Alayne's clear voice came to them:

"'She was silent and he got up and walked out of the house. From where she sat she saw him go, twirling his blond moustache with one hand, and viciously flipping at the flowers as he passed with the stick he carried in the other; a fine soldier-like man in appearance certainly, and not wanting in intelligence since he could comprehend her so exactly; but oh, how oppressive when in an admiring mood! This was her first feeling when she got rid of him, but . . .'"

Nicholas had seen the reflection of his nephews in the mirror. "Come in," he exclaimed. "Alayne is reading an old book of my mother's. Rather silly in spots but better than the new stuff she's been trying on me."

"This fellow," said Renny, putting Finch before him, as though he were an exhibit, "has done an amazingly good thing. He's bought Vaughanlands."

Alayne threw Finch a look almost accusing, as though to say,—"Here you go again—throwing your money away!"

Intercepting the glance Renny exclaimed,—"But he got it at a terrific bargain. He couldn't make a better investment."

"What is all this about?" Nicholas demanded. "I don't understand."

Renny pushed Finch forward. "Tell him yourself," he said, "in your own words."

Embarrassed, Finch mumbled what he had done.

"Selling more land," Nicholas said, in a tone of outrage. "Selling more land, eh? More developing! More bungalows! Ha—a good thing your Uncle Ernest didn't live to see this day." He turned his angry eyes on Renny. "If you are selling land, why don't you tell me yourself instead of asking Finch to do it?"

Renny laughed in triumph. "Not *selling*, Uncle Nick! *Buying*. This millionaire, Finch, is buying Vaughanlands."

As this was being explained to Nicholas, as his strongly marked features were taking on a look of deep satisfaction, Meg, Piers and Pheasant entered the drawing-room. They

had just come down from Ernest's bedroom where they
had been tentatively selecting their choice from his belongings. Ernest had, with great impartiality, bequeathed his
money and his personal property to be divided equally
among his nephews and niece. The money thus divided
among five did not amount to a great deal but was a
pleasant windfall, particularly to Piers and Renny.

The three had entered the room with traces of friction on
their faces, but this was erased, as by a magic sponge, when
they heard the news.

"Oh, I am happy about this," cried Pheasant. "You
couldn't have done a better thing for *all* of us."

"And a mighty good investment," said Piers. "Gosh,
I'm glad!"

"And I hope," put in Nicholas, "that we've seen the
last of those horrid Clappertons."

Meg asked,—"What are you going to do with the house,
Finch?"

"I'm going to use the good material to rebuild."

"Not to sell, I hope."

"No. To live in myself."

"Oh, Finch, how lovely!" She threw both arms about
his neck. Her eyes filled with happy tears. "And it solves
a terrible problem for me. I have been worried to death
to know what to do about my house. It is no longer a
comfortable place to live in, so near the road and traffic
getting worse every day. How different from the quiet
country road it was before the war! Dear heart, I am
pleased. Now I can sell my house, and Patience and Roma
and I will come and live with you and I shall keep house
for you. How happy we shall be—all at Vaughanlands
together!"

Finch, enfolded in that warm embrace, thought what a
dear Meg was . . . and yet . . . it was not what he had
planned. He would struggle against it. He would. He
would.

Piers broke in,—"That's right, Meggie, arrange everything for him. Don't give him a chance." He exchanged
an amused glance with Alayne.

Renny added,—"It seems a good plan to me."

"Poor devil," said Piers, with commiseration, "in the house with three women."

"We shall spoil him terribly." Meg patted Finch on the back. "But we'll love doing it. If there's one thing I enjoy above another, it is spoiling a man."

"Time enough to talk all this over later," said Renny. "In the meantime I'm going to get drinks, to drink the health of the new owner of Vaughanlands."

"Make mine double," said Piers.

Meg whispered to Finch,—"Up in Uncle Ernest's room we were thinking that you might like to have the manuscript of his book on Shakespeare for your very own. He always so much appreciated your interest in it. Not that I wasn't interested in it, for I used to sit and listen to him read from it by the hour, though I did realize what a waste of time it was."

"On your part, or on his?" asked Piers. Again he exchanged a look with Alayne.

Meg scorned to answer such a question, but continued,— "Piers would like to have Uncle Ernest's pearl studs and cuff-links, though I do think that's being rather greedy, and Renny could have the water-colours that Uncle Ernest painted, with the exception of the one done in Rome, which I myself would like. But above all I want the pair of Dresden china candelabra. I've loved them ever since I was a child. Patience would like the travelling clock and the silver things from his dressing-table and I thought Wakefield should have the books. However, you and he can settle that between you."

Renny now returned, carrying a tray on which there were a decanter of sherry, a bottle of Scotch and glasses. His walk, the light in his eyes, showed the exhilaration of his spirits.

"Good!" said Nicholas. "Good! Just what I wanted." Glasses were filled.

"Here's to Finch," said Renny, "and may he spend many happy years at Vaughanlands."

"Alone," put in Piers.

When the health had been drunk, Renny added,—"Not that there's any reason for him to keep up a house of his own. He's always welcome at Jalna."

"I've thought for some time," said Finch, "that I'd like a house of my own. I think it would be fun building it and furnishing it."

"I know what," cried Pheasant. "He's going to be married."

"Althea Griffith!" laughed Piers. "I've always expected that."

"You couldn't be more wrong," said Finch. "I want to write music."

Meg's face had fallen at the suggestion of marriage. Now it brightened again and a sweet smile curved her lips. "Finch has no need of a wife," she said. "I will look after him."

Piers uttered one of his peculiarly irritating hoots of laughter. Then he said to Finch,—"Three females and your own kid, to begin with! Why, you've gathered a family like a snowball."

Nicholas said loudly,—"I want to hear of this whole affair from the very beginning. My, how glad I am that we've got the best of old Clapperton at last."

Renny interjected, "Don't say anything against him, Uncle Nick. He died a hero."

"And lived the life of a horrid old fellow," retorted Nicholas. "Another drop of Scotch, please."

Meg said, while sipping her sherry,—"Gem Clapperton has been having a private sale of some of her belongings. I went in the other day and you'll never guess what I bought." Without waiting for an answer she went on happily,—"I bought that wonderful oil painting of the shipwreck which was saved from the fire. It wasn't in the least damaged. She practically gave it away and I simply couldn't resist. Isn't it rather nice to think that it will hang on a wall of the new house at Vaughanlands—just as it used to on the old?"

"No," shouted Finch. "No!" He set down his glass and left the room. He heard Piers laughing. He ran up the two flights of stairs two steps at a time. In his room he sat down on the bed and gripped the bedpost in both hands. What was the matter with him, he wondered. He was always making himself ridiculous in front of the family. Even today. He cursed the nerves that betrayed him. He pressed his thumb and middle finger against his temples and closed his eyes. Three women, a child, and that picture!

When he opened them, Dennis was standing in the doorway, his odd greenish eyes questioning.

"Are you really going to build a house?" asked the little boy.

"Yes."

"Am I to live with you?"

Finch tried to speak like an affectionate father.—"Yes, of course."

"Then I'll have a house, the same as Archer has." He came and put his arm, with a possessive air, about Finch's neck.

"Would you mind going?" Finch said. "I'd like to be alone."

"To think?"

"Yes."

"I want to be alone, too. I'll go to my own room and we'll both sit thinking about the house we're going to build."

Downstairs, by the fire, Nicholas and Alayne were alone together. He was tired from all the talk and confusion but he had something he wanted to say.

"Alayne."

"Yes, Uncle Nicholas."

"I'm afraid that sometimes I may not have shown you how much I think of you and how grateful I am for your kindness to Ernest and me. But I do think a very great deal of you and—I'm very grateful. That's all."

She rose and came to him and kissed him on the forehead. "You both have been very dear to me," she said.

Looking back over her life at Jalna, she thought how, in spite of the times when the continued presence of the two old men had seemed a burden and an irritation, it was true that they were very dear to her. In truth there had been times when life in that house would have been less bearable without them, for they had supplied in their talk and their reminiscences, something of the Old World which her spirit craved. They had been conscious of the cultivation of her mind. They had appreciated her. Now one of them was gone and for this one left she felt an added tenderness. For a while she sat talking with Nicholas, then left him to doze, sunk in his chair.

She went out on the porch to let the air cool her face. The sky was darkening. A streak of gold showed in the west without brightening it. The light from the hall and the drawing-room showed the crimson of the Virginia creeper with which the house was clothed. Soon the leaves would fall, but now they had a richness, a seeming permanence, as though frost could not harm them. A few indeed lay scattered in the porch and she picked up one and felt its smoothness and admired its vivid colour. Even when the leaves fell the stout branches of the creeper would enfold the house. It would cling against the walls waiting for the ever-coming spring to renew it.

XXIX

DENNIS ALONE

THE LEAVES were coming down, faster and faster. The elms had shed nearly all of theirs. The maples had a bright-coloured carpet beneath them, and at every gust they cast down another shower, some yellow, some red, some rusty green. The trunk of the old silver birch on the front lawn gleamed white against the evergreens.

Dennis was trotting purposefully in the direction of Vaughanlands and, though it was evening and an owl was hooting in the ravine, he was not nervous. He came up on to the lawn and looked at the ruin of the house, its roofless walls rising darker than the twilight.

A feeling of pride welled up from his quickly-beating heart. The lawyers had done their work, he knew, and this house and all the land that went with it now belonged to his father. Consequently it belonged to him too. "It is mine," he said out loud, and he walked up close to the house and looked it over. "Archer can't come here unless I say. I'll invite people here when I want them, and when I don't want them they daren't come."

The black skeleton walls looked grand to Dennis. He pictured them changing into a fine house in no time. He would have a bedroom next to his father's and they would have long talks together. They would drive in and out in their own car. They would be like two men, driving and walking and talking together. He would be as important as Archer, more important because there was Adeline at Jalna to order Archer about.

The front steps were still standing and the door with the knocker on it. He went up the steps and reached up to the knocker. He knocked vigorously.

He was not prepared for the hollow reverberations of the knocking. It sounded terribly loud on that door that led nowhere. The twilight deepened. What if the door opened and something strange and horrible appeared? He wished he had not knocked. Somehow it had made everything different. Behind that door rose the menace of a phantom house. What dreadful beings might not lie in wait for the summons of that knock? He pictured them stirring—rising out of the grey rubble—drifting forward to answer the door—towering high above him.

He wanted to run, faster than he ever ran before, but he dared not turn his back on the door for fear that it might open and skeleton hands seize him from behind. He stood with his eyes staring at those threatening panels, his heart ready to leap from his breast. The sound of the knocking still echoed in his ears. Now was added the sound of rain-drops—not pattering on a roof, but falling into that roofless cavern—onto *what*?

Tom Raikes, who was living with the Barkers, had, in complicity with Barker, bought several bottles of rye whiskey and hidden them in the cellar of the ruin where he and Barker could retreat when they chose, unknown to Mrs. Barker. On this evening the wife was out and the two men looked forward to some carefree hours together. Raikes had come to fetch a bottle of rye. He was startled by the sudden resounding knock. Down in the cavern where he crouched it sounded so eerie that, for a moment, he was shaken. Who or what was after him now?

His long legs bent, he emerged cautiously into the rubble-strewn passage, crept up the charred stairs and peered round the skeleton wall to the porch. The relief on his face when he saw the little boy was almost comic. His jaw dropped and a smile replaced his look of consternation. Only a little prying youngster at the door! And already he was frightened. Well, he'd give him a real fright. He'd larn him!

He crept along a beam till he reached the door. He laid his hand on the brass door-knob. Raikes was too subtle to fling wide the door and appear with a threat on the sill. All he did was gently turn the knob without opening the door. He agitated the knob a little, as though the hand that held it shook in ghostly fury.

Dennis had heard the creeping steps. Now his terrified eyes were riveted on the turning knob. What horror would appear when the door opened? He tried to run but his legs were rigid. Only his heart leaped and bounded.

Again and again the door-knob turned. At last, with infinite caution, the narrowest possible crack of door opened, barely wide enough for an abominable eye to peer through. The tension of the child's nerves snapped.

With a thin cry, like a rabbit's caught in a trap, he turned and fled. He hurled himself down the steps, across the lawn, through the shrubbery, into the ravine. It was shallow here but overgrown by brambles which tore at him, sought to hold him. But he struggled through them, whimpering in fear and pain. At the edge of the ravine the going was not so difficult. He could run. But where it grew steep he caught his foot in a root, fell, and rolled over and over into the stream. Frantically he struggled to his feet. The water was up to his armpits. He waded across and found the path on the other side. Dripping wet, his head and legs bleeding from scratches, he climbed the path. He went through the little gate at the edge of the lawn and the house rose in front of him, its windows alight.

The dogs heard him and, for a moment, made an uproar, but lay down again when he entered the hall. The house was full of the music of the piano. Dennis opened the door of the drawing-room and went softly in.

Finch was alone in the room. The light from a lamp fell across his supple hands as they flew up and down the keyboard, and across his long sensitive face which showed a tranquil pleasure in his playing. He glanced over his shoulder, saw Dennis standing just inside the room and smiled at him.

Dennis sank to his heels, his back against the door. The curtains were drawn against the darkness which had descended suddenly with the rain. The sweetness, the power, the gaiety of the music rose, as a wall, to keep out evil spirits.

"I'm safe," Dennis whispered to himself. "I'm safe, with my father."

XXX

THE READING OF THE PLAY

BEFORE the first snowfall, Wakefield arrived from New York. He was both elated and depressed by his visit there. His agent had been enthusiastic about the play Wakefield had written. He had a manager in view who, he was sure, would be interested. It was a comedy, and good comedies were rare. New York audiences were going to laugh a lot at this play. Wakefield had pictured them as enchanted by this different sort of comedy, by a young actor who was already making his mark on the stage. And he, of course, was to play the principal part. The manager had expressed a fervent wish to meet Wakefield. Indeed, at their first meetings, Wakefield had thought all was well. But a change had come, why neither he nor his agent could guess. The manager had avoided meetings and, as it turned out, was putting his money on another play. As the agent and Wakefield were accustomed to the vagaries of the theatre they were not disconcerted, and there were other managers.

Wakefield enjoyed his stay in New York. The bequest from his Uncle Ernest made him feel tolerably rich. It had come as a splendid surprise, for he had expected that only the older members of the family would benefit. Now he planned to spend some time at Jalna, convenient for overnight trips to New York, in case he were needed.

Finch now found a new pleasure in Wakefield's society. As a boy this younger brother had irritated him by his cocksureness. Perhaps he was envious because Wakefield had always been the favourite of the family, while he because of his unhappy mixture of awkwardness and vulnerability had often been the butt for teasing. This he had never been able to take well, and even today winced at

344

the remembrance of some of Piers' and Eden's sallies at his expense. Renny had indeed been a father to him, but he had, as Finch thought, been sometimes severe with him, in contrast to his leniency towards Wakefield.

Well, all that was in the past and he looked forward to Wakefield's stay at Jalna. Wakefield was excited at Finch's purchase of Vaughanlands. Everything was now settled, the price paid. The two brothers spent happy hours exploring every corner of the property. Of course, they already knew it almost as well as they knew Jalna but, in Finch's ownership, it had a new aspect.

Finch had builders at work, and on the old foundations a new house was beginning to rise. The solid plain exterior was to be the same as of old but there were to be fewer rooms and more spacious. A new bow-window was to be added to the largest, which was to be the music-room. The consultations with the architect, with the builder, were an entirely new kind of interest, pleasure and anxiety to Finch. He was surprised, though not alarmed, by the way the money went. His resources were a constant marvel to Renny. He was mystified; he was delighted; he was curious. He would have liked to know, to the last dollar, how much Finch had accumulated. But Finch, who was by nature candid and open, had learned by experience that the Master of Jalna could, with all good intentions, borrow and be unable to repay, or advise investment in the stables which had so often absorbed his own means. From Ernest's bequest he already was making improvements to them and had bought a valuable mare. Piers, on his part, had put his share of the legacy into stocks, excepting for a new fur coat for Pheasant.

Everyone was interested in Wakefield's play, though it was only to Alayne and Pheasant that it was of deeper interest than the building of Finch's house. One evening, not long after his coming, it was arranged that he should read it aloud. Nicholas, Renny, Alayne, Piers, Pheasant, Meg and Patience, Finch and Adeline were gathered to hear him. Nicholas, in his comfortable chair, was seated close to the reader, so that he might not miss a word. Finch, at the piano, was prepared to play certain snatches of music, for one of the characters in the play was a musician. Renny was sitting on the window-seat, and Finch, seeing him there, recalled that it was in this same spot he had sat when the family had forgathered after the reading of the grandmother's will—a painful recollection.

Wakefield was in his natural sphere. He was acting; he was, as his brothers said, showing off. It was evening. The lights were low, except for the lamp which illumined Wakefield's manuscript and his dark, mobile face. The audience could not have been more attentive. Alayne, her critical faculty alert, leaned slightly forward. Meg also leaned forward but it was with encouragement for the reader, her smile only waiting to turn into a laugh, for she knew this was going to be an amusing play. Nicholas, his best ear cupped in his hand, was paying the strictest attention to all the preliminaries. In his day he had been an ardent theatre-goer. For this occasion he had thoroughly brushed his hair; had, at his request, been freshly shaved by Renny, and had put on his best suit. Back through long years, the glamour of the theatre touched him. He said to Finch,—"Start it off properly. Play God Save the King."

Delighted to see the old man in this mood, Finch played the anthem. At the first note Nicholas struggled to his feet and remained standing solidly to the end. Then everyone sat down. Wakefield opened his manuscript and cleared his throat. At that moment the dogs decided that they wanted to come into the room from the hall. The Cairn terrier, who was an adept at scratching doors and who had left his mark on every principal door in the house, drew his sharp nails, in rapid succession, down the panels. The bulldog barked, the sheepdog whined. Alayne had been tolerantly amused at the delay caused by the anthem. She was eager to get on with the play and found this second interruption very irritating. Her decisive nature was offended. She never had liked dogs and now she exclaimed:

"What pests those animals are! Will somebody please drive them away?"

At that moment an unseen hand in the hall opened the

door, and the bulldog, the sheepdog and the Cairn terrier entered. The bulldog, with his rolling gait, went straight to the fire and seated himself on the hearthrug, facing the company, the picture of "what I have, I'll hold". The terrier trotted briskly to Renny and pawed his leg. Renny lifted him to his knee. Of the three the sheepdog was the only one who stood in awe of Alayne, and that awe was, in a strange way, mingled with derision. He would obey an order from her but would, at the same time, make a grimace at her, lifting his upper lip and wrinkling his nose. Now, as she pointed to the door, he gave her this look that was almost a smirk, and prepared to leave. Everyone but Alayne laughed.

"Let them stay," said Renny. "They'll be good."

"They ought to be put out," growled Nicholas.

Piers called to the sheepdog,—"Here, boy!"

Wakefield folded his manuscript. "I shall begin," he said, "when those brutes are under control." He was not indeed angry but he was tense.

Adeline dropped to the floor beside the sheepdog and drew him on to her lap. "Be good, my pet," she whispered.

Renny was taking a burr from the Cairn's tail and it now gave a sharp yelp. Wakefield, with great calm, lighted a cigarette.

"Keep your hair on," said Renny, addressing both Wakefield and the terrier. He deposited the burr in a fern-pot.

The invisible hand in the hall closed the door. There was an expectant silence. Wakefield cleared his throat and began to read. He read well. He threw himself into the different parts with zest, his audience giving him their rapt attention, till, when he came to a love scene and lowered his voice seductively for the woman's part, Nicholas interrupted.

"Speak up. I can't hear you."

Wakefield raised his voice a little.

"I still can't hear you."

"My God," cried Wake, "I can't shout and be subtle at one and the same time."

Piers put in, "I don't see anything very subtle about it. She's simply cooing,—'Oh, Bill, I love you so terrifically.'"

"Well, then, I can't coo."

"What's he say?" demanded Nicholas.

Meg came to the rescue. "Uncle Nick, dear, it's a love scene. Wakefield, as the girl, wants to coo."

Nicholas snorted. "Very well. Let him coo and have done with it."

"Listen, Uncle," continued Meg. "This girl is in love with a plumber. Her family are bitterly opposed to the match, though I don't think Wakefield has made it clear whether it is because he is such a conceited young man or because he is a plumber . . ."

Wakefield tossed the manuscript to her lap. "You take it," he said, "and read."

"Now, Wakefield," admonished Meg. "Don't get upset."

"I want to hear him read the play," said Nicholas, "but if he mumbles, I can't. I know the plot so far but, tell me, is this play a farce?"

"No, Uncle Nick," Wakefield answered. "It's a straight comedy but underneath lies the truth that, in spite of all this socialism, class distinctions are still pretty rigid. As for my plumber, he is not conceited. He is an intellectual and he knows his value."

"He's very talkative for a plumber," said Meg. "Most of them are so taciturn."

"I grant you he's not a typical plumber," said Wakefield, again taking up the manuscript. "He's extremely clever and, but for him, the entire family would be down the drain, as it were." An hysterical giggle came from Finch at the piano.

"Read on," cried Nicholas.

Wakefield had no cause for further complaint about his audience. It was necessary a few times to explain a humorous point to Nicholas but, once he understood it, he laughed with enjoyment and even slapped his thigh in appreciation. Observing the strongly-marked animated features of his family, Wakefield wished that a theatrical manager might have been present, to see and to hear. At the end there was

an outburst of applause, so hearty that the bulldog, the
sheepdog and the Cairn terrier all rose to their feet and
barked.

There was not one dissenting voice in the verdict that, if
the play could once find a backer, it would be a tremendous
success.

XXXI

ADELINE

ALONE in her room, Adeline was undressing. She was thinking of the play and more especially of the scenes between the lovers. They had been moving to her, yet most unsatisfying. Did Wakefield really know what it was to suffer in love? She had heard, though vaguely, of an unhappy affair of his own. But—did he know what it was to suffer?

As she brushed her hair she saw her reflection in the looking-glass—that glass which for so many years had reflected the chestnut hair and dark eyes of her great-grandmother—she noticed how large and luminous her own eyes had become, how pale her cheeks. "No wonder," she thought, "for I 'let concealment, like a worm i' the bud, feed on my damask cheek' . . . What a fool I am to grieve so! I'm sure he doesn't long for me or his letters would be more of a comfort. They're not a comfort. They're a torture. What is he trying to do? Cool me off with accounts of his everyday doings, of his mother's doings, of his troubles with Sylvia—when he must know so well what I want to hear?" She tried to think like a grown-up woman in love—not as a yearning child.

She brushed her hair fiercely, as though she would tear it out. She shut her eyes, so she might not see her reflection. She saw instead the face of Fitzturgis, so clearly that she stood petrified, the brush poised in mid-air, devouring those loved features with her inner longing.

But the sound of his voice, which she had thought the most beautiful in the world, escaped her. And, as she desperately tried to recall its tones, the memory of his face became obscured. Then, when it reappeared, it was distorted and wore an expression of such sneering scorn that her eyes flew open in her astonishment and pain. She had no photograph of him, not even a snapshot, with which to refresh her memory. "How horrible," she thought, "if I must carry that sneering face in my memory." Deliberately she recalled the few times when they had embraced, when they had lost themselves in the depths of each other's eyes. But, when she tried to recall his eyes, they were glaring at her in anger.

She took her towel from the rack and crept upstairs to the bathroom. Up there it was dark and the darkness was rounded by the snoring of Nicholas. She went into the bathroom and turned on the light. Someone had left the window open and the night air was coming in, heavy with the smell of falling snow. It came down thick and wet, clinging heavily to everything it touched. Now the bad time for the birds would begin. Before she closed the window she stood looking out into the whiteness. There was no crisp gaiety of winter but only the melancholy warning of its approach.

She shivered as she washed her face and hands. Her bare feet showed, pink with cold, on the bathroom mat. She always was forgetting to put on her bedroom slippers. She washed her face with warm water, then with cold, and felt somewhat comforted. Kneeling by her bed she said her prayers half-aloud, quickly, the same prayers she had said as a child, but that time seemed far away.

To be covered up, head and all, was what she longed for these nights. No matter how lively the evening had been, there came this longing, this loneliness at night. She would shut herself away from it, the bedclothes over her head, breathing in the warm sweetness of her body. But even in this seclusion she could hear the night sounds of the house, a creaking on the stairs, a sound of movement in walls and roof. The old house was saying to her,—"I have known tears before these you shed, and heard long-drawn sighs. Yours are not the first and will not be the last. Your grief is no more than the soft snow lying on my roof. But I have witnessed grief, sharp and glittering as the swordlike icicles that hang from my eaves in midwinter."

Oh, if only she could hear his voice!

Suddenly, like a shout in the darkness, the idea of a telephone talk came to her. She remembered how Pheasant had telephoned Mooey on his birthday. If Pheasant could do that, why not she? She would do it! She would ring him up in the morning. . . . But it would cost twelve dollars and she had not that much money. From whom could she ask such a sum? Uncle Nicholas. He would surely give it her. But no—she made up her mind that she would charge it to her father's telephone account and she would, before the account came in, tell him what she had done. It was a frightening decision, but do it she would.

Now, in her excitement, she threw the quilt from her shoulders and lay, wide-eyed in the darkness, imagining what the conversation with Fitzturgis would be.

In the midst of it she fell asleep and in the midst of it she woke.

She was full of purpose. Her opportunity came right after lunch. Nicholas was taking his afternoon rest and Alayne too was lying down. Finch and Wakefield were gone to see the progress of the new house. Renny was in the town making the final arrangements for the showing of his horses at the coming Horse Show. In the tenseness of waiting, Adeline recalled, she knew not why, her rides with Pat Crawshay in Ireland. How gay he had been—how almost tender! How happily they had trotted along the roads among the grey-green hills! How mild had been the sunshine on his fair head and the glittering hide and mane of his mount! And how few happy recollections of Fitz-turgis—moments of delight, yes—but no sustained happiness of an hour! And yet—with all the fervour of her spirit she reached out towards their troubled love.

At the first she was too excited to make clear her directions to the telephone operator, but finally they came to an understanding and she was told to wait for a ring. While she waited, she paced up and down the room. Wragge opened the door and looked in.

"Anything you want, miss?"

"No," she answered curtly, then added, "thanks. I'm making a long distance call. I don't want to be interrupted."

"I'll see to that, miss." He gave her an inquisitive look and closed the door.

After a moment she opened it and looked up and down the hall. It was empty. She closed the door and locked it.

Her mouth was dry, her palms moist, her heart thudding so that she was conscious of it through all her body. Time passed. It seemed interminable. Her mother would be up, her father returned from the city. What would she say if they tried the door? Had either of them, she wondered, been through anything equal to this? Had her great-grandmother? Surely they had married the people they wanted, and that had been all there was to it. . . .

The shock of the telephone bell startled her. She took up the receiver.

"Hello!"

"You are calling a party in Eire?"

"Yes."

"Here is your party," said the nasal voice.

She waited. There were noises. Several times she said 'Hello'. There was silence. Then,—

"Here is your party," repeated the voice. "Go ahead."

"Hello," she said shakily.

"Hello," answered the voice of Fitzturgis, as clear as though he were in the room.

"Oh, Mait, is it really you?"

"What is the matter?" he demanded.

"I . . ." oh, how dry her mouth was! "I had—to speak to you."

"Has something happened? Are you in trouble?"

"No—no. I just *had* to speak to you."

"But why?"

"Because . . . I love you so and I want to hear you say you love me . . . that's all."

He was silent. Surely he could hear the beating of her heart. What a thing that would be—right across the ocean!

"Maitland!" she cried. "Are you there?"

Still silence.

"Maitland! Speak to me."

Now his voice came no longer clear, but harsh and broken. "My darling."

"Are you sorry I called you?"

"No—no—I'm glad. Why—to hear your voice—so unexpected—it is unbelievable." His own voice shook.

It was too much for her to bear. She broke down and began to sob into the telephone.

"Adeline—my darling—if only I had you in my arms . . ."

"Oh, Mait . . ." She could say no more.

Again his voice came, rough and shaken by emotion. "If you wanted to hear me say it—hear me now—I love you and only you and always shall."

She could say nothing.

"Adeline? Are you there?"

He could not make out her incoherent reply.

"Listen." He spoke sternly. "You rang me up. You wanted to talk. Are you going to waste all our time in crying?"

"No."

"Then tell me that you're going to be brave and happy. You know how I feel. Even though my letters . . ."

"Your letters are so . . ." She could not go on.

"My letters?"

"Y—yes."

"What about them?"

"Oh—never mind . . . Maitland, darling, are you crying in Ireland?"

"I am not."

"But you were!"

"Well . . . almost."

"Oh, say you were. I can bear everything—if I think you're crying too."

He gave a short, uncertain laugh. "Very well. I'm crying too."

"No—you're laughing! You mustn't laugh at me, Mait."

Now his voice had great tenderness in it. "I only laugh because I . . . Oh, darling, how narrow the ocean seems! I feel that I can gather . . ."

The warning signal came. She tried to speak. She tried to cry out,—"Go on . . . don't stop . . ." She heard his muffled good-bye. "Good-bye!" she cried, and bent her forehead to the receiver.

It was over.

She went outdoors into the new world that the snow had made. She crossed the lawn and walked towards the orchard. The trees still held their leaves, and one old tree, the apples of which had not been gathered, still displayed them boldly red, though each was capped by snow.

On the road to the stables some grain had been spilt and the pigeons were collected there. Whether because they had had enough, or for love of her, they now left the grain and winged through the grey air with grey and white and puce and buff wings to where she stood. She remembered how Noah had put out his hand from the ark and drawn in the dove. She put out her hand and caught the willing white pigeon, her favourite, and set it on her shoulder. The others circled about her head, their coral feet held close, the jewels of their eyes shining. They curved, they floated, they dropped, as though to alight on her, then again swept upward, the white one on her shoulder cooing in pride. She felt the movement of its feet through her thin blouse.

She saw her father in his riding-clothes returning to the house from the stables. He saw her also and turned towards the orchard. At his approach, the birds, with a heavy whirring of wings, rose and flew back to their grain. As he drew near, her heart was bursting to tell him all. It was so hard for her to deceive. She would be forced before long to confess that she had telephoned to Ireland. Better tell him everything now, try for his sympathy. She called out:

"Hello, Daddy. I wasn't expecting you so soon."

"No? Well, everything is arranged. It's going to be a grand show. What have you been up to?"

Been up to! If only he knew! What would he say? Now is the moment for telling him . . . He put his arm about her. The white pigeon swept upward and soared lonely above the ravine. The sun came out and the clots of soft snow began to fall from the trees. Soon winter would again retreat.

"Why are you outdoors in that flimsy thing?" he demanded.

"I'm not cold." She looked up into his face.

Never could she love any man better than him. If she had to choose between the two, which would she choose? She would die, she thought, before making that choice. But there was no need to choose. Brace yourself, she thought, and tell him all—he will understand. Never had she asked understanding of him in vain. Yes, she would pour out to him the story of her love. She tried to choose the right words from the tumult in her brain. It should be easy, for she had been talking to Fitzturgis and now the ocean seemed so narrow. But no words came. She twisted a button of his jacket.

He repeated, carelessly curious,—"Tell me, what have you been doing?"

"Nothing," she answered, smiling.

She was so close to him that the fine check of his homespun jacket was magnified and she saw it as a miniature countryside of little fields, green and brown and mauve. He guessed that she had something on her mind, and he pressed her against his side, in encouragement.

"Come," he said, "what's up?"

"I've been telephoning," she got out.

"Yes?"

"To Ireland." Her knees shook and she clung to him for support . . . "To a man I love."

She raised her eyes to his face, eyes so like his own.

"Yes? And what did he say?"

He felt her body tauten. "Oh, Daddy," she cried. "You know! And I made Uncle Finch promise he wouldn't tell. He gave me his word."

"Wakefield told me."

"Are you angry?"

"I should be," he thought. "I should be the arrogant outraged parent, ordering her to put this rascal out of her mind for ever. But . . ." He looked down into her face, tracing in the pink-flushed marble of its contours the resemblance to the proud portrait of old Adeline. He had been waiting for this moment. He was glad now that it had come. He drew her along the path towards the house.

"No," he said, "I'm not angry."

In the porch, where her outgoing footprints stared up at them, he halted. "I've been in love myself," he said, smiling.

"I suppose you have. With Mummy."

"Yes." The back of his hand went to his lips, as though to conceal the smile. "Yes—with your mother. And I had to wait, you know."

"Oh, I'm willing to wait. I'll wait for years—if I must. Though waiting comes hard to me." Then she added, almost defiantly,—"I'll never love anyone else . . . not in this way."

"Of course not." He touched her hair soothingly. "One never loves two people in the same way. It's always very different."

She laid her hands on his chest. "Oh, if only you could meet him," she cried. "You'd understand everything. He's so sensitive, so proud——" She hesitated and then added, almost in a whisper,—"so *poor*."

"Yes. I gathered that."

Now her eyes flashed in pride of her lover. "But he's so clever. He can change everything, if only he's given a chance . . . What I want is to see you two together. You'd be sure to like each other."

He took a rather battered packet of cigarettes from his pocket, extracted one with care and lighted it. He said, in a matter-of-fact tone,—"I must meet the chap. I should like to meet him quite soon. How about you and me going to Ireland next spring and looking him up?"

Adeline stared at him speechless, in incredulous joy. She rose on her toes and raised her arms, as if about to fly.

The door opened and Finch stood there, with an enquiring expression.

"Want to catch your death of cold, Adeline?" he asked. "Will you come in or shall I bring you a sweater?"

"I couldn't take cold," she cried. "Nothing bad could possibly happen to me. I've just had the most glorious news. Come out and hear."

She caught him by the arm and drew him into the porch. The three dogs followed him to the door. They looked out to see if anything worth while was happening. Deciding that there was nothing, they returned to the warmth and lay down.